The World Under the Clock

Book I ~ The Festermunder Chronicles

Chris Jernigan

 FriesenPress

One Printers Way
Altona, MB R0G 0B0
Canada

www.friesenpress.com

Copyright © 2024 by Chris Jernigan
First Edition — 2024

All rights reserved.

ISBN
978-1-03-830875-7 (Hardcover)
978-1-03-830874-0 (Paperback)
978-1-03-830876-4 (eBook)

1. YOUNG ADULT FICTION, FANTASY, CONTEMPORARY

Distributed to the trade by The Ingram Book Company

For my family

TABLE OF CONTENTS

Chapter 1

Festermunder

Beatrix would forever refer to it as "the day it happened."

It was a Friday in November after school when Beatrix Voght spotted her doppelganger crossing the street. It was literally her exact twin. Beatrix thought she was hallucinating. But there it went, crossing Amsterdam Avenue at the 79th Street crosswalk, as plain as day.

Beatrix tried to sort it out, her mind refusing to accept what her vision was claiming. With the hair standing up on the back of her neck, her throat tightening, and her jawline burning, Beatrix clenched her teeth and jogged after it.

Struggling to keep up, she scampered as fast as her short stride and rarely tested lungs dared take her. Dumping her sacred leather satchel on a brownstone stoop, Beatrix made a mental note to return for it, then bounded off toward the park and her twin.

Her teeth hurting from mouth breathing in the 34°F air and her black hair flailing, fourteen-year-old Beatrix sprang across the Columbus Avenue intersection where W 79th dead-ended into the back of the Museum of Natural History. As only a New Yorker would, she timed it with the lights all red, not waiting for the white "walk" signal to permit her to cross.

"Hey!" a policeman yelled, trying to get her to slow down. Beatrix waved with an awkward grin while sprinting across Columbus, narrowly missing a passerby on a Citi Bike. The cop saw only a short girl in a plaid skirt and knee socks with a mass of hair, black framed glasses, braces, and teeth.

Her quarry approached a slow-moving throng of suit-and-tie-wearing workers leaving happy hour as well as a group of old ladies, then disappeared into the mass of people, darting with inhuman speed and agility. When Beatrix lost sight of her doppelganger, she stopped and doubled over with her hands on her knees.

Maybe I'm going crazy, she thought. *It must run in the family. I'll fit right in with Dad.*

A sound in the alley to her left drew her attention. Venturing into the alley, Beatrix rounded a dumpster, her stomach turned to jelly with fear, the burning in her jaw and throat rising, and her ears ringing. Suddenly, a dirty old cat leaped out and then scampered off. Beatrix let out a gasp, then began to breathe again.

How stupid am I?

The hairs on the back of her neck tingled, and Beatrix knew she wasn't alone. Spinning around, she beheld her quarry across the alley, standing in front of her in full view, not twelve feet away. She could finally see up close the person she had been chasing for blocks in the frigid evening air. It was as incredible as it was impossible. She was looking at a perfect representation of . . . herself.

Her knees weak and her fingers trembling, Beatrix reached for her phone to take a picture, only to realize she had left it in her bag on 79th.

Her eyes returning to her doppelganger, she realized it was surrounded by a faint aura of shimmering green light. Her likeness put its fingers to its lips as if to quiet her and then whispered a single word: "Thirteen."

Then, with a puff of black smoke and green lightning, the figure disappeared.

As Beatrix watched the soot dissipate, she became woozy. Then black wings of unconsciousness wrapped around Beatrix's mind, and the world went dark.

Earlier that day at Festermunder—4:38 p.m.

Don't even look at the clock, Beatrix. Don't even look at it . . .

Beatrix recited the words repeatedly as the class, and the school week itself, was dwindling down to the last fifteen minutes. The other students were feeling the same level of impatience as their attention spans, already hanging by a thread, began to stretch and break like gossamer in anticipation of the weekend. Beatrix couldn't wait for the interminable class to be over. World history was bad enough, Beatrix mused, made even worse when an academic overanalyzed trivialities that would never be on an exam. Beatrix thought the students should be turned loose to ride out the last few moments on their own.

"So, the symbols are widespread and all during the same time period, yet there was no means of transportation for explorers to complete them during the carbon date restrictions. Science doesn't lie. Your thoughts, Miss Voght?" Professor Lightheart asked. "Miss Voght? Miss Voght, are you listening?"

"Beatrix, answer him!" Demi Reeves hissed.

Nic Stooch and Becker McTeel were red faced, struggling to control their laughter.

"Ground control to Major Voght, we have a moron in orbit requesting permission to crash land on Uranus," Nic Stooch said.

The class erupted, snapping Beatrix out of her stupor. She had been doodling in her black composition notebook.

"Master Stooch," Professor Lightheart declared in his British accent, "if you choose to speak like a child, you will be treated like a child and embarrassed accordingly."

Someone, likely Becker McTeel, stammered like a baby, and Beatrix swore she heard another student whisper something about a diaper change.

"Miss Voght?"

"Yes, sir, I heard you. Perhaps the symbols aren't meant to be understood by our limited thought processes. Like, maybe they're a form of higher intelligence or a phenomenon we can't decipher. Maybe extra-dimensional? I think maybe, um, that could be a way of seeing it, sir."

"So, you're speaking of supernatural or 'extra-dimensional' origins?

Interesting, but we may be getting far afield here. All things ought to be defined in terms of the laws of the known universe. That conjecture, while creative, is perhaps a bit farcical."

Even though Professor Lightheart hadn't meant it in a mean way, the word "farcical" triggered another explosion of mirth from the class and an obscene sound from one of the boys, likely Stooch.

"Professor, please!" Beatrix protested over the din, then lowered her voice. "I'm saying the symbols being located all over places that were unreachable with the technology of the time is explainable only by gaining knowledge we can't access. The events likely mean something and are so random that the randomness itself must be a pattern. The key is solving that pattern, and to do that, we need a code. Maybe we're not ready to find these answers yet."

Lightheart started to reply, then stopped himself. Beatrix looked at him, anticipating a sarcastic response to her hypothesis, but seeing no malice in his face, she smiled, relieved at not being challenged again in the open.

Above all else, Beatrix Voght despised attention. Years of ridicule for being different, weird, and quiet had made Beatrix even more different, weird, and quiet. She ran her hand through her thicket of curly black hair, adjusted her glasses, then stood up as the dismissal bell rang.

Quickly, quickly. Be the first one out and make it to your locker before Awful Alexandria and Deplorable Darby show up and block yours to see if you'll say anything . . . which, of course, you won't because you're a loser. Ben would do something.

Beatrix started down the aisle but was restrained by a weight that spun her around, nearly clothes-lining her. A cacophony of noise ensued as her desk and its belongings crashed to the tile floor along with her.

Nic Stooch and Becker McTeel squealed with delight. "Nice going, Grace," Stooch said.

The effectiveness of tethering Beatrix's letter satchel to the back of her desk was dimmed by the low-quality verbal barb. Most of the class laughed at Beatrix as she lay on the floor.

The spectacle of her desk crashing to the floor didn't bother Beatrix nearly as much as the fact that the strap on her satchel had broken. Made of leather and worn beyond description, her satchel was one of the few possessions she treasured. The brass clasp that held its flap closed had long since oxidized and become tarnished, as it was over eighty years old. Lieutenant Waverly Voght, her great-grandfather, had used it to carry classified documents in Europe during WWII. Her dad had taken it on every one of his adventures, to wherever his passion for archeology took him. Inside the flap in small gold foil letters was an inscription: "Seek and Ye Shall Find. 273.025." The digits were some sort of military serial number. Her dad had given her the satchel prior to his trip to Scotland.

The trip that changed everything.

Beatrix got to her feet and then blew her stack. "Very mature, you imbeciles! Did Mommy and Daddy not teach you any manners? Or did the nanny who raises you not teach you when your parents were in the Hamptons?"

The entire class stopped, silence prevailing as Beatrix stood in a pile of papers and Post-its from her perpetually untidy desk.

"At least we have parents, Muffaletta," Stooch said, using the well-known nickname for Beatrix due to her hair density issues.

"Unless you call that cracked old man Wendell of yours a father. Where's your family, huh? Your mother—wait—your stepmother is a joke, and your fake dad is, at this moment, choosing his decor for a padded cell at the asylum! Or is he preparing for another midnight stroll in Central Park in his pajamas? Don't lecture us on family, loser. At least our parents saw fit to keep us, not make us wards of the state!"

As Beatrix framed her response, she felt a burning sensation in her face. Her neck felt hot as she felt tears welling up in the corners of her eyes.

Please no. Not now. Please don't . . .

Too late.

A plump tear rolled down Beatrix's left cheek. To hide it, she bent down with as much dignity as she could muster and gathered her belongings, sniffing and feigning a cough to cover her crying.

A skinny brown hand entered her view, holding a piece of paper—her class schedule for the following semester. The hand belonged to Malik Patel.

"Jerks," Malik said in his rich Indian accent. "They'll probably eat at Desmond's Dog Shack and get food poisoning, then end up being hospitalized with vomiting and explosive diarh—" Beatrix cut him off with a look of disgust.

Malik was not a friend by any stretch, but he was a charter member of the same fraternal order whose only requirement for membership was to be a loser, an outcast, or a freak. In the opinion of many, Malik was heaping tablespoons of all three superlatives.

Beatrix imagined Malik's dossier would read as follows: skinny to the point of emaciated, a shock of black hair sweeping into his monobrow, glasses rivaling that of Beatrix in terms of thickness, and an overbite that had him in braces since he was nine. Malik was 110 pounds soaking wet. He had a thing for corduroy pants, and he tucked his shirts in absurdly tight, leaving no slack whatsoever. He had a soaring intellect and was tragically friendly yet antisocial due to lack of opportunities. Malik was constantly called "Ma-Leek." It was supposed to be pronounced "*Mal-lick*," with the first syllable accented, which he never failed to make known. Adding irony to idiosyncrasy, Malik touted his knowledge and appreciation of gangster rap.

Beatrix sniffed. "Thanks. Enjoy your weekend."

"Maybe I'll see you around the block," Malik called out as she walked away. Beatrix exhaled with a sigh and rolled her teary eyes in disbelief.

Can you believe this guy?

"Fine. Whatever," she said, losing her patience at the broken rules of engagement, which she had been clear about many times before. "And for heaven's sake, don't tuck your shirt in so tight. You look freaking ridiculous."

"How should I tuck it? If it's loose, I feel drafty and might catch cold and get the tongue depressor—"

"Malik, shut up *please*!"

"But—"

"I said no!"

Malik smiled. "Oh well. Goodbye, Beatrix."

He gave her the "okay" sign with his skeletal thumb and forefinger to acknowledge he was being dismissed. "Sorry," he said, though it came out as "soddy."

Thank you, Malik.

It meant a lot that Malik was continuously concerned about her. He was compassionate to a world that offered him none in return. Malik had none of the boundaries or limitations that normal teens set for themselves on how to be cool. Beatrix had told Malik, in no uncertain terms, that their affiliation as neighbors and colleagues ended at the doors of Festermunder. They had a pact. They would associate amicably outside of school, but once inside those walls, Malik did not exist. The pact was unilaterally enforced by Beatrix. Malik was pleased at the arrangement, and Beatrix was disturbed at his self-deprecation.

Beatrix always thought it was because they lived on the same block on the Upper West Side that Malik had nothing to lose by trying to befriend her. However, Malik had no siblings, associates, colleagues, or buddies. Truth be told, Malik Patel had no friends.

Neither did Beatrix.

After vainly trying to pair her AirPods for the umpteenth time, Beatrix headed for the door, knowing full well the delay, courtesy of the Stooch/McTeel incident, would put her right into the path of Alexandria and Darby. Alexandria was a true mean girl in the time-honored tradition of middle school bullies. She was tall, blond, and flawlessly complete with perfect teeth and a British accent, having come from London at the end of the previous year. She had shot to the top of the social strata. When Alexandria walked by with her swiveling shoulders and exquisite posture, boys had trouble speaking and maintaining their train of thought. Girls hated her on sight. Only Darby, the sycophant, followed Alexandria around like a sick puppy, mimicking her every move. Alexandria enjoyed the stir she created around school, a smile always on her face. She was also first chair viola in the concert band, a position Beatrix once held and coveted, and captain of the varsity tennis team, all at age fourteen. It especially bothered Beatrix that Ben got along well with her.

Then again, everybody loves Ben.

"Miss Voght?" Professor Lightheart cleared his throat and then beckoned Beatrix to approach his desk.

Goodness, what now?

"Miss Voght—uh, Beatrix, I wanted to ask you about your response today in class. Not the content. I was more impressed with the conviction with which you spoke. You seem quite confident and knowledgeable about extra-dimensional phenomena. I, uh, fancy myself a bit of an amateur expert on this sort of thing."

Beatrix smiled. "Thanks."

"Years ago when your father graced these halls, he was instrumental in helping me think about things in a unique vein. Beautiful mind. Your father, he had . . . a *different* way of seeing the world."

"Yes, sir, I suppose he did," Beatrix replied.

"Had." Past tense.

Acting as if he had just remembered something, Professor Lightheart opened a locked drawer in his large mahogany desk and pulled out an old leather-bound composition book. "This was his. His notes and writings from when he was a student. It seems he left them here on purpose. We were classmates, you know. When I phoned him years ago to say I had access to his memorabilia, he told me to keep it. When I'm not perusing it, I keep it locked up in the central vault of Festermunder's library. Perhaps you'd like to flip through —"

"Professor Lightheart, sir," Beatrix said, "I really need to be going."

Lightheart's face became serious, and he stared at Beatrix for a full five seconds without blinking.

This is weird. Does he think I'm telepathic?

A look of disappointment on his face, Lightheart nodded, then locked the notebook in the drawer.

At the door, Beatrix turned back to apologize, but Lightheart raised palms in polite resignation, then nodded goodbye.

After Beatrix left, Professor Lightheart pulled the notebook out and walked over to the corner behind his desk where a beaten copper pipe ran from floor to ceiling. He turned a handle, and a plexiglass door, just large enough to fit a book, swung open. Placing the notebook inside with utmost care, Lightheart flipped it closed, then pressed a red button. The book was sucked away with a pneumatic *thunk*.

Back to the library. Back to the World Under the Clock.

Festermunder Academy ran from 8:00 a.m. to 5:00 p.m., including a sixty-minute lunch break. The goal was to simulate a normal American workday and prepare students for real life. The effect was to make the experience of attending ol' Festermunder miserable. After the 5:00 p.m. bell, the reward for a hard day at 'the Mothership' as students called it, was traveling home during rush hour in Manhattan's sea of humanity. The students thought it cruel, but their parents loved it. They usually all worked too except for the moms on the local "tennis and lounging by the pool" circuit. Festermunder School was for the economic elite. It also had some glaring idiosyncrasies, some well-known and others downright scary.

Beatrix and her brother, Ben, who seemed to agree on little, concurred that Festermunder had cornered the market on the five-percenters. As Beatrix once explained to Ben, "Everyone has their five percent—the small part of their personality that's an oddity. Like an idiosyncrasy or a trait that's out of character."

Beatrix tended to use an unreasonably complex vocabulary.

They had discussed this concept at length in Central Park weeks before. "You, Ben, are nearly a freak for Festermunder because you're cool and athletic. You never have to try at anything, and you always come out on top. Look at lacrosse or your grades. You look like you don't give two craps, and yet you make straight As. I mean, even Headmistress Grunnion-Paltine likes you! You have no five percent. Therefore, you're a freak. You'd be better off at the school for all the little perfects like Houssers Academy or even Broadmoor. I can see you wearing the purple-and-gold plumage of the Broadmoor Scots with your flawless complexion and perfect hair."

Ben's perfect complexion was a sore point for her.

"I have a five percent," Ben insisted. "I just haven't found it yet. Or maybe my five percent is that I don't have a five percent." Ben knew that would get Beatrix, seeing as her detector for understatement was calibrated at "super sensitive."

Ben walked with his shoulders relaxed and his hands in his pockets, as if he didn't have a care in the world.

Typical Ben. La-dee-da and life goes on, and it's probably awesome 'cause that's the way it is for Wonder Ben!

"Okay. Okay," Beatrix said, laughing. "But look at me. I'm a freak. My hair is a blasted bird's nest the moment I get out of the shower. It was a lost cause at that salon on Madison when Rosemarie made me get my hair done. The stylist quit mid-procedure and declared my hair unmanageable. My five percent is my normal. I'm ninety-five percent freak show with a five percent dash of normalcy that no one sees or wants to see."

The reference to their stepmother sobered the conversation, but Beatrix continued, undeterred, launching into a self-deprecating monologue as they walked on the traverse near the Tavern on the Green. "Yes, a freak! The hair. The glasses. And for some reason, I'm not a candidate for contacts or laser surgery. Sweet! Tell her what she's won, Bob!"

Beatrix held up her cell phone like a game show host's microphone and used a formal booming voice. "Well, Beatrix you've won an all-expenses-paid trip to Zitsville, the capital of Pimpletonia.'" She lowered her phone and reverted to her normal voice. "I wash my face more than anyone I know, and you eat total garbage, yet your face looks like a newborn baby's butt. And you want to know what else?"

Beatrix was on a roll, and Ben, who was entertained by her rant, let her continue as he shuffled his feet to spread the pebbles on the path near the Strawberry Fields monument.

"I'm five foot one, and I'm done growing. My growth plates are fused. I saw the freakin' X-rays. I'm short, and I'm not going to do anything but shrink as I age and my spinal column degenerates. Aces! Toss in these braces I've had since Rosemarie took me to that hack of an orthodontist in Tribeca."

"Isn't that where you met Malik?" Ben asked.

"Ugh. Yes, okay. That's great. We have that and unfortunately more in common."

"With Malik? Like what?"

Beatrix thought it surprising that Ben was the only popular kid she knew who would not take a cheap shot at someone like Malik. Everyone loved an easy target, but Ben seemed to be above it.

His five percent? Oblivious altruism? Wow. . . .

"We're both different. That's it. Just different. Okay?"

"Gosh, I was only asking. Hey, maybe you just have a little more of Dad in you than you thought."

Beatrix stopped on the bridge overlooking Wollman Rink and looked at Ben. "Really."

It was not a question.

Thanks a lot, Ben. You know just what to say. . . .

Beatrix kept the rest of her five percent to herself. For some reason, she'd been hearing the same song in her head since she could form memories, an orchestral piece that she couldn't identify. Meanwhile, she couldn't get her AirPods to function for her. Even though they worked on Ben's phone, they wouldn't work for her. So, she needed to be hardwired to her phone with a stupid cord.

Then there were the hand driers and touch-free water faucets, none of which ever worked for her either. The only place anything ever worked at all was at the Mothership: Festermunder.

Am I a freakin' vampire? Honestly?

Finally, there were the migraines and the intense "flash visions" of things that looked, most peculiarly, like stars and galaxies.

Festermunder - 5:01 p.m.

The coast was clear to her locker as Beatrix, who was simultaneously scrolling her social media feeds, ran as fast as her legs would carry her.

Thank goodness!

Grabbing her books and stuffing her satchel took less than thirty seconds. Beatrix ran down the deserted halls, slowing as she passed classroom windows. She remembered the technique from an old 1980s movie that featured a kid who was a lot like Ben. Then she made a hard right toward the stairs, eyes glued to her phone. After a quick stop in the powder room and another frustrating attempt to get the sensor for the faucet and hand drier to work, Beatrix continued to bolt down the halls.

As she rounded a corner, she ran into a large object that was both hard and soft at the same time, a monolith of humanity. It was thick and over six feet tall, and its breathing created a slight nose whistle.

Beatrix had just slammed, braces first, into the immovable object known as Headmistress Grunnion-Paltine. The woman sized up her prey as if she were about to devour her. Then, taking a deep breath, she spoke in a surprising shrill and feminine voice. "Miss . . . Voght."

Her eyes narrowed, and an evil grin spread across her face, revealing a large chasm between her central incisors.

Oh God, please no. Not today.

"Yes, Headmistress," Beatrix replied.

"It's Headmistress Grunnion-Paltine to you, Miss Voght."

"Yes, Headmistress Onion-Palpatine. I'm sorry." The headmistress seemed to ignore or not notice the mistake in nomenclature, which included a reference to a pungent vegetable and Darth Vader's master.

"Miss Voght, do you recall the penalty for running in my halls? Or do you need a reminder?"

"Ma'am, I'm not sure—"

"Silence," the headmistress said, her palm outstretched. Beatrix was transfixed by the size of the woman's fingers, which were as big as sausages.

"The penalty for violation of the code of conduct here at Festermunder Academy is . . . filing."

Filing. The dreaded job of coming in on the weekend and returning all the books issued to each class and student, and then reshelving them as per the Dewey Decimal System. Festermunder could have easily upgraded to a computer-based system, which would have been cheaper, more efficient, and less sadistic.

No, here at ol' Festermunder, we pay homage to Dewey, the creator of the obsolete in a library that's rumored to be haunted. Great!

Beatrix had heard all the stories. Everyone had. Rumors abounded about something evil down there. Something dark. There were stories about kids who had gone missing down there in the 1980s. A few years ago, a new kid had supposedly snuck down to the basement library, and the elevator never came back up.

A giant analogue clock with dozens of hands pointing to numbers and symbols hung above the elevator to the library. It was covered with incongruous shapes and objects that resembled planets and galaxies. Students mysteriously referred to the basement library at Festermunder as the World Under the Clock.

"You will be here next Saturday a week from now at eight o'clock sharp with the other miscreants to complete your assigned tasks. Failure to be there at the appointed time in the properly appointed uniform will result in further penalties. An additional term next summer is not off the table for you, Miss Voght."

"Yes, ma'am," Beatrix replied, then headed down the hall toward the stairs.

"Saturday night, eight o'clock sharp, at the library rotunda. Not one minute later, Miss Voght," the headmistress shrilly called out after her.

"Yes, ma'am," Beatrix said.

Wait a second, next Saturday a week? That's Thanksgiving break! Great.

Beatrix Voght was going to the World Under the Clock.

CHAPTER 2

A Night
in the Park

BEATRIX WAS FINISHING HER BREAKFAST ALONE ON THE balcony overlooking West 84th Street, pondering her yesterday and planning for her today. After recovering from her fainting spell in the alley, she had wondered if seeing the doppelganger of herself was real or just a dream. She still wasn't sure.

It was Saturday, November 20, and next week the Festermunder students would be dismissed for Thanksgiving break. Classes would be slow until they got out next Wednesday. She enjoyed having no responsibilities until the next weekend and her dreaded detention at the Mothership. Pulling her knees up onto the chair and drawing the blanket under her feet, Beatrix picked up her second mug of coffee, cupping it with both hands and blowing on it before she took a sip.

The sky was overcast, and it would probably rain later, but the cold November air did not bother Beatrix. She had always liked cold, cloudy days. Curling up in her "reading window" with her pug, Parfleet, over-looking the street and wrapped in a blanket against the gray melancholy was a sanctuary.

Her peaceful breakfast was broken by the rap of five-inch heels across the parquet floor in the den, signaling that Rosemarie was on a mission.

She opened the French door to the balcony and stuck her head through the drapes. Rosemarie Crerar-Voght was considered by many to be beautiful in the generic sense. Tall, slender, and fit, she was obsessed with her physique, continually asking Ben and Beatrix to check various parts of her body for cellulite. She was intensely concerned about the "suppleness" of her calves. Beneath her towering sense of self-importance and vanity, Beatrix thought Rosemarie had the emotional intelligence of a lost child. Her blond hair was long and flowing. No neighbor ever caught Rosemarie out in less than her best procurement. Even her workout clothes were more expensive than most people's formal attire.

Rosemarie had come from French-Canadian aristocracy, or so she would have others think. Beatrix thought she smelled like fake royalty. At age twenty-five, after a stint of modeling, she married Dr. Wendell Voght, then dashing and thirtysomething. Shortly before that, Wendell had adopted Beatrix and Ben at age five and six, respectively. At his core, he was a family man.

Rosemarie was none too happy about the arrangement and, at first, considered the prospect of children who were not her own to be an embarrassing knock on her spawning social status, and she even spoke of divorce. It was an empty threat, though. Rosemarie never wanted her own kids, stating that pregnancy would make her dreadful, fat, and irrelevant. Besides, Rosemarie was far too enamored with Wendell's financial status and the social pipeline he provided among New York luminaries to give up on the marriage just because of two rotten foster kids. Ironically, Rosemarie never inquired as to their origin when Wendell returned with Ben and Beatrix after a trip to upstate New York.

Wendell came from a well-to-do family who owned publishing houses in New York and the UK. He was not involved in the family business but, as an only child, was allotted a share of the family fortune. To his credit, Wendell could have taken much more but chose not to. He had inherited the apartment at Wellesley from his grandfather, Waverly Voght.

Beatrix thought she had figured out Rosemarie's true motive. Rosemarie planned to wait it out. She would endure until Wendell died of his malady or was committed to the funny farm; then she would have her lawyer friend redo the will and take over the family fortune. At that point, Ben and Beatrix would be shipped off to boarding school until age eighteen. Then she would dump them, and Rosemarie would be home free and the wealthy majority stockholder in several successful companies. Beatrix detested her foster mother for many things but, most of all, for how she treated Wendell. Rosemarie despised him.

"I'll be out all weekend and late coming home Sunday," Rosemarie said without making eye contact as she thumbed through social media on her phone. "Make no plans. Someone has to watch him. Your brother has football today. Let him know it's his responsibility to get transportation to and from practice—"

"Rosemarie, it's a lacrosse tournament, and it's all day, way out in Hoboken," Beatrix said.

"Ugh." Rosemarie feigned nausea. "Here's the Visa Black Card. Have him take an Uber."

"An Uber?" Beatrix looked at her in disdain. "You want a fifteen-year-old to take an Uber alone to New Jersey?"

"If I wanted your opinion on the matter, Beatrix, I would have asked you for it. Now, I'm off. Watch Wendell, and make sure he doesn't do anything stupid like burn the place down or walk down Amsterdam Avenue naked."

She stalked off, her hips swaying to each side, then picked up a piece of paper from the counter and brought it back. "I found this on our door this morning after my jog."

She angrily flicked it at Beatrix, who swiped it out of the air and then read it.

> Want to play Druidia today?
> I'm going to be bored.
> — Malik ☺

Beatrix shook her head and snickered. Only Malik was dorky enough to type a note. He couldn't text, as he had no phone per parental rules. Beatrix had her own means of contacting him.

"I thought I told you I don't want to see that little weasel up here on our floor. No one buzzes him in, and he still gets up here, slinking about the halls. Someone that creepy shouldn't be walking around the Wellesley. What will the neighbors think?"

"If you're right, Rosemarie, then I don't belong here either. I'm just an orphan, remember? Malik may be weird, but at least he doesn't judge people."

"Oh, you and your little mouth. Hmm . . ." Rosemarie reached out with mock parental compassion and fixed Beatrix's hair. "Spoiled little brat. Someday . . . Nonetheless, take a shower and do something with your hair. You'll look like a vagabond if you take that mongrel Parfait out like that. Mr. Keane doesn't like that dog in the building any more than I do. T'would be a shame if he went missing one day while you were away."

"His name is Parfleet, not Parfait, and he's like family to me. Besides Ben, he's the only one in this joint who cares about me." Beatrix checked her phone. "It's quarter to eleven. Aren't you late for a very important engagement? Are you speaking at the UN or doing brain surgery rounds at Sinai this time?"

Rosemarie gave an insincere grin to show her disgust. "Go wash your face with the cleanser the dermatologist prescribed. You're one big breakout."

Beatrix watched with amusement as Rosemarie stalked off on her clomping heels, slamming the front door behind her.

Life was so much easier before the Scotland thing.

Over the years, things hadn't been easy for Ben and Beatrix. As a result, they had formed a bond not easily broken. They called it the Rule of Two: "It's just us. We must have each other's back no matter what. We're all we have." It was an odd mantra for two kids in a four-person family. Being fostered and adopted wasn't the problem, at least back in the old days. Prior to Scotland, being adopted was the greatest thing that had ever happened to them. Being foster children since they could form memories was not something they ever talked about with anyone, including each other.

Dad, as they both thought of Wendell, was their hero and the most interesting person they had ever met. Professor Wendell S. Voght was chairman of the Department of Archeology and Anthropology at New York University. He also had a keen interest in astronomy and celestial physics. To "B Squared," as he used to call them, he was just Dad. They never considered him a foster parent. He was whimsical, funny, and adventurous, a renaissance man born too late. A life set to music.

In those rare, quiet moments when Beatrix caught Wendell alone, he seemed melancholy. She never told Ben about it, but she continued to watch Wendell from afar, glimpsing a different side of him—a preoccupation that betrayed something deeper.

Wendell had the saddest eyes she had ever seen. He also had an idiosyncrasy that belied his dashing nature. Never, not even when Ben and Beatrix asked him repeatedly, would Wendell speak of one subject, even though he was transfixed by it. It was like he was afraid. Even when pressed, he refused to discuss anything about his quiet obsession.

The stars.

Wendell was a shadow of his former self. At one time, the forty-five-year-old had been tall, rangy, and rugged. Now he was stooped, frail, thin, pale, and lacking in his former vigor. Wendell used to be loquacious and esoteric in his detailed retellings of his adventures, too much for people who preferred brevity or topical small talk. Although Wendell had enough brains to split the atom, he had the emotional forbearance of a kind father. He actually listened during conversations rather than just waiting for his turn to talk.

Wendell's former passion was travel. Most often, Rosemarie did not accompany him and the kids on their journeys. Wendell would have never called them something as pedestrian as vacations. Cruising the fjords of Norway. Staying a week on an Alaskan ice cutter. The Galapagos islands. Rappelling down a shaft into a South African diamond mine. Coming in to shore at a Normandy Invasion reenactment. Lists of future trips were recorded in his notes. Wendell had an old wooden globe in his study on which he had circled and annotated future trips. Beatrix and Ben had more stamps on their passports than any kids anywhere. He had no qualms about pulling them out of school and home-schooling them on the road.

These days, though, Beatrix wasn't even sure if Wendell knew them anymore. He had taken a journey into mental oblivion, muttering to himself. He had been committed to St. Julien in Saratoga and returned a week later even more out of sorts. Nervous and paranoid, he kept the blinds pulled while constantly peeking down the street toward Central Park with his telescope to identify who he could see. Wendell kept a journal of the people he didn't recognize. He also became transfixed with newspaper clippings and conspiratorial websites. Most were concerned with paranormal phenomena or kidnappings and missing persons. Most curious of all, Wendell had begun disappearing at night into Central Park.

It had all begun after Scotland and those eight hours.

GLAMIS CASTLE 11.19.2014 21:24PM REPORT NO.1753280

Subject: Summoned to investigate "large energy burst" at Castle Glamis near Forfar, Scotland. Sensors picked up gamma radiation swell emanating from secluded upper room. Another type of radiation not recognized by our spectroscopy was picked up that requires further study. Wendell S. Vogt, Ph.D was trespassing in areas forbidden by facility. Subject was incoherent and uncooperative. Subject stated he was only gone a few minutes but was unaccounted for 8 hours; all in one room with one door. Arrived by his own accord in the upper foyer and retrieved by Mr. Nigel Geddings who said he "appeared out of nowhere."

Conclusion: Dr. Voght suffered anxiety attack and has acute PTSD as well as retrograde amnesia. Dr. Voght was evacuated for a medical evaluation and will require further debriefing on something he kept referring to as a "rythrax" (sic). Claims he lost it in the "meridian." Dr. Voght babbled numeric gibberish that seemed astrological in nature and would not elaborate. We currently have no explanation for the unknown energy burst or how he disappeared in a 12' x 12' room.

Recommendation: This is decidedly a Section 16 Unexplained Phenomena case and does not concern Section 3 (Operations).

Priority Level: Orange (lowest)

Special Agent: Elizabeth Soames-Briggs, Mi5 (Sec. 3)

Beatrix heard the sound of pecking on a keyboard in the study and ambled over to check on Wendell. He was always up first, drinking coffee all day. She opened the French doors to the study and took stock of the room. Papers were strewn all over the place, covered in gibberish—unintelligible hieroglyphics, nonsensical mathematical formulae, and equations. Numerous star charts were pinned everywhere, and newspaper articles and printouts were pinned and taped all over the bookshelves. The room looked straight out of the *X-Files*. Most of his notes were a conspiracy theorist's dream. Wendell had taken a keen interest in disappearances, especially luminaries in the arts and sciences.

Beatrix stopped short of tapping Wendell on the shoulder as he hunched over his large desk, facing away from her. She wished last year had not happened. She wanted to hug her dad and for everything to have been a bad dream. Wendell continued typing as he muttered under his breath. He was no longer the tall, vital adventurer. Sitting there in his bathrobe and slippers, he looked like a frail, unshaven, broken old man.

Breaking out of her daze, Beatrix took note of the globe. It was a huge, hulking amber sphere, covered in annotations. Locations all over the world were marked with small pins, including places she had visited before the event in Scotland—Rome, Athens, Iceland, France—places they had traveled to before everything had changed.

Beatrix noticed that Wendell's fountain pen and inkwell were on the globe's orbital rim and had been used recently. New markings and lines connected points not referenced before. The lines formed a complex system of rays that looked like a spider's web and were oddly symmetrical.

"Uh, Dad?" Beatrix said, her voice barely above a whisper. "Dad?"

No response.

"Wendell!"

Wendell sat up ramrod straight and turned his head toward the intrusion, then returned to his computer the screen.

Beatrix sighed. "There's breakfast on the bar in the kitchen. Rosemarie said you need to shower and get moving today."

A lie but an innocent one.

Wendell stood up and shuffled off to the kitchen, mumbling and writing figures on a yellow pad as he walked.

Alone in the study, Beatrix stole a glance of the screen. It featured a PDF of what appeared to be architectural blueprints. Beatrix studied the blueprints for a moment and then clicked on a link, opening a new window for Rutherford Appleton Laboratory, Oxfordshire, Britain. Oddly satisfied, Beatrix closed the page. Glancing at Wendell's PDF, she saw the words "DIAMOND LIGHT SOURCE" inscribed in tiny text vertically up the side of the page. She glanced over her shoulder to ensure Wendell wasn't coming back. Then she slurped another sip of cold coffee as she clicked Wendell's search history. It mostly consisted of obscure scientific articles. As she clicked through them, her brain took snapshots of each page. It was a talent of hers.

One of my few.

Antimatter. Einstein-Rosen Bridge. Andromeda particle. Snap, click. Snap, click. Beatrix jotted them down in her mind.

After exiting the browser, she noticed Wendell's iPhone—which never left his sight—revealed a text that had come in twenty-two minutes earlier.

Oddly, Mr. Conspiracy theorist doesn't code out his lock screen. Freaking amateur night!

It read:

$$\pi - \emptyset - 1 / 12 / 15 / 14 / 5$$

The floor creaked and Beatrix took a sharp breath.

Then she exhaled, as it was only Parfleet coming to let her know he needed breakfast. Beatrix covered her tracks at the computer and walked out of the study, closing the door behind her. Not for the first time, she was keenly interested in the nocturnal activities of Dr. Wendell S. Voght.

Beatrix looked up the Greek alphabet on her phone and found no significance for π other than its mathematical usage with circles. She gave it up as a lost cause and spent the rest of the afternoon and early evening reading while listening to music, forgetting that she had not responded to Malik's note.

Ben rolled in at 7:45 p.m. and began eating as he stood with the fridge open. As usual, Rosemarie was nowhere to be found. Beatrix, wearing flannel pajama pants and a Coldplay T-shirt with slippers, appeared as Ben closed the fridge door, startling him.

"Hey, if someone said the words 'pi' and then the symbol for 'zero' what would that mean to you?" she asked, Parfleet in her arms.

Ben swallowed a gulp of water to wash down his pizza before replying. "Hmm . . . Is this a verbal conversation or a text?"

"A text! Duh."

"Assuming you're not inquiring about the pastry, pi, as in the symbol pi, like 3.14597 . . ."

"I got it, Einstein. What do you make of it?" Beatrix showed Ben her phone screen. "It was on Dad's phone with an 'o' with a slash through it. Then one dash twelve dash fourteen dash fifteen dash five. The sender was blocked."

"It sounds like instructions. I mean, you know he frequents the park at night. Maybe you've discovered a clue about his nightly activities."

Ben washed a green apple and then took a bite. His mouth full, he typed something on his phone. "It's a stupid code," he said once he had chewed and swallowed. "The numbers correspond to letters in the alphabet. I only know that because we know the context because of Dad's activities. It says, '3:14 a.m. Onassis Reservoir. A-L-O-N-E. Don't get followed.'" He took another gargantuan bite of the apple and walked past her, chewing confidently.

How did he figure it out so fast? I was on it for hours? Idiot! But I guess he knew this was going to be about Central Park.

Ben slipped off his sweaty lacrosse jersey and then stood in the kitchen in his brown Festermunder shirt and sweats. "I'm going too."

Beatrix raised an eyebrow. "Excuse me?"

"You heard me, Beatrix. You're going into the park tonight, and you intend to follow him. If you do, I'm going too, and my decision is final."

Beatrix wasn't used to Ben talking to her like that, and it set her off balance.

"Listen here, Ben, this is my thing, and I think it best that you aren't involved." Parfleet, still in her arms, got agitated, so Beatrix let him down. He darted for Ben, jumping into his arms.

"Right. So, I'm going too, and we'll take ol' Par here as our watchdog. Then if we encounter a cop, we can say we're walking our dog and didn't mean to violate the park curfew."

Beatrix regarded her brother's confident face for a moment before she gave in. "Okay, but I'm calling the shots tonight."

Ben snickered. "Was it really going to be any other way?"

If you knew what I saw yesterday, you might not be so smug.

They spent the next several hours in Beatrix's room, waiting for Wendell to leave. To pass the time, Ben would tie a knot in his shoelaces and Beatrix, while holding Parfleet, would try to undo it. When they heard Wendell leave at 2:11 a.m., they made preparations for their covert mission. Ben was tired, but Beatrix was amped up and in her element.

Suddenly, she noticed a green laser light shining onto Bono's forehead on the U2 poster by the door.

"Oh, I don't believe this!" Beatrix slammed the hoodie she was holding onto the bed and stormed over to her Celestron telescope by the window. "Some nerve!" She mouthed the words "not now" with a vehemence that went beyond her typical petty annoyance of dealing with Malik.

Across the street, looking through his own telescope, complete with night vision (which he had made himself, no doubt), he mouthed, "What's up?" then stood there grinning.

He doesn't even get how uncool he is.

Beatrix scratched some words onto a dry erase board and then held it up.

None of your business!

Then she stomped off to the bathroom to complete her ensemble for the reconnaissance mission.

Ben strode over to the Celestron and mouthed a salutation to Malik. Then he waved goodbye and pulled the shade.

Beatrix, clad in black sweats and a gray hoodie, emerged from the bathroom with Parfleet in her backpack. The pug's head was resting on her right shoulder as he looked at Ben.

"Ready?"

Other than the street sweepers and trash trucks, 84th Street was deserted. Beatrix and Ben hurried toward the park, bracing themselves against the cold air. Parfleet had burrowed down inside Beatrix's backpack and showed no signs of surfacing. The distance between avenues was considerable, and both siblings shuddered, their teeth chattering as they strode toward Columbus Avenue. Ben, a creature of habit, pushed the button to cross Columbus and intended to wait for the "walk" signal even though the street was devoid of traffic. Beatrix gave Ben a "you've got to be kidding me" look but waited until it was "safe" to cross.

As they crossed Columbus through the howling wind, they thought they heard a voice call out to them through the night air. At first, Ben and Beatrix dismissed it as a "night person" who had best be avoided. Suddenly, a cab flew down the avenue and slammed on its brakes, honking its horn. Standing dumbfounded in the middle of the intersection with his hands on the yellow cab's grill was none other than Malik.

Realizing that any hope of keeping a low profile had been blown to bits, Beatrix stalked over to Malik and unloaded on him as the cab drove off, the driver having yelled at Malik and shaken his fist at him through the windshield. "Are you freaking crazy?" Beatrix asked. "What's your problem, huh? What is it that you don't get? There was a reason—"

"Beatrix, it's alright," Ben said, only to be silenced by Beatrix's index finger.

"We have an arrangement, Malik! We're not supposed to get in each other's way!"

As Beatrix continued to berate her on-and-off friend, she realized Malik was shivering and sniffing, his nose running as he listened. He was dressed in striped pajamas, the pajama shirt tucked in as tight as ever. A Members Only jacket and slippers (no socks) completed the ensemble.

"Geez, dude, what the heck are you in PJs for?" Beatrix inquired, still angry but with a hint of concern in her voice that meant the world to Malik. "It's freezing out here."

"It's past my bedtime, and this is what I sleep in. Soddy, I don't understand what's going on."

"*We're* out walking Parfleet, and *you* were just headed home!"

"Beatrix!" Ben said with enough emphasis to indicate he had indulged her long enough. "I invited Malik along."

Beatrix stared at her brother, incredulous.

"I signaled it to him with the telescope when you were in the bathroom. I thought it would be a good idea. Don't worry; it's cool."

Beatrix looked at Ben, her mouth agape, then gestured for him to go on. "This better be good."

"Malik has night-vision goggles and laser pointers that we can signal each other with. It would have been rude to ask him for the stuff and not take him along. Besides, he's the only one of us smart enough to use this equipment. Malik's cool."

Having never heard those words used to describe himself throughout his fourteen years, Malik was stunned. After recovering, Malik opened his *Star Wars* backpack to reveal the goggles. "Fully loaded and ready to rock and roll, baby."

"Shut up. Keep up. And stay quiet."

Beatrix spun on her heel and walked off toward the park as Ben reached out and gave Malik a soft punch on the shoulder to say "it'll be alright" before they followed Beatrix to Central Park West.

Any normal parent would have considered them all missing and soon to be fugitives. Not having any normal parents, Beatrix was determined to find and follow the one person she did consider to be her parent—Wendell. Ben was determined to protect Beatrix. Parfleet was determined to stay warm. And Malik Patel was determined to be cool.

They entered the park three blocks north of the Museum of Natural History. Beatrix glanced to her right down Central Park West at the huge building where she had so many good memories with Wendell.

That was then. This is now.

The trio made their way to the 86th Street traverse and headed for the reservoir. No one else was out. The park had a strict curfew from 1:00–6:00 a.m., and only police and vehicular traffic were allowed. Ben made sure that none of Malik's sensitive equipment would deploy prematurely and blow their cover.

Striking out on the bridal footpath, they made it the 150 yards to the edge of the water before Beatrix motioned for Ben and Malik to join her in a thicket of trees.

"Stay hidden," she said. "We don't want whomever he's meeting with to see us. Besides, this is a recon patrol. Observe and report only. We don't, under any circumstances, want to get made or make contact."

And so, they waited. It was 3:01 a.m. and 33°F according to Ben's phone. They shivered and huddled close in the thicket for warmth.

"I need to pee," Malik said, breaking the silence.

"You're kidding," Beatrix whispered. "Hold it in."

"I can't. Soddy, I've been holding it ever since I left home. I was so excited to come along that I forgot to go."

"Malik, can you make it a little longer, dude?" Then a thought hit him. "Just go right here, man. It's all good. Just step around the trees."

Malik gave him a horrified look. "I'm veddy soddy, but that is not possible. I need privacy, and I need to wash my hands after. I have a cold, and my immune system is compromised. Any extra bacteria could be problematic for me."

"Malik," Beatrix snarled, "just go to the restroom then, but you're going alone. Don't take the footpath and stick to the tree line. The bathrooms are down about a hundred yards to the right, and they're probably locked anyway, but go see for yourself!"

Malik handed Ben and Beatrix a pair of night-vision goggles and a laser pointer and then set off at a modified scamper, crouching as he zigzagged through the trees like a soldier trying to avoid enemy fire.

Ben turned to Beatrix and grinned in the moonlight. Beatrix rolled her eyes and snickered, which broke the tension for a moment.

To his surprise and relief, Malik found the bathrooms were unlocked. After doing his business, he washed his hands, then looked in the streaky metal mirror and ran his fingers through his hair. "Hey, baby," he said. "Do you want to play video games with me?"

Just then, a toilet flushed with a deafening roar in the last stall. Malik froze, stricken with panic. He was afraid it was a policeman and that he, of all people, would be responsible for compromising the mission.

The stall door creaked open, but Malik stood there, accepting his fate. It turned out to be a scruffy old man with white hair and a beard, who appeared to be homeless. The stranger washed his hands, acknowledged Malik with a barely perceptible nod, then exited the lavatory. Malik exhaled with relief.

Malik raced back to the thicket, only to find it empty. He slipped on his night-vision goggles but saw no sign of Ben and Beatrix.

In fact, Beatrix and Ben hadn't moved an inch. Malik, however, had gone right instead of left when he left the restroom. Ben had watched the entire thing through their night-vision goggles. He considered using his laser pointer to direct Malik, but he feared giving away their position.

"That idiot is going the wrong way!" Ben said.

"Really?" Beatrix whispered. "No street smarts! Well, forget him. We can find him after we find Dad."

They continued scanning the circumference of the reservoir, looking for Wendell and his mysterious contact on the footpath. So far, nothing.

"Where are you, Wendell?" Ben whispered.

Beatrix remained mute. She was beginning to feel strange. Not herself. She felt the familiar pinprick of worry in her mind and of the hairs standing up on the back of her neck. Her heart was pounding, feeling like it wanted to crawl up into her throat. Ben noticed her distress.

"Beatrix? Are you okay?"

"Ben, I . . . I need to tell you something about yesterday. Um, it's going to sound completely freaking crazy, but on the way home from school I —"

Ben gasped.

Beatrix looked along the footpath, but it was devoid of people. Then she realized Ben wasn't looking at the path. He was looking at the water.

"What in the blazes?" Beatrix stammered.

Directing her view to the reservoir, she was choked with amazement, coupled with fear. Beatrix grabbed Ben's arm to support her, as she thought she might pass out.

Wendell was in the middle of the reservoir, and he appeared to be standing on the water's surface.

As Ben stared at the apparition, he removed his jacket. Feeling the adrenaline too, Beatrix removed her hoodie, hoping the chill November air would calm her nerves.

Only it's not cold, she thought. *It's as hot as a furnace out here!*

"Ben," Beatrix said, her lower lip trembling, "what the hell is happening?"

"I don't know, B. I don't know." Ben was shaking too.

The heat coupled with the cold water of the reservoir condensed into a steamy fog. Then the siblings noticed a green light dancing through the haze. It looked like a hopping firefly.

"Oh no. That's Malik's laser," Ben said. "He knows he's lost and needs help. We're blown."

Sweating profusely, Beatrix watched the Wendell apparition out on the water through the haze. He was standing completely still as if in suspended animation, his hands at his sides.

Suddenly, a path was cut approximately six feet wide and from the edge of the reservoir to where Wendell was. He talked and gestured for a few moments, then squatted into a ball. There was an intense flash of light; then a funnel of air appeared to suck Wendell down into the water. The path that had been cut through the mist refilled from the inside and disappeared.

Ben and Beatrix were dumbfounded, standing there motionless until they regained their senses.

"Beatrix, let's go! This place isn't safe. I need to get you out of here." They were about to leave when Ben stopped short. "Aw, crap! Malik!"

Beatrix took off at a dead run, heading east on the footpath. Shocked at her speed, Ben caught up to her as she raced past the bathrooms, then stopped and cast about for Malik. She flashed her green laser light in the hopes that he would see it.

"Malik!" she hissed. "Malik, come out!"

Ben put his goggles back on and scanned the reservoir's periphery. He was out of breath and sick with worry for their companion.

Beatrix saw a faint red-orange glow about 300 feet down the footpath. She exhaled with relief and they both took off.

"Weren't all the lasers green?" Ben asked as they ran toward it.

They both stopped dead in their tracks as the area exploded with light, pushing back the thick darkness. The streetlights and security lamps around the reservoir had been off, which they hadn't noticed during Wendell's disappearance. Now that they were on again, they saw a figure standing under a streetlight in front of them.

And it wasn't Malik.

The figure was tall, almost certainly a man. He was wearing a black fedora and a black suit. His head was tipped forward, as if staring at the ground. They couldn't make out his facial features under the shadow of his hat, but they saw the red-orange glow of a cigarette as it dangled from his lips.

Beatrix pulled Ben behind a tree. "Ben, who is that?"

"I don't know, but he's not friendly. We have got to get Malik and get out of here!"

When they peeked out again the figure was gone. Then they heard rustling in the shrubs behind them. They crouched behind the tree, Ben shielding Beatrix and Parfleet growling.

"Get ready to run, Beatrix. I'll cover you, but you need to go now while I hold it off."

Ben's body was coiled like a snake, ready to strike.

With his penchant for materializing and disappearing at the most inopportune times, Malik emerged from the thicket. Ben relaxed and let out his breath, as did Beatrix. At that point, they were both far too frightened to be angry with Malik.

"Malik, you good?" Ben asked.

Malik poked out his lips and flashed a hip-hop symbol with his fingers contorted in a non-ironic manner.

Beatrix shook her head, her brow furrowed in disapproval, then straightened up. "Let's go. We can talk this out later."

Getting home was cold but mercifully uneventful.

"Lock your doors, Malik," Ben said as they bid him goodnight. Ben said they would wait until Malik made it up to his family's apartment and signaled from his bedroom window that he was safe.

"It was stupid of you to come," Beatrix said, "but thanks. We needed the equipment."

Malik nodded, then climbed the steps to his building, his feet dragging from fatigue.

"And, Malik, you can't tell a soul about this. Understand? We'll meet up tomorrow. I'll buzz you in at noon. Okay?"

"Okay." Malik yawned and went inside.

Anxious to put a locked door between themselves and the night, Ben and Beatrix scrambled into their apartment. They were both overcome with thirst, and each downed a twenty-ounce bottle of water before either of them spoke. Parfleet had his fill as well.

"What do you think?" Ben asked. "Should we contact the police?"

Beatrix picked up a banana and held it like a phone. "Sure, good idea. Hey, 9-1-1 emergency. Hi, there. I'm fine too. Thanks! Hey look, uh, I'm Beatrix Voght, and I'd like to report a missing person. He disa-freakin'-peared while standing on the surface of a twenty-foot-deep freaking reservoir in Central Park. Yup, he was wrapped in green light and just vanished from the face of the Earth. What? Oh yes! Come to think of it, it was unreasonably hot in the immediate vicinity. Yes! It went from thirty-three degrees to freaking eighty-four degrees in ten seconds! Yes! I did see a seven-foot-tall man in black with a hat that looked like he came from the darkest place in the universe itself. And, oh wait, the day before I just so happened to see—"

"Okay, I get it. No police—yet."

"I'm tired," Beatrix said.

Ben nodded. "Me too, and I don't think I've ever felt so weak. Must be the adrenaline wearing off." He gave Beatrix a hug. "We'll find him, and we'll also find out what happened."

"Yeah."

"Goodnight, Beatrix."

"Goodnight, Ben."

"Beatrix?"

"What?"

"Why did you say that?"

"Say what?" Beatrix asked.

"The darkest place in the universe. Why did you say that?"

Beatrix looked at the floor and then shrugged. "Goodnight."

They trudged off to their rooms.

Ben fell asleep the moment his face hit the pillow.

Beatrix lay there awake. She was exhausted, but couldn't fall asleep.

When Beatrix finally dozed off, Parfleet in his usual spot by her head, she was troubled by her dreams. A man in a black hat and with a featureless face was following her down Broadway. She was alone, and there was no one to call to. She wanted to run, but her legs were like cement. The Hat Man disappeared into green light, leaving only a whisper of his presence in her mind.

All that was left were the stars.

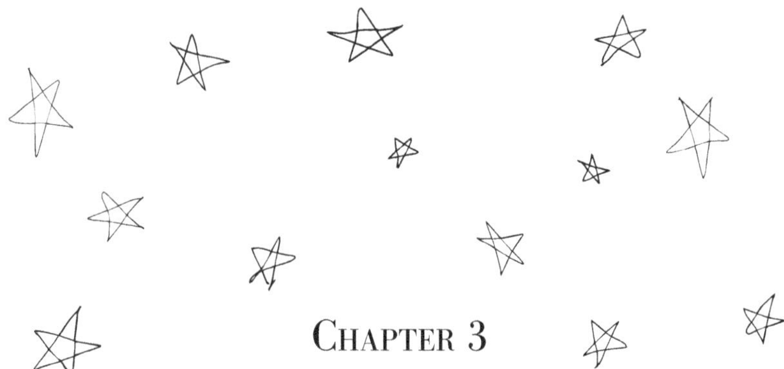

Briefing, Debriefing, and Mulligatawny

MR. KEANE, THE DOORMAN, BUZZED THE VOGHT APART-ment for permission to let up their guest. Not fond of children and even less inclined toward teenagers, Mr. Keane frowned at Malik. "You may go up. Fifth floor only." His headphones blaring, Malik gave a left-handed mock salute and then boarded the elevator.

It was noon. Beatrix and Ben were sitting in the kitchen sharing a microwave pizza. Rosemarie was still on hiatus to parts unknown, and Wendell, of course, had literally disappeared to parts unknown. The prospect of no authority figures around exhilarated Beatrix.

Malik took off his headphones as he entered the kitchen, then picked up the pizza box to examine it. "Gluten free?"

Ben shook his head as he chewed, indicating the pizza was fully leaded.

"I'll just eat my apple then," Malik. "If I eat gluten, there will be serious repercussions and —"

"Malik, we get it, okay?" Beatrix had things on her mind, and Malik's dietary constraints were not among them.

She gripped the counter with both hands and stared at her feet.

Realizing she was composing herself prior to launching into a monologue, Ben swallowed what he had been chewing and prepared to listen.

"Let me start by saying that everything that has happened in the last two days has been completely surreal for me, and my head is swimming," Beatrix began. "I'm sure yours is too, Ben. Malik, for better or for worse, you got dragged into this last night." She raised her eyebrows at Ben in admonishment. "And I'm sure you're confused as well."

Malik and Ben, who scooped up Parfleet, were sitting on barstools at the cream-colored kitchen island across from Beatrix, waiting for her to continue.

"The way I see it, we need to make a list of what has happened—a problem list—and then come up with possible explanations. It's way too early to think of solutions. We have no idea what we saw last night, but we have to get something out of the way first."

Beatrix grabbed a red felt-tip pen and a paper towel and drew a triangle on it. "This is us. We're the only three who witnessed Wendell vanish on the reservoir last night. Normally, we would tell our parents and the police, but that's out." She pointed at the triangle. "It's just us three. No one outside this triangle has any clue what we know, and I need your word of honor that that is all who will know. Dad used to say that the number of people that know a secret can count on a factor of three learning it. Three cubed is twenty-seven and so on. We can't have that, or we could all be hauled off by some government agency or to the nuthouse—or worse." Beatrix looked straight at Malik. "Can I trust you?"

"Yes. You can trust me," Malik replied.

"Good. It goes without saying that things may become dangerous. Who knows how deep this goes and what forces are causing it?"

Beatrix cleared her throat. "Wendell vanished at 3:14 this morning. We need to know everything about who contacted him. I haven't looked for his phone, but I can't imagine him leaving without it last night. I couldn't check the number because the caller was blocked. We need that phone! Someone set that meeting up."

Malik raised his hand like he was in class at Festermunder. "Who says he was taken?"

Beatrix's nostrils flared. "You saw it yourself, right? I mean what kind of—"

"Soddy, but who says he was taken? It may have not been an abduction. Maybe he planned it himself and meant to vanish."

Ben and Beatrix exchanged glances. Beatrix shook her head almost imperceptibly. *We're not talking about Scotland right now. In fact, we really never found out what Dad saw or how or why he "disappeared" two years ago anyway. No need for Malik to know all of our business and start a bunch of conjecture.*

Ben stood up and began pacing around the island. He attempted to hand Parfleet to Malik, but the pug growled and refused the transfer. Parfleet had no love for Malik.

"We need to go through all of Dad's personal effects, manuscripts, notes, memos, emails, and his Internet history," Ben said. "We have no witnesses besides us, and we can't talk to Dad, so we'll have to piece the information together, just like a detective might. Any detail, no matter how insignificant, is important."

"Agreed." Beatrix tore off another slice of pizza, stuffed it in her mouth, then went to Wendell's study to start digging.

With Parfleet in tow, Beatrix surveyed Wendell's study with renewed interest. Then she gathered her wits and started collecting papers and memos and placing them in an accordion folder for further investigation. Beatrix worked best in a tidy space.

Clean room. Clean mind.

She had always made sure that her room was spotless and organized before beginning her homework, telling herself that it would clear her mind of clutter.

Beatrix was happy to hear Ben and Malik talking in the kitchen, preferring them to be preoccupied with each other's company rather than bothering her during her search. It was a daunting task. Wendell was a gifted hoarder. It would take weeks to sift through so much information, and despite her preference for working alone, she realized she would need the others to help her filter through it.

What the heck am I doing?

Deciding to check the computer rather than collect papers, she flicked on the monitor and checked the desktop, but it was clean and devoid of folders and documents. Opening the browser, Beatrix went to the search history and found it had been wiped clean as well. The hard drive was empty too. Beatrix was startled. She was positive she had checked the computer shortly before they set out for the park, and the data had still been there. If Wendell hadn't been there to erase it, who did?

"Malik!" Beatrix called out. "Malik! Ben, come here!"

Both boys scrambled into the room.

"What did you find?" Ben asked.

"Have you been on this computer at all in the last twenty-four hours? Please say yes."

Ben shook his head. "No, not at all."

"Malik, can a hard drive be wiped remotely, or does it need to be in person at the terminal?"

Malik thought for a moment. "Anyone can bomb a hard drive remotely. It takes out the entire operating system, and the computer is kaput. It won't even turn on. I did that once to my cousin Anish. I napalmed his computer through a worm I sent through his email in retaliation for listing my profile on the eHarmony dating site. It was the most gangsta thing I've ever—"

"Malik, this PC is running fine, but all of Dad's files are gone. His search history has been deleted, his emails are gone, and the recycle bin is empty. He wasn't here to do that. This computer was not 'bombed' from the outside."

"Then someone must have been here while you were out last night," Malik said.

"I swear thought I locked the door, Beatrix," Ben said.

"We can see if any files have been modified or deleted and at what time," Malik said.

"That's possible?" Beatrix asked. When Malik nodded, she smiled. "Oh my goodness, Malik, you're a lifesaver! Let's do it!"

Beaming with pride, Malik stepped over a pile of papers and sat at the desk. He began typing furiously in computer code. Ben looked at Beatrix and shrugged, then turned and headed for the door. "Let us know if you need anything, Malik. We'll be in the—"

"Got it!" Malik exclaimed.

Ben and Beatrix exchanged an impressed look, then turned to Malik and gestured for more information.

"Some large files were copied to a compression software online and sent somewhere that's encrypted beyond anything I've seen. It doesn't even look like regular code. It's more like gibberish. These were huge files with tons of data. Impressive, three terabytes—"

"Malik, focus!" Beatrix said.

"At 2:56 a.m., last night, the files were duplicated, compressed, and dumped somewhere offsite, then deleted permanently and can't be retrieved. But it was done locally at this computer terminal."

The thought of someone sneaking into their home, made Beatrix's skin crawl.

Taking a more proactive approach, Ben went to the mud room to grab his lacrosse stick and began searching every nook and cranny of the apartment, Parfleet at his heels. It had become a much darker and more sinister situation than they realized. All three of them were scared, especially Beatrix.

"Malik," Beatrix said, "your parents are out of town, right?"

"Yes, they're on sabbatical in Calcutta until after Christmas break."

"Who looks after you when they're gone?" Ben asked. "Surely, you're not alone over there in your place."

"No, I'm not staying alone. My cousin Kasra is twenty-two and goes to NYU. He stays over to make sure I'm alright, and we have family in the Upper West near 101st. But Kasra is practically never around, as he works as a DJ. Like last night, I had no idea where he was."

"You were alone?" Ben asked, wide-eyed.

"Yes. After I got home, I slept in the closet with the light on covered in my old stuffed animals. It was quite claustrophobic—and sceddy." Malik pronounced "scary" as "sceddy."

"Can we stay with you tonight?" Beatrix asked. "I don't feel safe here."

Malik was overwhelmed. "My place? Sure, it'll be great! I've never had a sleepover before. Do you want me to stay there too?"

Ben smiled. "Yeah, Malik, we do. It's all good, dude. We'll be over at seven o'clock or so. Then we can make plans. It'll be fun."

Malik could hardly trust himself to speak. "I will make muffins," he said thickly. "Gluten-free, of course."

The rest of that Sunday day passed uneventfully. Malik took his leave, saying he had to make preparations for having them as guests that evening. Beatrix went to the Drip, the local coffee shop, to plug into the Wi-Fi and do some research. Ben locked himself in his room and took a nap, having not fully recovered from the previous night's chaos.

Finding her favorite corner table at the Drip unoccupied, Beatrix sat at a nearby table and plugged in her laptop, thankful for an unobstructed view of the street. She wanted to keep an eye on who was coming and going.

As Beatrix sat down, an image flashed in her mind of the figure under the streetlight in the park.

The Hat Man.

Beatrix shuddered, then positioned Parfleet on the bench closest to the wall to conceal him. While dogs were common in Manhattan, she was concerned that his presence could get her booted from the Drip, and she needed time to do research.

Beatrix opened Wendell's satchel, which she had claimed as her own. Pulling out a composition book, Beatrix jotted down everything she knew she had seen on Wendell's computer. References to scientific phenomena were numerous and populated with words she didn't understand.

Dark matter, event horizon, singularity, time dilation . . .

It seemed more like items of concern to an astrophysicist than an archaeologist. Wendell had always been interested in ancient symbols and talismans, though Beatrix had noticed he also had a quiet obsession with the stars.

In his notes, Beatrix noticed references to a person named "G." Other times, his name was interchanged with "Montavani."

G is aware of the necessary steps to coordinate the

Gateways. It's expressed as a simple calculation. Yet, I can't do it. . . .

Montavani can predict them now. Tiny singularities. Now large, man-sized gateways found.

We can control them!

The symbols all the same. Exactly congruent in every way conceivable. The dual triangle with apexes touching, superimposed over what appears to be an infinity symbol. Twin shapes tethered by an infinite distance. They're everywhere.

G and I have figured at least 14 so far: Franz Josef Land, Iceland, Zaire, Siberia, to name a few . . . Alaska, Arizona, of course the Prime one here in New York.

New York!

The gateways are doorways to the Infinite. Isolated pockets of singularity displaying aspects of relativistic time dilation. It stands to reason that the stars of the cosmos, eternally quarantined from one another by the distance/time constraints of light years, are now within our grasp. All I need is time, and I may be able to locate the exact data point in the time stream. I may yet find her and change things.

I may yet find her.

Beatrix turned up her headphones to drown out the sound of someone talking loudly on their phone. The song happened to be "The Scientist" by Coldplay.

By the time Beatrix was on her third cup of coffee, she had assembled quite a dossier on Wendell's activities. She was confident in her appreciation of the situation: Wendell's disappearance(s) were cosmic events beyond her understanding and not of this world.

Dad is missing, and he may or may not return. He returned from the incident in Scotland, so maybe he'll return here. Maybe I should wait this out. I just don't feel like he would leave us like this. Sure, he hasn't been right for the last year or so, but he's all we have. Maybe he didn't leave us. Was he taken? Could Ben and I be in danger? And what about Malik? Poor Malik! After Scotland, our lives have been so messed up. I—Scotland!

Beatrix thumbed through her notes for something she knew she had overlooked.

Where is it?

She found a page of Wendell's chicken scratch, then turned it over and drew in a sharp breath. It was a picture of Glamis Castle in Scotland with a single word under it: **meridian**.

Beatrix twisted her curls with her right hand and looked out the window as she thought about that revelation. Had Wendell's obsession with researching ancient symbols revealed something else?

Beatrix zoned out as she stared at the traffic. In her daze, she thought she saw a tall man with no face and dressed in all black standing across the street, watching her. He was wearing black sunglasses and a fedora. A city bus flew by and broke her trance, and when the bus passed, the figure was gone, like a whisper in her mind.

Outside the door of Malik's apartment, Ben and Beatrix heard the stereo blasting. They knocked on the door for a good two minutes before it opened, greeting them with the sound of hip-hop rap blaring through a subwoofer and the smell of spicy Indian food. Standing there, clad in a red kimono and tank top was Malik.

"Greetings!"

"What the hell are you wearing?" Beatrix asked as she stepped inside.

"These pants are called jams. And this is a kimono. It's very relaxing. I have extras, and I could grab you—"

"Never mind, Malik. It's great," Beatrix said as she set down her overnight bag.

"Hey, Malik, I'll take one," Ben said, ever the gracious guest. "What colors do you have?"

Malik delivered a blue kimono that Ben put on and modeled for Beatrix. She shook her head in mock disgust, though she thought it was funny. Malik had delivered on his promise to make muffins. In fact, he was a shockingly good cook. Never one to turn down a meal, Ben was in heaven. Malik had also made a spicy soup called mulligatawny. Malik turned off the stereo, and the three of them ate in silence.

"Malik, that was great," Ben said when he was finished. "How did you become such a good cook?"

"Well, my mom and dad are rarely home. They're biochemical engineers with tenure at Columbia and Rutgers, and both are publishing research and traveling. I spend a lot of time on my own. I sort of fend for myself. Kasra, my cousin the DJ, has no home of his own, so he crashes in various places, but this is his crib. Otherwise, I'm a one-man wolf pack, as they say." Malik's use of hip-hop vernacular was common. "That won't be the case any longer now that I have you guys."

Beatrix opened her mouth to respond, but Ben beat her to it. "Sure, Malik. We're friends. You can hang with us any time, dude. School too. Look us up."

Beatrix's jaw dropped open, then slammed shut. She had decided that, in light of recent events, she would order a temporary ceasefire on Malik. Regarding those recent events, Beatrix had come to another decision.

"We need more information on Dad, and I know where the motherlode is."

"We're all ears," Ben replied. "Where?"

"You're not going to like it," Beatrix warned.

Ben leaned forward from where he was sitting on the futon in the living room. "Are you going to make us guess?"

Beatrix sighed. "The Mothership." She let that sink in before she continued. "Professor Lightheart said Dad's manuscript is in the archives in the library's basement."

Malik flinched. "Crap, the World Under the Clock? I hate that idea. It's supposed to be haunted."

"I have a bunch of stuff I gleaned from Wendell's papers. It's nothing concrete, but I have a name—"

"Montovini, right?" Ben said.

"Montavani," Beatrix replied. "He's referenced dozens of times in Wendell's notes, but I have no clues to a location or a contact. That's all I have to go on. And like I said, Dad's manuscripts are kept in the basement of Festermunder's library, though I couldn't even hazard a guess at the reason."

"I understand he was a graduate in 1993, but when did the school get the composition book from Dr. Wendell?" Malik asked. "Was it recent or when he was a student there?"

That's a good point, Beatrix thought. *I never thought of that. Were his manuscripts deposited in the archives years ago, prior to our adoption, or more recently? Wendell never expressed any of his tendencies toward the bizarre until after Scotland. It would have to be recent, right? What does Lightheart know?*

They retired to Malik's bedroom, where he had made space on the floor for sleeping bags. Ever the gentleman, Malik offered his bed to Beatrix, saying he could sleep on the floor. Distressed and slightly repulsed, Beatrix declined and stretched out on the floor next to Ben instead.

As she stared at the ceiling fan spinning away, entranced by the sound of Malik's bedside Optimus Prime humidifier, Beatrix had an epiphany. "That's it! Here's what we need to do." She sat up. "Ben, can you get into school next Saturday night when I have data and book filing?"

Ben propped himself up on his elbow and yawned. "Sure. I have access through the athletic department to pretty much anywhere in the school at any time. I have a QR code on my phone to scan into the building."

I can't believe I'm going to say this, Beatrix thought. "Malik, I need you to do something that may get you into a lot of trouble, something you have absolutely no experience with."

Malik gulped. "Yes?"

"You, Malik, are going to get a detention."

In theory, the plan was so simple that it hardly merited discussion. Malik, having never bent the rules or broken them in his entire life, had to do something to upset Headmistress Grunnion-Paltine. Uncomfortable with affording creative license to Malik, even for something as easy as getting into trouble, Beatrix laid things out for him.

"Don't hatch your plan until Wednesday before Thanksgiving break. Anything sooner and you may be sentenced to something other than night filing. I need you and your memory next Saturday night in Mothership."

"I could do something terrible!" Malik said. "Maybe not wash my hands before lunch! Or even . . . oooh, speak without raising my hand. Aw, that would be so gangsta!"

Beatrix smiled. "I can see you're going to need some coaching. . . ."

It was judgment day: the Wednesday before Thanksgiving break. Beatrix had given Malik some parameters but allowed him some creative space to develop his masterpiece in order to secure a detention with her. Beatrix also wanted to maintain her usual low profile with Malik in the halls of Festermunder Academy. Ben, on the contrary, seemed to have taken up with Malik, which triggered the Law of Unintended Consequences. In Beatrix's estimation, although she still considered him a complete tool, Malik was becoming slightly more redeemable in the social climate.

As Malik and Ben walked down the second-floor hall past Nick Stooch and Becker McTeel, neither made a move to hinder or hurt Malik, who had braced himself for the inevitable barrage. Later in algebra, Malik went to the board and completed a factorization problem, and no one jeered at him and called him by his normal monikers — My Leak, Loser, or Bones.

Beatrix surmised that these changes had come about as a result of Malik's association with Ben. She felt jealous that she did not have the same effect on Malik.

What's wrong with me?

Shrugging off her insecurity, Beatrix yanked Malik by the strap of his *Star Wars* book bag, replete with Ewoks, into the vestibule by the water fountain.

"Hey! Wud up, B?" Malik said with ridiculous bravado.

"Shut up!" Beatrix hissed, attempting to bring Malik back down to Earth as she vainly tried to get the infrared sensor on the water fountain to work. "Are you solid? We have one more period to get this done. What are you doing?"

Malik was messing with the contents of his book bag, giddy with excitement. "Oh, yes I'm solid. Solid as granite, yo."

At 3:00, they went to ELA with Old Lady Proche. Professor Proche was at least seventy years old — some said older. She was British, prim, proper, and incapable of being fun or even recognizing it. If fun were shot with a tranquilizer dart, tagged, and put into captivity, Proche would not even have it in her presence. Proche demanded unyielding behavioral standards in her classroom. Malik had picked a good place to stage his spectacle.

Some professional athletes find that doing something challenging in front of thousands of screaming spectators is easier than performing under the quiet scrutiny of a coach and a few teammates in practice. There's less pressure to get caught up in the minutia of technique and mechanics. Beatrix realized that Malik, being neither professional nor athletic, would not succeed in his endeavor to do something so seemingly easy as to get in trouble in a place with such a strict regimen that the students tiptoed on eggshells. He would need help or divine luck.

Beatrix looked over at Ben, who was seated across the room, and conveyed her displeasure at the situation with a furrowed brow, pursed lips, and a shake of her head.

"Now, in *Jane Eyre*, Charlotte Bronte's placement of Jane Ingram into the story as she's planning to marry Mr. Rochester serves what purpose?" Proche asked the class, peering over her glasses. For eons, teachers had failed to understand that method guaranteed no one would answer.

In the ensuing silence, Beatrix noticed that Malik had slipped on Ben's lacrosse helmet and was leaning back in his desk, having achieved about four to five inches of anterior lift off the front legs.

He's trying to flip his desk!

At that point, physics took over. Malik, at approximately 107 pounds, coupled with a thirty-pound desk, was struggling. The desk's wide-set legs prevented him from getting the angle to form a lever-and-fulcrum system, and his slippery-soled Converse Chuck Taylor All-stars (light blue) did not provide the necessary friction. His shoes slipped across the varnished hardwood floor, creating a high-pitched squeaking noise that sounded like a bodily function. Embarrassed, Malik slipped off the helmet and tried to reproduce the noise (as one does), but his attempts were in vain. The classroom exploded in laughter.

Old Lady Proche, whose hearing was not as acute as her foul humor, didn't hear the quasi-flatulent expulsion, but she boiled over at the class disruption. As she opened her mouth like a barracuda, ready to devour her prey, a much larger and far more dangerous predator appeared in the doorway, blocking out all of the light.

"Anges, are we having trouble controlling our classroom?" Headmistress Grunnion-Paltine bellowed. "Surely, you don't think that just because we break for the remainder of the week that you can allow a class to be disruptive."

"No, ma'am—Headmistress," Proche said. "I would never undermine—"

"Silence!" HGP commanded. "Masters Stooch and McTeel, you are to be held here this coming Saturday for detention in the library."

The order was completely arbitrary, HGP having singled them out as the usual suspects. Stooch and McTeel were silent but furious, mostly at Malik, whom they labeled the instigator. There would be payback.

As Headmistress Grunnion-Paltine scowled at the class, she looked down and was confronted by Malik's quivery likeness. "Master Patel, why is a useless parasite like you out of his desk unbidden, hmm? Professor Proche, did you ask Mr. Patel to leave his seat? In fact, do you have any ability to control this classroom? What say you?" Grunnion-Paltine demanded with uncharacteristic vehemence. Her face was beet red, and she had the characteristic neck sweat prominent among the angry and simultaneously rotund.

Then "it" happened—something that would be talked about in the annals of Festermunder Academy for years, eventually becoming the stuff of legends. Desperate and bereft of all other options, Malik pulled a move that was beyond comprehension.

During lunch, Malik had been pecking away on his laptop, working on something called "Operation Kings of Rock," and as HGP glared down at him, he put it into action.

A loud, bass-heavy sound began to emanate from the speakers in every hallway and classroom. At first, it was a musical hodgepodge of hip-hop vernacular; then the sounds of "It's Tricky" by RUN-DMC blasted throughout Festermunder Academy.

As the music played, Malik began to dance, slowly at first and then with more speed and emphasis, gyrating in sync with the music. His moves were angular and jerky and horrifyingly atypical.

The class was awestruck at first. Then they joined in, pumping their fists, clapping, and "woof-woofing," creating an unforgettable spectacle that had never been seen in Room 212 and never would be again. All HGP could do was stare, too dumbfounded to respond.

Completely committed to his performance by that point, Malik had no choice but to go all in. Climbing onto Proche's desk, he introduced his repertoire of hip-hop moves, complete with pelvic thrusts with both arms behind his head.

When Headmistress Grunnion-Paltine finally recovered from her shock, she tried to impose order on the chaos, yelling over the music, to no avail. As the song reached its crescendo, Malik leaped into the air and assumed a mid-flight seated position as he flew toward HGP. She instinctively caught Malik just as the music stopped, cradling him like a fourteen-year-old baby.

HGP was silent, completely caught off guard. Her mouth agape, she took a deep breath, no doubt in preparation to unleash the loudest tirade ever rendered in her tenure or that of any other headmistress at the fabled school. She was apoplectic. But before she could speak, Malik cemented his legend.

"Headmistress, did anyone ever tell you how stunningly beautiful you are?"

With that, still cradled in her arms, Malik reached up with his bony index finger and caressed her hairy chin.

All Beatrix and everyone else in the room could do was sit and stare, too shocked to say anything.

HGP gathered herself, then heaved Malik onto the floor. He lay there in silence in the shape of a cowering fetus.

"Blasphemous! How dare you? Mr. Patel thinks he's funny. He desperately seeks the approval of the popular kids, but he will never get it. Look at you, little filth! Data filing for you this Saturday. Your parents will be informed in the next fifteen minutes. You may be paddled as well once I get a waiver!"

"They're in Calcutta," Malik said. "My cousin Kasra, a DJ, is my guardian. He actually mixed that phat jam. As in p-h-a-t—"

"Silence, maggot!" Headmistress Grunnion-Paltine hissed.

Beatrix looked at Ben, who smiled as if to say, "Well, you got what you wanted."

Beatrix couldn't help but grin. *The guy actually came through for me!*

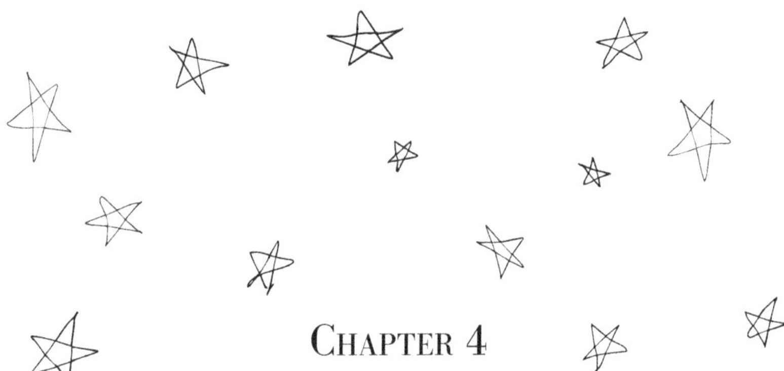

CHAPTER 4

The World
Under the Clock

T HE GIANT CLOCK WAS PERCHED ABOVE THE BRASS DOORS of the elevator leading to the library. It was huge, at least eight feet in diameter, and made of tarnished gold. It had twelve hands—some short, some long, and some curved, all moving in different directions and at different rates. They pointed to the hours and the minutes as well as other symbols. There were planets on the clock and what appeared to be the orbital patterns of celestial bodies. At the center were two pyramids, their apexes touching, superimposed over an infinity symbol.

Beatrix opened her eyes and focused on the distorted reflections of the students jammed into the elevator. She could barely make out her face in the scuffed brass plating. She couldn't help but wonder what she would do if the tall man with the hat appeared in the reflection. Would she have the strength to run?

As soon as Beatrix got into the cramped, musty elevator, she wanted out of it. The descent was slow, and it seemed impossible that the library could exist so deep under a city that had a warren of subway tunnels.

"This is making me queasy," Malik said. He belched with his closed mouth as if to portend things to come. "We need to get out of here."

Mercifully, moments later, they heard a chime, and the doors opened.

They assembled in a semicircle in the basement rotunda, all twelve of the condemned students. It was the Saturday after Thanksgiving, and outside it was a cruel, cold night. Inside the library, things weren't much better. There was no heat down there. All of the students relegated to spending a holiday evening doing trivial work for the school as a consequence of their failure to abide by the Festermunder Articles of Discipline saw the task for what it was — sadistic.

Beatrix and Malik were anxious to get started on their search through thousands of books for a single manuscript written by Dr. Wendell S. Voght. As they focused on how to tackle the problem, their proctor for the evening entered the foyer through a mahogany door and stood in the center of the room on the scarlet carpet, which Beatrix sardonically labeled as "Episcopalian Red."

Their proctor, Professor Gregory Brecourt, was short, in his mid-thirties, portly, ill-tempered, and witless. He reminded Beatrix of a garden gnome. In fact, he was known throughout the school as the Gnome.

Professor Brecourt/Gnome cleared his throat and spoke in his exaggerated aristocratic tone. "Ahem. Attention, students. This evening, we have a lot of work to do. The twelve of you have, let me see, ahem, 3,218 books and periodicals to file. And each one must be cross-referenced in the card catalog according to Dewey. When you're done filing each item, sign your name to each index card and then place it in the stack. The final stack must have 3,218 cross-referenced cards. These cards will be refiled in the catalog as well. You may break into teams, but no one can leave until all items are filed."

Stooch and his partner in crime, McTeel, glared at Beatrix and Malik. Beatrix held her satchel close, trying to conceal what was inside while also allowing its contents — Parfleet — to breathe.

After they all signed up in teams, Professor Brecourt grabbed the clipboard and read off names.

"Patel and Voght?"

"Sir?" they said in unison.

"You have sections zero-zero-zero to three hundred."

Section 000 was general works, computer science, and unspecific information. Sections 100 to 300 were concerned with philosophy and psychology, religion, and social sciences.

Not exactly the area we need to be, but it's a start, Beatrix thought. *Then we can break free and search.*

As the Gnome assigned the other teams to their areas, Beatrix's attention was drawn to Alexandria Thacker and Darby St. Vincent. As per usual, Alexandria looked flawless with her china-doll skin and long, straight blond hair. Inexplicable meanness seemed to ooze from every pore as she stood there. Darby, ever the pretender, did her best to pull off the Alexandria Thacker starter kit, complete with a fake British accent. Beatrix wondered what Miss Perfect and her lap dog had done to get the detail in the basement.

"There will be snacks preserved from this week's throw-outs here in the rotunda at ten o'clock that Headmistress Grunnion-Paltine was generous enough to provide. I'll be in the admin office, but don't disturb me unless absolutely necessary."

"One last thing: In case you haven't noticed, the library is circular, and the stacks are, in fact, rings. The breaks in the rings are random, which makes it easy to get lost. Write down the turns you take, or you may never be found."

Pleased with his warning, the Gnome chortled before he continued. "The center of the library is roped off and off limits due to construction with the boilers. It's also hazardous. Those not wishing to have their skin burned off should stay on the periphery. It's now 8:30 p.m. Your first check-in is 11:30." He paused, hoping to conjure another verbal javelin tipped with irony to spear the students' hearts, only to come up short. "Okay, go!"

Though the ceiling was low, Beatrix and Malik were stunned by the library's size. Looking down the stacks, Beatrix could hardly make out the distant walls. She was reminded of a trip they had taken to the Bois Jacques woods in Belgium, near the town of Bastogne, for a WWII excursion with Wendell. His grandfather Waverly had carried secret documents for the Allies through those very woods, where two seemingly infinite rows of pines had been planted in perfect linear symmetry.

Who made the first straight line, from which we base all straight lines? she wondered. Then she shook away the cobwebs of such intrusive, useless thoughts and tried to focus.

"Aw, dude. Look." Malik drew Beatrix's attention to a seven-foot-tall heap of books behind them. Looking up, they saw the reason for their ramshackle state. An old beaten copper chute extending from the ceiling opened with a bang and a clatter as more books spilled out and landed on the pile. Beatrix wondered why a school the size of Festermunder needed such a huge library and why no students were allowed direct access to it — the books had to be circulated by the faculty, and even that didn't happen often. For the most part, book distribution was overseen by Professors Brecourt and Lightheart.

If Professor Lightheart were here, at least we could get help, Beatrix thought. *I should have taken the composition book from him when he offered it. He was literally throwing it at me! Later that day, I had different priorities, or so I thought. Now it seems there could be a connection. Beatrix, you idiot!*

She and Malik grabbed a nearby cart and began checking numbers until they found some books in the 000–300s and began stacking them. The system was ludicrous. They should have reconvened without Brecourt and designed a new system by which to sort the books.

Alexandria and Darby, as well as Stooch and McTeel, simply piled books on their carts and then disappeared down a distant row. Beatrix and Malik figured they had no intention of doing their jobs and would just push the task onto the two of them.

After an hour, Malik and Beatrix had sorted several hundred books in separate numeric categories. Only then did they set off toward their respective sections. Section 000 was all the way to the left, so they went there first.

"Where should we look for Wendell's manuscript?" Malik asked as he walked alongside Beatrix, who was pushing the cart. "We have no reference point and nothing to go on."

"I have no idea. Just hold on."

Beatrix was transfixed by the library. It was exceptionally — and unnecessarily—beautiful for a place like Festermunder. Wooden beams crisscrossed the ceiling. The scarlet carpet created an acoustic void, absorbing every sound as they walked. Every ten feet or so, old-style filament bulbs hung from the ceiling. Not even the New York City Public Library, one Beatrix's favorite places on Earth, had as much character. And the musty smell of old paper entranced her. Beatrix was in her element.

When she heard someone approaching from the adjacent row, she held her breath. Then a book slid forward and extruded itself from the shelf as if by magic, followed by another and another. Malik and Beatrix flattened themselves against the bookshelf and waited for some new devilry to occur. They were both startled to see a hand extend through the gap at eye level. The ring finger extended forth to produce an innocuous flip of the bird. The imposter avian metacarpal waggled back and forth; Beatrix let out the breath she had been holding and snickered.

"It's alright, Malik."

Beatrix went over and grabbed the finger

"Ouch!" their owner whispered.

"What kept you?" she inquired.

"I got in as fast as I could," Ben said. "But there were security guys that I hadn't seen before, all of them dressed in black. I had to go through the gym and the locker rooms to the freight elevator."

"Security? You meant faculty, right?" Beatrix said. "Were you spotted?"

"No, not teachers; creepy dudes in suits. And no, I wasn't spotted. I'm good."

Ben nodded to Malik, then repaired the hole he had created by pushing the books out.

"Okay," Beatrix said. "Let's check periodicals. Maybe they keep notes there and annotated drafts rather than formal texts. It's all the way in the back."

The boys followed Beatrix down the last row of bookshelves. So caught up in their search, none of them noticed the lights grow dim, nor did they realize they were not alone.

The trio did some cursory book filing before Beatrix delegated that responsibility to Ben and Malik. In true fashion, Ben jumped in with a positive attitude and proceeded to do the job the only way he knew how—his best. Malik, happier than a pig in slop to be a part of the "adventure," worked just as hard to file books and jot down the data on the index cards, cracking bad jokes the entire time.

Beatrix decided that as long as they were quiet and didn't disturb her process, she was fine to let them carry on. Watching Malik and Ben having fun together also made her happy. It was an incongruous relationship. The best-all-around boy wonder and the nerd-for-all-time finding common ground.

Taking a chance, Beatrix removed Parfleet from her satchel, seeing as he was making a federal case about being confined.

"Hey, Ben, do you know what language Professor Brecourt speaks in?" Malik asked, a goofy grin on his face.

"What's that?" Ben asked, anticipating a corny reply. Malik did not disappoint.

"Gnomen-clature."

Ben thought it over, then burst out laughing.

"Hey! Would you shut up?" Beatrix whispered. "Are you trying to get us in trouble? Quiet!"

"Yeah, man," Malik replied. "They might put us in detention."

Ben lost it. He had a habit of screaming as he laughed, and he issued forth a burst. Malik fell to the floor, beating the carpet with his fist, gasping for air. "Stop it, dude!" he pleaded. "You're gonna make me fart."

"Shhh!" Beatrix said, her index finger mashed against her lips as she glanced around, listening for the Gnome's inevitable approach. As Malik and Ben composed themselves on the floor, even Parfleet looked up at her.

"Something's not right here," Beatrix whispered.

She walked to the outer ring with Malik and Parfleet behind her. Ben brought up the rear, keeping an eye out for trouble. Although the room was enormous, only about forty feet was visible in front of them at any given time. Beatrix walked with her body bent slightly to the left to peek around the turn without exposing herself.

"Beatrix, it's getting darker in here," Ben whispered as he looked around. "The lights have dimmed. Do you think that's the Gnome's way of calling us back? What time is it?"

Malik checked his Casio. "It's only 10:50."

"Yeah, I noticed a while back that I was having trouble seeing," Beatrix said. "We'll have to get creative with our search so we make it back by 11:30 and don't arouse suspicion."

Suddenly, two figures jumped out in front of them—Stooch and McTeel. Standing behind them were Alexandria and Darby.

"What's up, losers?" Stooch asked. "Are you guys at home in the 'we have no social life' section?"

He gave Malik a two-handed shove in the chest. Malik fell to the floor, but not before jarring some books loose, causing them to fall all over him.

"What's wrong, My Leak? Not going to do crap if your big bad protector isn't here, are you?" Stooch said. "Huh? You can't even stand up for your—"

Stooch stopped mid-syllable as Ben materialized from the gloom.

"Hey, Nic. What's going on?" Ben asked, knowing that his passivity was more intimidating to Stooch than aggression. Both parties knew that Nic stood no chance against Ben.

Ben pulled Malik to his feet. Then he stood and smiled as he watched one of his tormenters squirm for a change.

"Nic, why don't you take your little gang of single-digit IQs to your own section?" Beatrix said. "We'll call you for arts and crafts and finger painting momentarily."

"Shut up, orphan," Stooch said. "This doesn't concern you."

Ben stepped in front of Beatrix. "If it concerns me, it concerns her."

At that moment, Beatrix realized Darby had been looking on in silence during the entire exchange. Alexandria had been staring at Beatrix the entire time.

What's up with that?

As they turned to go back to their section, Darby made an awkward attempt to score a point for the opposing team. "Beatrix, your hair looks dumb."

Alexandria smiled at Ben and gave Beatrix a curious look, but she made no attempt to join in the name calling as they melted back into the stacks.

Following the interruption, the trio searched through hundreds of annotated manuscripts, but they didn't find anything resembling Wendell's notebook or any mention of the name "Montavani."

"The heck with this," Beatrix said. "We're wasting our time. We need to try another section. Maybe astronomy."

Ben raised his eyebrows in surprise. "Astronomy?"

"Malik, what section is it?" Beatrix asked.

"Five twenty," Malik replied as if he had anticipated the question.

"Let's go," Beatrix said.

"B, it's clear across this maze of a place. We have to map it out as we go, or we're going to get lost."

They had to switch back and forth through several shelf breaks and would have been hopelessly lost if not for Malik's memory. He ticked off the moves aloud. "Three rights, six lefts, four rights . . ." He knew they would have to reverse the right-left order to find their way out.

As they walked, Beatrix noticed the beams in the low ceiling radiated out like spokes on a bicycle, and she could tell they were getting close to the center of the library based on the ever-diminishing distance between them.

Up ahead, Beatrix saw a light. They slowed down as they approached it. The light appeared to be emanating from the floor like a digital bonfire. The center of the library was sectioned off with crude cyclone fencing complete with concertina wire. Beatrix had only ever seen such things in documentaries about prison camps. Somebody was determined to keep people away from the area.

Incredibly, Ben found the gate to the partitioned area was ajar. Compelled by curiosity, the trio navigated some bookshelves that seemed to serve no purpose other than perhaps to afford concealment, then they finally reached the source of the light.

In the floor at the center of the basement library and the vertex of the beams was a circle approximately twenty feet in diameter. From it emanated a tiny blinding white light. It was a focused beam no more than two inches wide.

Ben and Beatrix crept to the edge and leaned out as far as they dared.

Malik hung back with Parfleet. Beatrix hunkered down on her belly and shimmied the rest of the way, then placed her chin on the edge. Placing a finger on the nosepiece of her glasses to prevent them from slipping off, she gazed down into nothingness. It was like a deep black eye with a white-hot pupil. She traced the beam up and then gasped.

"Look!"

Above the circle was another of the same size in the ceiling. The light beam blasted forth from the floor into the upper chamber's center. Shielding her eyes to remove the light beam from her field of vision, she attempted to look beyond it. What she saw took her breath away. The void was full of stars, tiny pinpricks of light that seemed to go on forever.

As Beatrix lay there, entranced, the rest of the world fell away, as did all of her worries. At that moment, she was the only person in the universe.

"It's so beautiful," she mumbled, her eyes glistening with tears.

"We've got company," Ben whispered, breaking the spell.

Seeing the fear on Ben's face, Beatrix scrambled to her feet. Then she noticed something else. The air had become dry, and it was getting warmer. She stared at the oculus on the floor and the ceiling and beyond to the stars. Then she noticed the upper oculus had symbols on the borders — two triangles facing the sides of the circle. Spanning the circle was the symbol for infinity, like the number eight lying on its side. The light pierced the center of the symbol.

"Beatrix!" Malik said. "It's time for us to leave."

Scurrying away from the oculus, they retreated into the stacks to regroup. When they were a hundred feet from the epicenter, Ben chanced a look back, his eyes widening in fear. "Run!"

Approaching behind them was a figure. Not Stooch, McTeel, or any other student. Nor was it the Gnome. Dressed in black and wearing a fedora strode a shadowy, faceless being.

The Hat Man.

Beatrix screamed as the three of them, and Parfleet, bolted through the labyrinth of rings. Ben took up the rear, instinctively protective of Beatrix and Malik. Parfleet was in the lead and going berserk. The Hat Man was walking, not running, but he seemed to be gaining on them. He would disappear and then reappear at each aperture.

Once they lost sight of him, they stopped to catch their breath. "It's him, isn't it?" Malik said, gasping. "We're dead!"

"Hold on," Ben said, then disappeared to their left, back toward the middle of the library. Beatrix knew he was going to try to draw the man away, so she, Malik, and Parfleet could get to safety.

A rumble began, growing louder and louder until it seemed to be on top of them. The bookshelves tumbled over, coming from the direction Ben set out, creating a huge domino effect. Ben had started the chain reaction by bracing himself against a column and tipping the first shelf over. The shelves, being on a curve and irregular in length, clipped others in front and created a massive phalanx of deadly tonnage that threatened to consume the entire library and all of its inhabitants. As books and shelves thundered and crashed, the trio hoped the diversion would seal their escape. In fact, it served to seal them in further.

Beatrix, Ben, Parfleet, and Malik sprinted as the wave of falling bookshelves pushed them to the left, into Section 500. Then a much larger series of crashes ensued.

"Oh no!" Beatrix was the first to see it. Someone—or something—had started the process from the opposite side. The roar of falling shelves made the floor shake like jelly. "We'll be trapped!"

As the row they were in disintegrated behind them, it looked like a giant zipper was being closed, the tipping shelves forming a tunnel. The kids were like toothpaste in a tube that was being squeezed, but the cap was still on.

"We're gonna die!" Malik cried. "We're gonna die!"

"Not today," Ben declared. He spotted a huge book cart and flipped it over. "Get under! Quickly!"

Ben waited until the others and Parfleet were under the cart, then crawled under it himself at the last second. The shelves above them smashed together with a thunderclap.

As Beatrix lay sprawled on the carpet, she groped for her belongings. Her satchel was open and hanging upside down on one of the filing cart's supports. Beatrix studied it for a moment, reading Waverly Voght's inscriptions upside down. Right side up, the series of numbers was "273025." Reading them upside down, though, they made a different impression on her: "520.372."

"Ben, I know where it is. Just tell me we haven't destroyed the section it's in," Beatrix said.

Malik picked up a book near where he was lying and read the Dewey Decimal number on the spine: 510.989.

"Thank goodness," Beatrix said. "It's just up ahead. Let's grab it and go."

The faceless man was nowhere in sight, but Beatrix could feel his presence and knew he was lurking nearby. The distant booms of falling shelves continued as the entire library imploded.

"Five sixteen, five seventeen, five eighteen . . . Almost there. Five nineteen. Okay, the five twenties. Here we are!" Beatrix was ecstatic.

"Beatrix, hurry," Malik said. "He may come back!"

Ben remained on guard with Parfleet, ready to pounce to sacrifice himself to protect the others.

"Cosmos, Carl Sagan, Copernicus's essays, Kepler, Hawking, *A Brief History of Time* . . . Here we go 520.371 . . . 520.372!" Beatrix's excitement was at a fever pitch.

"He's coming!" Ben yelled. His breathing was heavy; his voice was shaking with fear. "We're cut off!

Malik was frozen in terror. He grabbed Parfleet and held him close. For once, the pug didn't protest. "For goodness' sake, hurdy, Beatrix! I'm too young to die. I was meant to see the next *Star Wars* movie!" A hot wind blew across the library, originating from the center, sending papers and books flying.

Beatrix grabbed the book corresponding to the number on her satchel; then her heart sank. It certainly wasn't Wendell's composition book.

That's it. Now we'll never know . . . because we're going to die. And it's all my fault.

She glanced at the tattered green hardback and checked the number again. It was correct. Unable to make out the title on the spine, she opened it.

Ben and Malik screamed for Beatrix to hurry, their only means of escape being a small gap in the bookshelves farther down and to the right. Ben was attempting to hold it open.

Just as Beatrix was tempted to toss the book away and run, the tiny and faded title caught her eye: *meridians*. Her chest ignited with fire, and her mouth went dry. As she flipped the page, her heart jumped into her throat. It was written by Guiseppe Montavani and W. S. Voght, and scribbled in pen in the bottom margin of the page were the following words: "The answer is always up."

Stuffing the book into her satchel, Beatrix turned to run to where Ben and Malik were hollering for her. Debris was flying everywhere. Suddenly, her path was blocked by a wall of bookshelves that came crashing down ten feet away. Hemmed in on all sides and with the ceiling too low for her to climb over, she was trapped.

He's coming for me, she thought.

The bookshelves behind her began to bend and distort like a liquid gel. Then through the distortion, she saw a tall, dark figure.

It's him. The Hat Man.

Beatrix suddenly had a thought.

The answer is up.

Beatrix started to climb. There was barely enough space to make it over the top of the bookshelf, but sensing the intruder behind her, she tried to sling herself over to the other side. As she fumbled for a handhold, her fingers swiped something. She grabbed it and held it up. It was a worn notebook, tattered and covered in dust.

Dad's notebook! The answer is up! As in up on the top shelf! Now to get out of here!

She heard a voice call her name on the other side of the shelf; then a small hand appeared and grabbed hers. Beatrix felt herself being pulled back by something else, back into the pit with the Hat Man. The small hand jerked her down, assisted by gravity, and she landed on the floor of the adjacent row. It was too dark for her to make out her rescuer's features, but she could hear the person's voice over the din.

"Come on! Run! This won't hold him for long!"

Beatrix and her rescuer sprinted along the room's outer edge, feeling their pursuer's presence right behind them.

As they rounded the last curve, they saw Ben and Malik struggling to hold the door open against a storm of wind and flying books, Malik clutching Parfleet in his other arm. Beatrix and her rescuer burst through the doors into the carpeted rotunda, and the heavy wooden doors slammed behind them with enough force to send Malik and Ben flying across the room. As the storm inside the library abated, they all lay there catching their breath.

Beatrix checked her satchel. The text and the composition book were safe inside.

"Are you okay?" her rescuer asked from behind her, her words tinged by a slight accent.

Beatrix turned toward the voice. "Yeah, thanks. I —" She stopped short, dumbfounded, as she finally realized who her rescuer was.

Alexandria Thacker.

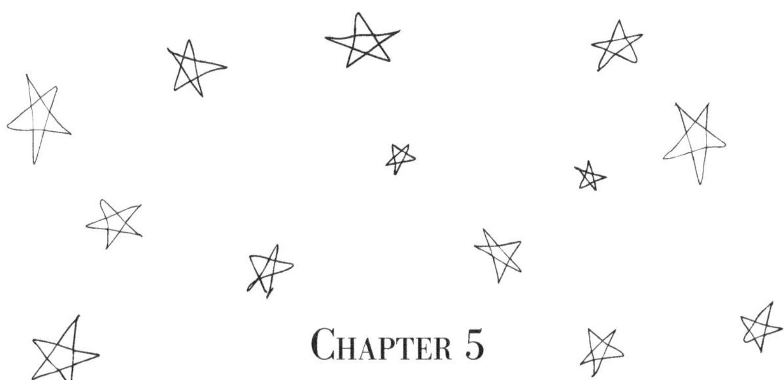

CHAPTER 5

Of Clues
and Lemons

T HE FOURSOME SPRINTED OUT OF THE ROTUNDA AND escaped by way of the freight elevator. At no time did any of them concern themselves with the destruction they left behind. Nor did any of them care about the repercussions that would beset them courtesy of the Gnome or Headmistress Grunnion-Paltine. All they cared about was putting as much distance between them and Festermunder as possible.

Ben flagged down a cab, and they all piled in. Ben, Malik, and Beatrix got in the back with Parfleet. Alexandria sat up front with the driver. She gave him instructions, and they sped away from Midtown toward Queensborough Bridge.

"What the hell is happening?" Beatrix asked, her adrenaline wearing off. She looked out the back window at the East River and watched the city fade behind them. "And where are we going?"

Beatrix smacked her hand on the plexiglass window to get Alexandria's attention. Alexandria just nodded to Beatrix, then looked straight ahead.

Malik nudged Ben. "Why are we going to Queens?"

"I don't know, but we'll find out soon. Maybe Alexandria knows a place where we can hunker down and collect our wits. At this point, I don't care. I'm fried. Just hang on."

The cab pulled up to a row of shabby apartments next to an overland railroad bridge. Alexandria got out, and the trio followed her.

"Alexandria, why did you tell the driver to take us way out here?" Beatrix asked. "It's past midnight, and we're in Queens. Is this your idea of a joke?"

"I live here," Alexandria replied. She turned to enter the apartment and stopped when she realized the others weren't following. "Well, are you guys coming or not?"

It was cold, and they were all scared, so without any further encouragement, they followed her in.

Alexandria's split-level house was meager to say the least. Beatrix felt as if she'd stepped back in time. The shag carpet was old and mustard yellow. The couches and chairs were covered with homemade afghans. An old cuckoo clock hung over the mantle in the small living room. Alexandria led them into the kitchen, which was even more pedestrian. It had a light-blue ceramic tile backsplash, a white Formica countertop, and sunflower wallpaper. Beatrix, Ben, and Malik seated themselves at the small kitchen table.

"Hot cocoa?" Alexandria asked.

They all nodded, then waited in silence, not wanting to disturb whoever might be sleeping in the house.

"Alexandria, did you lock the house?" Beatrix asked.

"Yes, of course. But I'll check again if it will make everyone more comfortable." She set their mugs on the table and walked out of the kitchen, leaving the trio alone.

Beatrix sipped her hot chocolate, Parfleet in her lap. "What do you think, Ben?"

He shrugged.

Malik held his latte cup up to his face, completely obscuring it. Still in shock over their escape from the library, he had surprisingly had little to contribute.

Alexandria returned and seated herself at the table, blowing on her hot chocolate before sipping it. As Beatrix looked at their host, she saw something she had never seen before. Alexandria's eyes pinched tight, the corners of her mouth turned down, and her face wrinkled into a decidedly ugly contortion. Beatrix realized Alexandria was crying. It was soft at first; then she caught her breath between sobs, her shoulders bouncing up and down. Beatrix was incredulous. She had never seen Alexandria let her guard down.

Ever the saint, Ben patted Alexandria's shoulder. "Hey. Hey, Alexandria, it's gonna be alright."

Beatrix was a speechless mixture of sympathy and doubt.

"They didn't deserve this," Alexandria stammered. "It's all my fault. They're gone . . . gone! It's all my fault."

"No. No. We're all here. We're safe," Ben said.

"No, we aren't. And what about the others?" Alexandria asked through her tears.

"What others?" Malik inquired.

"Nic, Becker, and Darby."

Everyone was silent for a moment, so intent on escaping that they had forgotten about the other students in the library.

"What about them?" Beatrix asked.

"They're gone! Gone! And they're not coming back. They didn't deserve that!"

Beatrix set her cup down and placed her hands flat on the table, looking into Alexandria's eyes for the first time ever. "What do you mean 'gone'?"

Alexandria got up and closed the door to the kitchen, as if that offered any more privacy. Then she stood in front of Ben, Malik, and Beatrix, taking a moment to compose herself. To Beatrix, she was still the prettiest girl she had ever seen in person, but somehow, she hated Alexandria slightly less than she had two hours earlier.

"Gone as in *gone*. I saw it. They disappeared into the void."

"The void?" Ben inquired.

"Nic and Becker were messing around and wanted to see the restricted area, and Darby and I followed. It was stupid. They picked the lock to the gate and left it open for us. That's when we saw it."

"Saw what?" Beatrix knew what Alexandria was going to say, but she wanted to hear it in her own words.

"The hole. The tunnel. Whatever it was. Nic, that duffer, threw a coin into it, and it came alive."

"Alive?" Ben asked.

"It started to give off light. I was frightened and backed away, but it was too late for Nic and Becker. They were sucked in. I couldn't help them. Darby tried to run, and I tried to hold on to her, but . . ." Alexandria started to cry again. "But it was too strong. It pulled us both down, and I couldn't hold onto her. I lost my grip, and Darby . . . was taken into it. She's gone."

Although Beatrix despised bullies like Nic, Becker, and Darby, she never wanted any harm to come to anyone. She felt sorry for her lost classmates but most of all for Alexandria. Beatrix knew about loss.

"I wrapped my bag around my wrist and held onto the gate. It felt like it was going to cut my hand off." She held up her right hand, her wrist ringed by a bruised and slightly bloody. "Then the hole stopped pulling, and more and more light came out of it, getting brighter and brighter. I ran away and hid until I heard you scream." She looked at Beatrix.

"Well, thank you . . . for helping me," Beatrix said.

"Don't mention it," Alexandria replied.

Beatrix looked down at her empty cup.

Of all of the paranormal activities I've personally witnessed, Alexandria Thacker may be the most unbelievable. She might be sort of nice.

Later in the powder room, Beatrix looked at her reflection in the mirror as she tried to conjure up the laundry list of reasons why she detested Alexandria. She found it considerably difficult to find any direct reasons that weren't born out of jealousy. Alexandria's looks, height, hair, musical and athletic ability, and her British accent were not her fault. It was Alexandria's self-assuredness and confidence that needled Beatrix the most. But when she analyzed it further, Beatrix was forced to confront the truth.

Alexandria isn't the problem. Maybe I am. Maybe my lack of something makes me feel incomplete. Like half a person. . . .

A gentle knock on the door broke Beatrix from her daze. "Malik! Not now."

"It's me," Alexandria said.

"Yes?" Beatrix replied.

"Are you decent?"

Beatrix looked herself over. "Uh, sure." She opened the door.

Alexandria came in wearing a T-shirt and plaid flannel pajama pants. She handed Beatrix a stack of clothing and linens. "Hopefully, they fit. They belong to my little sister, Gwen." Her eyes looked apologetic as she continued. "What I mean is—"

"It's okay. I'm not offended. I'm short. I'm used to it. Your kid sister's pajamas are fine. It's nearly two in the morning, and we're going to have to stay tonight, and I need some clothes."

Beatrix noticed that Alexandria was wearing a U2 *The Unforgettable Fire* shirt. "Nice shirt," she said. "One of my favorite bands."

Alexandria perked up and smiled. "Right! Brilliant, aren't they?"

Beatrix smiled, then an awkward silence ensued.

"Look, Beatrix, I'm not who you think I am," Alexandria said.

"It's okay, Alexandria. It's probably me. I—"

"Alex."

"Excuse me?"

"Alex. My friends back home called me Alex. I'd be pleased if you called me that."

Friends?

"Sure. Alex."

Alex smiled, then went out and closed the door.

Beatrix looked in the mirror and smiled despite herself.

The four companions and Parfleet slept in sleeping bags on the floor in Alex's room. Alex's bed was closest to the door. Next to her was Beatrix, then Parfleet on a floral pillow, then Ben, and then Malik, who was wedged in and against the wall. He didn't seem to care; just being included in the adventure exhilarated him. He either didn't mind or failed to perceive that some or all of them could have died that night. All Malik seemed to care about was that for the first time ever, he had companions.

They were all amped up from their night in the library, wondering what it all meant and who they should tell. Despite having called a truce with Alex, Beatrix wasn't ready to bring her in on every secret and mystery just yet.

Ben thanked everyone for their courage and spirit in helping each other escape the library. He was in his element — good-natured, competent, and self-aware. A born leader.

Parfleet rustled and seemed out of sorts, unable to settle down.

"Goodnight Beatrix," Alex whispered once the boys were asleep.

"Goodnight, Alex." She closed her eyes, then a question rose in her mind. "Alex?"

"Yes?"

"Why were you in detention?"

Alex lowered her voice even further. "Your brother. I, uh, I rather fancy him. When I saw your name on the list, I figured he would show."

"Oh."

Ten seconds later, Beatrix snorted, then started to snicker. Alex giggled. They began to laugh while trying to restrain themselves. For a moment, they were just two teenage girls doing what fourteen-year-olds do. They both shushed each other and turned over to try to sleep.

As Beatrix lay there, ready to fall into the ocean of fatigue that was consuming her, she felt an odd sense of satisfaction that warmed her heart. Even with the danger they were facing, she felt somehow at home. As an overwhelming sense of happiness swept over her, she realized what it was. She, Beatrix Voght, belonged. Just like Malik, for the first time in her life, Beatrix had friends.

Outside, clouds veiled the stars. A storm was gathering.

They roused for breakfast at 9:00 a.m. Alex's parents were off to church, but they made breakfast for her "guests." Alex created a cover story that was easy for them all to remember because of its simplicity. Beatrix had to respect her ingenuity. Alex had told the truth.

Well, part of the truth. She left out the life-sucking hole of space-time continuum in the library, the loss of three students to said life-sucking hole, the implosion of the entire basement at Festermunder, and the chance meeting with a hatted monster who had no face.

Alex's parents, Robert and Evelyn Thacker, were fantastically polite and perfectly British. They introduced themselves, drew the kids' attention to the breakfast fare, then excused themselves to go to church. For a moment, Beatrix thought she caught Evelyn staring at her.

Only Malik was potentially problematic. He was overly effusive in his praise of the accommodations and lavish in his approbation of the breakfast, laying it on thick. A quick stomp on the foot from Beatrix silenced him.

"Cut the crap, moron," she whispered. "You made it look like we're trying to cover our butts!"

"Duh, Beatrix. We are," Malik replied. "It's called *strategy*."

Beatrix rolled her eyes, then turned to Alex. "What do your parents do?"

"Mum stays home and keeps the house and takes care of me and Dad. She used to have a high-level government job back in the UK but gave that up a few years back. Dad is a delegate for Great Britain at the UN."

That kind of job and you live here? Gosh! I should quit complaining.

Once breakfast was devoured, Ben got down to business. "We've got to back to the Mothership on Monday. You all realize that, right?"

The three others didn't respond, but Beatrix arched an eyebrow.

"What?" Ben asked.

"Are you mental? We can't go back. We need to ditch. It's a crime scene. We're going to be held responsible. Three kids are missing, and we're witnesses. Not to mention someone was trying to kill us!"

"I know, Beatrix, but we need to find out what we can about what happened to Nic, Becker, and Darby." Ben glanced at Alex as if to show empathy for the loss of her friend. Alex smiled in thanks. "Look, Beatrix," Ben continued, "we need to see what's going on, and it won't interfere with our original mission at all."

"Mission?" Alex asked, looking at each of them in turn.

Looking as if he might burst, Malik chimed in at machine-gun speed. "Ben and Beatrix's dad disappeared into thin air last weekend on the reservoir in Central Park, and somebody nuked his hard drive by breaking into their home. They thought there might be clues in the library as to what happened. It's not the first time we've seen that sceddy man with no face, and we found a book that mentions the name of Dr. Wendell's colleague—Montavani. We also found a manuscript, and we hope it has clues relating to the disappearance of Dr. Wendell and explains where he might be. And I personally think what happened last night is related. Oops."

Ben stared at Malik with a barely perceptible grin. Beatrix wasn't smiling, though.

"Dude, really? Nice going, James Bond."

"Thank you!" Malik beamed, not realizing he had just been insulted.

"Is that your 'strategy'?" Beatrix asked, making air quotes.

"Yes!" Malik replied. "You should try it sometime."

"Okay. Okay." Ben said. "Everybody calm down."

Alex looked neither shocked nor surprised at the story Malik had belted out. "Beatrix, maybe we should go back to school to see if the disappearance of Nic, Becker, and Darby are connected to your father. Maybe we can get answers to both."

"Sounds good," Ben said. "Beatrix?"

"Okay. You're right, Ben. We'll go back to Festermunder tomorrow. Sorry, Malik."

"It's all good." Malik turned to Alex. "Are these English muffins gluten free?"

She shrugged. "I have no idea. I doubt it. Why?"

"No reason! Bee-tee-dubbs. Where's the loo?" Alex pointed it out, and Malik bolted down the hall, leaving his three companions laughing hysterically.

As she gathered her belongings to leave, Beatrix scanned Alex's room with passive interest. Amidst the memorabilia, trophies, and citations for various accomplishments, she noticed a collage of family pictures over a desk stacked with books. One picture interested her, and she leaned over to study it. It showed a slightly younger Alex, a little girl, and a tall, thin scarlet-haired man with a large, toothy smile. They were eating ice cream, and it was smeared all over their mouths and faces. They looked happy.

"My uncle Freddie," Alex said from behind Beatrix, startling her.

"I'm sorry. I was just looking," Beatrix replied, straightening up.

"It's alright. By all means." Alex took the photo off the corkboard and showed it to her. "Freddie is Mum's brother back in London."

"Is this Gwen?" Beatrix asked.

"Yes."

"Cute." Beatrix wasn't accustomed to using the word other than in reference to pets.

"Yeah," Alex replied, then fell silent.

"Alex, have I done something wrong? I'm sorry I pried into your stuff. I was just—"

"We lost Gwen a year and a half ago," Alex said. She offered Beatrix a taut smile, as if she felt sorry for her.

"Oh my God! I'm so sorry," Beatrix said.

"It's okay. It's just what we deal with. That's sort of our life after Gwenie was lost." Alex stared at the photo. Beatrix had no idea what to say.

Leave it to me! Constantly inserting my foot in my mouth!

"What happened?"

Alex sighed, then set the picture down. "Let's just say you and I have a lot more in common than you think."

Beatrix stared at Alex, wondering what she meant.

Alex fidgeted with her necklace. "We were on holiday. A day trip. Uncle Fred took us out to Oxfordshire to visit relatives. We had a blast, me and Gwenie riding in our great-gran's convertible, which Freddie borrowed. We stopped at an ice-cream shop on the outskirts of a little hamlet. That's where we took that picture. Freddie took us out to a park, and Gwenie saw a bunny."

Alex began to choke up, then continued once she got hold of herself. "Normally, I watched her like a hawk. Freddie was replying to a phone call from work when I let Gwenie follow the bunny to the edge of a wood. I . . . I was playing with my phone or texting someone, I don't know. After a few moments, when I called out for her, she didn't answer.

"Freddie and I searched for her, getting help from local folk and then the police. Even MI5 got involved. But we couldn't find Gwenie. We never found her, Beatrix. My poor little Gwenie vanished. It was my fault, but Uncle Freddie will never forgive himself. He's made it his life's mission to find out what happened. He thinks she's still out there somewhere. I think . . ." Alex broke off and began to cry. "I think that's why I took last night so hard with Nic, Becker, and Darby."

"It's alright. I understand how you feel," Beatrix said. "In fact, I understand perfectly."

"I know, I know. After that, Mum retired from her government job and Dad applied for a transfer to the states. We just needed a change. We couldn't find a flat in Manhattan — not on our budget — so we live here. It's cozy, and I like the neighborhood.

"Mum and Dad spent their life savings and borrowed everything they could to find Gwen. Uncle Freddie went broke, and maybe a little cracked, after that. He lives with his granny in Hackney. He even changed divisions at work to research Gwen's disappearance."

"What does he do? Fred, I mean?"

Alex almost snickered. "Believe it or not, he works as an investigator for MI5. He refers to his area as the 'investigation of the unexplained.' Everything from black cats crossing your path to little green men."

Beatrix snickered, as did Alex, signaling the end of the tell-all.

As they walked out of the room, Beatrix turned to Alex. "Isn't it strange that the two of us both lost people the way we did, and we both wound up at the same school?"

Alex smiled, her lips pressed together. "Something is wrong with that place, and we both know the secret of what that is lies with your father. I want to help. I need answers just like you do."

Beatrix grabbed Parfleet and her satchel as she prepared to leave. Malik and Ben were already waiting at the door.

"Okay, Alex," Beatrix said. "You're in."

"Thank you!" Alex hugged her, but Beatrix stood with her arms at her side not reciprocating, as was her style, a cucumber hug. "See you tomorrow."

Their plan was to return to Festermunder and try to find out what happened. No operational creativity was required, nor was it possible. The four companions had no idea what to expect upon their return. They fully anticipated they would be taken into the custody of the police and/or Headmistress Grunnion-Paltine, offered up as sacrificial lambs into the maw of guilt and uncertainty. But it was Ben's plan, and they trusted him.

They passed through the gates together, then huddled under the covered causeway prior to going inside as Beatrix laid down some ground rules.

"Okay, here's the deal. We act normal and do nothing to arouse suspicion. If anyone gets called in for questioning, text the rest of us so we can get the hell out of here."

Malik raised his hand. "I don't have a smartphone."

Alex handed Malik an iPod Touch. "You can use it to send and receive messages over Wi-Fi. I programmed all of us into it. All you need to do is identify yourself as the new owner."

Malik was overwhelmed by the gift and the fact that Alex had spoken to him. "Thanks! Should we use code names? If so, I prefer Tupac Sh—"

"That'll be enough," Alex said.

"Okay. Just keep it all under wraps no matter what," Beatrix said. "And for God's sake, no one talks. Oh, and avoid the Gnome at all costs! If we have no contact at all, meet up at Rockefeller Center on the 5th Avenue side of the ice rink."

"Ooh, the LEGO store?" Malik asked.

"Yes, fine, meet at the LEGO store," Beatrix replied, smiling slightly.

With that closing edict, they headed into Festermunder and into a new unknown.

Shockingly, there was no mention of anything averse happening at the school over the weekend. In fact, the faculty and administration continued their educational duties unabated, as if none the wiser. Astonishingly, Headmistress Grunnion-Paltine simply welcomed everyone back from Thanksgiving break and admonished them not to slack off for the next three weeks until Christmas break.

Ben passed by Beatrix in the halls between classes, and they both looked at each as if to say, "I don't get it; it's like it never happened."

Only later in the day in Lightheart's ancient history did the chaos begin to spin out of control.

First, Professor Lightheart no longer displayed his polite, self-deprecating manner. Knowing full well that Lightheart possessed information about Wendell's matriculation at Festermunder and the notebook itself, Beatrix was overcome with the urge to talk to him in private, but she resisted.

It was only after class began that Beatrix, and, to a lesser extent, Malik, noticed something odd. Seated in the back row in the usual spots were Nic, Becker, and Darby. When Beatrix saw them, her jaw dropped.

They were gone! Alex said they were pulled into that thing. Is she nuts? Is she lying?

It didn't take long for Beatrix and everyone to realize that something was dreadfully wrong with the three students.

Lightheart asked a question to the ever-buffoonish McTeel: "Master

McTeel, do you know any reason why the Phoenicians were so proficient at spreading their alphabet?"

McTeel simply sat there, his face blank, neglecting to offer up a sarcastic answer, as he was wont to do. "I . . . I . . . I have nothing."

Almost in unison, everyone turned to face Becker. The response was so out of character that even Lightheart was incredulous. "Master McTeel, are you unwell? What's the matter with you?"

Becker sat there, his face as blank as an unmarked gravestone as he fidgeted with his hands. Normally, Stooch would have initiated some time-honored bully versus bully ragging, but he seemed to be mentally and physically detached as well. Darby wasn't much better. She had turned in her desk to face the back wall, which was covered in shelves full of books. When Lightheart asked her what was the matter, she replied in a dull, somnolent voice. "The daylight . . . it hurts me today. It just . . . hurts."

Beatrix realized the three students had been taken, and they had seen something — something they would like to forget. Beatrix had experienced such behavior before and was familiar with the repercussions. The unintelligible mumbling. The lack of visual focus. They were not themselves.

This is Wendell all over again. There are too many coincidences surrounding Wendell and Festermunder. We have got to locate this Montavani!

Ben had put the composition book and the Montavani text in the bottom of his duffel bag and locked them in his locker in the varsity locker room. He later gave it to Beatrix to study during the day. It was safer there than at home. Who knew what sort of snooping the police would do at Rosemarie's behest?

She had made one or two appearances during the previous week to coordinate with police regarding Wendell's disappearance. Oddly, she said it was likely Wendell had taken off on a road trip or something. If he had flown somewhere, he would have been flagged at immigration upon entering a foreign country.

Ben and Beatrix knew better. Wendell was gone, likely forever.

Beatrix sat in a daze in Lightheart's class, racking her brain for clues. A sliver of insight. But so far, all she had were several facts she scribbled on her notepad.

1. Wendell — Gone
2. Nic, Becker, and Darby — Gone but returned different
    (see item 1)
3. Montavani textbook — meridians
4. Wendell's manuscript — a bunch of nonsense; full of
    unintelligible coordinates and equations

As she itemized the clues in her head, Beatrix realized there was more to add to the mystery. These she did not jot down on paper, as they seemed too far-fetched and too incendiary to commit to paper. The pursuit by the faceless man.

The Hat Man.

Who is he? He lives in my dreams and thoughts, but he's real. Ben saw him too. I'm not going mad.

Beatrix traced her mind back to Wendell's trip to Scotland.

Was there a chance his study of those symbols led him there? Was it an accident? Or like Malik suggested, were Dad's vanishings intentional? Did he know he was going to be taken?

Seeing my doppelganger in the streets is going to stay my little secret right now. Nobody needs to know about that, not even Ben. But things really took off in the wrong direction after that day, to say the least.

Someone tapped her foot, and Beatrix noticed Professor Lightheart returning a paper to her. It was her essay on Viking colonization and exploration. She received an eighty-eight. Under the grade in faint handwriting was the word "over." Beatrix flipped the paper over and saw something else written in tiny handwriting.

West 54th Street and 9th Avenue. Pizzeria, third booth
on the left. Read this again. And keep it quiet. Bring
W's composition book.

Read the back of a stupid test paper at a specific booth at a pizzeria? Great. What I need is Lightheart alone for an hour to find out what he knows about Dad and who this Hat Man is. Wait! The composition book?!

Class ended, and true to Beatrix's continual bad luck, she couldn't seem to send or receive a text to Malik, Ben, or Alex. They were going to wind up at 30 Rock, and Beatrix was going to try to follow Lightheart's instructions. It could be her first and only break in the case.

When school was dismissed, seeing no sign of Ben, Malik, or Alex, Beatrix trusted the system and hightailed it over to 54th and 9th. She found Tony's Pizza easily enough, and when she walked in, she was greeted with the smell of freshly baked pies. Her stomach gnawing with hunger, Beatrix sat at the third booth on the left.

Well, when in Rome!

Beatrix ordered a fully loaded twelve-inch pizza and a Diet Coke. Glancing around she saw no one familiar. The black light above her head issued forth from a Tiffany-style lamp. Breaking out her test paper, she gazed at it again. Nothing. Then she held it up to the black light as surreptitiously as she could so as not to attract attention. She looked for clues in the manuscript as well but was drawing blanks.

Well, this stinks! What was I thinking? That I'm freaking Nancy Drew?

The server, who looked like the elder patriarch of the pizza joint, approached her table. "Need any lemon for your soda, dear?"

Beatrix smiled. "No, sir. Thank you, I'm good."

He smiled through his white beard, his eyes blue and kind. "I'll leave them here for you just the same."

Beatrix watched as he walked back toward the kitchen. She felt as if she knew him, but he couldn't place him. She shrugged, then became lost in thought.

Lemons . . . Lemongrass . . . Mr. Lemoncello. When life hands you lemons, make — wait!

Beatrix flipped the test paper over and sprinkled lemon juice on the back. Then, using a linen napkin, she rubbed the acidic juice into the paper. She held it up to the black light and gasped as numbers and words appeared on the page.

Page 121 bottom right margin
answers await
be careful who you speak to!
— GM

P.S. bring the dog

Beatrix tore open the manuscript and was disappointed to see page 121 was covered in more crazy calculus and elliptical diagrams. She checked the bottom right margin, where something stuck out from the rest:

34.987 x - 80.231

Ok? Now what do these numbers mean?

Puzzled, Beatrix scribbled the numbers on a napkin and tried to work things out in her head but to no avail. After gulping a swig of Diet Coke and devouring a slice of pizza, she went to the register to pay.

"Is that older gentleman still here?" Beatrix asked. "You know, the manager guy who came by my table? White beard, kind of tall?"

The cashier, who was no more than thirty, hollered toward the kitchen. "Hey, Tony! Anyone else on shift tonight?"

He shook his head. The cashier turned back to Beatrix. "Sorry, kid, but it's just me and my uncle Tony. We don't have no old folks working here."

Beatrix nodded as she scanned the perimeter of the pizzeria. Only a few patrons were there, and none of them were the old man.

Stepping back onto a frigid W 54th Street and not thinking, Beatrix threw the napkin in a trash bin while hailing a cab.

"Rockefeller Center off Fifth, please."

The traffic was so heavy that Beatrix realized she would have gotten there much faster on foot. When she finally arrived at the appointed place but didn't see Ben or the others, she pulled out her phone to check it for texts.

"Psst. Beatrix." It was Alex. She motioned Beatrix to follow her, then headed toward the back of the LEGO store.

"You good?" Alex asked when Beatrix caught up to her. "We were worried. None of our texts would go through."

"I'm fine. My phone has been acting up all day too. I have news. Where are Ben and Malik?"

"They're coming. We've got news too," Alex said as she cupped her hands to blow warm air on them. It was bitterly cold.

They each grabbed a clear cellophane bag and began picking out colored custom pieces as they talked. Malik was visible across the store, eyeing a *Lord of the Rings* castle (Minas Tirith). Beatrix had yet to spot Ben.

"Did you hear?" Alex asked.

"About what?" Beatrix.

"Professor Lightheart announced his retirement effective today. He resigned. Then the HGP and some suited security types I hadn't seen before escorted him out."

The message!

Beatrix was dumbfounded. "What?"

"Yes, he's done, they say. Completely washed up and basically was marched out of there. It was awful. They treated the man like rubbish."

Ben entered the store carrying four hot coffees, and Beatrix mouthed a heartfelt "thank-you" to him. Then she summarized her tale from the pizzeria and the old man giving her the lemons to see the message from the mysterious "GM."

Beatrix produced the numbers the composition book and the message from the test paper and showed it to the others.

"Is it an IP address?" Ben asked.

Having finished his appreciation of Sauron's fortress (Barad-dûr), Malik strutted over. "What gives?"

Beatrix held up the napkin. "What sort of numbers are these, and what do you think they mean?"

Malik squinted at them, then pulled back. "Easy. Those are map coordinates. Latitude and longitude." He pulled out the iTouch Alex had given him and typed the numbers into an app. "Okay."

"Okay what?" Alex and Beatrix said in unison.

"These coordinates are a location in the Catskills Mountains. Upstate New York."

The four companions stood in the middle of the LEGO store, looking at each as if trying to figure out who was going to take the lead.

Then Ben smiled. "When do we leave?"

Several hours later, at 54th Street and 9th Avenue, a tall, obscure man in a fedora and trench coat approached a trash receptacle. He opened the top and rummaged through it. After securing a wadded-up napkin, he replaced the top to the bin, then headed off down the street, disappearing like an apparition into the cold, dark night.

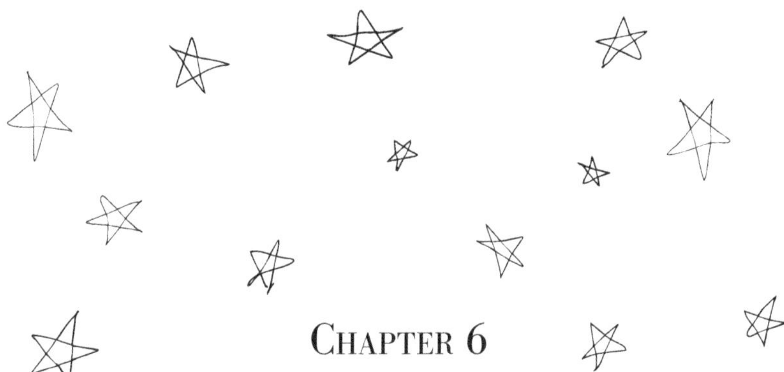

Chapter 6

Escape from New York

"Compass, pocket knife, extra belts—one, two, three, four of them—backup glasses, rubber bands for my braces from Dr. Fesler, inhaler, extra socks, and Skechers if there's snow. Beatrix, do you have a satellite phone by any chance? I really—"

"Malik! We don't even have a plan yet. You're packing like you are parachuting into Normandy, and all we said is we *may* try it."

Beatrix counted off on her fingers. "We have no freaking money, at least nowhere near what we're going to need. We have no alibi for Alex's parents, Rosemarie, the cops—who are positively watching us—your cousin Kasbah—"

"Kas*ra*, as in Rock the Kasra," Malik said, grinning as he packed his bag.

"Kas*ra*," she corrected herself, then stopped. "Okay, that was actually pretty funny. Anyway, as I said. We're kids, and if we just up and disappear, we're going to be missed! Even Rosemarie will want to know what we're doing. Not to mention, Mr. Professor, how the heck are we even going to get to this place in the Catskills *if* we can even find it?"

Malik walked across his room to Beatrix and placed his bony hands on her shoulders. "Oh, bless you, my dear child. Trouble yourself not in the ways of geniuses."

Beatrix looked at Malik with her usual contemptuous sneer as he fished around in his back pocket before withdrawing his wallet. In typical Malik fashion, it had all of the expected characteristics: red, frayed, Velcro closure, and sporting the Member's Only logo. Malik opened it, then pulled a card out of the front sleeve and held it close to Beatrix's face. "Call me if ya gangsta. What? What?" Malik completed the reveal with a dance move that made him look like a gyrating robotic scarecrow.

"A fake driver's license? Where did you get that?" Beatrix was beside herself.

Malik shrugged. "Kasra had it made for me. He charged me two hundred and fifty bucks too. It's all good. We're set."

"Set? For what? You can't drive, and neither can I. Only Ben has had driver's ed. Where the hell are we going to get a car from anyhow? I mean, dude, this is lame even for you. And that's saying a lot." Beatrix invoked the old rules of engagement of treating Malik poorly. But he didn't seem to notice, as usual.

"Calm down, woman. I got this covered, I tell you. Kasra never uses his car, okay? He uses the subway or Citi Bikes or just bums rides from his posse. He keeps it over in a park-and-ride in Queens, and I know where the keys are. Problem solved."

Beatrix stared at Malik. "You want to steal your cousin's car and drive over a hundred miles into the mountains of Upstate New York?" She paused to let that sink in. "Do you even know how to operate a car?"

"How hard can it be? Look at all of the idiots who can drive. I have an IQ of 172, and I made a 1475 on the SAT as a seventh grader. I just need some time on the simulator, and I know I can get us there." Malik was so sincere that Beatrix believed him.

This is beyond stupid. But it may be the only chance we have to find Wendell.

Malik and Beatrix joined Alex and Ben in the kitchen as they worked on a list of items they would need for the trip. They were sitting closer together than necessary as they pored over a topographic map that Malik had downloaded and printed out.

"Ahem." Beatrix cleared her throat, startling Alex and Ben, who looked up and separated slightly. "Have you guys found the route?"

"Yep, as well as the general area of the coordinates," Ben replied. "But I have news for you. Google Earth is up to date, and nothing shows at the coordinates you gave."

Beatrix said, "Maybe this person doesn't want to be found by anyone else, only us."

"Or maybe we're being drawn into a trap," Malik said as he stood in front of the open fridge door. "Right into the spider's web." He stuck a spoonful of Nutella into his mouth. Beatrix gave him a cold look, but he just gulped, then took another spoonful, straight from the jar. "Look, people, have you ever heard of chaos theory?" The other three looked at Malik as if he were speaking a foreign language.

"Look at the situation. No patterns. Nothing predictable. The present doesn't determine the future as it normally should; then the approximate present doesn't determine the approximate future. Get it? Guys, have you ever read Tyson or Hawking? Geez!" Beatrix, Ben, and Alex remained mute, mesmerized.

"Look it. I want to go. I do. I really want to go. Saying this, I have the least invested in this situation of anyone here. But don't be naïve. We have no predictive value in what will happen when we follow this letter. We could get hurt or vanish like the others. Or be killed. Yes, I said it. I think we need a contingency for what we do when we find out that what we might be looking for is something we should be running from instead."

The last words settled like smoke over the group. No one spoke for several moments.

"Right. I have something to say," Alex replied. "We're going to need to put aside our doubts. Malik, I'm afraid to go, but I'm also afraid to stay and watch my friends face danger without me. But Malik's right; we need a plan for how we approach the sender of the message. We can't communicate with him, so the sender has the advantage when we encounter him."

Ben was chewing on the drawstring of his hoodie. He finally spoke after an interminable pause. "Malik has a point. When we meet our contact at these coordinates, we have to be ready for anything. We need to find a way to draw him out into the open so we can meet in conditions of our choosing. For now, we need to worry about alibis and transportation. Beatrix and I are fine. Rosemarie is usually non-existent during the Christmas holidays, partying with friends. We go days without seeing or talking to her. Malik?"

"I'm cool until January ninth, when my parents come back. Kasra doesn't care where I am, of that I'm quite certain." Malik shot Beatrix a look with his lips poked out, having not forgotten their verbal altercation in the other room.

"Alex?" Ben asked.

"I'm good. No need to worry."

"What do you mean?" Beatrix asked with a cold look. "Your folks are at home, and you're leaving around Christmas."

"My folks are picking up my uncle Freddie at JFK the day we get out of school, and he's staying throughout Christmas break. I'm sure I can come up with something."

The others eyed Alex with doubt.

Alex smiled. "Guys, I got this. I can go. I'll be there."

Ben stood and clapped his hands. "Okay. We'll go the day school gets out for break, December nineteenth, right after dismissal. Now, how are we going to get there?"

Beatrix rolled her eyes as Malik presented his plan.

In London at that very moment, it was 6:52 a.m. as Frederick J. Hardingham approached the door to the largest office in the building. As he whistled and fumbled for his keys, he looked up at the sign on the door, which read "Area 51." He snickered despite himself as he unlocked the door and entered his office.

At his desk, he turned his computer on. It was another frigid Monday in the basement: Storage C, Hall 5, Annex 2. Other than the occasional rat, Fred was the only resident of BC52. To say it was morning at all in BC52 was a stretch, as there were no windows, only creaking, sweaty pipes and conduits along the walls. The eerie feeling of claustrophobia, mixed with the specter of a perpetually nocturnal environment, didn't seem to bother him.

As his computer took its time booting up—he had been promised another one months ago, but as of yet, the IT department seemed to have overlooked him—Fred took a sip of tea from his mug.

"Ah! Hot! Right, okay, that was not good. Burned me tongue." Fred set his Princess Leia mug down and grabbed a water bottle to negate the pain. "Blimey, that hurt."

Fred needn't worry about keeping his voice down, as not a soul worked in the basement with him. Fred had the distinction of being the only agent in Special Section 16. His basement office was at least 6,000 square feet, and he had it all to himself. SS-16 was a subunit of an upstairs bureaucracy that remained cloaked in secrecy. BC52 may have been a dark dwelling no one heard of, but everyone had heard of the resident organization of Thames House, 12 Millbank, London, for Thames House was the headquarters for MI5.

Although Fred was doing work that was vitally important to him, no one else at MI5 seemed to agree. In fact, no one else at MI5 seemed to know he existed at all.

That was what made him a true spy!

SS-16 was cloaked in obscurity, though not as a necessary cover for covert activities vital to British national security as its own version of the CIA. On the contrary, SS-16 mattered to no one, it seemed, except Hardingham. His section dealt with the investigation of the unexplained. This obfuscatory designation was the intelligence equivalent of a doctor's "throwaway" diagnosis—a waste basket full of investigations that no one could get to stick to any other department. A collection of crazy files made by crazier complainants about any and all uncategorized phenomena. The "upstairs" agents viewed SS-16 as window dressing, a bureaucratic answer to filing away issues in order to not throw them away. But to them, sending cases to SS-16 was the equivalent of throwing them away. For, as of yet, in the two years the department had existed, Fred had yet to solve a case.

From the Loch Ness Monster to lights in the sky to someone hearing voices when they turned on the microwave to filing reports on little green men, Fred had covered a lot of ground. But progress was slow. To his relief, there was very little pressure from upstairs, as most had forgotten about Hardingham's subterranean existence. His only moments of visibility were when he was allowed access to the break room and the employee cafeteria.

The other agents, mostly the hotdogs in Section 3 (Operations), really poured it on poor Fred when they saw him in the cafeteria. Always eating alone while reading comic books like *The Avengers* made Fred an easy target, as he already stuck out like a sore thumb. Fred was a towering six foot, four inches but did not have much in the way of meat on his bones. Not even weighing 175 pounds made it hard to find clothes that fit. What he did find was cheaply made and loose around the collar. His pants were slightly short, which contributed to one of Hardingham's nicknames: Flood. They also called him Spooky due to his line of work and his pale skin.

Fred had flaming-red hair and a prominent Adam's apple that danced up and down when he laughed, which, ironically, was quite often. He was self-deprecating and so mannerly to others that he was uncomfortable to be around. Fred would apologize for his very existence if he could. His granny Olive said his first words after being born into this world were "I'm sorry" and that he would have "I beg your pardon, sorry I took up so much space" on his headstone one day.

Fred lived in a modest first-floor flat in a modest London neighborhood of Hackney with his granny Olive. As a widow, and not entirely in control of her mental faculties, Olive needed looking after, and Fred was happy to help. In return for repairs, upkeep, cleaning, and doing the wash, the shopping, and the cooking, as well as assisting his gran with various appointments, Fred lived rent free. This was helpful on a meager salary such as his and as he tried to rebuild his credit following a financial mess from a couple of years back.

Granny Olive made Fred's life more difficult than any of the Op-3 blokes at work. She was up at all hours. Thanks to faulty hearing aids, which she refused to replace, his gran constantly blared music, especially a band called Earth, Wind, and Fire. The tele was stuck at top volume as Gran watched her game shows, during which she would yell at the screen and insult the contestants about their stupidity, their beliefs, their mothers, or their respective regions. But worst of all, Gran was difficult to control socially. She was forever meeting and dating elderly men, connecting with them on Craig's List or a new dating site for the very mature called BlueHair.com. Poor Fred was stuck chaperoning Gran on her various dates and having to keep track of her whereabouts. She often stayed out past midnight and, one time, called him from Sheffield to say she was staying over for a few days with her girlfriends to go to a football game. The only benefit to such outings was that Fred gained vital experience in tracking down and surveilling someone's whereabouts. He looked forward to it as a challenge, telling his cat, Moresby, it was time to play a game of "Find Gran." It also offered Fred an outlet and got him out of the house.

"Freddie, ya should find yer a gal," Gran said to him one day. "Ya got to git out, dearie. No gal is goin' to notice you if yer stuck in the flat all day. Is there anyone special? Anyone at all besides that blimey cat?"

"Gran, my work is my life right now," Hardingham had replied. "And looking after you and Moresby is plenty enough action for me. Besides, the ladies don't fancy me."

"Oh, bloody hell, Freddie. I was out on dates during the Blitz, and a few Kraut bombs didn't keep me from meeting my Tommy. Them lasses? They don't fancy ya because ya don't try. Don't expect one to like ya 'cause they feel sorry for ya. Are ya on Snapchat? Facebook? Are ya even on Insta?" Granny Olive was surprisingly adept with her iPhone, which she held up in triumph. "Think I'm due a free upgrade."

"This is fine for me, Gran," Fred replied, holding up his Motorola "dumbphone." Fred could text on it, but he had to go through all the number choices to find each character. It took a while, so he rarely did it except to text himself reminders. Looking at his phone, he saw a message he had sent himself.

> 12/20/2016
> Depart: 08:00 a.m.
> Flight 1880 Heathrow to JFK
> Evelyn Thacker

Fred smiled, looking forward to his trip. It would do him good to go to the States and see his sister, Evelyn, and his brother-in-law over Christmas. He had accrued so much unused personal leave and vacation time that his superiors had ordered him to take a holiday.

Packing up Granny Olive and leaving her with his cousin Howard made him uneasy. Although Gran was high maintenance, Fred loved her dearly and appreciated her company.

Without her, there's only Moresby.

"You'll be fine with Gran Olive, mate," Fred said as he stroked Moresby's fur. "It'll be good to get across the pond and see my niece and sis."

Wrapping up the last day of the year for himself at work, Fred finished his memo reviews, which were due upstairs. He also finished his report on a man in Grimsby who said he saw an object in the sky that resembled a kielbasa sausage on six consecutive Tuesdays.

After straightening out his desk and arranging his pens and pencils, Fred opened his work email one last time. He had a new message in his inbox. The subject line caused Fred to sit up ramrod straight:

> Section 3 meeting, January 3, 2017, 8:00 a.m.
> — Special Agent: E. Soames-Briggs

Fred's pulse quickened, Section 3 was Operations. The email was time locked not to open and decrypt itself until December 31.

Am I to be working with the field agents directly? Fancy that! Maybe they need my case work and want me out in the field. Blimey, maybe I can finally become a field agent!

Fred switched off his computer and cast a brief look in the mirror. "Don't kid yourself, Freddie. They don't want you."

Checking his desk one last time, careful not to leave out any sensitive materials, Fred arranged a photo next to the banker's lamp. It showed him and two little girls laughing and eating ice cream, which was smeared all over their faces.

Fred smiled as he focused on the smaller of the two girls. "One day, sweet girl."

Beatrix tossed and turned in her sleep. Ben and Malik, who had made beds on the floor in her room at the beginning of the Wendell crisis, watched and listened to her, their faces distressed. Seeing as it was the night before their planned embarkation to the Catskills, Alex had decided to stay home in Queens. The car was parked there, so they could pick her up on the way.

"She's getting worse," Malik whispered.

"I know," Ben replied. He worried sick over Beatrix. The burden of what they were going through seemed to hit her the hardest. She kept repeating the same phrases in her sleep: "Half a person. Not real. Not true."

Ben scooted over to the bed and patted his sister's back, then covered her up with her favorite blanket. "It's okay, Beatrix. It's alright."

At 2:33 a.m., Beatrix was turned away from Ben, so he didn't realize she was awake and staring. She readjusted Parfleet near her head and then closed her eyes again, but sleep would not come.

The days leading up Christmas break at Festermunder Academy came and went without incident. Now it was the last day before winter break until January. Beatrix texted Ben, Alex, and Malik a vague message that only they would understand.

Go/No-Go

They replied immediately.

Ben: Go
Alex: Go
Malik: Crap are we sure about this?

Beatrix was perplexed at Malik's response. Annoyed that Malik had been so gung-ho before but was suddenly getting cold feet.

Headmistress Grunnion-Paltine gave a final announcement over the loudspeaker. "Students. We adjourn for two weeks. I, on behalf of all the faculty, staff, and administration here, wish you a hearty, happy holidays from ol' Festermunder."

Then the HGP asked everyone to stand. The students knew what was coming next, and they faced it all with a quiet dread—the singing of the alma mater. HGP started in hear shrill voice and required each student to join in as a choral echo to the words.

(tinkling on the piano in D♭ major)

Who is the best?
The very, very best?
The positively best.
The absolutely best!
Better than the rest . . .

(the piano rising to a crescendo then getting quiet)

Long ago, Dear Anton,
On the banks of the Hudson Found,
This sweet charming oasis,
On this our Hallowed Ground.
Travelers from distant realms,
Riders from all lands,
Paid homage to the mighty spot,
That showed us where Earth stands.

Festermunder!
Festermunder!
Hail unto thee!

Festermunder!
Festermunder!
Dear Anton would agree.

Other schools are dodgy,
A token point of fact.
We'll create a prodigy,
Who has no use for tact.
A strong mind and body,
To 'Munder's banner we flock,

Another place is shoddy,
We'll watch you like a hawk.

Festermunder, Festermunder!
Hail unto thee!

Dear ol' Festermunder . . .
We adore you certainly

Fester School, you are the best,
And the rest — quite pungent.
Fester School, you pass the test
Any other — quite repugnant!

(quickened pace)

A robin lays an egg,
A pirate with one leg,
A round hole without
A square peg.
Dear ol' Festy!
You are like a perfect match,
And contain a perfect batch.
If you were a rainbow trout,
You'd be a perfect catch.

A freckle to a mole,
A mouth without a hole,
A bridge without a troll.
Dear ol' Festy!
I love thy fairest halls,
And if they have the gall
To disparage our dear Festermunder,
We'll truly make them crawl.

Hail!
Fester-Fester-Festermunder!

More brazen students oft whispered the optional last phrase ("help, this place sucks") while the headmistress sang one last "Festermunder."

Headmistress Grunnion-Paltine dismissed the students at 5:00 p.m. precisely, according to the normal routine.

Having already packed and prepared as much as they could, the four companions made their way home via taxi. Malik went home to use the last reliable bathroom he thought he might see in the next few days. Back at their apartment, Ben and Beatrix made final preparations for the journey.

"Phone chargers?" Ben inquired.

"Yep. Got us each one and a backup. Also got one for the car."

"B?" Ben yelled from his bedroom. "You got any spare glasses? If something were to happen to yours, I wouldn't want you to —"

"I only have one pair, so they'll have to do. Look, we're good. Let's call a cab, grab Par, and go."

"Malik," Ben said.

"What?"

"Malik. Aren't you forgetting our science officer?" Ben asked, grinning.

"Oh, yeah, whatever," Beatrix replied.

They found Malik waiting in the lobby with his bag packed and book bag loaded. Mr. Keane eyed Malik with suspicion. His eyes widened substantially when he saw Ben and Beatrix, similarly loaded.

"Going on a little holiday trip, Master Voght?" Mr. Keane asked.

"Yes, sir, Mr. Keane, we are," Ben replied. "We're heading upstate."

Beatrix shot Ben a look of venom for letting that little nugget of information out. Mr. Keane knew Rosemarie well and was fond of her. It alarmed Beatrix that their little jaunt upstate could be a source of small talk between the two adults.

"I suppose you're taking Mr. Patel with you?" Keane asked, a hint of derision in his tone.

"No, sir," Beatrix replied. "He's going on a trip of his own, back to his . . . homeland. Yep. Going back to India, right?" Beatrix poked Malik.

Malik missed his cue. "Huh? India. No way. I'm going with you."

Beatrix's eyes narrowed; then she picked up her stuff and walked out past Malik. "Don't mind him. He gets confused and often stays that way."

The ride to Queens to get Kasra's car and pick up Alex was quiet. Beatrix was lost in thought in the back of the cab with Ben. Malik was up front, trying to convince the driver to let him control the radio station.

The Queensborough Bridge loomed, and the car began to climb. Beatrix looked over her left shoulder at the lights of Manhattan. The stars were out, and for a second, she realized how beautiful they were. But she had never felt so out of sorts.

At the park-and-ride, Malik had some difficulty locating the vehicle. Finally, they found their chariot: a gold 2002 Honda Accord.

"Okay, this is it," Malik said as he fumbled for his keys. "Let me do a 'pre-flight' check!"

Ben smiled and looked around. Beatrix could tell he was scanning the perimeter of the poorly lit parking lot for a threat. He slipped past the car to look down the rows. Ben didn't say it, but Beatrix could tell he was nervous about something. As for Beatrix, her stomach was in knots over the thought of Malik driving them the two miles or so to Alex's house in rush-hour traffic during the holidays.

As they piled in the Accord, they were met by the pungent odor of stale Cheez-Its and Black Forest Musk. Malik started the car and put it in reverse, pulling out of the spot and executing a majestic three-point turn.

"Easy on the gas and don't ride the brakes," Malik muttered, quoting the instructions from the driving simulator.

"How many hours did you log on your simulator?" Ben asked.

"At least a hundred, and I did some driving under adverse conditions like snow, rain, and even driving while being attacked by criminals!"

He pulled out of the lot and accelerated up the road. The gold Accord, complete with a rear window sticker that read "#jazzyphatnasty" disappeared from sight.

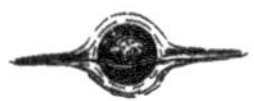

Under a streetlamp, a tall figure watched the tail lights disappear up the turnpike ramp. He raised his hand, palm up, and a small, dense cloud of black smoke issued forth, expanding until it was quite large. The faceless figure stepped into the void, and the smoke began to diminish. After it cleared, the Hat Man was no more.

When they reached Alex's house, they were early. Beatrix and Ben were impressed with Malik's driving. So was Malik.

Alex's cover story was that she was on a school trip for the "gifted and talented" at Festermunder and would be returning in four days. She had gone as far as engineering fake forms, waivers, and other documents for her parents to sign. Having no reason not to trust her, her parents wished her well.

Beatrix, who was growing fond of Alex, was puzzled at how untroubled Alex seemed with how hollow her scheme was. She had already said goodbye to her parents as they were leaving for a Christmas party that specified no kids. Mr. and Mrs. Thacker had dragged Alex's poor jet-lagged uncle Freddie along with them.

Alex came out with one bag in hand and a book bag slung over her shoulder. Beatrix could tell she was anxious to leave.

Gosh. She even looks perfect in a sock hat.

As Beatrix opened the door for Alex and got out, she realized something wasn't right. Checking her phone, she saw that it was 7:48 p.m., but the streets were deserted. No cars or pedestrians, and no one moving in the windows of the homes.

"Hello, all," Alex said as she stuck her head into the car. "Beatrix, Ben. Alright there, Malik? You look good behind the wheel."

Malik beamed.

Alex stood up and looked across the car's roof at Beatrix. "Well, it's now or never, right?" Looking off to her left, Alex squinted at something then her eyes widened. "We have to go. Now!"

Alex heaved her bags into the backseat and jumped in, as did Beatrix. "Let's go, Malik! We need to leave now!"

Triggered by the fear in her voice, the other three looked behind them and saw a large void of billowing black smoke creeping down the street, seeming to consume everything in its path, including light. It was about a hundred yards from the car and closing. From its center, five forms materialized, all of them wearing black cloaks. Beatrix looked into the rearview and gasped as she realized another thing they all had in common.

No facial features.

As the faceless forms advanced, they seemed to be in no hurry, a sense of inevitability to their movement as they trudged forward in a lockstep of doom.

As if compelled by a force outside her body, Beatrix opened her door and ran out into the middle of the street.

"Beatrix, no!" Ben yelled.

Ignoring him, she faced the advancing hoard and the billowing void, her hands balled into fists.

As Beatrix drew closer, the five figures parted and another, larger one stepped out of the black smoke.

It was him. The Hat Man.

Beatrix recoiled; then a cry bubbled up from the depths of her lungs. "Nooooooo!"

The word burst forth like a thunderclap. Nearby windshields shattered and exploded. The five lesser figures scattered and seemed to fade from sight. The Hat Man turned his head to the side as if weighing his alternatives.

A blaring sound came from within the black cloud, followed by screeching and bright light. The Hat Man opened his palm and appeared to disappear into it. The sound was revealed to be a car horn and screeching tires. A car had barreled straight through the black mass, coming to a halt inches from Beatrix.

Beatrix stood there, shaking. Malik, who had run up to help her, looked into her eyes, and for the briefest of moments, he could have sworn her irises had flared bright purple.

Beatrix stood with both hands gripping the hood of the car whose headlights were blinding the others. Gripped by adrenaline, she looked into the driver's eyes.

"Oh, dear! My goodness, young lady, are you alright? Are you hurt?" The driver, a skinny man who spoke in a prim, polite British accent, got out and approached Beatrix, who was still dazed. "I nearly hit you! Are you sure you're not injured? You're lucky I saw you at the last—"

"Uncle Freddie!" Alex ran over and threw her arms around the man, and he reciprocated, though initially startled.

"Allie! Hello, my dear. I was on my way back to your house. I was jet-lagged and feeling quite dreadful, so Evie let me take the car back early from the Christmas party. The hors d'oeuvres were abominable and—"

"Uncle Fred —"

"But the car. Blimey, I can't drive on the right side. Nearly totaled it three times on the way back. Oh dear, I —"

"Uncle Fred," Alex said. "It's happened. What Mum thought. We found something. It's here! We're leaving to find the source."

Fred was taken aback, a look of amazement on his face.

"Gwen. We may learn something about her," Alex said.

That statement snapped Beatrix out of her daze. She was suddenly very interested in Alex's knowledge of the situation.

"Alex," Fred said, "perhaps we should all sit down for a rest and discuss this. I —"

Parfleet started barking. Beatrix looked down the street and saw why. Another black mass was developing about a quarter mile away. Beatrix's heart raced as panic set in.

"Gotta move!" she yelled. "Now!"

Already on the driver's side, Ben jumped in with Beatrix and Parfleet up front with him. Alex jumped in the back. "Malik, this is my uncle Freddie. He knows our business. He'll help us. Can you ride with him and follow?"

Though clearly unhappy with the arrangement, Malik recognized the emergency and nodded his understanding.

With the cloud closing in on the vehicles, Malik dove into the car with Fred. The cloud was almost on the bumper of the trailing car as Ben gunned it, and Fred followed. As they sped away from the dark shroud, the mist disappeared into a manhole, and the stars became visible again.

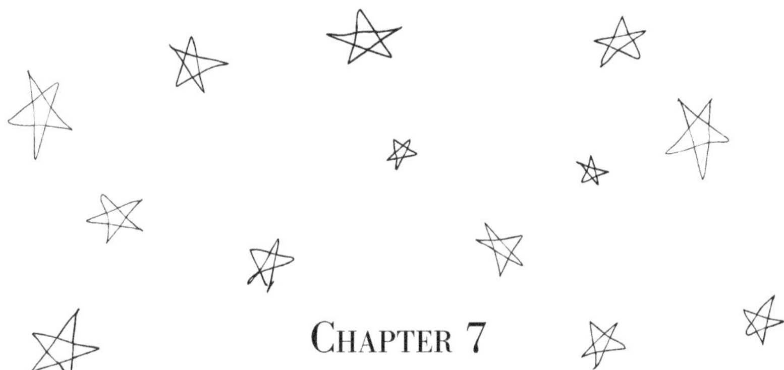

CHAPTER 7

Drones on the Mountainside

IN THE ACCORD, THE TRIO EXPERIENCED MOUNTING STRESS as the minutes ticked by. They took solace in the fact that each minute put more distance between them and their pursuers. The holiday traffic was congested and slow, which made it easier for a neophyte driver like Ben to negotiate the lanes of the busy turnpikes heading out of town. Alex and Beatrix collaborated on their smartphone GPS apps to make sure they didn't get turned around. Beatrix was most concerned about them being pulled over by the police.

The party's over if that happens, she thought. *Rosemarie likely won't post bail and just let us all rot in the clink.*

The mood in the follow-up car was quite different. While nervous at the overall situation, Fred began to get the hang of driving on the left side of his rental car and the right side of the road. He also found his passenger, Malik, to be affable and talkative. Fred liked him instantly in the way that kindred spirits graft to one another, not realizing that they're birds of a feather. Fred allowed Malik unrestricted access to the satellite radio and found he was adept at maintaining a continuous flow of pleasing music. When "Take a Chance on Me" by ABBA came on, the odd couple fell into a synchronized head bob. True to form, Malik took the first thirty minutes of the journey to unabashedly bring Fred up to speed on the situation, leaving nothing out and completely breaking the napkin oath he had sworn to Beatrix the previous week.

"So, Alex," Malik said out of the blue. "Like, what's her deal?"

"I beg your pardon?" Fred replied.

"You know. What's up with her? Is she cool? She only started talking to me this week."

"Oh, yes, I see," Fred replied. "She's quite nice and very gifted. Like her mum. She could easily take over for her . . ." Fred trailed off as if realizing he had said too much.

Malik didn't seem to notice. "Well, she's super pretty, but I'm not sure Beatrix likes her. Correction, I don't think Beatrix *liked* her. She seems to be fine with her now, though, I suppose."

"Right. Well, a book judged by its cover is never appreciated on its own merit," Fred replied, talking from experience.

Fred's phones rang. Surprising Fred, Malik snapped it up and answered.

"We need to stop soon and gas up," Alex said. "We're not sure when we'll see another station."

"Red-Five, roger that," Malik replied.

By that point, they were about sixty miles outside of the city and on Highway 87 North toward the Catskills. They pulled off at a gas station called Snuffy's Last Resort. In addition to getting fuel, they stocked up on water, soda, snacks, and candy. Fred was left to negotiate the gas pump, though unaccustomed to serving his own "petrol." The attendant, who was not the famed Snuffy himself but someone wearing overalls and a bushy white beard, was standing by the entrance to the store, flipping a coin over in his hand.

"How much longer to the hamlet of Phoenicia would you say, kind sir?" Fred asked.

"Up the road aways," the attendant said, pointing northeasterly while not looking up from his coin. "About sixty miles as the rabbit runs and forty-five as the crow flies."

"Thank you. I hope you have a pleasant evening, sir."

"Pleasant?" the old man said. "It'll be what it'll be, and no events in the cosmos will influence it any further at this point."

Fred turned toward the man. "I beg your—"

Fred stopped and turned about, only then realizing the old man was gone.

The group resumed their journey with the understanding that they would regroup and hash out their further plans when they arrived in Phoenicia, New York (population 331). Alex jumped in the car with Fred and Malik, leaving Ben and Beatrix in the lead car.

Sitting in the passenger seat of the Accord, Beatrix watched her GPS. Pinching out on her screen, she saw the purple pin signifying the coordinates on the map; they were getting closer. As road branches and tributaries sprang up on Beatrix's map, she turned to Ben.

They rode in silence for several minutes. Then Ben sighed. "Maybe we have this all wrong. I just feel like we should have talked to someone. Maybe the police or something. We have no one to guide us."

"We've got Fred!" Beatrix replied, smiling as she continued to follow the dot on her GPS. Then her head shot up. "Professor Lightheart! Oh my goodness! How could I be so stupid! Ben, Lightheart was the one who gave me the test paper that led to page 121 of the manuscript!"

"He what?" Ben asked.

"I guess in all the confusion, I forgot to mention it. Before Lightheart was escorted out of Festermunder, he directed me to the pizzeria, and that's where I read the message."

"The message from the old guy who had no record of ever working there?" Ben asked.

"Yes!" Beatrix. "The message was already on the paper when I got it from Lightheart. I was only able to decipher it at the pizzeria because of the lemons the old man gave me."

"Makes sense," Ben admitted.

"What does?"

"Lightheart knows everything. You've always said he was interested in

Dad. He tried to give you the composition book himself. Then he was fired with no explanation. He tried to help us. But he couldn't run the risk of . . ."

"Of what?" Beatrix asked.

"Headmistress Grunnion-Paltine," Ben said. "The library. It all goes back to the library. We know what they're hiding down there. We saw it, and it isn't books. I bet Lightheart knew too much and was removed. In fact, I wonder if he's even safe at this point."

"I never thought of that," Beatrix admitted. "I've lost track of things, like everything has been a dream or . . ." Beatrix's voice trailed off as she looked out the window into the dark, leafless woods to her right. "What's that?"

"What's what?" Ben asked, not taking his eyes off the road.

When Beatrix didn't reply, Ben looked to his right, and his eyes widened when he saw where she was pointing. Deep into the woods were flashing lights, tiny white and blue lights buzzing and swerving like fireflies.

Beatrix's phone buzzed with a text from Alex.

>   Alex: ???

Beatrix returned with a simple "IDK."
"Tell them to follow closely," Ben said.

>   Beatrix: Stay close on our tail
>   Alex: K
>   Beatrix: We don't know what it is. What u think?
>   Alex: Don't know scared tho
>   Beatrix: What does uncle think?
>   Alex: No idea scared 2
>   Beatrix: Malik?
>   Alex: Thinks we need 2 go faster
>   Beatrix: Faster?
>   Alex: Behind us now what do we do?
>   Beatrix: Hang on

"We're close, Ben. Only three miles off now. There is a left coming up soon—Furgett Road—let's take it. These lights make me think we're about to have another encounter like back in the city."

"Wait a second," Ben said, and rolled down the window, letting in a blast of frigid air. "Take the wheel and hold it steady on the straightaway."

Beatrix complied and held the wheel as best she could. Her hands were shaking, but not from the cold. Ben craned his neck out the window and the car had slowed to twenty-five miles per hour as he took his foot off the gas.

"What do you see?" Beatrix hollered.

"Not sure!" Ben bellowed back as he rolled the window back up. "But they aren't friendly. We need a plan! Look around. See anything in here that we can use as a weapon? Can you access the trunk?"

"Not sure. Hang on," Beatrix replied as she texted Alex.

> Beatrix: Ask M what's in the trunk
> Alex: K he says LARPING stuff
> Alex: LARPING?
> Alex: Live action role play
> Beatrix: One sec!

Beatrix shot into the backseat with surprising agility and peeled the back seat down so she could rummage through the trunk. She turned up a Viking helmet, a cape, a pair of pointy felt boots, and a stick that was four feet long.

"This help?" Beatrix asked as she shoved the stick through to the front seat.

"A bo staff? Okay! Beatrix, you're going to have to fight them off while I try to lose them."

The objects were disk-shaped and black. Blueish-white light emitted from beneath them. They were flanking both cars, and one was over them from above. There were seven of them, and the two cars were surrounded.

"These aren't lights! They're drones!" Ben exclaimed. "We've left most behind, but I see a few in front. How many do you count on Fred's tail?"

"One, two, three, four, five! Five of them!"

Beatrix unbuckled her seatbelt and turned around, crouching on one knee. Before rolling down the window, she wound the seat belt around her thigh in case she fell out of the car. When she lowered the window, the frigid night air blasted into Beatrix's face with cold fury. Ben was doing 50 mph on the winding back country road.

"Careful!" Ben screamed over the wind.

"Obviously!" Beatrix yelled back as she clutched the bo staff.

The drones, as black as night, swooped toward Beatrix's side of the car with astonishing speed. There were ten of them now, all positioned vertically with their white-hot undersides pointed away from her. The drones formed a circle and began to rotate, forming a ring in front of Beatrix. The ring steadied over Beatrix despite Ben's mad swerving of the car and Fred's honking of the horn and tailgating dangerously close.

"Beatrix, get back!" Ben bellowed.

Entranced by the spinning shape of the obsidian drones, Beatrix didn't hear him. She stared straight into the spinning wheel of black drones until they formed one confluence. One circle. Inside she saw stars. And space.

Then she heard a voice. It came forth from the deep recesses of her mind. At first, it was unintelligible. Then a single word took shape, and through the diffusion, she finally recognized whose voice it was—her own.

Fight.

Beatrix felt a rush of energy in her chest. A deep, unquenchable fury. Clutching the bo staff with both hands, feeling a foreign sense of strength and focus, Beatrix swung it into the center of the spinning circle. Then she extended her body out of the window and began to spin the black circle like a hula hoop. With a long sweep of the staff, she flung the circle away.

The drone circle broke apart into individual discs and exploded past Fred's speeding car. The undersides of the drones glowed as they rocketed into the woods.

Both cars screeched to a halt just in time for everyone to watch the mountainside come apart. Like combustion in the vacuum of space, there was no fire, only an explosive concussion. For several hundred yards in every direction, trees were mowed down as if cut from a scythe.

Dumbfounded, they marveled at the level of devastation. Then, one by one, Alex, Malik, Fred, and Ben turned to look at Beatrix. She was leaning against the hood of the car, both hands grasping her head, her fingers outstretched as if trying to contain a migraine and her face concealed by her curls. Beatrix began to cry and hyperventilate. Looking up, the irises of her eyes blazed violet, then went dark again.

What's happening to me?

The voice. Beatrix shuttered it away in her subconscious. She was losing her grip, feeling the black pressing in just as she perceived the sound of footsteps

Then nothing.

"Is she dead? Oh my God, she's dead, isn't she?" Malik cried as he knelt beside Beatrix and nudged her.

"Bugger off," Alex said. "She's not dead. She just passed out."

"I'm trained in routine medical care. Let me check her," Fred said. He looked Beatrix over for wounds and found none, then checked her pulse and breathing. Alex stepped back from the vehicles to assess the demolished road and landscape behind them, Malik joining her.

"She's alright. She's actually asleep," Fred said. "She's just fine, otherwise."

Squatting by Beatrix's head, Ben took in Fred's assessment and prognosis with an intense glare. His formidable expression seemed to intimidate Fred, so to break the tension, Fred extended his hand.

"Uh, we've never been introduced officially. I'm Frederick Hardingham, Alex's uncle on her mother's side."

Snapping back to his usual courtesy, Ben smiled, then reached over Beatrix's sleeping form and shook Fred's hand. "Ben Voght."

"Maybe we should get her off the road, huh?" Fred suggested.

Ben slid his arms under Beatrix and lifted her as Fred tried to assist. Feeling the role of the responsible big brother, Ben gave Fred a firm look that implied he would carry his sister alone. He laid her in the car's backseat with Parfleet, who was all worked up, as Alex and Malik returned.

"It looks like a bomb went off down there," Alex said.

"Well, we won't be discovered by anything from that direction, at least not by road," Ben said.

"That's a freaking comfort," Malik quipped, "because whatever the heck is after us will surely drive up in rental cars and attack us by land. We're dead. What are we going to do? Face it, we're lost!"

"Easy, Malik," Ben said. "It'll be alright. Alex, check your GPS and the compass on your phone, please. Are we close to the destination?"

"Checking," Alex said as Fred looked over her shoulder. "Okay, well. This is weird."

"What now?" Malik asked.

"It won't ping."

"Come again?" Ben asked.

"It won't ping a location anymore. Look." Alex held up her smartphone for the others to see. The arrow indicating the compass was spinning.

"Oh, crap. We've seen this before," Malik said. "Something is close."

"Let's just relax and think for a min —" He broke off when he noticed Beatrix was sitting up, looking dazed and weary as she pointed down the dark road ahead.

Fred flipped on the car's headlights, revealing a figure on the road about one hundred feet ahead of them.

Ben strode toward it and then stopped when they were about ten feet apart.

"No further. Come no further, sir," Ben said with authority in his voice.

The figure complied, then raised his right hand and waved. When he spoke, the figure, who appeared to be an old man, disarmed Ben immediately. "Well, well. Benjamin Voght. I would say this is unexpected, but that wouldn't be wholly true, would it?" He smiled. "I'm the one you seek. Now, young man, can you tell me my name?"

"Montavani," Ben replied without thinking.

The old man stepped forward and smiled. "It is I."

"We . . . we're in trouble. My sister, she's not well. She's —"

"Is she hurt? Injured in any way?"

"No. No, I don't think so. She's passed out."

"Lucky are you. You don't know your peril."

"What were they? The drones?" Ben asked.

"Reconnaissance elements gathering intelligence, no doubt—but also with deadly capabilities. Tools used by servants of the Black. And that is all I'll say here. We must go. Immediately. They will return, and in greater numbers."

"Where to?" Ben asked, feeling an unwitting trust in the old man.

"Why, my home, of course, young man," Montavani said with a reassuring grin. "All of you. I understand I'm the objective of some sort of mission, correct?"

"Yes," Ben replied.

They walked back to the cars, where Montavani introduced himself. Out of all of them, Fred was the least trusting of the old man, but at Ben's insistence, they agreed to leave the scene.

Montavani gave Parfleet a playful but firm smack on the rump to get him off the passenger seat and into the back with Beatrix, who was asleep. Then Montavani got in while Ben got behind the wheel.

The two cars drove deep down a trail that disappeared into a gorge on the left side of the road. Sheer cliff walls rose on either side of the road, and everyone became claustrophobic, the cars having only two to three feet of clearance from the cliff walls that rose at least one hundred feet into the air. They drove for about a half a mile before Montavani instructed Ben to pull over in a clearing.

"We must go the rest of the way on foot. And the vehicles. I'm sorry, but we have to dispose of them."

"Dispose?" Ben stared at the old man, incredulous.

"Yes. It's quite necessary. Lest my home be discovered by what just had you as they're quarry."

Ben shrugged in agreement and then motioned for the others to get out of the cars. They dragged Beatrix out, and Fred and Ben helped hold her up.

"Step back, please, fine folks. This won't take but a moment," Montavani said. "Do you have all of your belongings and that accursed mongrel?" he added as he pulled a small device out of his pocket.

Ben glanced at the others, who nodded. "Yes, we're good to go," he said.

"Ah! 'Good to go,' he says!" Montavani replied with an ironic degree of mirth in his voice as he raised the device. A thunderclap ensued, and Freddie's rental car disappeared in a mass of black smoke and green light.

"Sweet Mama Harriet, that's bloody brilliant!" Fred cried.

The other car was next. It seemed to implode into the darkness without a trace.

"Kasra. He will be bummed," Malik lamented.

"Now then, let's get indoors," Montavani decreed as he led the way down a narrow, winding path into the darkness.

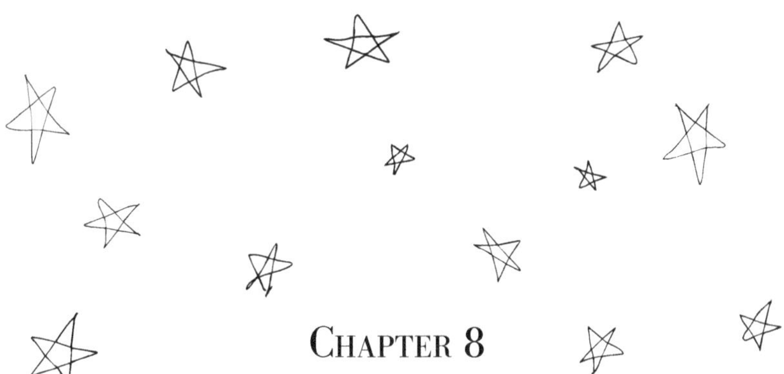

CHAPTER 8

Moving to Mars

GUISEPPE MONTAVANI'S HOUSE WAS NOT A HOME IN THE conventional sense. The dwelling was literally invisible from the outside world. In fact, even when standing straight in front, no one would notice anything but a tall, snow-covered edifice. The door, if one could call it that, was concealed and pointing sideways back into the mountainside. Walls of rock, one hundred feet high, were on all sides and covered with leafless hardwood trees. The snow was light but covered most of the ground. Lapping up to the side of the ridge that held the door was a small spring-fed pond no more than seventy-five feet in diameter. A tiny footpath circumnavigated the pond to the door. No other approach to Montavani's home was discernible.

The heavy oak door had a large metal knocker under a small, round window the size of a man's face. Upon closer examination, Beatrix, who was still in a daze, noticed many more windows, all small and round, facing the pond and the cliff walls. She found the home to be cozy and warm. Its ivy-covered entry reminded her of a fairy cottage from a storybook.

Surprisingly, Parfleet left Beatrix's side and wandered off into the home unbidden. Beatrix shrugged, then cast her eyes around the home, taking it in. The front room was a parlor of sorts. Its stone floor was warm and comfortable on the feet. All at once, Beatrix realized why the room seemed so peculiar. No electrical technology of any kind was visible. Only oil lamps and a fireplace in the corner provided light. There was no phone, television, or computer.

Beatrix peered at a picture that caught her attention. It was a tracing of a constellation whose celestial bodies, when connected, formed an infinity symbol, flanked on each side by inverted triangles.

I've seen this before. The library.

"Familiar?" Montavani asked, his voice thundering across the room. Although his voice was authoritative, it was also suggestive of kindness and benevolence.

Startled, Beatrix turned toward the old man and gave him a once-over. He looked to be in his early seventies. He was tall and thin. His beard was closely cropped, and his silver hair was combed back, extending halfway down his neck. He was wearing a navy-blue nautical sweater and dark khaki pants with scuffed brown boots. Most telling feature was his eyes. They were crystal blue and nearly phosphorescent. Beatrix saw humility and good humor in them, a sense of sincerity that made Beatrix trust him.

Reminds me of Wendell.

"Yes," Beatrix replied, the sound of her own voice surprising her. "We have met before, right?"

"Not formally," Montavani replied.

"Where?" Beatrix asked.

"Where? When? How? Why?" Montavani sighed. "It's always questions with you, isn't it?"

"Yes," Beatrix replied. Then her eyes lit up as she realized where she had seen him before. "You! You were at the pizzeria. The message. The lemons. I also saw you on the street. And Malik said he saw an old man at the reservoir on the night my dad—"

"You have seen me," Montavani said as he stared into Beatrix's eyes. "I've been watching you."

"Watching me? Watching for what?" Beatrix couldn't help but feel agitated.

"Not what. *When.*" Montavani took a deep breath and laid his hand on Beatrix's arm, then pulled away and seemed to draw himself up to his full height. "Introductions. I am Guiseppe N. Montavani, PhD. My colleagues call me Seppe. Others call me Gee. I would be pleased if you called me Gee." He reached out his right hand. Beatrix reluctantly shook it.

"It's nice to meet you, sir—I mean, Gee. Listen, I'm wondering what's going on. I have, like, a million questions—"

Montavani broke into polite laughter, which caused Beatrix to pause. "Just like ol' Wendell, always angling for answers."

Beatrix stood there, mouth agape.

Beatrix could wait no longer and burst forth a volley. "Tell me! Please tell me everything! Mr. Gee, er, Montavani. I'm desperate. I need to know the truth, and you have the information I need, sir, please!" Beatrix's chest was heaving, and she felt light headed. "I think I'm going to faint . . ."

Beatrix collapsed, but Montavani broke her fall, then helped her over to a chaise lounge where she lapsed into unconsciousness.

An undetermined amount of time later, Beatrix awoke to a cool, damp cloth being wiped on her forehead. She assumed Montavani was tending to her, but when Beatrix's eyes pulled focus, she realized it wasn't.

"Hello, Beatrix. You alright?" Alex asked.

"Hey. Um, yeah. I'm fine." Beatrix struggled up onto her elbows. "Where's Ben and Malik and your uncle Fred?"

"All here. And all safe and sound. For now."

"For now?"

"Just rest, Beatrix. We're going to meet in the morning. Gee wants to talk to all of us. He said there were some things that we should be made privy to."

Alex pulled out her iPhone and checked the time. "It's 12:48 a.m. We're all beat. Gee has us set up in two rooms with an adjoining bathroom. And thank heavens, there are fresh towels and linens and hot showers awaiting us."

Beatrix was incredulous. "Alex, I need to see Ben. We have some things to sort out about how we got here and the trust we're placing in Montavani and—"

"Gee." Alex corrected.

"How do we know he's the real Montavani? After what we've all been through, I wouldn't accept anything as fact without proof."

"Proof? Okay, let's go get it. C'mon."

Alex helped Beatrix to her feet, then led her down the hall. They rounded a candlelit corner and came face-to-face with Montavani, who was smoking a pipe as he brooded. He cut an intimidating figure when he wasn't smiling.

"Proof." The lines on Montavani's face creased into a large smile. Neither Beatrix nor Alex could find a trace of malice in his eyes. "Ask me a question to which only Wendell Voght would know the answer."

Beatrix was stumped at first. Then an idea popped into her head. "What's my favorite band?"

"Coldplay," Montavani replied without hesitation. "Four lads from London. Wendell bought you a copy of their first album, *Parachutes*, on vinyl two Christmases ago. An understated masterpiece in the opinion of *Rolling Stone* magazine."

Beatrix was dumbfounded. *Okay, but let's keep checking your bona fides.*

"What was Dad's — I mean Wendell's — favorite place to eat in New York?"

"The Brooklyn Diner, East Fifty-seventh Street. He would get the western omelet and typically have three cups of black coffee and a side of fruit."

Oh, geez, Beatrix thought. *This guy knows everything about us.* Then a wild idea hit her.

"Okay, who are my original parents?"

Montavani gave Beatrix a quizzical look, then smiled. "Parents? Parents. I have to say that your parents' origin is not immediately clear."

Their origin? Immediately clear? What the heck does that mean?

As Beatrix pondered his last statement, her thoughts were disturbed by a familiar voice calling her name.

"Beatrix!"

The voice belonged to Malik. "You're up!" He reached out to hug Beatrix, who recoiled at first before awkwardly embracing her friend. "You feel okay after all that? I can't believe it. You're like a superhero from DC comics. I'm going to start calling you Diana Prince!"

"Beatrix!" Ben slid past Malik and wrapped her in a bear hug. "We're safe. We did it! We're here. Montavani is going to help us now. We have nothing else to worry about."

"Yeah, sure," Beatrix replied. Through the door to the next room, she saw Fred talking animatedly with another gentleman whose back was to her.

"Everyone! Everyone!" Montavani said. "I believe it would do us all good to retire. We're far into the small hours, and the night is getting short. Let us say goodnight, and we shall have a fine feast in the morning, during which we can exchange information. Leave behind your worries for tonight. Everyone is perfectly safe and sound here, that I promise. Tomorrow, we will unravel mysteries and perhaps create a few more in turn." Montavani laughed at his own wit. "So, let us all bid one another goodnight."

Montavani bowed and then disappeared into the warren of underground halls as the others retired to their appointed bedrooms. Alex and Beatrix were in one room, and Ben, Malik, and Fred were in the other. After showering and putting on clean clothes, Beatrix fell asleep almost immediately. Her last waking thought was of Parfleet and his whereabouts. He had never spent a night away from her, but he had not returned from his explorations. Too tired to ask about him, Beatrix turned over and fell into a deep, dreamless sleep.

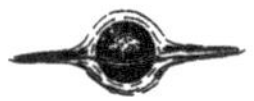

The following morning, Beatrix awoke before the others. She looked over at the other single bed and saw the comforter-ensconced lump that was most assuredly the form of Alex Thacker. As was her custom, Beatrix slipped her socks on prior to getting out of bed. After stopping in the powder room, she peeked into the boys' bedroom. Ben was asleep, only the top of his head exposed. Fred was stretched out on a mattress on the floor, the beds too short for his frame. Malik was in the other single bed. He was on his back, snoring with his mouth open. His portable Optimus Prime humidifier was set up on the nightstand. Beatrix saw no sign of Parfleet.

This is so strange. Where is Parfleet? It's 5:28 a.m.!

After contemplating going back to bed, Beatrix decided to try to locate the kitchen.

Surely there's a cup of coffee in this freaking place.

Beatrix felt her way around the home's curved walls until some oil lamp sconces came into view. A familiar, splendid smell wafted through the air. She knew it well. . . .

Coffee!

It smelled better than anything at the Drip or anywhere else in New York. She turned to her right, following the smell until she found herself in what could only be the kitchen. Sitting on the butcher block island was a white ceramic mug filled with steaming black coffee. Beatrix looked around for whoever had timed the cup perfectly for her to enter the room, but not one was around. A yellow Post-it note had an inscription on it in pen.

> Good morning.
> Join me in the study before the others get up.
> Two doors down on your left.
> — G

Beatrix scooped up the mug and made off down the dimly lit windowless hallway. After several meters, she found the study, which had a brick-lined arched entry but no door. Beatrix found Montavani seated in a rocking chair by the fire, his hands clasped around a cup of coffee.

"Did you sleep well?" Montavani inquired.

"Never better. Thank you, by the way. Your hospitality is most gracious."

"Anything for a friend in need," Montavani said while adjusting the pillow in the small of his back. "And you do appear to be in need at this moment, are you not?"

"I'm not sure," Beatrix replied.

"Aren't you in need of something? Is there something that you require of me?"

Beatrix noticed that Montavani was pressing her into revealing her purpose without revealing his.

I surrender!

"Where's Wendell?" Beatrix blurted.

Montavani took a long sip of coffee, then seemed to hold it in his mouth forever before swallowing. "Mind if I have a morning smoke?"

Without waiting for an answer, Montavani drew out a long wooden pipe and brought it to life with a single match stroke. After a few puffs and complementary mutterings about the flavor, Montavani exhaled and seemed to relax. Finally, he leveled his gaze at Beatrix. "What I'm about to tell you will change your life and possibly your destiny on Earth, as you know it."

Beatrix sat across from Montavani in suspended animation, a stupor of exhilaration and cold fear gripping her.

What in the blazes?

"Let me ask you something. You sensed that Wendell was quite different after Scotland and the missing time incident at Castle Glamis, correct?"

Beatrix was too stunned at that revelation that he knew about that incident to answer.

"Let me start from the beginning, Beatrix. I have known your Wendell for a long time. I did research with him in the nineties, and we became professional acquaintances and then friends. Did he ever mention me?"

Beatrix shook her head.

"Not surprising, really," Montavani said with a hint of laughter. "He was always a bit secretive when it came to what you and Ben were exposed to. Now let me ask you something, Beatrix. Do you know what a meridian is?" Montavani raised his eyebrows in anticipation.

Beatrix groped for an answer, wanting to impress upon Montavani that she was intelligent. "Uh, a dividing line? Like longitude and latitude?"

"Yes. Very good. Now, other than land masses, what else can be separated or divided? Do you believe that time and space can be divided and portioned as well?"

Beatrix snickered. "Like a portal or something? Sure, I've seen that in movies."

"Let me put it to you as an example. If I were to stand on the edge of a black hole in space and shine a flashlight into it, if it were actually possible to send a beam of light over the event horizon of said black hole, what would you say would occur?"

"Light would enter and not escape, just like in the movies. Nothing can escape a black hole." Beatrix was confident in her answer, as she had just finished a unit about gravity in physical science with the dreadful Professor Null.

"Very good and proper. Now, let me postulate something by asking another question. Where does the light go?" Montavani leaned forward in his rocker, anticipating her response.

"I dunno. Uh, it goes nowhere. It disappears or just goes to infinity."

"Ah! Infinity, you say. A never-ending bottomless pit of space and time. Very right and proper. Yes. Very proper. Emm. Hmm . . ." Montavani pulled on his pipe once more.

"Let me reveal to you a truth of the universe that you don't know. Nor do most living people on Earth, as we know it. True, some black holes have singularities with infinite densities with infinite gravity, but some are not infinite at all and are connected to others. Light and matter enters and escapes elsewhere."

"Like, you mean in space, right? These two-sided black holes are in space?"

"Yes and no."

"Where are they then?" Beatrix's throat began to tighten as she suspected she already knew the answer.

"Right here on Earth. They're here amongst us. They're everywhere and still being discovered as we speak. These small, soft singularities we call meridians."

"The book, your book that Dad co-authored, it's about meridians? That's what you and Wendell researched, right? We found a copy of it."

"Ha! There aren't many copies of that piece of fine literature."

"So, you're saying that's what happened to my dad? He got sucked into a meridian or something in Scotland and then again in New York, where he disappeared?" Beatrix felt her eyes sting with bitter tears.

"Again, yes and no. Wendell discovered the first meridian long before Scotland. He was borderline obsessed with the subject. He didn't get 'taken' in Castle Glamis. He left willfully 'into the Black,' as we call it."

This can't be true.

"Your father was indeed different when he was returned from his misadventure in Scotland?" Montavani asked.

"Of course. He was traumatized. He had PTSD!"

"Think you that Wendell was again inadvertently taken in New York that night a few weeks back? Hmm? Beatrix, you think that was 'your' Wendell who left you? Search your feelings."

"Wendell disappeared. He was the only father I ever knew. He had changed since Scotland. Sure. Who wouldn't? Who knows what he experienced being trapped between walls in the dark for hours and hours? Dad did the best he could after that!" Beatrix was growing upset at being repeatedly challenged by the old man.

"No." Montavani raised his index finger and smiled. "He was a changed man—literally. That man who returned was not your Wendell or mine. Beatrix, the man who returned was not Wendell Voght at all. He was a replica, a duplicate. He was what we call a simulacrum." Montavani paused to let his words sink in.

"A what? That's preposterous. A copy? Of a human?" Beatrix stood up with her hands on her hips. "This is crazy!" Beatrix's mind was spinning. "I don't know what's going on or who you are, exactly, but this isn't true. What you say is—"

"Impossible?"

"Yes!"

"Improbable?"

"Absolutely!"

"Against all of the laws of the known universe, as matter itself does not behave that way and this sounds like complete rubbish?" Montavani smiled.

"Yes!" Realizing she had raised her voice to the point of yelling, Beatrix flushed with embarrassment. "I'm sorry. This is, after all, your home."

"Beatrix, it's true. And there's more. Much more that you and Ben need to know."

Ben.

"Replicas. Simulacrums?"

"Simula*crum*. The plural is simulacra."

"They're real?" Beatrix asked as she sat back down and took a sip from her mug.

"Yes. Far too real. And it's because of them that I have been attempting to summon you."

"Tell me everything," Beatrix said. "I want to understand. Is there proof?"

"Proof? Again, huh?" Montavani smiled. "No problem. Just pardon me for a moment."

He eased himself out of the rocker and walked to the threshold of the study. "Percival! Percival, my good man, would you join us in the study, please?"

Following the clang of pots and pans came a response in Scottish drawl. "No. I'm not up to it!"

"Dear Percival, please! Join us for a bit. I have someone who would like to see you." Montavani glanced back at Beatrix and smiled as if they were both in on some practical joke.

"Blimey. Alright, but this is beyond poor taste for even you, Seppe!"

Footsteps approached down the hall, and a figure appeared in the doorway. He was in his late sixties, slim and trim and of slightly below average height. Wearing circular glasses and a pencil-thin mustache, he looked studious.

"Ah. Good man, Percival. Beatrix is here." Montavani spoke of Beatrix with a sense of familiarity that she did not fully understand.

"Seppe, I meant what I said. I'm just now getting acclimated to my condition, and this is patently inappropriate and uncalled for!"

Montavani grinned as he held his palms out in mock apology. "Oh, alright, you old duffer. But here she is."

"Hello, Beatrix." Percival extended his hand and shook hers. While clearly angry at Montavani, Percival was clearly fond of Beatrix.

"Hello, Mr. Percival." Beatrix couldn't help but feel heavy traces of familiarity with him although she didn't know why.

His aftershave maybe?

She turned her attention to Montavani. "I don't understand. I asked you for proof."

"Ah, yes! Well, we have a bit of a demonstration for you!" Montavani replied.

"Seppe, I mean it! I'll lose it . . ." Percival warned.

"Oh, bugger off, you old duffer."

"Seppe, stop!" Percival commanded.

Beatrix's heart was racing with anxiety.

"Damn you, Seppe!" Percival raged.

Montavani pulled a metal device from the mantle and opened it near Percival. "Introducing Dr. Percival Julien Parfleet!"

A puff of black smoke rose out of the device and spread all over Percival, followed by a crash of green light. Beatrix didn't know which was more of a surprise — the green jolt of lightning in the study or the fact that standing on the floor in front of her as the smoke cleared was her pug, Parfleet.

Parfleet? What the hell is going on here!

Parfleet was going bananas at that point, trying to balance his appetite for biting Montavani with his desire to snuggle with Beatrix.

"What did you do?" Beatrix asked.

"I provided you with proof," Montavani said over Parfleet's barks.

"Parfleet. Parfleet is a simulacrum?" Beatrix asked, her lips quivering.

"Sort of. Not really. But he'll do for the moment. The dog was all I could muster at the time, and I was under extreme duress!"

Beatrix shook her head, utterly confused. "Tell me everything. From the beginning."

"Let's adjourn for a few moments and then continue the conversation after our canine friend has calmed himself. Isn't that right, ol' Percy?" Montavani rubbed Parfleet's head, clearly trying to get a rise out of him, and the pug growled in response.

Well, this is going to be good!

Montavani walked Beatrix and the dog she now knew as Percival J. Parfleet through the maze of candlelit halls. He stopped in a wide hall with a large bay window facing west. Beatrix realized they were looking in the opposite direction from where they came in. The morning sun was rising behind the mountain, casting a beautiful pink-orange hue on the valley below. It occurred to Beatrix that Montavani's house was more than a home; it was an underground castle that occupied the interior of the mountain.

Beatrix sat on some cushions in the bay window and allowed Parfleet to jump up and take his usual place next to her. She felt awkward having him around now that she knew his real identity, but he cuddled up and fell asleep next to her for his usual morning nap without making a fuss. Montavani sat opposite Beatrix, eyeing her. Feeling nervous under his gaze, Beatrix removed her glasses and cleaned them on her shirt. When she was done, she put them back on and looked him in the eye. "Everything. Tell me everything. From the beginning. I need to understand."

Montavani exhaled with resignation as if preparing to deliver a monologue he had waited his entire life to give. "Long ago, eons before recorded history, the universe was shaped and made; then the cosmos changed. I believe a Maker, a Creator, started it all. Don't let my reputation as a scientist bely the fact that this universe was made; it is not the result of a cataclysm of celestial accidents. Someone or something got it started. For centuries, astronomers have researched the origin of the galaxies, and they have all agreed that most galaxies—past, present, or future—are associated with a singularity, or, as you may call it, a black hole. There are moderately sized ones like Sagittarius A in our galaxy, and there are some so large they defy measurement called supermassive. What you need to know is that at some point in the timeline of our planet, a key discovery was made.

"A small black hole was found first. This was termed a meridian. Neither I nor Wendell applied the term to this phenomenon. These are micro black holes or quantum-mechanical black holes for the astrophysicists in the house." Montavani laughed at his own lame joke, then straightened himself. "We became interested after Wendell made discoveries as a student."

"At Festermunder?" Beatrix asked.

"Yes. While a student there, young Wendell, at age fifteen or sixteen and fancying himself an amateur Illinois Jennings-type archeologist, made his first discovery."

Beatrix pursed her lips to suppress a laugh at Montavani's misstatement of Indiana Jones's moniker.

"At the time, young Wendell was already a consummate adventurer and a hopeless romantic. However, he made his discovery purely by accident, made possible through his devil-may-care attitude and mischievous behavior."

Tears stung Beatrix's eyes as she smiled at the description of a boy who would become the only man she knew as a father. "How did it happen? Was he on a trip? What country was it in?"

"Oddly enough, the discovery was made right there at your school. Wendell found the meridian buried under Festermunder and began to perform tests on it and, eventually, on himself."

"The library! I've seen it. I've been there, and we lost people there! Three kids!"

Montavani nodded. "Stooch, McTeel, and St. Vincent. I know. They went into the Black. Of that I am aware."

"You know? How?"

"They returned, of course," Montavani replied, ignoring her question. "Notice you any changes?"

"Yes. They were quiet. Robotic. And when they spoke, none of their thoughts were complete."

Montavani muttered, "That was what they were—incomplete simulacra. Anaphora."

"Them?"

"Yes. Replicas. Like your Wendell after Scotland. What you must understand is a question that I'm surprised you've yet to ask." Montavani leaned in and smiled. "What's on the other side of the equals sign? If the simulacrum is on this side, where are the originals?"

"Are they . . . dead?" Beatrix ventured.

"No, not dead. But a different fate may await some of them that could be worse. But more on that later. There's another world that is like and yet unlike ours and seeks to be interwoven and melded together with this one. It's an alter world. Wendell and I call it the Divide. Some call it the Sanctuary, but more on that later. For now, all you need to know is that it's real, though quite different from the reality you know. More primitive. Less advanced. Though in many ways, some would say it's better. Its discovery and existence will change history. And recent events tell me that could be a huge problem."

"Why?"

"The original meridian wasn't discovered at Festermunder by accident. The school was built on it. In fact, the original school building was the first structure on Manhattan Island. As far back as the 1600s, a gateway existed there. The school was built over it to protect it from accidents, discovery, and, later on, the British. Just delve into that putrid alma mater that you all recite. It's there in plain sight.

Beatrix's brow furrowed as she tried to discern what part of the alma mater he was talking about.

"Over the years, the school used it for evil purposes, and several students disappeared in experiments as test pilots."

"How do you know this? Did Wendell tell you?"

"No." Montavani looked into Beatrix's eyes. "I was in the Divide. I was there, Beatrix. I saw them, the travelers, coming out on the other side."

This revelation sent Beatrix reeling. Her mind refused to accept what she was hearing. And yet, she had every inclination to trust the old man.

"That was how I initially met Wendell. Undoubtedly, it lines up when he went into the Black in Scotland. He knew he would go. His research was complete. He also knew some of what he might discover from his prior experience with the meridian at Festermunder."

Beatrix looked out at the snowy valley. "Eight hours. He was missing for eight hours in the castle. How did you get to know him in so short a time?"

"Ah, yes. Time is a strange thing. On Earth, Wendell was missing for eight hours, but in the Divide, we have quantified that as eighty-eight years. He was with me that entire time. Few friendships last that long."

"Eighty-eight years? Didn't he age?"

"Yes. Technically, he aged eight hours. You see, time is dilated in the Divide. So, Wendell was missing for eight hours here, and we had him with us for eighty-eight years. He accomplished a lot."

"Accomplished? What do you mean?"

"After getting acclimated in the Divide, Wendell sought out others to establish friendships with like-minded people. We met and did our assigned tasks quite well until our circumstances became untenable. Beatrix, there are others there. There's a system, so to speak, to how people conduct their activities."

"Like a government or something?"

"I guess it's not unlike a government. People are given duties, tasks that fit their strengths or talents, all for the greater good."

"The greater good," Beatrix said. "What was the greater good that my dad left us for?"

"Beatrix, you must understand that we were doing great things! Making unimaginable advances! We were given classifications: framers, scripters, time keepers, engineers. Wendell and I were known as architects. All of us were working to establish a plentiful natural world. A gift of unlimited natural resources for a humankind that was going to squander theirs. We viewed our position as vital to the survival of all people in the here in our world. We were building another—a sanctuary connected to our world through the meridians. That's why your father felt the mission was important enough for him to be separated from you. That's why he stayed in the Divide and why he sent his simulacrum back, to serve as a placeholder while vital work was being done. It was a gut-wrenching decision to make for such a worthy man, but he made it, nonetheless."

"So, what happened? Why are you here? Why didn't everyone live happily ever after once they created this alternate world refuge?"

"A talented engineer, a master creator, or so he calls himself, began to gain power over the meridians, and he closed some of them, sealing them with dark matter. Several of our colleagues were lost that way. Great scientists and inventors, beautifully gifted people. This master creator began to rally others under his banner. His goal was to limit the Divide to just us rather than the rest of Earth's inhabitants. Then we discovered he had an even more dreadful plan."

"What sort of plan?"

"The master creator, who is known as Seraphim, seeks to mine our world of all progenitors of science and enslave them while he pursues his real goal—to gain mastery over them and destroy our world and all of its inhabitants."

"Why?" Beatrix asked, fear growing within her.

"Why share something? Why not limit the Divide to those who are already there? Power is available to Seraphim that he yearns to possess but cannot obtain." Montavani shook his head. "I should have known from the outset. I was taken like countless others and should've realized that his final purpose would not be noble."

"Taken?"

"Yes. Like many other scientists and academic luminaries, I was taken through a meridian as a hostage. Look back over time. Philosophers, scientists, and even self-proclaimed mystics have been disappearing for centuries. Some have been snatched from the past. History changed. Rewritten. Heard you of the Greek mathematician Erudinius?"

"No. Just Pythagoras. And wait, uh, Archimedes." Beatrix pictured her horrible mathematical experiences at Festermunder.

"Well, you should have heard of Erudinius, as he's the greatest and most knowledgeable mathematician of all time. He came up with the original theory of relativity before that hack Albert Einstein plagiarized him. But, of course, you wouldn't know about him. You see, Seraphim learned to go back through the meridians in time. Through one of those wormholes, he snatched poor Erudinius. You see? History was rewritten. We did not learn of E equals mc^2 for many a century after that. Young Erudinius was 'unwritten.' He was with Wendell and me in the Divide. A brilliant mind if you could get past his truculence and his tendency to talk over others. But he was a fantastic cook, though he was quite dreadful company to keep most of the time. . . ."

Montavani mused for a moment and then straightened. "So, after the initial shock of being taken, I began to do what only a scientist could do. I worked. I read. I experimented. Over time, I began to believe in my work and take pride in what we were doing. But we were deceived. All of us. The self-styled master creator, Seraphim, has designs to destroy this world and to assimilate it into his own. And it looks as if that may happen. We have tried to stop him, but we need more resources. We also lack leadership."

"What do you mean?"

"Seraphim is supported by thousands of followers. Wendell, your incorrigible Parfleet, and I are part of an underground movement, the keepers of a secret faith. Our aim is to put an end to the Divide and Seraphim. Of course, that will likely mean that we, too, are destroyed. But if it is our destiny . . ."

"Surely there's something you can do," Beatrix said. "Why not send everyone back here? You sent Parfleet. And somehow you got back."

Montavani shifted in his seat. Beatrix suspected he was figuring out how to phrase his next response so as not to reveal too much. "I've yet to tell you the rules of the Divide. To the best of our knowledge, no one can come back to this world without a simulacrum on the other side. I mentioned the equals sign?"

"Yes."

"If an original goes to the same side of the meridian as his or her simulacrum, they both cease to exist. Think of simple algebra. An equal positive and negative integer cancel each other out. The polarity of their existence must be maintained. Once a simulacrum is developed, it can't be on the same side of the meridian. If that happens, they become unwritten, passing out of all memory and knowledge. Their possessions, works, and even their relationships cease to exist. This has far-reaching consequences, rippling forward through time. Children aren't born. Technologies aren't developed. And we've discovered something else that's much, much worse. Something that precipitated our coming to know each other."

"It gets worse?" Beatrix asked, realizing she was raking her fingers through Parfleet's fur.

"Yes. Using the power of the meridians, Seraphim has gained enough strength to take people from our world and send back the template and the simulacra. Obviously, if he did so, the result could be disastrous. The original would immediately be unwritten, and the replica would run amok. Seraphim has programmed them to do his bidding. Some of them are thrown together and appear quite dreadful. They look like us, but they're not like us."

"Is that what's after us? The man with no face? Is he a simulacrum?"

Montavani hesitated, then exhaled in a way that suggested an apology. "Yes. It's exactly as you say. You and your companions are being hunted by the evilest of simulacra."

"Who is he?"

"He's called Luka, one of Seraphim's most trusted lieutenants. An 'incomplete,' as they say. No eyes and no face but highly skilled and dangerous. Able to pass through meridians at will. He can even create them using devices like this."

Montavani pulled the metal object from his pocket that he had used earlier. "A rythrax. This was lost by one of them here. A cube full of dark matter from the Divide. It can concentrate enough dark matter to create a small meridian. They can also help us reanimate the simulacra that are incomplete." Montavani nodded at Parfleet.

"Why does Luka want me?" Beatrix asked.

Montavani sighed, looking tired and sad. "I'm sorry. Don't you know?"

"Don't I know what?"

"In the history of the Divide, no one has ever occupied the same side of the meridian as their simulacrum. Not once, not ever. It's impossible." Montavani raised his head and locked eyes with Beatrix. "No one except you."

Beatrix's eyebrows shot up. "Me?"

I know.

"Yes. We can only postulate that you are special in some way. All of us in the Divide became aware of your existence. Of course, we always had a theory that someone like you would show up eventually."

"What? Why?"

"There's a theory that has circulated for ages in the Divide, a mathematical probability, although highly unlikely, that this could occur. It's the Theory of the Andromeda Particle, an arbitrary title for a trait carried by one who does not have to comply with the rules of the Divide or the meridians. They would possess power over dark matter with this mutation. The carrier of the Andromeda particle could pass unobstructed anywhere anytime they wished. They could also do something heretofore impossible—bring materials and matter through the meridians. Technology, weapons, even other people. Now, by default, we believe you fulfill the hypothesis."

"What, like a prophecy? I've seen this movie before okay?"

"Ah, yes. You think I jest. Tell me, Beatrix, what thought you of the simulacrum you saw in the city? It was you. It has been following you. You inadvertently caught up to it."

Beatrix hung her head.

No more secrets.

"I feel like my world has been turned upside down. It's been hard enough for me without being the holder of some key to the space-time continuum. How do I have this . . . this Andromeda thing? I'm just a regular kid. Sure, I was adopted out of foster care, but I'm just me.

Just Beatrix! I'm not special. I'm certainly not talented or gifted. I'm the average of the law of averages!"

"A fugitive from the law of averages would be closer to the mark. You have talents and gifts that will be discovered in time."

"Well, I've been waiting fourteen years and have yet to see any!" Beatrix said. "But tell me this, why the dog? What's Parfleet's role in all this?"

"Percival is a great scientist and was a fine architect in the Divide. I saved him from Luka's agents many years ago when he was caught spying on Seraphim's engineers. He owes me. We sent him back through to you due to the risk of discovery by the Mechanix."

"The what?"

"The Mechanix, agents of Seraphim commanded by Luka. Servants of the Black. Ravers full of dark purpose and madness. They serve the master that they hate. They're a matter of discussion in and of themselves. Later."

"The dog?" Beatrix urged.

"Yes, of course. We knew a dog would be easier to assimilate than a person. So, Percival was reanimated as our furry friend and sent to you. You found him in the park, close to a meridian. He will do as I wish because he owes me. Of course, he does so begrudgingly. As you can see, he's an impossibly negative person. Incapable of fun and not a shred of human warmth could be found in the dark recesses of his even darker soul." Montavani smiled at Parfleet as he said that last bit. The dog raised his head and gave Montavani a look that was as human as a dog could muster before he shook his head.

"He can understand us?" Beatrix asked.

"Of course, the mangy little scallywag can understand us. Right-o there, boy?" Montavani shook the pug's back fat. "Alas. Okay, enough is enough, I s'pose." Montavani produced the rythrax from his pocket and held it up to Parfleet. "Beatrix, darling, do us a favor and back up a bit."

There was a flash of green and a wisp of black smoke, and Percival J. Parfleet was standing in front of Beatrix and Montavani, his hands balled into fists at his sides.

"A'right! That's it, you mad bastard! I'm not a stinking toy to be trifled with! Do that again, Seppe, and I'll 'ave you. You hear me? Fisticuffs next time."

Percival calmed himself with a deep, soothing breath and then turned to Beatrix. "I'm sorry for allowing my mouth to run away with me. Please forgive me while I step away and get reacclimated to my condition." Parfleet glared at Montavani.

"No problem, Parf—er, Mr. Percival. Uh . . ."

"Parfleet is fine. I'm a friend." With another sharp look at Montavani's mirthful face, he left the room.

Beatrix watched him walk down the hallway, pausing to acknowledge Malik, who cowered in the man's presence.

"Dr. Montavani, it's me, Malik, sir," he said as he entered the study. "I have more than a few questions. . . ."

Following a none-too-brief debriefing for Malik, Montavani took his leave. Beatrix noticed that he was quite transparent with Malik and treated him with respect, something Malik wasn't used to. Montavani left out the part that identified Beatrix as having abilities that were, to say the least, odd.

"Ben and Alex need to know," Malik said. "So does Fred. We've risked so much. They deserve to know the truth. To be aware of what's at stake."

"Just so you know, Beatrix, I'll be here for you no matter what. Until the end, however this ends. I can't offer much, but I can and will be your friend."

Beatrix half hugged Malik in an awkward sisterly fashion. "C'mon. Let's go find Parfleet and the others. There's something you need to see."

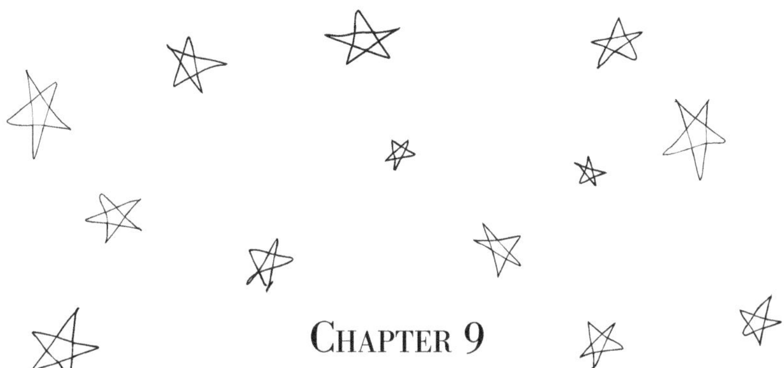

CHAPTER 9

A Fireside Chat

THE DRY AUTUMN LEAVES SEEMED TO BLOW THIS WAY AND that with the most effortless whisper of the wind. The sky was overcast and gray, the air chilly. It was one of those New York City Saturdays that seemed to incentivize solitude.

Beatrix was sitting on a quilted blanket on a hillock in Central Park, reading. The slope of the leaf-covered hill was so steep that Beatrix had difficulty not sliding down to its base. As she listened to an atmospheric song by Pink Floyd on her headphones, her mind wandered.

Beatrix lay on her back and let her imagination drift out to sea and her body slide to the bottom of the hill.

Soon, she found herself wandering down an empty path strewn with small pebbles. As she walked, the trees became thicker and more numerous, replete with thorns. The park transformed before her eyes into a dark bramble. Glancing around, Beatrix noticed that the park was devoid of life. No people or animals. Not even birds chirping. Only the gentle whoosh of the wind through the trees and her own footfalls broke the silence.

The sky darkened to a slight amber-yellow, and the leaves on the sides of the path looked gray and broken. The trees also showed signs of rot and decay. Looking up, she realized the distant buildings were dilapidated and covered in detritus, some of them falling apart. Beatrix's pulse raced as she jogged down the path toward a noise she could barely hear as it floated on the wind.

Her jog turned into a run as she realized something was pulling her; a voice seemed to demand her attention.

Looking up, she saw the moon eclipsing the sun. As the sun's light faded, Beatrix sprinted down the path toward the voice wailing in the wind.

The path split, and Beatrix stopped, wondering which branch to take. She decided to go left.

Racing forward, she rounded a bend and then stopped. A small figure was standing on the path in the dim light.

The simulacrum spoke in a whisper. "You going to have to choose."

It smiled, then vanished.

"Help! Anyone, please help!"

The child's plea snapped Beatrix out of her stupor, and she broke off running back down the path to where they split. She took the right fork toward the child, who was now screaming with fear. Suddenly, the source of the wailing was standing before Beatrix.

It was a little girl, nine or ten years old, with blond hair and a yellow flower in it. She was holding a bunny, which she was patting to calm herself.

Gwen!

"Help us! Please help us!" she cried.

Beatrix went to her, but her hand passed right through the child.

Gwen continued to cry out as the sky turned dark.

"Why did they leave me? Help me! He's here!"

As Gwen's voice faded, Beatrix looked around, yelling to anyone who could hear. "Stop this! Go away!"

With a flash of green light and distorted air, a figure in a black cloak appeared on the path, its face obscured.

She knew immediately who it was.

The Hat Man.

She suddenly heard laughter. Deep, droning, horrible, and mocking. It was followed by another flash of blinding light.

Stunned, Beatrix realized she was alone once again. The sun pulled away from behind the moon, and daylight returned. As her surroundings brightened, the decay diminished, and the sounds of people talking and children playing returned.

Beatrix looked down the path where Gwen was but saw no trace of her or the Hat Man. Noticing something on the path, Beatrix bent down to pick up a yellow daisy.

With that Beatrix awoke, promising herself that her dream was just that.

"I understand completely. This all makes sense. Strangely, I'm not surprised," Ben said after Beatrix finished telling him about her long talk with Montavani.

"Obviously, I have additional questions, but in the meantime, I'll say this: that business with your dog is freaking me out."

"I don't like dogs," Malik added as they walked down the hall toward the dining room where Montavani had organized a meal and a meeting. "And they don't like me."

"Do you think he'll tell us the next steps we should be taking?" Alex asked. "I dearly want to make a plan."

Beatrix kept her thoughts to herself as they progressed down the dank, candlelit hallway of Montavani's underground castle, which Montavani called the Verge. The little company of companions already felt at home at the Verge, which was keeping them safe and insulated from the problems and dangers that awaited them in the world outside.

Fred trooped along behind the group, muttering about his inability to get a signal on his work phone. He was never to be out of contact with work, and as a consummate rule follower, his inability to connect alarmed him.

The group stopped when they reached a massive chamber flooded with light. The elliptical room's stone walls rose at least a hundred feet. The roof was a glass atrium with ornately crafted frameworks holding the glass panels. A long table ran down the center of the room, flanked on three sides by fireplaces. The evening sun was too low to be visible in the atrium, but it cast an orange hue over the room.

Montavani was standing at the fireplace on the far right, his back turned as he chatted with another gentleman whom no one recognized. When the group entered the room, Montavani and his companion turned to them in greeting.

"Welcome, friends!" Montavani bellowed, his arms stretched out wide. There was mirth and sincerity in his eyes. However, as the others stepped toward the table, which was laid out with a feast, Beatrix was transfixed by the other gentleman.

"Hello there, Beatrix," he said as she approached the duo.

"Hello, Professor Lightheart," Beatrix replied.

"Begging your pardon, but you don't seem surprised to see me," Lightheart said.

"No, sir. Respectfully, I'm not."

After the meal, the food and dishes were cleared and the company got down to business. Percival, in the role of chef and concierge, brought out a rolling cart with after-dinner treats and drinks. The kids settled on hot cocoa, and the adults, save Fred, who drank cocoa, had tall steins of ale.

Montavani was seated at the head of the table and seemed intent on allowing everyone to settle themselves with their snacks and drinks and let the inevitable chit-chat die out of its own accord. When things declined to murmuring and throat clearing, Montavani began.

"Friends, some old"—he nodded to Lightheart and Percival—"and some new"—he looked at Fred and the teens—"welcome to the Verge."

The group nodded and smiled in acknowledgment—except for Percival.

"We're gathered by need, will, and, I also believe, by cosmic fate. By now, all of you know most of the information that I have told Beatrix this morning." He paused to smile at Malik. "You also have much to contribute to the matter due to your experiences, which are extraordinary in their own right. We have all been apprised that this world faces an imminent threat and I—"

"Pardon me, er, Dr. Montavani, for the interruption, but would you please expound on the threat of which you speak?" Fred asked. "Begging your pardon, sir."

"Expound, huh? Expound I shall, my dear fellow." Montavani took off his glasses and stood up and rested his hands on his chair, looking down at his boots as if searching for the right words. Then he looked up at the group. "In five years, the world, as we know it, will be destroyed and all its inhabitants annihilated or lost forever to oblivion. It's up to us to stop it. How's that for expounding?"

The words hung in the air like a dark cloud. Already aware of the situation piecemeal, the company seemed to be galvanized by hearing the fate of the world announced so succinctly.

"Seppe, if I may, please?" Professor Lightheart asked, standing up.

"Ah, yes, most certainly." He gestured to his friend. "I give you Elias Lightheart, an ally and friend who knows our business well."

Lightheart smiled, then looked the group over, nodding at Ben and smiling at Beatrix. "Thank you, Seppe, for your kind words. Everyone, we now know that the meridian at Festermunder School was the initial 'discovered' gateway. However, that does not mean it's the first. In fact, it isn't. These are as ancient as time itself."

"How did they form, Professor?" Ben asked.

"We think the meridians are aggregates of dark matter spun off from supermassive black holes. Dark matter was perfused all over the universe, and small 'sequestra' were left behind, forming the gateways we call meridians here on Earth. These gateways are, in fact, wormholes. Shortcuts through space-time. Some terrestrial and some not." Lightheart glanced at Montavani. "In truth, Ben, we simply don't know, so we do what scientists do in such situations."

"You guess?" Alex asked.

"We postulate and we hypothesize," Lightheart replied. "The small remnants of the supermassive black holes scattered throughout the universe are not unique to Earth, although their concentration here seems astonishingly dense. The globe your father possessed traced the pathways all over the planet. One could use the meridians to travel from New York City to Prague in microseconds. With these meridians marked and mapped, we now have the means for instantaneous travel."

Fred raised his hand. "Professor Lightheart, how is time traversed if travel is in 'real time'? And what about the Divide? How was it discovered?"

"Ah, my friend, you have cut directly to the core. Very good. Like most notable inventions, the ability to traverse time was discovered by accident. There exists a coordinate system by which the meridians can be passed in a certain order, and the result is a hyper-fold of space-time. There are currently forty-eight two-way meridians that we know of on Earth. That's a forty-eight factorial of time possibilities, i.e., 1.2413916e plus sixty-one possible destinations, some of which undoubtedly lead to places that aren't here."

"Aren't here?" Fred asked.

"As in not on Earth but elsewhere in the cosmos."

The group gasped as Lightheart continued. "Originally, Wendell Voght stepped through the first meridians in random order, thereby discovering the Divide by accident. We also know that some meridians aren't bilateral. They're 'export only,' straight to the alter world. The most powerful of these one-way meridians is at Festermunder."

"So, if I understand you correctly," Alex said, "a number of meridians could be joined together like a combination lock to travel through time?"

"Very good, Miss Thacker," Lightheart said. "For instance, the most common triad traverses to the mid-thirteen hundreds in Europe by taking the New York-Franz Josef Land-Verdun group. But, as we stated before, the meridian at Festermunder is the prime meridian. It will take you straight to the Divide unhindered. Understand that space allows us freedom of movement through all three dimensions. Through the meridians, time, the fourth dimension, is not fixed in one direction anymore."

Is it not sort of an odd coincidence that if I'm the Chosen One, or whatever, that I just happen to be a student at the school harboring a time bending wormhole? Beatrix wondered. *That's far too convenient.*

"The replicas," Ben said, prompting Lightheart to continue. Instead, Montavani jumped in.

"The replicas, the simulacra, they're another matter entirely. We discovered them immediately upon our arrival to the Divide. It was apparent those who had gone into the Black that there was a balancing facsimile of our own existence in the Real World."

"Who makes the simulacra?" Malik asked. "Or do they simply exist in the Divide of their own accord?"

"Very astute question, Master Patel," Montavani said. "They do not originate anywhere. The simulacra all exist as we do. It would appear that every living being on Earth has its replica in the Divide, making it a true alter world, and no being can occupy the same side of the meridian as their likeness." Montavani directed that last sentence to Beatrix.

"This Luka and his Mechanix," Ben said, "what would happen if they were killed? Is it even possible to kill them?"

Montavani pondered the question for several moments. "We're not sure, Ben. No one who has faced the agents of the Black Path has ever survived the confrontation. They've all been destroyed. All of them . . . except her."

Montavani was looking directly at Beatrix.

Okay, she thought. *I've had just about enough of this. When is the part where the old man tells us about the quest he has to lead us on? If this is the secret council where I'm entrusted with something that the enemy wants, I guess that makes me Frodo. . . .*

"What now?" Beatrix asked, breaking the silence. Everyone else turned to look at her. "Where do we go from here?" she continued. "You spoke of a plan. What plan?"

Montavani looked at Lightheart as if to warn him to keep quiet about something.

What are they hiding?

"Yes. The time has come for us to decide on our next move against Seraphim. Of course, this will be highly dangerous. The sacrifices we make might benefit humankind, but those sacrifices could include our lives. Young and old, some or all of us may fall prey to the servants of the Black. But there is hope that we may prevail. With faith and strength in each other, we can close the meridians—"

"Close them?" Ben said. "Why not destroy them?"

"Ah. Yes, destroy them. Why haven't we thought of that, Elias?" Montavani laughed good naturedly so as not to offend Ben.

"The meridians are made of space-time and dark matter," Lightheart explained. "There is not sufficient energy anywhere to destabilize them. Only antimatter could possibly bring about a critical mass that could destroy a singularity. Antimatter does not exist in sufficient quantities on Earth, and what is here is kept under close guard."

"Where?" Beatrix asked.

"I beg your pardon?" Lightheart replied.

"You said that antimatter is here on Earth. Where?"

"My dear, you're referring to heavily guarded particle accelerators."

"Like CERN, the Large Hadron Collider in Switzerland," Malik said. "That's the most heavily guarded place on Earth. Security is pimped out tighter than the White House."

"They ain't just handin' out antimatter like popsicles. Elias, Seppe, don't give these kids the idea they can obtain or use antimatter," Percival spat.

"Who said they would just give it to us?" Beatrix asked. Everyone turned to look at her. "Obviously, we'll have to steal it."

Percival was not at all happy with Beatrix's suggestion, and he took her aside to explain why. "Beatrix, I have known you for years. I'm here to help you, to protect you, and I'll follow you wherever you go — to the end and, if need be, into the Black. But I won't watch you stoop to this level. Lyin', stealin', cheatin' — let someone else be party to that . . . like that fool, Seppe. Besides, how the bloody hell would you know where to steal antimatter from. Come clean, Beatrix. What cards are ya holdin'?"

"Parfl — I mean, Percival, I understand, okay? I do. I won't let you down. Dad had this on his radar. He had all types of stuff about dark and antimatter on his computer, including information on the Diamond Light Source, a.k.a. the DLS particle accelerator in Oxfordshire, in the UK. It's a softer target than CERN. I know this is far-fetched and dangerous, but we have to make compromises here, and Montavani is right. He knows —"

"Seppe would have us all die right now if it meant bringing down Seraphim. It's personal for 'im. But Seraphim isn't my responsibility. You are. I promised your father that I wouldn't fail you. . . ." Percival trailed off, realizing he might have said more than he intended.

Before Beatrix could ask him about it, Montavani came over to where they were talking by the fireplace. "Ideas, my dear Percival?"

Percival kept the interruption in stride for once and allowed Beatrix to be led back to the table, where Montavani continued his explanation.

"We have concluded that the best course of action is to begin closing the meridians. The most powerful of which is at Festermunder. Forty-eight of them are scattered across the world. These are mapped and known to us. Other than obtaining the necessary antimatter and the means of disbursing it over the target area, we have a bigger philosophical issue."

"And what issue is that, Dr. Montavani?" Fred asked.

"The issue, Sir Hardingham, is that we may be trapping the Taken forever in the Divide. They will be sealed and unwritten. Most assuredly, Seraphim will strike out at these poor souls if we close all access points to our world. However, we must also do two things. We must lure Luka and the Mechanix into the Black. They can't stay here, which raises a troubling issue."

"What issue, Seppe?" Lightheart asked.

"Someone must go into the Black and seal the prime meridian from the other side." Seeing the questions on the faces of the group, Montavani continued. "Just like the singularity in that accursed Festermunder School, there's another prime meridian in the Divide. A mirror image. Remember the equals sign? It must be shut. If not, the Mechanix, and perhaps one day Seraphim himself, could cross over to our world again and all our work will be for naught."

"I won't be party to any sacrifices like that in this group, Seppe," Percival said. "That's a death certificate for anyone who crosses over. And that's a fact! The prime meridian is in the Deep."

"The Deep is just a place, just like this place, which means it has weaknesses. We have information that they don't know we have. Seraphim has no idea that we have one distinct advantage."

"Which is?" Alex asked.

"We have someone on the inside," Montavani replied.

After an hour of going over Beatrix's proposal to attempt a heist on DLS, Percival followed Montavani down the hall toward an ancient elevator. "Seppe, I think we should talk about this. They ain't ready for this —"

"Oh, shut up, you old fool. They know as well as you do what the risks are," Montavani replied.

"Risks? They're children! And that poor sod of a British agent is in over his head and totally unreliable."

"I can hear you!" Fred said.

"I meant no offense, mate, but you ain't exactly mission worthy, are ya? What did you do over there for Her Majesty anyway? Sniper school? Military intel? Interrogations? What of it, mate?"

"Section Sixteen," Fred replied.

"What the bloody hell is Section Sixteen? Special ops? Black ops?"

"Analysis," Fred replied. "Of unexplained phenomena. Mysteries. UFOs and the like."

"Oh, bloody hell! We got a sodding pencil pusher, Seppe! Seen Nessie yet? How about the Sasquatch? Little green men? Great news! I feel much better about a mission to break into a secret facility under armed guard to capture some sodding piece of damn black hole likely to blow my arse and everyone else to —"

A thunderclap of sound and green light exploded in front of the elevator, silencing Percival and startling the group. Only Beatrix seemed unfazed as she bent down to scoop up Parfleet. She nodded and smiled at Montavani.

Montavani exhaled with satisfaction. "That . . . is an unpleasant man." Then he pushed the elevator button and the doors opened.

The group piled into the elevator, expecting ancient buttons and mechanisms. Instead, Lightheart opened a panel, revealing an LED touchscreen. Lightheart placed his finger on his tongue and then touched it to the screen, bringing up a numeric thermal touchpad. Malik gasped at the breach of hygiene etiquette as Lightheart entered a code, and the elevator began descending.

Beatrix glanced at Ben, whose brow was furrowed, a concerned look on his face.

Here we go again.

The interminable elevator ride was of the deafeningly silent variety, common among groups confined to tight spaces. Everyone faked preoccupation with something. Fingernails became of dire interest, and the metal walls quite compelling. As the levels ticked by, the elevator also became warmer.

"Level twenty-four?" Malik said. "What's on the other floors?"

"Nothing. Absolutely nothing," Montavani replied. "We just thought it would be easier on the occupants if the journey were quantified, lest they become agitated." He cleared his throat. "You don't look like your usual strappingly unflappable self at this moment, Master Patel."

"That's because I'm not. I want to get off. Make it stop, please," Malik pleaded as he held his hands on his lower stomach. "My guts are bubbling. This sucks."

"Hmph. Your foul words, young man. Almost there. There's something you must all see before we finalize our plans."

At that moment, the doors opened without a chime or any other warning. The group filed out into a large, open space, only to be taken aback by the sight before them. The chamber was dark and dank, covered floor to ceiling with castle-like stones. In the center of the room, the stones rose two feet off the floor to form a large ring about fifty feet in diameter. Spanning it was a footbridge at the level of the containment wall around the ring. The bridge was about eight feet wide, and it had a hole at its center that corresponded with the center of the circle. Extending down from the high ceiling, a ray of white light pierced the darkness through the footbridge and into an endless black chasm below.

Alex ran to the edge of the circle, only to be pulled back by Lightheart. "Careful, Alex."

Still restrained by Lightheart, she peered over the edge into the abyss. "I don't see anything. No light. Nothing. Is it functional?"

They all glanced around for Montavani, having lost track of him during the initial commotion.

"So this is it? A meridian. Elias, what powers it, sir?" Fred asked. Malik wandered over, keenly interested in the answer.

"The meridian isn't powered by anything," Lightheart replied. "It's self-sustaining dark matter, likely spun off over here eons ago from a cataclysm like a destroyed neutron star. This meridian is as old as time itself. It's simply dormant now."

"Okay, where does this one lead?" Beatrix asked as she stepped out of the shadows, Parfleet in her arms.

"This meridian is unilateral or, as we say 'afferent.' Through trial and error, we've determined that its destination isn't far from your home, Master Hardingham. It's in Kingston upon Thames outside of Central London."

"Brilliant! When do we try it?" Fred asked.

"Ah. Okay, we don't just ride these like sliding boards at the park, Master Hardingham. There are inherent dangers and the omnipresent risk of being intercepted by agents of the Black."

Lightheart had their attention now. Ben in particular seemed keenly interested in any information on the potential dangers involved with Seraphim and the Mechanix. Lightheart explained that the Mechanix were aptly named, as they, as incomplete simulacra, had abilities that allowed them more access to the spaces between meridians. He even postulated that, by their nature, all meridians were connected and were part of the same network.

"It's my thought, not shared by others per se, that the Mechanix can drift between meridians, not unlike a car moving at high speed down a freeway and instantly changing direction on another freeway. In fact, they may look separate, but I think of them as one large room with many doors. Gateways into a slipstream of incalculable destinations. Infinite doors. An 'ethernet.' Some leading to other doors, like this one, and some leading to the Other Place. . . ."

"The Divide? Have you been there?" Beatrix asked.

"Me? Heavens no, child. I haven't taken the Black Path, but my time has come, it seems."

"It has indeed," a voice from across the meridian said.

It was Montavani, standing by the oculus on the footbridge. He was holding the rythrax in one hand and a bright-red apple in the other. He activated the device, and a tiny beam of green light pulsed into the chasm below.

The others made their way to the edge of the meridian, which began to awaken from dormancy. Then Beatrix gasped.

It's full of stars!

Montavani held the apple aloft. Then he cast it into the meridian. A blast of heat and white light was followed by silence. Then he looked at the group and grinned.

"Want to take a ride?"

CHAPTER 10

Through the Never

"SEVEN, SIX, FIVE, FOUR, THREE . . ." MALIK MUTTERED to himself as the others prepared for the journey. "The journey into the unknown," Malik continued. "Probably into death or worse."

"What's worse?" a voice asked. It startled Malik, who had been crouching as he packed his book bag with some essentials for the trip. Looking up, he saw Ben standing in the dimly lit prep room immediately adjacent to the meridian in the great hall, deep in the heart of the Verge.

"Huh?" Malik said.

"Death. What's worse than that? Pain? Torture?"

"What's worse?" Malik stood up. "What's worse than death may be infinity. A timeless journey into forever. A void of nothing forever and ever. No life and no death. That's what's worse."

Ben stiffened and raised his eyebrows at Malik's rare display of indignation. "You don't trust Lightheart and Montavani? How can you not believe everything about the meridians at this point? We've seen so much. We've seen miracles. Supernatural stuff. Beatrix alone would qualify."

"Beatrix will be fine. She's the strongest. She's different. Different than she was even a couple of weeks ago back at school. What will I do if I'm confronted by one of these bad people? I'm the weakest link."

Ben looked Malik in the eyes and placed his hands on the boy's shoulders. "Beatrix is strong, but so are you. We wouldn't be here without you."

"But . . ."

"Stop. I've got your back, Malik. I won't let anything happen to you. You have my word."

Malik continued to stare at Ben, then nodded. "Okay. It's cool. I'm cool."

"Cool," Ben said with a smile before he released Malik's shoulders and smacked him on the arm.

Pausing in the doorway on his way out, Ben turned back and said something that Malik would not forget for the rest of his life. "You're my best friend, Malik."

Then he was gone.

Malik stood there alone, facing the stone wall of the prep room, shifting his weight from one leg to another for a full minute, not trusting himself to speak. He knew he had sixty minutes left before he would take the leap into the never.

The problem was, Malik was harboring a terrible secret, and that was this: he had no interest in Wendell Voght, Festermunder, meridians, Seraphim, or even the end of the world. He did, however, have an insatiable need for friendship and the security and happiness—nay, the joy—that Ben and Beatrix provided for him. That was all that had propelled him along so far. Now Malik was feeling pressured to remain involved in a set of circumstances that were dangerous and clearly going to claim his life at the ripe old age of fourteen.

Malik reached down and doubled the knots on his red Converse All-Star Chuck Taylors. Then, checking himself one last time, he made his way out of the prep room.

Pop.

Malik turned. Sitting on the floor was Beatrix staring at her phone and chewing gum. She was wearing headphones, and Malik could hear the bass and four/four beat of an anthemic song by Arcade Fire. Taking a chance at stirring up trouble, Malik tapped her shoe, and she looked up.

He was expecting a rebuke, but instead, she took off her headphones and patted the stone floor next to her. Malik accepted her invitation to sit, surprised at the request.

"Well?" Beatrix said.

"Ready," Malik replied, though his voice was shaky.

"Liar."

"Yeah. I'm not ready. I've peed twelve times in the last hour. What if I need to pee while I'm in the portal?"

"Montavani said it'll be fast, like, instantaneous. I'm sure you'll be able to hold it until we get to London." Beatrix grinned.

"Are you ready?" Malik asked.

Beatrix rubbed her hands over her face, displacing her glasses into her thicket of curls, then let them slip back over her eyes. "Yeah, I guess. I dunno. Who can be ready for something like this?"

"It'll be alright, I'm sure," Malik said with false bravado.

Beatrix let out a long exhale, then let her head sink to the right, coming to rest on Malik's shoulder. He froze and gulped.

"Relax, idiot. Just because we may be dead in thirty minutes doesn't mean I'm going to tell you I've always loved you or anything."

Malik giggled. "Okay."

They remained that way for several moments until Beatrix broke the silence, her voice soft and feeble. "I'm scared, Malik. Help me not be."

As a lump grew in his throat, Malik wisely decided that silence was his best option.

As Malik and Beatrix spent what they thought were their final moments on Earth in silence, a secret conference was taking place elsewhere in the Verge as Montavani, Lightheart, and the newly reanimated Percival J. Parfleet finalized preparations. Montavani's voice rose above the others.

"So, in summary, you will take the portal to its customary afferent location, Elias, in Kingston upon Thames in Central London. The adorable little Telegraph Cottage sits out front. Just take the five of them — and Percy, I suppose — to execute the plan."

"Five? My God, you can't mean it, Seppe," Percival said. "Why not let us just go? We're older and have experience. Why the children and that Brit agent? Hell, I'll go alone if I must."

"Because, you fool, would you like to travel bereft of all accouterments?" Montavani asked. "How about clothing? Remember the time you showed up in the town square in Rangoon without a stitch of clothes on? We had an unbelievable mess getting you out of the asylum under the eyes of the Burmese government. And how about that issue on Darech-7 where you offended an entire alien culture? No, you imbecile, we need our . . . resources."

"The girl," Percival said.

"What?" Lightheart asked.

"He needs the girl. Beatrix. He means to use her," Percival said, a hint of sadness in his voice as he was already resigned to it. "She has this trait, the Andromeda particle. With her, we can go over intact. Just like them. Just like the Mechanix."

"Enough, Percival," Montavani said. He turned to Lightheart. "We're at war whether we like it or not. That means compromises must be made—and sacrifices. Besides, taking her into the Black will confirm her powers and their limitations."

"It's only a start, Percy," Lightheart said. "A quick trip. Only nanoseconds to us."

"Yeah? Yer sure, are ya? Okay, Professor, pop quiz. We think she has this Andromeda trait, right? This sodding particle. How do we know for sure how she's going to respond? We have no idea what will happen to her." Percival's Scottish drawl grew more intense the angrier he got.

"Percy, the math checks out," Lightheart insisted. "We have enough data. Look at how she performed against the servants of the Black Path. She's seen him, Percy. She faced him in New York several times. No one has ever done that before. She could destroy the Mechanix."

"She could destroy us," Montavani said.

"And maybe herself, and don't call me Percy, Lightheart. You ain't earned it."

"Bah! Enough of your drivel. We go." Montavani looked at his antique timepiece. "Seventeen minutes."

With that, all three of them filed out of the room.

"Beatrix. Beatrix, it's time." Montavani reached his weathered hand down to pull her off the floor where she was slumped, listening to music.

"Right," Beatrix said, then she got up and followed Montavani to the edge of the prime meridian. The thin white beam was brighter and more intense than before, and stars were visible deep in the core.

The group assembled in a tight circle off to the side of the meridian. Out of deference to Beatrix, all of them parted to allow her a place in the circle.

"Alex?" Montavani said.

"Ready," she replied.

"Master Hardingham?"

"Uh, I suppose yes, I'm ready." Fred was sweating and shuffling his feet.

"Ben?"

"Ready."

"Master Patel?"

"I . . . I . . . I have no saliva," Malik said as he swayed on his feet. Beatrix patted him on the arm and nodded in encouragement. He nodded back. "I'm good. Ready."

"Beatr—"

"Ready," Beatrix replied.

"Beatrix," Montavani continued, "for us to pass unhindered with all of our personal effects, we need a token of yours that identifies with your DNA. You have the trait that we do not possess."

"The trait. Uh, right, like what?" Beatrix asked.

"A lock of your hair for all the travelers will do," Montavani said, then produced a pair of red scissors and handed them to her.

Beatrix exhaled, shrugged, then reached back and grabbed a thick wad of hair and began cutting. Everyone else watched in respectful silence, the moment feeling ceremonial. She handed the first piece to Fred, then gave the next to Alex, who seemed ashamed for Beatrix to have to do such a thing.

Why is she acting that way? Beatrix wondered.

Beatrix handed a lock to Ben, who nodded as he pocketed it. Percival stepped forward and held his hand out, causing Beatrix to look at Montavani for guidance.

"Did you really think he was going to let you out of his sight?" Montavani asked.

Beatrix smiled in thanks to Percival and then gave him the lock.

After handing a lock to Lightheart, who looked nervous, she turned to Malik, whose body was quivering.

"Don't do this for me. I'm not comfortable with it," Malik said. He was on the verge of tears.

Sensing his anxiety, Beatrix reached to the front of her hair and pulled out a long curl that, when outstretched, extended to her chin. Then she held up the scissors and cut it, never taking her eyes off Malik.

"Open your hand," Beatrix whispered. "It's okay."

Beatrix laid the strand of hair in Malik's small, sweaty palm and then closed his hand. "We're going to do this," she said. "We'll all be together. It's okay."

Malik nodded.

"Four minutes," Montavani said. "Let's get you all into position."

"What, you're not going?" Ben asked.

"No, Ben, I am not. I can't."

"What? Why?"

"Now is not the time, young man. Get Percy and Elias to tell you sometime. But for the moment, just know that I can't go. I'm . . . how should I put it? Marked."

Montavani instructed the group to assemble on the footbridge over the meridian. The time had come for them to make their leap through the hyperfold provided by the singularity. Montavani appeared anxious to get the group off, but his preoccupation with something else piqued Beatrix's interest.

"What's up?"

"Up? Hmph. Nothing is up. We have need of haste, is all. Using the meridian runs the risk of exposing ourselves to those we're trying to avoid. The minute we power it up, the Enemy will become aware of us."

"Power up? How so?" Beatrix asked. "Isn't it always on?"

"No, it remains dormant until it receives a substrate."

"What's a substrate?" Beatrix asked, suspecting she already knew the answer.

"You all. The travelers." Montavani was staring into the meridian, and Beatrix followed his eyes downward.

"Is Wendell out there?" Beatrix asked as she stared at the pinpricks of light in the meridian.

Montavani said nothing for several seconds, then exhaled with resignation. He looked at Beatrix, his eyes sad. "Child. How could I know? I can't explain how or why his simulacrum left the final time. My only assumption is that the duplicate Wendell was recalled to the Divide by some master plan of Seraphim."

"Wait! You said the two can't occupy the same side at the same time. If the simulacrum went to the Divide and Wendell was already there, then he would be . . . he would be . . ."

"Unwritten," Montavani said, finishing for her.

She nodded. "Yes, unwritten."

"He is not. I'm quite sure of that, Beatrix."

"What? How do you know?"

Montavani fished into the top of his sweater and pulled out a necklace with a metal talisman on it—the twin apex symbol superimposed over infinity. "This." He took it off and handed it to her.

Beatrix held it in front of her face as she waited for an explanation.

"Wendell gave me this. So, you see, we know he's not unwritten. He lives, Beatrix!"

Beatrix shook her head. "I don't understand."

"Child, remember you not our conversation? The unwritten have no works, no kin, no influences. Everything is swept away."

"So as long as this exists, he's alive," Beatrix said, excitement rising in her voice. "If Wendell was unwritten, this would have disappeared! This means we have a chance. We can find him and bring him home!"

Montavani sighed and looked as if he would like to speak further on the matter but merely nodded. "Yes, perhaps so."

Moments later, on the footbridge, they all stood in a circle surrounding the oculus. It was treacherous to look down into the starlit void. Other than Parfleet, only Alex seemed at ease. Beatrix dared not look into the meridian. Ben stood close to her and remained silent. He, too, was preoccupied with his own thoughts. Malik was a mess, his red-rimmed eyes revealing that he had been crying. Fred assured the others that all would be well in merry London in a few seconds, but Beatrix noticed his body was shaking and his voice was wavering. Lightheart seemed pensive, keeping his thoughts to himself.

Beatrix knew that jumping into a pit of nothing was incompatible with human instinct. She equated it to trying to drown oneself.

How can anyone just jump into the black nothingness?

"Percival, would you do us the honor of making the first jump? It will help reassure the newcomers."

"Right. For them I will, old man," Percival said. He checked his pockets one last time and made certain the lock of Beatrix's hair was in the breast pocket of his crushed-velvet suit. He also shut down his iPhone. "Ready."

"Then proceed, my good fellow," Montavani said.

"See you all in London," Percival said as he saluted the group, a wry smile on his face. Then he turned and walked backwards off the edge of the oculus and plunged into the void.

Malik yelped in astonishment as they watched him fall for several hundred feet. Then the meridian flared purple and white, and he disappeared. The group continued to stare in silence. Montavani's cell phone chimed. He glanced at the screen, then snickered, passing the phone around.

Incredibly, on the screen was a selfie of Percival standing outside Telegraph Cottage in London and rendering an obscene gesture with his middle phalange.

"That's bloody brilliant!" Fred exclaimed. "Can I go next?"

"By all means, my good man," Montavani said.

Smiling broadly, with his eyes squeezed shut, Fred summoned all the courage within him, then turned and jumped into the abyss. As they had with Percival, the group followed Fred with their eyes until the void flared and then went silent. Montavani's phone chimed moments later. No picture this time, just a single word: "Limey."

Needing no prompting, Alex went next, diving into the void with ease.

Moments later, another text came: "Limey brat."

Malik began to shake, and tears welled in his eyes. "I can't. I'm sorry. I can't do this."

Ben reached out to steady him. "We can all go together."

Ben looked at Montavani for approval and received a nod of affirmation.

Ben hugged Beatrix. "Love you," he said.

"Love you too," Beatrix replied, her heart racing.

Then Ben positioned himself on Malik's right, and Beatrix stood on his left.

A tremor ran through the room, causing dust to fall from the ceiling. The trio looked to Montavani for an explanation. "You must go," he said. "We have alerted the Enemy, and the portal must be reduced. Farewell, travelers."

Montavani squeezed Ben and Malik's shoulders, a warm smile on his face. Then he leaned in close and whispered Beatrix's ear, "Enter through the narrow gate, for wide is the gate that leads to destruction, and many are those who enter by it."

As she looked at him for an explanation, the room began to shake as if from an earthquake. Shards of stone fell from the ceiling, and the footbridge began to sway so hard they feared it might break.

"Go! We're discovered! Go!" Montavani yelled. "The Enemy is in the Verge. You must go!"

"What about you?" Malik protested. "You'll be killed!"

"I'll be fine! Away with you, now!" With that, Montavani loosened a buckle on the bridge, then produced the red scissors and cut the support rope loose. The bridge tipped forty-five degrees, spilling the three companions through oculus.

As if in slow motion, Beatrix made eye contact with Montavani. To her surprise, in his eyes, she saw neither fear or anxiety.

Only sadness.

The night air was chilly in the London suburb of Kingston upon Thames. Telegraph Cottage was well concealed by large oak and elm trees. The idyllic little cottage was made of brick and stucco and had been restored numerous times since World War II, during which, incredibly, it had been occupied by General of the Army Dwight D. Eisenhower. An ivy-covered trellis surrounded the cottage's front and sides. Montavani and Percival had agreed that it was a supreme irony that it, of all places, was the efferent for the captive portal from the Verge. They were even more aware of another supreme irony, that Lt. Waverly Voght, Wendell's grandfather, was once an intelligence officer on Eisenhower's staff and was once billeted there. Percival was ever skeptical of that fact, thinking it far too convenient.

Percival and Fred stood behind a giant elm, waiting on the next arrival from the Verge. Fred was still coursing with adrenaline from surviving his first instantaneous intra-stellar trip.

"Pipe down, mate," Percival said. "You had a one hundred percent chance of survival. You don't get a sodding medal."

To Fred, Percival appeared surprisingly unsettled. He kept checking his phone and scanning the tree and fence line, though he said nothing of what he was looking for.

A flash of green and a black cloud materialized in the backyard. After their eyes adjusted, they went out to retrieve Alex.

Two to three minutes passed, longer than Percival was comfortable with, before there was another flash as the final group arrived. Percival and the others rushed forward to check on them.

Across the world, Montavani was running out of time. Sprinting down a long, dark tunnel in the Verge to a more secluded and secure location, he barreled forth without the need for light, as he knew the catacombs from memory. The sounds of destruction above seemed to please him, and he snickered as he scurried through the darkness. The reverberating sounds of explosions were not from the Enemy but had been designed by Montavani to go off in case of an emergency. He had sealed off the meridian lest the Mechanix break through to take control of it. If he had left it dormant, he was certain they would have figured out how to prime and ignite it again.

As he paused to catch his breath, his phone vibrated with a message from Percival. When Montavani read it, he could hardly believe what it said.

WHERE IS BEATRIX?

CHAPTER 11

Special Agent Libby Soames-Briggs

I N A DARK PLACE, A CHILD'S VOICE WHISPERED "Help . . . Help me, please!"

The detention area was a seemingly endless dark hall, lined with stones and illuminated by a white glow in the distance.

The girl's voice was drowned out by a deep, doom-like droning sound. All at once, the dim hall became as black as space. Something was blocking out the light.

It approached the child, knowing exactly where she was. Then it stopped in front of her cell and pressed its expressionless face against the bars.

The girl recoiled in mock horror, although she had seen the deathly face countless times in real life and in her dreams. She couldn't apprehend why she was not as afraid as the others. Being younger than the rest of the internees, she should have been more afraid, and she should have shown proper respect by fearing them. She knew her captors fed off it. They were spawned and nourished by fear. They couldn't process strength, nor will, nor love, nor courage as they were incomplete and not wired that way.

The girl knew that calling for them could cause her to be taken to the lowest reaches of the Deep. Many of the others had disappeared there, likely cast into the Black.

Wiped. Deleted. Unwritten.

Or worse yet, some of the others could be punished for her defiance. She was fond of them and they of her. She would use fear as bait. Fear of the Mechanix and of the prospect of being taken to the White Room for conditioning—the place she desperately needed to go to complete her mission. She could make contact with her ally there.

"Do not speak of the places in the Deep or you shall be made to visit them," Luka said, his voice seething with hatred. "And worry not, child scum. The Master has need of many travelers, and you all will visit the White Room as soon as you are bidden."

"Please no. I'm too young."

"You are old enough to know fear, child. And you will do the Master's bidding. You entered the Deep Fell without permission, and your punishment isn't complete. I need not tell you your destiny. Like that of the others, it is only doom."

The Deep Fell. . . . The Haunted Woods. I wasn't afraid.

"Luka, it's time," a deep, gruff voice said.

Her tormentor disappeared in a flash of black vapor, leaving the girl alone. She retreated to the back of her cell, where she had a small bed and table. A shelf of books was above her bed. There was a candle, which she lit with a flint and piece of tinder stolen by one of the other Taken. She opened her favorite book, *Alice in Wonderland*, her prized possession, and continued reading.

As her mind wandered in the dim cell, she thought of someone she used to know. A friend from another time. Another place. She flipped to the title page and read the inscription.

> My dear Gwen,
> What does a raven have in common
> with a writing desk?
> For I have no idea. . . .
> P.S. Watch the sky

As she thought about her plan, she began to fall asleep. As she drifted off, she thought about the others. About how to watch the sky. And mostly about *Alice in Wonderland*. Her last thoughts were of the rabbit hole.

And how deep it went.

Elizabeth "Libby" Soames-Briggs had been awake for all of six seconds, but she was already piping mad. The messages had come in all night. Incessant texts to her work phone. All of them encrypted and all of them rubbish. She was to have been off for a three-day break before Christmas. This already had her incensed. As she had no immediate family, the suits at work had made themselves a priority during the holiday and would take time off over Christmas and New Year's. Libby could hardly complain. She had asked for this. In a profession dominated by men, she had jockeyed for advancement, volunteering for anything and everything, even hazardous duty.

Still, for heaven's sake, you'd think I could get one night of uninterrupted sleep!

When her phone vibrated again on her nightstand, she scooped it up.

"Bollocks! Alright, enough's enough. Another one of the blokes in Op-3 can be rung up. I'm not the only one on call! They're just avoiding their duty. Do you hear me?"

"Libby? Dearie, you sound right stoked up. Are you okay?" a voice that sounded like a middle-aged parent asked on the other end of the line.

Pulling the phone away from her ear and looking at it, Libby realized it was her personal phone, and it was her mother who had called.

"Bloody hell."

"Libby?"

"Yes, Mum. Yes, I hear you. Sorry, I was just—"

"It's alright, Lib. I just wanted to tell you good morning on your special day and to say happy birthday to my sweet Lib-Lib. Thirty years old today."

Crap. I'd forgotten. It's December 21. Ugh. Don't remind me.

As she sat up in bed and looked around for her glasses, Libby assumed her typical propriety. "Right, Mum. Thank you. That's very kind of you."

"Any plans for your big day, my love?"

Thinking about the list of emails to return and case files to review, not to mention being on call, Libby was sure she had plans. Lots of plans.

"Oh yes, Mum. Big plans. Loads of plans. Plans and plans. You know, that's what young people do."

"Okay, Lib-Lib, well your step-papa sends his love." Libby heard him say some sort of salutation in the background. "Make sure you get a piece of cake with your friends while you're out, dear. That's important. Smell the roses and all, you know."

"Yes, yes. Oh, how I love a good cake. Always have." Libby wanted to puke.

"Love you, Libs," her mum said.

"Okay. Right. Love you too. And give my love to George. Right. Goodbye."

"Honestly." Libby exhaled as she flung herself back onto the bed and pulled a large pillow over her face to stifle her scream of frustration. Things were not going how they were supposed to go.

C-4 is known in military circles as an extremely combustible, high-explosive putty capable of powerful concussive detonation and a large blast radius even if deployed in small quantities. The nickname fit Libby to a T.

Her coworkers at MI5 found her to be all business, with zero tolerance for even the smallest piece of stupidity. A by-the-book martinet to the point of self-ostracization, Libby could be difficult to spend time with. Fierce and humorless. A joyless heap of human intensity. "Call the fun police, everyone," her coworkers would joke when she showed up. "It's Lib. Put down your fun!"

Standing at just an inch over five feet had never stopped the diminutive yet formidable young woman. She competed in and won several triathlons, once outperforming several men from the British SAS commandos on their annual fitness invitational. Never afraid to tuck her amber hair into a tight ponytail and play with the boys, Libby was ultra-competitive. Whether it was athletics or academics, case investigation, or advanced hand-to-hand combat training, it became abundantly clear to others: Libby Soames-Briggs did not just want to win; she wanted others to lose and do poorly.

Being the only female in Op-3 (Investigations), Libby was oblivious to her standing with the others. Caring only for advancement, she miscalculated the need for teamwork and delegation. She would rather do things herself. The right way.

Her way.

Libby flipped on her computer and entered the activation code for the mandated spyware and worm sweep. MI5 was understandably very serious about security with those working from home. Special security clearance and weapons training were imperative and required annual proficiency exams.

Checking her work email, she came upon a subject that raised an eyebrow.

SUBJECT: AGENT IN U.S. ON LEAVE OFF-GRID HAS
NOT REPORTED

Clicking on the email, she read that some moron in Section 16, whatever that was, was crapping out on the job and not checking in. As she read further, Libby sipped her coffee and pulled a knee up under her as her house cat, Henry, jumped into her lap. Her interest growing, she read that the Company (as MI5 called itself) had tried unsuccessfully to ping his GPS and he hadn't checked in. It was a serious breach of security and had set off alarms with Internal Security (IS-1).

Poor fool. You never want to get involved with IS-1. They don't play.

Libby was just about to close the email and move on when she saw the name of the agent along with a photo.

SPECIAL AGENT: FREDERICK J. HARDINGHAM,
Section 16

"Goofy bloke," she whispered, then swallowed another sip of coffee.

Her interest piqued, she highlighted the name and searched it, which brought up one of her own emails.

What the hell?

Setting Henry on the floor, she read further. Apparently, Libby had sent a message two weeks earlier to the same Frederick J. Hardingham, requesting a meeting on January 3. Now it all came back to her. Section 16. The investigation of the unexplained. She had been given orders from above to look into some disappearances that some idiot upstairs thought required Op-3 involvement.

"A load of crap," Libby said.

Libby had only had one other interaction with the vaunted Section 16 a couple of years back when she had been made to go up to a castle near Dundee.

What was it called? Glam something? Castle Glamis.

The case was something of a one-off write-up of some type of missing person's issue. Some idiot went missing in the castle for hours, apparently disappearing into thin air, and Libby was ordered to file a report.

Feeling energized, Libby decided on a path for her day. She would skip CrossFit, as she was still quite sore from the double session the day before. Instead, she would go to the office and take advantage of the fact that because it was a Sunday, only a skeleton crew would be staffing the place. Then she would take a look in the offices of Section 16. Distressed that her name was on an email to an agent who was off the grid, she did not want to be connected to anything like that. It could hurt her upcoming review or at least raise eyebrows.

She left her flat fifteen minutes later, having taken a quick shower and whipped up a kale smoothie, ready to head out to Thames House and determined to get to the bottom of this business with Frederick J. Hardingham.

Although boarding a trolley in London on a Sunday morning would have been a cinch, Libby decided to ride her bike. The cold December air would clear her head and allow her to think about her predicament.

It was just another hiccup in a life full of hiccups and setbacks that Libby was constantly battling through.

Born in Sheffield, UK, it had been clear for as far as she could remember that she would succeed. In primary school, young Libby was distressed that the other kids weren't cut from the same cloth as she was. They would babble unintelligibly and play pretend and chase bugs in the schoolyard. Meanwhile, Libby would sit against a tree and do extra-credit homework. Early on, Libby developed a lack of self-awareness about how her behaviors were seen by her peers. In high school and in college, she was always focused on some unknown future. She seemed to be chasing something she couldn't identify. Few people ever got close to her.

Practiced in high-level analysis, which was paradoxically balanced by her lack of self-awareness, Libby had never thought of herself as pretty. Had she been more self-aware, she would have realized most people regarded her as fiercely beautiful. However, the off-putting nature of her dogmatic personality caused others to shun her. Libby had no real close relationships. She classified those who were relationship seekers as needy, codependent leeches. Still, deep down, she couldn't help but wonder why she had never had a companion.

So far, no one's been good enough.

Pulling her sock hat down tighter over her ears, Libby rode the last half kilometer to Thames House, listening to her music and lost in thought. A passing motorist honked and rolled down his window, hollering a question about her relationship status. Ignoring him, Libby entered the check-in area. The duty officer scanned her ID badge and signed her in. Unlike the movies, there was no sophisticated retinal scan. A simple voice match was sufficient.

"Special Agent Soames-Briggs, Elizabeth."

Her voice pattern was confirmed, and the gate buzzed and unlocked.

With no expected Sunday morning salutation to the duty officer, Libby walked past the control room toward the elevator bank. Having unrestricted access to all floors in the building, save two — the evidence floor and another with the obfuscatory name of Management Analysis — Libby voiced her destination to the intercom in the elevator. She knew all too well that the voice recognition system was used as a means to track the whereabouts of the agents while in the building.

Paranoid idiocy. They already have our iPhones and Apple Watches practically surgically grafted to us and track us through GPS for our own "safety." A load of bollocks. That's just Management Analysis's way of watching for the next crack-up to go off the grid. We all know there's been an issue with agents on "extended leave." My foot. They went rogue. The world just swallowed them up. Like this Hardingham chap.

When Libby started down the dimly lit halls of BC52, she couldn't believe that anyone had to work under such conditions. Leaky, steaming boiler conduits lined the ceilings and wall, looking like something out of the turn of the century — the nineteenth century.

The door to BC52 was unlocked, as per protocol, and marked with a cheekily humored "Area 51" sign. Libby allowed herself a smirk, then went inside and locked the door behind her.

"Bloody pigsty," Libby spat. As she cast her eyes around the room, it became clear that Special Agent Frederick J. Hardingham was a disorganized slob who occupied a room reminiscent of the mad scientist from her favorite movie, *Back to the Future.*

Where to bloody begin?

Libby sat at the desk and turned on the computer monitor. The Company's protocol dictated that the computer itself was never to be turned off. The servers backed up the data each day at midnight.

When the screen brightened, Libby went to login. She looked around at the memorabilia and personal items for password hints, then began typing in ideas when they came to her.

> tatooine
> *FAILED*
> tk421
> *FAILED*
> tusken raider
> *FAILED*
> dr. who
> *FAILED*
> maytheforcebewithyou
> *FAILED*
> floopowder

FAILED

Beginning to despair, Libby stood up and paced around the disheveled room. Looking at portraits, she scanned them with half interest. There was a picture of Fred clad in a Starfleet uniform standing next to William Shatner at a *Star Trek* convention. Another photo featured a grandmother type. There was also a picture of a little girl with blond hair and ice cream on her face. Intrigued, Libby popped the photo out of the frame and flipped it over.

Gotcha!

On a random hunch, Libby typed in a name.

Gwen

PASSED

Libby's research into Special Agent Hardingham's comings and goings was surprisingly simple at first. She was able to log in to Fred's emails and find his plane tickets to JFK and then his return flight to Heathrow on December 30. His correspondence with Evelyn Thacker in Queens, New York, was of the humdrum variety—hardly a plot to go rogue or any hints of nefarious activity. All she discovered was that Fred appeared to be a total bore and a complete nerd with even less of a life than she had. Libby began to think more in terms of him cracking up and going AWOL. It was understood by everyone at the Company that one couldn't just decide to quit. There was a debriefing protocol. Agents had to be processed out by IS-1. Many around Thames House referred to the process as "purging." As a point of fact, going off the grid was synonymous with desertion with classified material. Libby assumed IS-1 had probably already been activated and agents in the United States were looking for Hardingham to bring him in.

Following Fred's deplaning at JFK, he rented a car from Hertz and was traceable by GPS all the way to Queens. Libby logged on to the GPS software that monitored each agents' phone. She made her way to the recent activity window, then sat up straight in the chair when she realized something out of place. The telemetry monitor, highly sensitive and sophisticated as it was, recorded an anomaly at 7:17 p.m. on his first night in New York.

Ionizing radiation? That's not normal.

Additionally, the gyroscope had been knocked off kilter, his compass sent spinning. This same phenomenon happened again at 1:14 a.m., except this time in Upstate New York near a town called Phoenicia.

What the . . .?

Libby zipped up her hoodie and shuddered in the damp air. Craving tea, she looked around to see if the poor bloke had anything to brew. As she scanned his office, Libby noticed a corkboard with newspaper clippings thumbtacked to it.

Nessie Seen Twice This Year

Cat Does Algebra

Lights in the Sky near Devon

Wow, ol' Freddie. Some top-level work they've got you on down here.

Libby was about to close up shop and grab a coffee upstairs when she spun back on her heel and stared at a news clipping she had missed at first glance.

Girl, 9, Vanishes While on Holiday

Libby pulled the clipping off the corkboard and sat back down at the computer. She scanned the article, looking for pertinent data, as was her custom at work or at leisure. A name stuck out in her mind—Gwen Thacker.

Gwen. The password.

Reading on, Libby learned that Gwen was the nine-year-old daughter of Evelyn and Joel Thacker.

Evelyn Thacker.

On a whim, Libby returned to the computer and did a Google search for "Evelyn Thacker." She was surprised by the discovery of two facts and was unable to decide which of them was the most shocking. First, Evelyn Thacker was a former MI5 agent who had gone into early retirement following the loss of her daughter. Second, Evelyn's maiden name was Hardingham.

When Libby searched the MI5 database for Evelyn's name, she came up empty. Libby found that odd, as the Company routinely surveilled and investigated former agents. It was as if Evelyn had never existed at the Company.

Purged.

Libby pulled up Special Agent Hardingham's file. It said he was thirty-three years old, unmarried, and had one sibling. Both of his parents had died in an accident when Fred was a teenager.

Doesn't have it easy, does he?

His only next-of-kin in the UK was Esther Olive Chapman, eighty-four years of age. Oddly, she had the same street address in Hackney as Hardingham.

Lives with his granny. Poor bloke.

Careful to leave the office in the same condition in which she found it, Libby tidied up and returned everything to its place. After logging out the computer terminal and turning out the lights, Libby failed to notice two seemingly trivial facts. First, she had inadvertently kept the newspaper clipping about Gwen Thacker in her pocket. Second, Libby had failed to notice a small camera that had been installed in the banker's lamp on Fred's desk. The twenty-four-hour video feed was neither installed nor monitored by Fred. It was directed to a department on the fifth floor, the Office of Management Analysis, a.k.a. IS-1.

His fingers quivering, James Manafort downloaded a video feed from BC52 and ejected the thumb drive. He hated working with the IS-1 people. As a tech support engineer, Manafort detested that his top-secret security clearance exposed him to such people. They were more than mysterious. "Dangerous" was closer to the mark. They went only by coded monikers, not their real names. Rarely, if ever, were the IS-1 operators seen, only their sub-lieutenants, who were glorified proxies and messengers to those who operated in the shadows.

Manafort walked the thumb drive down to the elevator and out of the building, then went to the tube terminal on Church Street. No one else was down there, which wasn't surprising on a Sunday. Following instructions, Manafort descended to the lowest level and stood at Platform A3.

After a few minutes, Manafort removed his scarf and gloves, feeling warm. As he fidgeted with the thumb drive in his hand, he noticed the fluorescent lights flicker on and off.

Casting a nervous glance right and left and then up and down the tracks. Manafort worried, but knew that the sooner he made the drop, the sooner he could get far away from his contact and back home.

Suddenly, the security camera behind Manafort exploded with array of smoke and sparks. Wheeling about, he saw a figure materialize out of a small cloud of black, sooty smoke. The figure was tall and dressed in black. A fedora obscured his nondescript face.

"Place it on the ground and step away."

Manafort complied, then reeled as the figure lifted his arm, and the thumb drive appeared in his gloved hand as if transported by an unseen force.

Manafort was gripped by ice-cold terror as the figure reached out and grabbed his wrist. Before his world was consumed by black fog, his last mortal thoughts were of a man with no face. Then James Manafort was no more.

"Luka, it's time," a guttural voice said.

Luka turned towards the voice down the tube and faded into nothingness.

Libby pedaled back in the cold to her flat. Once there, she fed Henry, then ate a quick bite of lunch. Ever a creature of habit, Libby did fifteen dead-hang pull-ups in the doorframe to her bedroom. After a quick trip to the powder room to wash up, Libby headed for the door, but not before reaching into the small of her back and pulling out her sidearm to inspect it.

Safety on. One in the chamber.

Libby was consumed in thought as she boarded the trolley, and headed to Hackney, wondering who Evelyn Thacker was and if she was involved in Hardingham's disappearance.

Jumping off the trolley while it was still moving, much to the chagrin of the bell captain, Libby trotted the last half mile to 12-B Manchester Street.

When she got there, she knocked on the door. Getting no response, Libby knocked again, then rang the buzzer without pause. Finally, she heard a voice on the other side.

"Alright! Bloody hell, I'm coming!"

When the door opened, Libby was presented with a mental image that would take weeks to shake off. Standing in the foyer was an elderly woman in a fuchsia leotard with fluorescent green tights. She was stooped over, fumbling with her Bluetooth headphones, and Libby could have sworn she heard the opening bars of a song by Neil Diamond.

"Well, speak, will ya?" the old lady said. "It's as cold as a witch's teat out there, and yer lettin' all the hot air out!"

"Fred Hardingham's residence?" Libby asked.

The old lady leaned in close and examined her visitor, raising an eyebrow in suspicion. She suddenly began to giggle. And chortle. Then the old lady broke into uncontrollable guffaws and held her sides, barely able to speak. "Freddie? You? Are you sure you got the right name, dearie?"

"Ahem, yes, ma'am. Frederick J. Hardingham." Libby smiled, hoping to get inside and have an audience.

The old lady stopped laughing and straightened up, her face turning serious. "Is something wrong with my Freddie? Tell me, is he hurt? What do you want him for?"

Libby smiled her most charming smile. "Heaven's no, ma'am, he's fine. Freddie is still on vacation in the States. I'm a friend from work, and, uh, he asked me to get something he took home from work and bring it back to the office."

The old woman narrowed her eyes at Libby before she smiled and turned back into the flat. Libby remained on the porch, having yet to be invited in.

"Well, come on in for a spot of tea, dearie," the old lady said as she disappeared down the hall. "You'll freeze your bloody arse off out there!"

Libby made herself comfortable in the living room and waited for the old lady to bring her tea tray out and set it on the table. The old lady sat down and handed Libby a cup, and they both took a sip.

"Olive," the old lady said.

"Olive? No, ma'am, thank you, but I'm fine with the chamomile," Libby demurred, playing dumb.

The old lady giggled. "No, dearie, my name is Olive. My baptized name is Esther, but I wouldn't be caught dead using that sodding name if me life hung in the balance."

Libby laughed, then introduced herself. "I'm Libby. Libby Mathews."

Olive eyed Libby as if she knew a secret that would embarrass her and then shrugged. "Tell me more about how you know my Freddie. I must say, I was a bit shocked to see a lass like you call fer 'im. The ladies aren't too keen on Freddie, 'specially ladies of yer caliber."

"Like I said, I work with him at Thames House. MI5."

"Oh, you must be a spy like my Freddie. He's always on dangerous missions. Carrying on, doing things for King and Country."

Libby suppressed a laugh. *Hardly.*

"So, Gran Olive"—Libby thought using her affectionately termed name may make her more likely to cooperate—"where's Freddie's part of the flat?"

"Freddie's room is next to the loo, and that dratted cat of his, Moresby, stays in there too."

Olive's iPhone chimed with an obnoxious disco ringtone. Olive held up her finger, got off the couch, and headed for the kitchen.

Sensing it was a good time to snoop for clues, Libby stood up. "Just going to the loo!" she called out.

Libby headed down the hall toward Fred's part of the flat. Once she reached the bathroom, she turned on the light and the fan, then closed the door and crept down the hall to where Fred's room should be.

Unlike his office, Fred's bedroom was in excellent condition. Even the quilt on his bed was immaculate and wrinkle free. The room was spartan, without much decor. On the nightstand were pictures of Evelyn Thacker and her husband. Gwen was pictured as well, as was another young girl, a teenager. Another photo showed what could only be young Freddie Hardingham being pushed in a swing by his parents.

Now deceased. Poor guy.

Finding nothing but dead ends, Libby returned the bathroom to its normal state and then joined Gran Olive in the living room.

"Fred asked me for some stuff with his sister, Evelyn, in it. Like some pictures or memorabilia. He's always going on and on about the Thackers in the US. Got any picture albums or anything?"

Olive snorted. "Hmph. The whole lot's cracked. Cracked, I tell you. They leave London for America. I mean, who wants to live there with a bunch of loud and braggy Americans? Especially after Gwen. They leave! Evelyn and her husband are cracked, and it wouldn't surprise me if Alex isn't more bloody cracked than all of them."

"Alex?" Libby said.

"Evelyn's other daughter. Must be about fourteen now."

An awkward silence ensued. Then Olive brightened. "I do have something, though it's not much. Pretty stupid, really." She went behind the sofa and opened a dusty trunk that had an afghan covering it. Olive coughed as the hinges creaked. "Bloody dusty mess."

She returned with a thick photo album and plopped it into Libby's lap. Seconds after Libby began flipping through it, Olive pointed. "There!"

As Olive stood close to Libby, she was momentarily overtaken by the old woman's pungent perfume. Olive stabbed at a photo with her finger, and Libby leaned in close.

It was a picture of Evelyn and some strangers. One was a thin, kind-looking man in his thirties, an academic type. The other was a rotund woman with a severe expression and a military bearing. On the back in cursive was written "first meeting, 03/14/01."

Libby pulled out her phone and snapped a picture in HDR mode, then opened an app furnished by the Company. It allowed her to zoom in while increasing the resolution. Libby zoomed the picture in on the large, severe woman to read the monogram on her navy-blue uniform blazer. Then, turning off her phone, she sat back and mouthed the name she had just read: "Festermunder Academy."

Olive seemed to snap out of a trance as she turned to Libby with serious eyes. "That place, dearie . . . is evil."

Playing the dutiful houseguest and trying to respect Gran Olive as an elder, Libby had acquiesced to an overture to remain for dinner. It turned out to be an underwhelming affair consisting of Chinese takeout. Now Libby was frustrated with herself for being drawn into a conversation with Olive for several hours.

When Libby finally said goodnight to the old woman and made her way back onto Manchester Street, it was nearly 10:00 p.m., and it was already dark and bitterly cold. Few cars and even fewer pedestrians were out.

Damn! I'll never catch a trolley home now. Stupid me! Getting sucked into that old bag's kill zone.

Despite her regrets, Libby had learned a rather intriguing background of a school in the States where pupils were rumored to have disappeared and then turned up again. It was probably urban legend bollocks, but still, there were some interesting coincidences. Fred was missing in the US, and his sister, Evelyn, a former Op-3 operator, had had contact at one time with the headmistress of the school that was associated with paranormal disturbances and missing students. Plus, Fred's niece, Gwen, had gone missing in the UK.

Makes me wonder, what the bloody hell is Festermunder Academy? Libby thought. *And why did Olive call it evil? And just who is the other chap in that photo?*

Dressed in black yoga pants, a hoodie, scarf, and gloves, Libby strapped her bag around her body crossways and took off at a trot in the cold night air. Being alone after dark was not smart, and she knew it, but, as usual, Libby was aware of any and all threats.

As she jogged toward her flat in central London, Libby sensed she was not alone. It was a sixth sense that most special operators possessed, an innate ability to perceive threats.

Libby spun on her right heel and darted full speed into an alley to her left. Covering the one hundred yards into no time, she cut back left one block later and made another left. Having essentially reversed her course to come in behind her previous point, Libby peered around the corner into the gloom.

Just ahead under a streetlamp stood a figure. He appeared to be speaking to another person. The tall figure, clad in black with his arms crossed, spoke in guttural hushed tones. She felt she had seen him before near King's Cross.

Am I being tailed?

Libby crept down the street, remaining concealed behind parallel-parked cars. She didn't risk pulling her sidearm, as the sound of her working the action would reveal her position. Trusting herself not to breathe, Libby crept to one car length away from the two figures and then lay flat on her stomach, peeking out at them from under the car. Not daring to move, she listened as they spoke in hushed tones.

"No more games. Where?" the large one clad in black said, his voice deep.

"You must understand, I have no leverage. When I give you what you seek, you'll—"

"My master demands the truth. Where? I won't ask you again."

The smaller man seemed to falter. "Kingston upon Thames. A small place. Telegraph Cottage. I need assurances—"

"Be silent. The only thing you can be assured of is that I have further need of you. If I find you've lied, you'll be cast into the Shadow. What will I find at this location?"

The man's voice was filled with malice, making Libby shudder.

Who the hell is this?

"I have not lied, Luka. There is a captive portal there. Behind the cottage in the trees. An efferent, just like I said."

"Name me not, fool," Luka replied. "Not one more time."

"Be that as it may," the small man said, "I'm being tracked by agents from MI5, and there will be a tail. Will you just put down another one? That was a dirty trick you played on that poor fool Manafort. Killing will not win you more followers to your cause."

Manafort! He was with us at the Company. That nervous tech support guy? Dead?

Luka leaned into the other smaller man. "I have another who must be eliminated. You have seventy-two hours to find him. Then contact me." Luka reached into his black trench coat and pulled out a photo. "Be where you say you'll be, Geddings. You'll meet me at the captive portal when we have information of efferent usage from the targets from New York."

New York!

Luka held out his hand and seemed to disappear. Libby shrieked and recoiled in fear. She peered over the edge of the car and saw that Luka was indeed gone without a trace. As for Geddings, he was scurrying down the street.

Libby ran after him, but by then her adrenaline had worn off, and she lacked the energy to give chase. Feeling tired and hot, she was relieved when a taxi drove by, and she waved it down. Libby didn't feel safe until the taxi door was locked, and it sped away.

On a hunch, Libby pulled her phone out and accessed the London Department of Transportation web archive of traffic cameras. She found the Manchester Street camera and then looked for the date and approximate time.

Come on, damn it! It's got to be here! Gotcha!

Libby found the still pictures of the men in the street, but she was frustrated to discover their faces were concealed by the angle of the camera. She focused on the photo Luka handed to Geddings, using her MI5 app to increase the resolution. When the face in the photo finally came into focus, she gasped.

It was Frederick J. Hardingham.

CHAPTER 12

Shut the Way

THE SHIFT CAME SOON AFTER THE JUMP. BEATRIX HAD Malik and Ben in sight for only a few seconds during the fall. Then she felt pulled, sucked down into the void, and a slipstream of stars engulfed her. S

An explosion of silence followed, unlike anything Beatrix had experienced before. It terrified her. She was in a nightmare, but couldn't wake up, nor scream for help.

Then she heard a voice in her mind.

Let it in.

Unconsciously, Beatrix opened herself to the fear and let it in. At first, it felt like being stabbed with black sabers of terror, and she fought against it. Then the tenseness in her mind and body dissipated, followed by clarity.

The stars continued to explode past, forming continuous lines. Her fear gone, Beatrix became enraptured by freedom.

I'm flying!

Beatrix couldn't tell if she was accelerating or if the meridian was speeding past her.

She saw a white dot at the end of the slipstream and was hurtling toward it — or it was hurtling toward her. Either way, it was coming up with astonishing velocity.

I'll hit it!

The white dot became so large, it engulfed everything. Beatrix shielded her face with her hands as she disappeared into it.

Silence was all she knew. Feeling herself being sucked down, she saw the ground racing up to meet her.

This is it!

Beatrix clamped her eyes shut and prepared for the impact that would claim her life. But it never came. She opened her eyes.

Beatrix was lying in grass, staring up at the clearest sky she had ever seen. Although Beatrix couldn't see the sun, it warmed the air and the grass. She felt an irresistible urge to lie there and sleep, overcome by a sense of peace she had never known.

Beatrix sat and looked around. Hills and grass-covered pastures extended as far as she could see. A lone tree sat atop a hill in the distance.

As she scanned the skyline again, Beatrix noted a peculiarity. Above the tree in the distance was a small dark spot. Though barely perceptible, it was there nonetheless, hanging in the sky, small and motionless.

As Beatrix realized she was not at home, a gnawing fear began to grow in her belly.

Ben? Malik? This isn't where I'm supposed to be. Something has happened! I've been redirected somehow.

Beatrix got up and walked toward the distant tree. It stood large and withering against the fertile pastureland. Feeling energy she had never possessed before, Beatrix broke into a run.

When she reached the tree, she grasped its trunk, hoping the bark's rough texture would bring her back to her senses and break her from what surely was a dream. However, the moment she touched it, Beatrix was slammed with a force that sent her hurtling back into the void.

The slipstream was much faster this time. And there were voices. Thousands of voices. Some whispering. Some laughing. Some crying. One voice rose above the din.

"I am here. You're close."

The slipstream faded, and Beatrix saw the ground rising up, preparing once again for a crushing impact that never came.

The ground was rocky and devoid of vegetation. Beatrix was on a precipice. Hearing the clinking and banging of metal, she crawled forward and peered over the cliff. Then she gasped.

Hundreds of feet below stood a structure. Huge and menacing, it rose out of a narrow support stem and widened into a massive citadel complete with ramparts and battlements. A gun-metal gray castle that was incomprehensibly "backwards" in every way. Wider at the top than the bottom, it was obsidian and foreboding. Tiny orange lights illuminated windows along the walls.

Looking down at the valley floor, Beatrix saw a fog-covered hollow. The vegetation was a thorny bramble that looked impassable.

Then the voices began again. Cries and pleas riding on the air seemed to splinter in Beatrix's mind. Confusion reigned, but Beatrix assumed that in the woods below dwelled something that did not sleep.

Feeling an impulse to run, Beatrix turned to look behind her and saw that the black spot in the sky had moved, and was positioned right over her.

Beatrix closed her eyes as a voice pierced her thoughts. A man's voice. Calm and reassuring, the voice grew in her mind.

Forcing her eyes open, Beatrix found herself in a cave, luminescent with white-blue light from the cave floor. She was standing on ice. The light was coming through the ice and cast the entire chamber in a blue hue. The cave was flanked on all sides with stalagmites and stalactites hanging from the high ceiling. The chamber resembled a beautiful underground ice-skating rink, but it was not the least bit cold.

"Listen," the voice whispered.

"What?" Beatrix said, her voice ringing out but no echo returning.

"Shhh . . . listen."

"Where are you? Where am I?"

"Heed me. Listen, Beatrix."

Beatrix stood poised on the ice, waiting for more instructions.

"Beatrix!" the voice whispered, the sound reverberating all around her and inside her head. "Beatrix, I'm here!"

"Dad!" Beatrix cried.

"Beatrix!"

"Father!" Beatrix stammered.

"My child. It's you, Beatrix."

"Dad, where are you? I'll come for you. I have help—"

"There's no time."

"Where are you? Ben and I know the truth. We know about this place. We can get here. We can bring you back home." Beatrix began to cry.

"Shh . . . listen, please, Beatrix. For your sake, please heed these words. Do not come for me. I have failed, Beatrix. I am beyond the stars to you now. I am no longer your responsibility now."

"I don't understand. Why? Where are you? Just tell me."

"I can't. It's far too dangerous. I'm only a figment coming to you. Your responsibility is elsewhere. Just heed me. Don't under any circumstances come for me. Destroy it, Beatrix. The meridians. This place. Destroy it all. Close it all off. Shut the way."

"Will I see you again?" Beatrix stammered through her tears.

"Perhaps in the afterlife. Beyond the stars. I am part of another place. I can't return. Countless times, I have tried to come back across, and each time, I was trailed by the agents of the Black."

"What? Dad? What . . . what am I?"

"You? You are everything. Alpha and omega. You're all of it, Beatrix. It will take time to realize that. Trust your friends. Trust in Ben. Never under any circumstances shall you be estranged or removed from Ben. Let nothing tear the family asunder. Do you understand?"

"Don't go!"

"I must. Child, hear me. Your heart . . . it's a stone that hides a light deep down. Crack the stone! Crack it in two and then move it away!"

"What? I don't understand what that means." Beatrix was nearly hysterical, realizing the voice was fading.

"I love you. I'm sorry, Beatrix."

"For what?"

"Beatrix?"

"Yes?"

"Shut the way!"

Beatrix snapped out of her daze and opened her eyes, looking up at the starlit sky. She flipped onto her stomach and prepared to shimmy over to the precipice to view the citadel once more, but instead before her, she saw an ivy-covered stone cottage with dim lights coming through the closed drapes.

Footsteps approached from Beatrix's left, and she froze in fear. A figure crouched next to her, silhouetted by the stars. Beatrix heard the person's raspy breathing as they examined her. Then it lifted its head as if to speak. Beatrix cringed in fear.

"Holy crap! It's Beatrix! Where have you been?"

A flashlight popped on, and through the fog, Beatrix saw Malik's face.

"Shut off that sodding spotlight, ya bloody imbecile," Percival growled in his Scottish brogue.

Only then did Beatrix realize she had made it across to London safely with her friends.

CHAPTER 13

Telegraph Cottage

THEY GATHERED IN THE KITCHEN AROUND A LARGE WOODEN butcher-block island. All the shades and blinds had been drawn as if they could provide protection from the evils that might be lurking in the night. After Percival made doubly certain that no light could escape to the outside, he informed the others that they could turn on a few lamps. He went even went out into the backyard and across the street to be sure nary a photon could be seen.

After coming across the meridian, Percival had assumed the role of de facto commander of the little expedition until such time as the plan Beatrix had begun concocting was brought to fruition. Having experience with the meridians and the agents of Divide made him a natural choice as their tactical leader. The problem was, now that Montavani was no longer with them, they had no strategic leader, no one to define the objectives and strategy.

Beatrix, in particular, was puzzled at Montavani's behavior during their final few seconds in the Verge. She wondered what was being left out of the story and if it was for her benefit or her detriment. That age-old skepticism that had dominated Beatrix's mindset at Festermunder was raising its weary head regarding the old man. Now in London, Montavani's sage advice seemed worlds away from their new reality: across the world with no strategic vision, a motley crew trying to save the world but with no real idea how.

Lightheart, who had gone out an hour earlier to get provisions, returned with groceries and laid out a large honey-baked ham with trimmings on the table. Everyone was famished, and they all served up. Only Malik was disappointed, as he would not eat pork. Although he was not devout, he had standards. Beatrix was impressed.

"Alright," Percival said, "we need to move quickly before we're discovered. The particle accelerator is in Oxfordshire, fifty-six miles northwest of London. We should have no trouble gittin' there undiscovered. But we can't hope to git past the most basic security. I have other issues, but those can wait. Ideas?"

After a long pause, everyone looked at Beatrix. Feeling an urge to laugh at the ridiculousness of the current moment, she finally gave in. Alex also snickered, realizing the complete idiocy of the situation where a fourteen-year-old was going to plan an operation to steal the most powerful and well-guarded substance known to humankind. Lightheart frowned in confusion.

"Alright, that's enough!" Percival said. "I get it, you bloody fools. The old man has buggered us up right and proper."

"I think we should recon the place and see what ideas we come up with," Lightheart said.

"Eh!" Percival made a beeping sound like Lightheart had just given a wrong answer on a game show. "Negative, Professor, they film and scan everyone coming in and going out of there and then try to match them again based on thermal and visual algorithms. You'll get flagged. Nice thought, but try again, Elias."

"We need intel, I agree," Beatrix said, drawing everyone's attention back to her. "We can't go in blind, if we can even get in. We have to snoop around there somehow. Diamond Light Source does tours for schoolchildren as well as VIPs. Some of us could go in as part of a school tour and try to break off and get the lay of the land."

"The synchrotron is being shut down at the end of this week for routine checks and safety evaluations," Lightheart said. "That means we have two days to make a move."

"Two days? What the bloody hell?" Percival said. "On Christmas, for Pete's sake? Out of the question, we're aborting this manure pile right now!"

"My good man, please pipe down. We can come up with a—"

"Pipe down? Sodding pipe down? Who the hell are you to tell me to pipe down? You have no idea what we're up against here, Mr. Professor." Percival leaned in close, his nose almost touching Lightheart's. "Ever seen a man die? Hmm? Ever watched a friend tortured? A child lost?"

A skinny hand politely squeezed Percival's shoulder, followed by a nervous voice. "Sir, the children." Percival wheeled toward the voice and was chagrined to see Fred, cowering slightly in the face of the Scot's anger.

"I'm sorry," Percival said.

"Why do we have to go in the front door?" Malik asked. "Why can't we use a meridian to open a portal right there in the antimatter chamber?"

A snort from Percival was followed by a deep breath. He was intrigued.

Beatrix nodded to Malik. "Go on."

"Why not open a meridian to arrive at the time and place we desire? Dr. Montavani did that to the dog." Malik cast a nervous glance at Percival, who crossed his arms and raised his left eyebrow in disapproval. "We need that device. A rhythax—"

"Rythrax," Beatrix corrected.

"Which we seem to be lacking at this moment," Percival said, his anger swelling up again.

"Surely there's another," Malik said. "Or can't someone go back to the Verge and get the one from Gee? All we need is a lock of Beatrix's hair, right? Traversing the gap is instantaneous. Heck, you can go get it and have it on this counter in sixty seconds if you want."

"The meridian is one-way, Malik," Ben said. "Montavani said this was a one-way captive portal. We can't go back the way we came, right?" He looked at Lightheart and Percival for an answer. Lightheart sipped his water and eyed Percival as if one or both of them knew something that the rest of the group didn't.

"What?" Beatrix asked. "What aren't you telling us? We were told it was a captive portal from the Verge with no other options."

Lightheart looked at Beatrix for a full ten seconds before he replied. "That . . . that is not a hundred percent accurate. There are axonal and dendritic branches from many portals, and one exists from this meridian here."

"Oh really," Beatrix said. "Great. More secrets. How can we trust you when you withhold information from us?"

Percival sighed. "It's for your protection. To guard you against peril."

Bull crap. They don't want me to know stuff in case I fall into the wrong hands. This isn't about protection for me but for them against Seraphim. Also, not one person has made mention, save Ben and Malik, of why I came through the meridian later than the others.

"I know where there's a rythrax, Beatrix, and you do too," Ben whispered into her ear. She pulled back and looked at Ben in confusion. She thought about it, staring at her feet and racking her brain. Then Beatrix's eyes grew wide, and she looked at Ben, hoping he was wrong.

"Oh no," she said.

"Castle Glamis, Scotland."

Beatrix looked at Lightheart, who had overheard Ben, but he just looked at the boy with a peculiar gaze.

He doesn't know, Beatrix realized. *No one told him about Wendell and Scotland. Why would Montavani and Percival withhold that information?*

The plan was as simple as it was impossibly complex. Beatrix, Ben, and Percival would journey north to Glamis and attempt to infiltrate the castle and abscond with the rythrax. It was believed to be in the room where Wendell had experienced his disappearance. The "talisman" that Wendell manipulated to go into the Black, Percival confirmed, was indeed a type of rythrax or a hybrid thereof.

Concomitantly, Lightheart, Malik, Alex, and Fred would attempt a clandestine reconnaissance of the Diamond Light Source synchrotron facility. They reasoned that both operations were mutually supporting: one would be of no use without the successful implementation of the other. As always, when teams were being sorted, there were arguments and a near physical altercation involving Percival and Lightheart.

"A'right! That's it. No use in splittin' up Ben and Beatrix. They're together, obviously."

"Percival, I should go with them to Scotland. The Oxford mission will need your skill set with infiltrating security," Lightheart replied.

"They don't need a sodding 'skill set,'" Percival said, making imaginary quotation marks using his fingers. "They're observin' and reportin' the layout so we can find the chamber. And more besides, Elias, where Beatrix goes, I go. Are we clear, lad?"

"You're making yourself clear, but I wish to protest—"

"Tell it to Seppe when we get back. That's if we ain't dead in a week, which, at this point, the sodding forecast calls for highly likely! Enough! The Voght kids are going with me to Scotland. Besides, I'm from the Highlands, and I want to get a pint at the Green Griffin while I'm there."

The group laughed dutifully at Percival's failed attempt to lighten the tenseness.

"Elias, you take Alex and the wizkid (Malik) along with 007 over here to Oxford," Percival continued. "The plan is recon, right? Technical layouts would be ideal, but that's highly unlikely. Remember, lad, we need the location of the storage chamber for the antimatter. The stuff is no damn good to us if we don't have it in a form that can be transported. So, we need to know where it's kept. You hear? Not where it's made, but where it's stored."

Fred gulped and then nodded in reluctant agreement. Alex, as always, seemed purposeful and confident, which continued to puzzle Beatrix, her skepticism of her newfound friend continuing to fester. Malik was unhappy with being separated from his friends, but he didn't openly object, as he was tired of all the arguing and was scared of incurring Percival's wrath.

"Okay, we set out tomorrow. It's December 22, so we must make our move before Christmas Eve. I'll leave tonight with Ben and Beatrix, as the trip is eight to nine hours at least. Both DLS and Glamis have tours tomorrow but not the next day. We'll rendezvous on the twenty-fourth, in front of Westminster Abbey in Parliament Square. By the statue of Churchill. Are we clear? Questions?"

Everyone looked around the circle, but no one said anything. Then Ben, who was standing next to Fred, furrowed his brow. "What's that?"

"What's what?" Beatrix asked.

"That sound. Hear it?"

Ben scanned the room, then looked down at Fred's right coat pocket. Fred fished his phone from his pocket. It was vibrating. He thought he had turned it off. Fred held his phone up, staring at it. He was about to see who had texted him when Percival plucked it from Fred's hand.

Everyone froze. Lightheart covered his mouth with his hand. "Oh my God. No."

"This phone was to remain off," Percival said through clenched teeth.

Fred was incredulous. "It . . . it was off. Oh my! Oh my . . ."

"What? What? Good man, tell us?" Lightheart said.

"My work phone. It must have been auto-activated. It's a safety mechanism for agents off the grid. It means . . ."

"It means we're being sodding tracked!" Percival said. He turned to Beatrix. "We need to leave." Looking around and seeing everyone staring at him, Percival's eyes and nostrils flared. "Now! Two minutes, grab your stuff and any food you can, and we're bloody off."

Percival handed a sum of cash to Lightheart. "Go. No credit cards and no phone calls. All phones off. That's O-F-F! Use only paper money or coins. Meet in Parliament Square tomorrow evening at eight o'clock. We can be tracked anyhow. They have infiltrated law enforcement and government. Don't trust anyone who claims to be a cop! By the way . . ."

Percival threw Fred's phone onto the floor and stomped on it until it was a useless pile of electronic components. Then he slung his bag over his shoulder and stuck his face within inches of Fred's face. "Take care of those children, Hardingham. They're your responsibility."

Looking at Lightheart, Percival shook his head as if to express the futility of the situation and then stalked off.

Malik and Beatrix stood in the hall, speaking quietly. Malik was close to crying, wishing he could go with his friends.

"Tomorrow night, Malik," Beatrix said, trying to calm him. "We'll be back tomorrow night."

She held her hand in front of Malik, and he grabbed it. She covered his hand with hers. "It'll be alright, Malik. We'll be apart one day, that's all. See you in the Square."

Beatrix smiled and nodded, then walked out back where Ben, who had taken several minutes to say goodbye to Alex, was waiting with Percival.

Malik slumped against the wall and closed his eyes for a few seconds, snorted his runny nose, then joined Fred, Lightheart, and Alex for their journey to Oxford.

Libby was lying on the couch with Henry, her cat, watching the news on TV. Two journalists with opposing views were arguing with increasing vehemence. Half awake, Libby switched to another channel that featured the local news and listened to it with her eyes closed.

"MI5 agent disappears, and the family fears the worst," a reporter said.

Libby slipped out of her dream-like state, rubbed her eyes, and sat up as the reporter continued to expound on the story, saying there were anonymous reports of several missing agents.

Manafort. Hardingham!

Henry settled himself on Libby's lap as if to say, "Go back to sleep." Libby yawned and rubbed her eyes and cheekbones. At that moment, 1:14 a.m. on December 22, her phone pinged with a new message. It was encrypted from the Company.

More rubbish, she thought, then immediately realized this message was different. An app was launched called TRACE-XR, and Libby watched as a file autonomously imported into a folder from MI5. Libby yawned as she waited for the message to decode. When it was complete, it read:

S16-SA-0415

Libby's heart jumped into her throat. The coded message was simple to interpret. Section 16 Special Agent 0415 was Frederick J. Hardingham.

Oh my, he's back on the grid!

Another ping and another message had Libby standing and reaching for her trainers and her sidearm.

S16-SA-0415 GPS trace
1612 Brentwood Avenue
Telegraph Cottage
Northwest London, 76543-2871
1:14 a.m. local time

Libby tore through her closet, looking for additional clothes and personal items. Racing into the powder room, she grabbed a toothbrush but was so flustered, she dropped it in the toilet.

"Bloody bollocks!"

She blasted through the kitchen and grabbed some bottled water and protein bars, stashing them in a book bag. She turned on Henry's auto feeder and gave him a quick scratch. "Back soon, old boy, okay?"

Libby sped downstairs to the street and then decided to take the bus rather than her government vehicle.

The less the Company knows about this, the better.

Ever vigilant, she scampered down to the train station and was relieved to see no one waiting on the platform. She was even more relieved to see that the train was full of revelers coming home from a concert at the O2 Arena.

Libby plopped down at the back of the train so that no one could position themselves behind her and read her phone. She was taking no chances this time and became increasingly alarmed the more she thought about her predicament.

Alright, Hardingham is back in London. I must find him and bring him in. God knows what he's done back in the US, but we're tethered together now that I stuck my bloody nose into this situation.

Libby looked up and thought about the ripple effect of the last thirty-six hours, and her heart filled with dread.

If I don't find Hardingham before those fellows on the street do, he's dead. They got Manafort. The poor bloke doesn't stand a chance.

Thinking it over, Libby understood now. The ping was autonomous upon his return to the UK. It went out to all the operations agents and, undoubtedly, the IS-1 people.

The men on the street knew where he would be. How? Has IS-1 been compromised? What is Hardingham into? Telegraph Cottage, Northwest London. They knew he would be there. "The travelers from New York would arrive on the captive portal." What the bloody hell is that?

One thing Libby knew was that she did not want any part of the Hardingham situation as it was. But she thought that perhaps she could remedy it by her investigation of the matter as well as bringing Hardingham safely into custody at MI5.

While at the same time finding out who the hell these people are and what their interest is in our agents!

As the outskirts of town whisked by and the train moved northwest of town, Libby had a disturbing thought.

I opened that bloody message! I'm just as trackable as anyone. I've talked to no one about this situation except . . . oh bloody hell, old lady Olive! Surely, she's far enough removed from this to be safe. Surely . . . Bollocks!

The bell on the train sounded at the hub where Libby needed to get off. She surveyed the train, but other than some teen boys smiling at her, which she ignored, everything looked normal. Libby exited the train and trotted the three blocks to Telegraph Cottage.

Looking across the street, Libby recognized the tall, skulking frame of her red-headed quarry. Then, as inconspicuous as possible, she followed him and his three companions onto another trolley.

Fred, Malik, Alex, and Lightheart, who was growing increasingly troubled, had a predicament. Their train left for Oxfordshire the next morning at 11 a.m. local time and would basically carry them to the doorstep of the Diamond Light Source Facility. However, in the mad rush to leave Telegraph Cottage, they forgot they had nowhere to go for the night. So, they boarded a trolley and decided to ride it until they figured out a solution.

Huddled on the trolley, whose only inhabitants were the sort of "night people" who frightened Malik but meant no harm to anyone, they spoke in hushed tones. The stress of the situation, laid bare now that the adrenaline had worn off following Percival's edict to vacate the cottage, began to manifest itself under the trolley's stark fluorescent lights. They were also out of sorts, as none of them felt comfortable without the habitual pastime of taking out their cell phones and checking social media. After Fred's mistake with his phone at Telegraph Cottage, the others dared not turn theirs on, fearing they could be tracked.

"What do we do now? Just stay on this trolley all night?" Malik asked. "I'm hungry, and there's no bathroom."

Lightheart sighed and shook his head like a man who'd been given a job, and his heart was not in it.

"Uncle Freddie, your flat? Where do you live? Let's go there," Alex said as she rubbed her hands together and then cupped them in front of her mouth, blowing on them to warm them.

"Uh, um, well, we could. It's just that, uh . . ."

"What is it, Uncle Fred?" Alex asked.

"Well, I don't have my own place right now. I'm residing with family in Hackney."

Lightheart, who had been looking out the window, turned and looked at him. "Is it secure? Who do you live with, man?"

"My grandmother. She's a brilliant old bird, but I think it best if we stay away from her place. She would be quite riled to see us all roll in, in the middle of the night."

"Please, I beg you, just take us there!" Malik said. "I need a place to lie down, and I really wouldn't mind a shower. Professor Lightheart, please just say yes."

Lightheart was surprised that Malik had addressed his plea to him when the imposition was clearly on Fred.

As kind and clueless as ever, Fred didn't seem to notice. "Alright, but this is my sweet gran, and we'll have to be quiet going in there. With any luck, she'll be asleep at this hour anyway." Fred turned to Alex. "She would love to see you. You're her great-niece and she loves to see family. But I think it best if we just slip in and out unnoticed."

The group had to transfer trolleys two times but finally made it to Fred's grandmother's neighborhood of Hackney (the dodgy end).

All the while, they failed to notice an amber-haired, stocking-capped young woman with a slight build following them. She was wearing leggings and trainers with a book bag over her shoulder and sat concealed on the trolley several rows behind them. She had heard every word they said. Shockingly, she had been to that very address in Hackney the day before.

The Oxford-bound party stole up the stoop of 12-B Manchester Street. Ice had formed on the steps, and Fred nearly slipped.

"Careful! Careful," he whispered as harshly as his persona could muster (which wasn't much). "Now, please be as quiet as possible, and we may not wake her. Oh, and step where I step as certain floorboards tend to creak!"

When the door to the flat swung open, the group was greeted by a waft of air that smelled like the homes of elderly, a mixture of moth balls and soup.

"It smells like old people in here," Malik whispered. Alex suppressed a giggle.

"Shh," Fred implored. "Please be quiet. Gran will hear us."

The others crept behind Fred as he led them to his bedroom, mindful to step exactly where Fred stepped in his exaggerated manner as if he were showing them the path through a deadly minefield. Only when Fred closed the door to his room did he relax. Alex plopped onto his bed, and the others stood with eyebrow-raising expressions that made Fred uncomfortable.

Fred proved to be a good host. One by one, with Malik going first, he ushered them to the bathroom and gave them fresh linens. He even provided each of them with a toothbrush from his personal supply, and when they voiced they were hungry, Fred snuck to the kitchen and brought them snacks, for which they were most grateful. Then he turned on a fan to create white noise, so they could talk.

"I need to get Moresby fed before long," Fred muttered to no one.

Lightheart raised his eyebrows. "Who's Moresby?"

"Me cat." Fred said it with such longing in his voice that it made Alex giggle. Not realizing he was the butt of a joke, he continued. "We should get a little rest. We can wake at seven and be off before Gran gets up to go to spin class."

They spread blankets on the floor and soon everyone but Malik drifted off to whatever sleep would come.

Malik lay awake, reflecting on the events of the last several days. It seemed like a lifetime ago that he got the okay from Ben, through the telescope, to join them in Central Park. Now he was in London via the space-time continuum and on the run from evildoers and British law enforcement. He wondered what Beatrix was doing at that moment.

As he gazed at the shadows the Venetian blinds made on the ceiling due to the streetlamp outside, Malik noticed a figure pass through his field of vision. Turning toward the window, Malik blinked several times but saw nothing. He relaxed somewhat yet found himself slinking down farther into his sleeping bag.

Then it happened again. On the ceiling, Malik saw the shadow of a figure. It was a man in a hat. He stood there on the sidewalk, his shadow stretching up the wall and across the ceiling of Fred's room. Malik felt the figure's presence even when he shut his eyes, realizing he had felt the same presence in the library at Festermunder when they were attacked and then again in the street outside Alex's house in Queens. Malik was a seasoned expert on fear, a veritable connoisseur. And at that moment, he was petrified. But this fear was different. It was cold. It made his bones hurt. Paralyzed, Malik couldn't bear to look at the Hat Man's shadow, but he couldn't look away either.

"Hey," he whispered. "Hey!" Only then did he realize he wasn't making a sound, his mouth having gone completely dry.

Suddenly, the Hat Man turned to his left as if something had caught his attention. When the Hat Man turned to walk that way, Malik finally broke free of his fright and dared to stand up and peek through the crack in the blinds.

"It's him," he whispered, still not making a sound. The man was tall and dressed in black. Malik knew immediately that he was looking at one of them. The Hat Man stepped aside to position himself behind a van as another figure approached. It was an elderly lady who was sashaying to the music in her headphones as she walked down the sidewalk with a cat.

Malik returned his gaze to the menacing figure who stood out of the old lady's view behind the van. The boy felt a lump of fear in his throat, mixed with empathy for the old lady who was about to be a hapless victim.

Just as the two were about to meet on their collision course, Malik was startled by a shrill sound from the opposite side of the sidewalk. He ducked down until his eyes were barely over the windowsill.

"Hey, you!" a younger woman yelled. Her voice was high pitched but brimming with authority and venom.

The Hat Man wheeled back toward the woman, who had darted to her left between parallel-parked cars. Then he turned back to his original prey, who was still dancing down the sidewalk, oblivious to the threat, though her cat was hissing at the Hat Man.

An explosion of broken glass was followed by a wailing sound. The woman had broken a window in a parked car, and its alarm was blaring. After taking a moment to weigh his options, the Hat Man disappeared in a cloud of black soot.

The woman materialized from between cars and crouched, poised like a tiger protecting its cubs. She appeared to have a weapon concealed in the small of her back.

When she approached the old lady, who finally looked up, the old lady appeared to recognize the stranger. Malik was stupefied by the exchange, which was made even more incongruous when the old lady produced a key and began to unlock the very apartment in which Malik and his companions were hiding, inviting the younger woman inside as well.

"Oh crapola," Malik whispered.

"What is it?" Fred asked, startling Malik.

"The old lady was out. She just came in. Your grandmother—"

"What? Oh, bugger! We're done for! Gran Olive's about!" Fred shrieked.

"Shhh!" Malik hissed. "She has someone with her."

"Someone's with her? Is it a man?" Fred asked in disgust. "I knew it. I say, 'Gran, it's time to settle down and stop trying to meet these strange old geezers,' but—"

"No! It's a lady. A jogger from the street. She's just come in after—"

"What's going on?" Lightheart asked, awakened by the commotion. Alex was awake as well.

"I beg you all," Fred replied, "please be quiet. For the love of all things sacred, my gran can't know what's going on. She's fragile and old and doesn't need this. I implore you, let me handle this, and please stay quiet!"

As soon as he stopped talking, they heard the young woman's voice. "Thank you very much, Olive. I'll just be a bit." They heard the bathroom door across the hall shut and the fan turn on.

Alex and Lightheart were standing with Malik in the middle of Fred's bedroom, listening. That's when the door to Fred's room creaked open, and all four of them came face-to-face with Special Agent Libby Soames-Briggs.

Fred was speechless. The woman was dressed in black stretch pants, white trainers, a dark blue hoodie, and a black sock hat. Locks of amber-red hair stuck out of her hat, and her fierce green eyes burned holes into him. She stood there with her hands on hips, eyeing the group with a mixture of suspicion and contempt. Everyone was transfixed on her, not knowing what to say, as they dared not compromise the mission.

Without preamble, the woman sprang forward and slapped Fred across the face.

"Ow!" he cried, recoiling as he held a hand to his cheek.

"Cheeky bastard," the woman said as she straightened herself up. "Special Agent Elizabeth Soames-Briggs, MI5. This gentleman is now in my custody. We'll—"

"What's all this? Ha! Freddie. My dear little Freddie is back!" Gran Olive slipped past Libby into the crowded room and kissed Fred on the same cheek that was still smarting from the slap.

Libby fell silent as if wanting to spare Olive the embarrassment of arresting her grandson right in front of her. Lightheart in particular, stood there with his mouth agape. He was incredulous that just three hours after Percival's rapid deployment order, they had been compromised by an eighty-four-year-old ballroom dancer and an MI5 agent.

When Percival, Ben, and Beatrix made it to the cavernous Paddington Station, Percival ushered the others into a small alcove next to a closed coffee shop. It provided concealment and allowed them to see who was coming and going. He provided them with blankets from his pack and told them to rest on the benches while he took first watch. Their train would not depart for two hours, and he had no intention of being seen by security cameras. They could be tracked by the forces of good and evil, with the result being negative either way.

As they settled down, Beatrix giggled.

"What?" Ben asked, his eyes just barely visible over his blanket, though she could still tell he was smiling.

"Me? Oh, nothing. I was just thinking about Montavani and this whole thing we're involved in. Doesn't it seem surreal? Like, last week, I was just a kid trying to eke my way through life, and now I'm—"

"The world's last hope?"

Beatrix scoffed, then realized Ben was serious.

"Ben, I'm not anything. In fact, I'm nothing. And you know what. Now that I've been told I'm something, I'm determined more than ever to go back to being nothing—I mean nobody. As soon as this is over, I'm—"

"When this is over?" Ben said. "Beatrix, I don't think we're both meant to be here for the aftermath. I . . . I've had dreams. Like, it's hard to explain, but I've this sense that I'm not here for the long haul."

"Hey! Quit with that crap, okay? Enough! I'm done with it, Ben! We all have dreams. They aren't meant to be taken literally. I swear half my dreams don't seem like mine anyway. They seem like invasions into my psyche, or I'm just crazy. I hear songs. I see visions, like freaking hallucinations. . . ."

"What?" Ben asked. A sense of familiarity came over his face, his interest piqued.

"Ben, what happened to us? You know, when we were little. I can't explain it, but I seem to have memories that I know aren't mine. And more recently . . ." Beatrix paused and looked down, then at Ben. He waited for the next part, poised on a precipice of curiosity. "Because you aren't in them."

Ben sat up on the bench and leveled his gaze on Beatrix. "Can I ask you something?

Beatrix raised her eyebrows as if to tell Ben to continue.

Ben breathed in and out and closed his eyes, then opened them again. "Beatrix . . . how do you know that we're brother and sister?"

CHAPTER 15

Questionable Quests

THE TRIO BOARDED THE EUROSTAR TRAIN FOR THE NORTH-bound journey. Built in 2002, the Eurostar was capable of speeds up to 186 mph from London to Edinburgh. That meant the trip to Edinburgh from Paddington Station would take just over two and a half hours. That would give the group plenty of time to rest, Percival having purchased the last remaining private club car ticket.

As the train sped away from Paddington, Beatrix checked her watch. It was 4:14 a.m. They would be in Edinburgh by 7:00 at the latest. Then an hour-and-a-half car ride to Dundee and onward a few miles to Castle Glamis—plenty of time for her to reflect on Ben's supposition that maybe they weren't brother and sister.

Entranced by the city lights whipping by, Beatrix pondered her origin while Ben slept. He was in the opposite corner of the rear-facing dark-green seat across from her. Percival slid the translucent pocket door closed and then turned the light off before taking a seat across from Beatrix. She offered him a feeble smile, then let her thoughts drift.

"Not sleepy?" Percival asked, his voice soft so as not to wake Ben.

"Tired? Yes. Exhausted? Yes. Sleepy? No."

"It's hard sometimes," Percival muttered.

"What is?" Beatrix asked, her gaze fixed on the blur of city lights flowing past the train window.

"Everything," Percival replied. "All of this is focused on you."

Beatrix finally met his gaze, nodding for him to continue. Percival took a deep breath, then rubbed his face with his hands, as if preparing something. "What did Seppe tell you about me? Where I come from? Why I'm here?"

Beatrix shook her head. "I don't know. Nothing, really. Just something about there being an emergency. He said he made you come back here. For me."

"That old fool. Always speaking in riddles and partial truths. Not lies, mind you. Just carefully constructed omissions. He's always been that way."

The cabin was dark by then, except for the dim light from the small outer hall projecting through the translucent door. As the city lights sped by, it started to rain. An eerie feeling descended over the train car. Ben turned into the corner, cocooned in his gray wool blanket, and slept on.

"So, what happened?" Beatrix asked.

Percival removed his glasses and cleaned them on his flannel shirt. For the first time ever, he seemed not wholly comfortable. "We were discovered, all of us. The Keepers of the Faith. Exposed. Laid bare to him."

"Seraphim?"

"Yes," Percival whispered. "A name that I won't utter here. But yes. It was him. We had been working on a plan to send the simulacra back to the Above to warn others — the scientists, the inventors — that they were being targeted. We had names, but we had no time! We couldn't get organized. And incredibly, we could only send back simulacra of those who had been taken. Just like Wendell after Scotland. People wouldn't believe them or think they were slap crazy, just like Wendell. If we send back a replicant and an original remained in the World Above, they would be unwritten. You understand? The Taken were the key. Their simulacra could go back but were basically running amok. They were like . . . signal flares. Flares being shot at random with no meaning. On their face many of the 'mentally unstable' aren't that at all, just incomplete simulacra we call anaphora.

"We were afraid we'd be discovered. Rumors circulated that the

Mechanix had penetrated our underground, and no one could be trusted. Great men and women were taken and cast into the Black merely on the basis of suspicion! These were beautiful souls, Beatrix, lost forever in a captive portal. To an infinity that we can't define. Sealed and unwritten for eternity in a lost dimension of space-time. A fate far worse than death or any other contrivance of the agents of the Black."

"Sending back the replicas? The simulacra? What was your and Dr. Montavani's part in this? I don't understand."

"Don't forget that I'm a scientist myself, young lady." Percival smiled and grabbed the lapels of his velvet blazer in mock pride. "We had — Seppe and I, that is — stolen away with the closely guarded secrets of how to prime a simulacrum and prepare it for its passage back to the Above. These steps were known only to the closest agents of the Master himself, the progenitors who knew how to harness and manipulate stellar material and cosmic elements. We had the technology and the know-how to send back copies of the Taken. There was nothing else we could do, Beatrix! We were desperate. We needed to get word back somehow to the World Above. We knew no one would understand except for a few. At first, we thought that fool who left the writings behind was going to lead others into a trap, but it turned out his manuscripts were meant to warn people."

"Whose writings? Dr. Montavani's?"

"No. Wendell Voght's."

"Wendell? He was warning people?"

Shut the way.

"Not people, Beatrix. He was warning you. You must understand that while he was off 'saving the world,' he was a trifle unbalanced."

"Where is he now?" Beatrix asked. "Montavani wouldn't say."

"He's gone, girl. Taken. Cast into some far-off place."

"Like the others? Unwritten?"

"No. He was removed from the others and taken off to . . . him. We have not seen him since."

Seraphim has Wendell. Great. The one place I need to go to find him is the one place I shouldn't go. The dream. Wendell said to "shut the way."

"This still doesn't add up," she said. "Where do I come into the story? Why were you sent back to accompany me? What was the emergency?"

"It was your . . . foster father, or whatever you call him. Wendell. When he was taken off to the Deep, we feared that you could be taken as leverage here in this world. The Mechanix were looking under every stone and taking no chances. Seppe had no time whatsoever. The agents of the Black were in our hiding place, and we were at risk of being discovered, so he took some of my DNA and used the rythrax and a poor mongrel. Well, you saw the result. I was sent to look after you and to take every opportunity to keep you away from the meridians, but you discovered them anyway."

Then another question sprang to life in her head. "Why was Wendell targeted and taken? What was he doing that was so important that he had to be taken straight to Seraphim?"

Percival raised his eyebrows in disapproval. "Wendell had many pursuits that were unnatural. For one, he was gallivanting around the cosmos, looking for something that he would not speak of, and he was helping us at the same time. Wendell was a convert to our cause. It was Wendell, Seppe, and me who were leading the underground. We wanted to end the whole thing once we realized Seraphim's true aim — enslavement."

"How were you going to achieve your goals, though? You can't destroy Seraphim. Montavani said that's not even a remote possibility."

Percival shifted in his seat and hesitated before he spoke. "We were, uh, constructing a, uh, a counter to Seraphim. An aggressive defense. We had gained forbidden access to stellar material and began using it for our cause."

"For what?" Beatrix asked. The train lurched as it slowed on the outskirts of Edinburgh, the first leg of the journey coming to an end. "What was Wendell helping you make?"

Percival shifted in his seat again. "A weapon."

The commotion quieted as Fred escorted Gran Olive into the kitchen and took a moment to explain things. Surprisingly, Gran was enthused that Libby was there to arrest him and take him down to Thames House. She thought the situation was grand and exciting, unconcerned that

Libby had used a false name when she interviewed her earlier. "I use the name Victoria when I'm on a first date myself."

"Gran, please understand! I have no idea what's going on. I want you to be as far removed from this business as possible. Do you hear me?" Fred asked as Gran continued her failed effort to light the pilot light on the stove to make tea.

"Oh, you and your bloody caution! Never mind about me. Now, Freddie"—Olive smiled—"she's quite the brilliant bird, isn't she?"

Olive was excited at the prospect of having intrigue, danger, and houseguests—one of whom was bearing an arrest warrant.

Moresby growled as Libby entered the kitchen, trailed by Lightheart. "Right, Special Agent Frederick J. Hardingham, I'm Special Agent Libby Soames-Briggs, MI5. I'm now placing you in my custody." Libby produced a pair of handcuffs. "Am I going to need these?"

Fred swallowed, his Adam's apple bobbing. "No, ma'am." Then a most peculiar thing happened that Fred never could have portended. He made a most mundane comment. "Soames? Like the soap?"

Libby rolled her eyes at Fred with a look of pure disgust. "What?"

"Gilchrist and Soames. The hotel soap."

"Charming," Libby said with a sneer. "Right, we need to evacuate this place immediately, and I'm taking you with me."

"What about the rest of us?" Lightheart asked.

Libby looked him up and down, clearly unimpressed with the academic. "That's none of my concern. And who are you, by the way?"

"Elias P. Lightheart, professor of history at Festermunder Academy in New York, New York."

"Listen here, Professor, I don't give a right blue damn about you or your—" Libby caught herself mid-sentence. "Festermunder? What the bloody hell is going on here?" Libby wheeled on Fred. "Hardingham. Who are these children?"

Though six feet, four inches tall, Fred was clearly intimidated by the five-foot-one agent. "They . . . they're students. Students at Festermunder School. My niece is one of them. Neither of the kids have done anything wrong."

Libby was unmoved by Fred's request for clemency. However, she also had a responsibility to keep civilians safe, especially children. Standing in front of the stove with her arms folded and her brow furrowed, she hatched a plan.

"Right. We're going to sort this bloody thing out, but not here. That godawful thing will be back. You." Libby pointed at Lightheart.

"Ma'am?" he replied with instinctive obedience.

"Gather the kids out on the back patio. We'll skip through the back garden to the side street. I have to get you all on the subway." She turned to Fred. "You! You will not leave my side." Then they turned to Gran Olive, her tone softening, "Ma'am, is there anywhere we can drop you that's safe? Is there someone you can trust?"

Olive was texting without looking up. "Wait a tick."

Fred rolled his eyes and shrugged at the futility of the situation.

"Right. My best girlfriend, Muffet, will be picking me up in five minutes." Olive smiled, pleased with herself.

"Oh my, Gran! Old lady Muffet is ninety!" Fred shrieked. "She can't drive. She's certifiable at this point. Pete's sake, anyone but her!"

"It's settled then," Libby said, ignoring him. "We go out the back on my signal. Olive goes with her friend. We'll escort her to her ride. Everyone stays in a tight group, and no spreading out. I mean it. Anyone runs, I have a Taser and I'll drop you." She said the last part looking at Fred, then Lightheart.

Libby removed her sweatshirt and tightened her hair tie. Fred swallowed thickly when he noticed her arm muscles, which were far more defined than his.

"Standard two-by-two cover formation just like in *Die Hard*?" a voice said from behind Lightheart.

"Who the bloody hell are you?" Libby asked.

"Malik Patel at your service," he said, bowing low.

"That'll be enough, Malik," Alex said; then she nodded at Libby, who ignored her as well.

"Okay, that's it. We—"

Suddenly, an explosion rocked the little house. The air itself seemed to shake and bend in slow motion before it was sucked out of the apartment. None of its occupants could hear, temporarily deafened and disoriented. There was no fire, just a concussive blast. Dust filled the air, obscuring their vision. The front door had exploded into thousands of splinters.

Outside, two dark figures were standing on the street. One was wearing a hat. He pulled an object out his pocket and walked up the steps.

It was the Hat Man, and he was coming for them.

But Libby Soames-Briggs was already moving.

No one noticed earlier that knowing they might have to make a stand in the apartment, Libby had turned on the unlit burners to leak gas when she had stood in front of the stove — 12-B Manchester Street was now a primed 1,300-square-foot hand grenade. She had only to pull the pin.

"Don't just stand there! Out the back, you bloody fools!" Libby screamed. Lightheart and Fred responded by pushing the kids out the back.

As the Hat Man's footfalls thudded up the stairs, Libby's heartbeat matched each one. He walked slowly and methodically, like the Grim Reaper himself. There was no hurry in his pace, only inevitability.

"Take cover!" Libby yelled as she flew out the back door. "Run on my signal!"

The Hat Man was heading down the back hallway of the flat, now only forty feet away.

"What signal?" Fred hollered.

Cradling something in her sweatshirt, Libby landed on her side and rolled into a crouching position, simultaneously removing her Taser. It crackled to life with purple-blue sparks. Locking the trigger in place with her hair elastic, Libby stood up and threw the sparking Taser through the open back door, right toward the Hat Man's face.

The blast was deafening and far more explosive than Libby had predicted. Blue-green flames coursed throughout the house, consuming the Hat Man. The back of 12-B Manchester Street simply no longer existed. The home itself had been blown in two. The street rocked, and the ground shook like jelly.

"My goodness, woman, you just blew up me gran's house!" Fred cried. "My poor Moresby. You just killed me cat! Oh, Moresby! Blown to bits." Fred began to sob.

He was greeted by a furry feline mass (quite alive) thrown at him by

Libby. "You're welcome," she said as she slid past Fred and opened the back gate. "Hurry. To the street and directly across to the train station."

"It's too dangerous," Lightheart protested. Libby surprised them all by agreeing, appearing temporarily off balance. But then she recovered and urged them all to get moving. They poured out the gate and traversed several more back gardens to the curb.

Across the street sat an ambulance with its lights off. There was no sign of old lady Muffet.

"Why not the subway?" Malik asked.

"Shut up!" Libby snapped. "Let me think!"

Lightheart tapped her on the shoulder. "Excuse me, ma'am?"

"Shhh!" Libby spat.

"My God! Look!" Lightheart pointed across the street.

"Oh no!" Alex whispered.

Incredibly, Gran Olive, whom no one had realized was missing until then, had given them the slip and was standing across the street peeking in the windows of the ambulance. It was parked in front of Fluffy Clouds Convalescent Home, a place that Gran Olive had frequented until she was banned for unspecified indecent behavior.

Olive scurried over to the hideout. "The lorry over there, it's always parked out front in case one of the old bags stayin' there pops an artery or blows a hip. It was unlocked." Olive produced a key.

Libby was energized at the find. She was also impressed that the eight-four-year-old woman from Hackney was the only member of the group with any ingenuity. Suddenly, a car approached—on the wrong side of the road. Its stereo was booming, clearly audible even though the windows were up.

"That'll be Muffet! Toodle-loo!" Gran Olive said as she tossed the ambulance key to Libby. She hugged Alex, then pulled Fred down and kissed his cheek. "Love you, dear Freddie. Proud of you." Last of all, she whispered something in Libby's ear. Libby gave the old woman a quiz-zical look as Olive walked toward the car. The door opened, and "Night Fever" by the Bee Gees blared before the door closed and the car sped away, once again down the wrong side of the road.

"Bye, Gran," Fred said, his voice somber.

"Let's get out of her before the police show up!" Libby commanded

"To the ambulance. You're with me," she said, pointing at Lightheart. "You three in the back," she added, indicating Alex, Malik, and Fred.

They dashed across the street to the ambulance. By then, it was 5:45 a.m., and day would break soon. Alex, Malik, and Fred got in the back, but not before Malik protested, saying something about bathrooms and claustrophobia. Ignoring him, Libby slammed the door behind him.

Climbing into the cab, she looked at Lightheart. "Alright. Where to?"

"Oxfordshire," he replied with trepidation.

Libby programmed the GPS to the location Lightheart had specified. Then the ambulance sped off.

On the other side of the dark street, the Hat Man picked up his charred and smoking fedora off the ground. He placed it on his head before he and another man slid into an unmarked vehicle. Blacker than the night itself, the car eased away from the curb, following the ambulance. Speed mattered not. It was being tracked.

In Edinburgh, Percival, Ben, and Beatrix rented a car for a hefty price, as they did not want to use a credit card. To guarantee the cash-only transaction was untraceable, the rental dealer was the essence of shady. Even the rental company's name, Best Bet Rentals, portended a feeling of hurried unreliability and a no questions asked mentality. Who else would be open twenty-four hours a day?

In a small sedan, they sped onto the M90 highway, embarking on the two-hour trip to Dundee. Percival drove while the two children slept, classical music by Wagner playing on the car radio.

When they arrived in Dundee, they left the car in a parking lot and boarded a tour bus to Glamis, which was seventeen miles away. Percival seemed stressed, continually watching the other people on the bus. Beatrix picked up on it but said nothing.

The weather had grown cold, the sun retreating behind the clouds in typical Scottish fashion.

The castle seemed to burst into view from the lifting gloom, taking

Beatrix's breath away. Though reaction wasn't the product of excitement or exhilaration. It was fear.

Following Wendell's disappearance, Beatrix had studied the legends about the place. One story was burnt into her mind—the Monster of Glamis. A family who lived in the castle had a child who was born with hideous birth defects. They hid the deformed child in a room deep within the castle, feeding it through a dumbwaiter system, never letting it out, not even in adulthood.

When he died, they walled off his room, his existence disappearing into legend. It was said that at night a single candle could be seen from the outside of the castle, but no one was able to access that room. It had been shut off from the world.

Shut the way.

Beatrix thought the legend a convenient means of hiding access to something else that no one wanted found. She also had another thought. *Glamis might have been built on a meridian to guard it. Just like Festermunder! Oh, crap!*

"Check the basement," Beatrix muttered.

"What?" Percival asked.

"Nothing," Beatrix replied, not realizing she had spoken the thought aloud.

The bus rolled to a stop in the roundabout, and the passengers filed out, then entered the castle's antechamber. Their guide, Mr. Oseary, issued instructions to the group of twenty or so vacationers.

It was critical they give Oseary and the other tourists the slip, or they would never make it deep into Glamis to find what they were looking for.

Mr. Oseary conferred with another man whose back was turned to them, then returned to address the group. "As it's the last day we're open before Christmas, we're on a skeleton staff here, so we'll allow groups to tour the castle without a guide. However, we must have you all back by four o'clock, as we close at five. Please respect our protocols, and good day to you."

The man to whom Mr. Oseary had been talking went into the administrative office and began texting on a cell phone. Then he looked up through the glass partition straight at Beatrix. Beatrix got a queasy feeling in her stomach she did not understand, and her mouth went dry. She urged Ben and Percival into the castle.

The phone chimed. A man with light skin and a dark beard looked down and read the message.

The girl.

He sent a reply:

Don't let them leave.

He was tired of dealing with that fool, Nigel Geddings. The man had no idea why Luka hadn't disposed of the witless worm on many occasions before. He extinguished his cigarette and sped up the highway. The trip from Dundee's outskirts would only take half an hour. He had them.

The trio sprinted down the halls of Glamis, unhindered by other tourists and guides. Ben had made a map from sketches Wendell drawn in his manuscript. Still, it took them nearly twenty-five minutes to reach their destination.

"One more left, then stop at the fourth tapestry," Ben said.

Following his instructions, they made it past a false wall, the stone door behind it opening with ease. After walking several hundred feet in a long, round hall, they reached the antechamber. The small door at the far end was locked.

"Oh crap!" Beatrix muttered.

"Not a problem," Percival said. "Just keep an eye on the way we came to make sure no one is coming."

Percival produced a lockpicking kit from the breast pocket of this jacket and got to work on the padlock. The lock was new and made of shiny stainless steel, seeming out of place.

"Okay, my compass is totally off," Ben said. "It's spinning!"

Percival nearly exploded with rage. "Your phone is on, boy? That's it! How the hell are we supposed to—"

"Relax. I have the cellular data, Wi-Fi, and Bluetooth off," Ben cut in. "Besides, how were we going to have light in there since you didn't bring a flashlight?"

Percival's anger subsided somewhat. "Alright. Score a point for boy wonder here. Just be careful!"

The lock snapped and clicked, and Percival removed it. "Okay, let's go. Ben, your light, please."

When they entered the chamber, they saw the familiar mismatched wine-colored carpets as those on the floor in the other halls. The window was painted over in flat black tar. The air was stale, and it was much hotter than it was in the antechamber.

Percival walked over to the far corner of the chamber, Ben shining his phone's light to guide him.

"Grab it and let's go!" Beatrix said. "I want out of here, Percival!" Her voice was shaking, and she was close to tears.

Percival reached into the cleft on the wall to pull down the talisman that they had come for. The rythrax was a carved piece of metal. It looked ancient and non-functional.

"Careful! Don't manipulate it," Beatrix warned. "That's what took Dad!"

"It's . . . it's not here," Percival said. "This isn't it. It's some piece of bloody artwork! A sodding facsimile. Someone has beat us to it. I don't understand it. The old man lied to me. Seppe promised it would be here, that we would have access to the device from this room. Damn him—"

"*From* this room?" Beatrix said. "Wait a minute. Ben, pull back the carpet."

Before Ben could react, they heard a noise. All three of them froze, and Ben turned off his flashlight, leaving them in total darkness, save for the oil lamps out in the antechamber.

"Footsteps! Somebody's coming!" Ben whispered.

"Those sound like hobnail boots," Percival said through clenched teeth. "That ain't good. Ben, kindly shut the bloody door."

"But it's our only way out!" Ben protested.

"There may be another way, you fool, now shut the door!" Percival was in no mood to be lectured by a fifteen-year-old.

Ben peeked toward the hall and saw a figure in a dark-gray suit. The man had pale skin, almost albino, and he was tall and thin, with a dark beard and black eyes. When he saw Ben, the man unleashed a sadistic grin. "Benjamin Voght! Don't be afraid. It's me, Bram! Surely, you remember me?"

Ben stared, dumbfounded, until Percival lurched over and slammed the door with surprising agility. Then he locked the deadbolt knob from the inside.

"Ben, it's me!" Bram called through the door. "My friend, hear me! I'm your ally. It's only Bram! Let me help you!"

Percival put his finger over his lips and shook his head, indicating Ben shouldn't reply. Beatrix looked on in terror, but Ben was unafraid, seemingly desperate to open the door. He leveled his gaze at Percival and Beatrix, and when he spoke, his voice sounded alien and detached. "It's Bram." He stared at the door as if hypnotized.

At Beatrix's urging, they lifted the carpets and found what they sought—a hidden trapdoor. Percival pried it open and looked down. Nothing prepared them for what they saw. Below the floor was an endless black expanse.

Full of stars.

"Diamond Light Source facility, all tours register with the control room. School tours meet at the reception desk," Lightheart said, reading the instructions aloud. "Well, that's it. We're blocked."

"What school would be touring on December twenty-second?" Alex inquired.

With Malik trailing, Libby walked off to the left and watched a van full of kids get out. Then she returned to the group. "A tour for some teenage science club. This is your chance. Hardingham and I have no chance of going in there. We'll get made on camera. You kids are going in. And you"—she turned to Lightheart—"will be their teacher. Clear?"

"Clear," Lightheart replied.

The fact that Libby was agreeing to and participating in the reconnaissance at the DLS facility was beyond the group's—and Libby's—comprehension.

I'm officially off the grid. I've gone rogue. Am I crazy? But what choice do I have? Who can I possibly trust at the Company now? I have no one. No one will believe me! I just have to see this through for now. When the moment presents itself, I'm sure I can bring out the truth and be exonerated.

In the ambulance ride out to Oxfordshire, Lightheart had brought Libby up to speed on the situation and the story in which they found themselves, though he left out a few details for the sake of brevity. She could have easily dismissed it as fantastical, pure rubbish. But she had seen the Hat Man herself.

This Beatrix and I will have a little chat soon enough, Libby thought.

The plan was for Lightheart, posing as a teacher mentor, to guide Alex and Malik through the tour with the other kids. It was 1:45 p.m. They were in the last group of the day. Libby resigned herself to waiting outside the facility with Fred, who was clearly unsettled, realizing the good guys and the bad guys were after them.

Lightheart briefed Alex and Malik on the way in. They were to attempt to find the synchrotron, then ascertain where the antimatter was stored. He repeated Percival's admonition that knowledge of the presence of antimatter in its active state was worse than useless—it was profoundly dangerous. They needed to know where it was stored in its inert state. Ideally, a state that was transportable.

They were all given lanyards and ushered in together. Their guide was a scientific type, a dark-skinned English woman who introduced herself as Dr. Abernathy. She was tall and thin and wore black glasses and a white lab coat.

"Welcome to Diamond Light Source," she began, "the second-largest particle accelerator on Earth. Only CERN, with its Large Hadron Collider in Switzerland, can boast more power or sheer audacity as we smash together particles near the speed of light. If you will all please follow me, I have something to show you."

Dr. Abernathy seemed excited about her work. Malik, albeit on a mission concerning the future of the planet, was overcome by her intelligence and beauty. Noticing Malik staring at Abernathy with this mouth agape, Alex elbowed him in the ribs.

"Focus, Malik."

"How?"

"Malik, stop it!" Alex hissed.

Lightheart shushed them both. "Please, for the love of all things sacred, you're going to get us tossed." He leaned in closer and lowered his voice. "We don't actually have to do anything. We just need to determine the precise location of the antimatter storage chamber. Then when Percival returns with the device, we can open a portal and snatch it."

The tour group was stretched out about one hundred feet along a large, tubular hallway. The walls were silver like the bottom of a stainless-steel skillet. The group was headed to the synchrotron's control room. As they walked, Dr. Abernathy moved ahead and continued her lecture on particle physics.

"We have to break away," Lightheart whispered to the others. "The storage area must be near. They would never risk moving something so volatile a vast distance."

"Why not ask Dr. Abernathy where it is," Malik suggested. The others gave him an incredulous look, shocked that such a simple solution hadn't occurred to either of them.

Just then, a scream echoed down the tube from the front of the group. Lightheart realized immediately that some ill fate had befallen their mission.

"It's almost three o'clock. This is bollocks," Libby said. "Something's happened. Hardingham, did you see anything out of the ordinary on the way here? Anyone tailing us?" Before he could frame his thoughts, Libby pressed further. "Think, you moron. This is life and death. They could be walking into a trap."

"I thought it odd that all the teachers were female, except this one bloke. He looked a bit out of place. Tall fellow."

"You bloody fool! Out of place? Did he have a lanyard? Was he talking to any students?"

"It did strike me as odd, come to think of it—"

An alarm sounded, tearing through the air with a screech right above their heads from a loudspeaker in the parking lot. Libby hesitated for a split second. Then she made up her mind.

"That's it. We're going in.." She reached into the small of her back and drew her sidearm. She worked the action, then replaced it in her waistband. Fred gulped. While intimidated to the extreme, until that precise moment he had never seen a more beautiful person up close in his thirty-three years on Earth. Fred Hardingham would follow Libby Soames-Briggs anywhere.

"Let's go!" Libby broke into a trot, crouching as low as possible with Fred trying, and failing, to do the same, as they entered the facility's main lobby.

The first thing they noticed was that the lobby was empty. Not a soul was there. Not even the security team. Then Libby discovered why. They were lying motionless on the floor behind the counter. They were breathing, but they were stunned and immobile, their eyes wide—and black.

"This is bloody unbelievable," she said. "We must get to them. They got here before we did somehow." Libby rummaged around the security personnel, looking for lanyards. "Here," she said, throwing one to Fred.

"Who? Who got here?" Fred asked.

"You bloody tell me! How would I know who these people are or where they come from? If it weren't for you, I would have never been bloody involved!"

They ran down the entry corridor until they reach a T intersection. Libby chose to go right.

The tour group had gone left.

Kids and faculty members screamed as they ran from something down the hall beyond them. Lightheart, Alex, and Malik could only watch and wonder what it was.

"We need to leave," Lightheart said, fearing the agents of the Black had gotten there ahead of them. "While we still can." He kept cleaning his glasses while running his hands through his hair.

"Dr. Abernathy, she didn't run past us," Malik said.

"What?" Alex asked.

"The nice guide lady, Dr. Abernathy. She wasn't with the others. She's still out there! We have to find her!"

"Absolutely not," Lightheart replied. "We can't compromise the mission for a stranger. She could be dead already and probably is if what they're running from is . . . him."

"I agree with Malik," Alex said. "Let's go forward."

"Let's go forward?" Lightheart exclaimed. "Excuse me, young lady, but I'm in charge here, and moreover, I'm your teacher. I don't care a thing about your pedigree. I put my foot down."

Alex shot a look at Malik to gauge his reaction and then nodded in response. "Lead on, Malik."

With Lightheart reluctantly trailing the rebellious duo, they dashed down the corridor toward the threat.

"I don't see her. How could we have missed Dr. Abernathy?" Alex asked as she cast her eyes around the tunnel but saw no sign of the tour guide.

Malik and Lightheart, both gasping for air, looked around in vain as well.

The trio was at an intersection of six metal tubes, all identical in shape. They couldn't see the end of any of the tubes, which seemed to go on infinitely.

"She's gone, Alex. Face it," Lightheart said between gasps, his hands still on his knees. "We tried. We should go now. Someone or something is down one of these tubes—"

"Yeah, and Dr. Abernathy is down there too. We have to find her.

We should split up and each take a different direction before things get worse," Malik said, having recovered from his sprint.

A loud, repeating whoop-whoop sound exploded in their ears, and everything went black. The three companions seethed with fright as they flattened out on the cement floor. Yellow emergency lights, which had been concealed along each tube, began to rotate, casting the corridor in an amber glow.

"It's worse," Lightheart said. "Let's go! Right now. The way we came!"

Alex looked at Malik as if to say, "I'm sorry."

"Alright, lead on, Professor," Alex replied. Lightheart was only too happy to comply with the order from a child who wasn't even half his age.

The trio headed back down the tube the direction they had come. After running several minutes, seemingly covering a mile, Malik noticed something wasn't right.

"Stop!" he yelled. "We've gone too far!"

"We must have gotten off track without noticing," Alex replied, doing a 360 and looking about.

"How did we get lost running in a straight line?" Lightheart asked.

"Wait," Malik said. "Something's not right here. Something's changed. It feels . . . different."

"What—"

"Shut up!" Malik said, cutting Lightheart off. "Wait a minute!" He walked over to the nearest wall and poked it with his index finger. Incredibly, the wall bent like distorted liquid metal. It was shiny and buoyant, and silver ripples emanated from Malik's finger.

Alex gasped as she and Lightheart looked on in bewilderment.

"What the bloody hell is this?" Alex asked.

"Malik, don't!" Lightheart protested as Malik poked his entire hand into the wall and, making a fist, pulled out a large chunk and tossed it. The clump of black liquid floated in the air.

Alex reached out to catch it, then gasped and pointed at the hole Malik had created. "Look!"

The others turned and saw it. A void. All black.

Stepping closer to peering into it, Malik froze. It was full of stars.

Malik was looking into space.

Down the corridor ahead of them, the flashing emergency lights were no longer visible. Something black had blocked them out. Then they heard it: a voice, high and shrill. A woman's voice. It froze their blood.

"Help!" she screamed.

"It's her," Malik said. "Dr. Abernathy."

"Let's go," Alex said, already moving toward her voice.

Lightheart gulped, then strode after Alex. Malik tore out another chunk of wall and trotted after them.

Screams and wails echoed down the corridor. "Help! Please! Anyone!"

The trio broke into a sprint, certain Abernathy was the source of the cries.

"Help me! He's here!"

They were sprinting headlong and into the pure darkness when it occurred. Lightheart was thrown backwards several yards as if shot from a cannon. Lightheart laying on his back, semi-conscious, had been hit with a pulse of pure energy, perhaps a magnetic field. Jabs of pain raked through his body. He looked up and saw a figure.

It wasn't Dr. Abernathy.

His lips trembling, Lightheart uttered a single word: "Luka."

CHAPTER 16

The Dark
Fellows

THE KNOCKING TURNED TO POUNDING, AND BEN SEEMED to shake out of his stupor. The man calling himself Bram had ceased calling out and focused on trying to force the door instead.

Ben laid on his belly and peered through the trapdoor. The starscape was infinite. He looked up and locked eyes with Beatrix, then shook his head as if to apologize for his behavior earlier.

Percival flopped onto his back. "All for nothing but a sodding wild goose chase. Now we're buggered right and bloody proper."

Beatrix turned back to the expanse. "There! Below us."

Cupping his hands over his eyes, Ben could just make out the silhouette of a wrought-iron bridge spanning the chamber. The ends weren't visible, as the chamber didn't seem to have any walls. It looked like a vast expanse of space.

"It could be a way out!"

"It's not a way out, you fool! It's to the Other Place," Percival said. "This is Wendell's path. We can't take it. We're as good as lost forever if we do."

A thunderous smash struck the door. Around the corners, a crack of intensifying green light sliced through.

Percival stood up. "Children, please get behind me and under no circumstance say or do anything."

Having never heard him talk like that before, Beatrix and Ben took up places behind Percival, as instructed. Beatrix was hollow-eyed with fear.

This is it. No escape.

As the green light intensified around the door, Beatrix returned to the open trapdoor and threw the carpet back over it to conceal it.

The chamber door seemed to vaporize in a cloud of dust and green light. When the dust settled, a figure standing in the doorway, tall and foreboding, was revealed. He raised his hands, a white light emanating from a flat black disk.

A rythrax!

"Traitor!" Bram hissed as he eyed Percival.

Percival was unmoved. He stood, all five feet, six inches of him, a solid as a sentinel in his crushed-velvet blazer. "Well, well. Bram the Corruptor. Or should I call you the Emulator? What, are you miffed that you missed arts and crafts time with Luka and the rest of the hostile boys?"

Bram's eyes turned obsidian. His voice expanded, seeming to enter Beatrix's brain. "Laugh on, mongrel man. You'll be put down soon enough."

Then Bram's eyes normalized, as did his voice. Ben couldn't help but be drawn into the newfound benevolence in his face. Beatrix, however, stayed concealed behind Percival and Ben, yearning to dive into the meridian.

"You, dog man, I know. And you," Bram continued, eyeing Ben, "no greetings for old Bram? Haven't we met many times before? Would you deny my friendship?

"Ben, don't listen to him," Percival said. "He's trying to poison your mind! He's a soul-soothing demon and a liar!"

"Silence, old fool!" Bram said, his eyes flaring as black as night. Then his face and voice softened again. "Star Child," he whispered. "Gray Witch, I see you. Come to me. Come to Bram."

Star Child? Gray Witch? Beatrix thought. *I want to dive in right now.*

Bram held the rythrax aloft and then stepped toward the trio. "No words for Bram? Hmm? No matter. The Master has agents capable of taking everything he wants. Yes, soul stealer, even you get to be broken.

Except, you old fool, today will be the day of your death. I'll take great pleasure in snuffing out the existence of the traitorous Percival J. Parfleet."

Beatrix was overcome with anger, a seething red fire burning in her chest. She stepped between her brother and Percival and stared up at Bram.

"If you want us, come and get us!" Beatrix said.

With nearly instantaneous speed, Bram flashed across the room at Beatrix.

For Beatrix, however, it looked like he was moving in slow motion. Everything was moving at one tenth speed but her. She could see the action unfold frame by frame in detail.

Bram reached for Beatrix, but she ducked, a green plasma blast from the disk just missing her and exploded against the wall. Bram reached out, but just as his fingers touched Beatrix's shoulder, he lost the advantage, and he knew it.

Bram was already falling.

The floor seemed to consume him, and he groped the edges of the trapdoor in vain as the carpet pinched him tighter, the force of the dark space pulling him down. As he struggled to grab the edges of the trapdoor, Bram fumbled the rythrax, and Ben saw his chance.

Diving onto his stomach, Ben wrenched the black disk from the corruptor's hand. Bram struggled against the force of the meridian, but he couldn't break free from its grip. Before he succumbed completely, he looked at Beatrix, who was crouching on one knee, staring at him.

"Enjoy the surface," he said.

The last thing Beatrix saw of him were his black eyes before an explosion of silence pulled Bram down into the void. The starscape flared white and then went dormant.

Percival looked at Beatrix and shook his head in disbelief. "You . . . are one stubborn teenager." It was not a compliment. He was thoroughly incensed. "Let's get out of here right now," Percival continued. He stood and held his hand out to Ben. "Give it to me, please."

Ben hesitated, then surrendered the disk to Percival.

"The meridian. We could go there, right? We could find Wendell," Ben said as he looked down into the meridian.

"Ben."

"This is our opportunity. We should take it."

"Ben, please."

"I want to."

"Ben!" Beatrix said. "That's enough. Stop it!"

What am I saying? I want to go too. But I don't know why.

"Listen to her, mate," Percival said. "You're not ready. None of us are." He glanced at Beatrix as if to indicate that last comment was directed toward her. "We should go. We have what we need now. This phase of the mission is complete."

Ben hesitated again.

He's not himself, Beatrix thought. *Did Bram tell the truth? Did they meet before?*

Percival heaved the trapdoor closed, the slam echoing through the chamber. Ben seemed to snap out of whatever had gripped him and covered the trapdoor with the carpet.

"Let's leave this Monster of Glamis for now," Percival said as he sped out of the chamber. "Come!"

He glanced back at the others as he trotted. "The agents of the Black knew we would be here. We've been compromised somehow. The gateway consumed that beast of a man, Bram, and you can bet that he's already being debriefed in the Deep by the agents of the Black. They will make use of him before he's unwritten. And we'll be surveilled as sure as bloody hell."

Panting, Percival paused at the top of some stone steps and looked left and right to regain his bearings. He let out a sharp exhale. "I feel the need for a pint like I never thought a Scotsman would."

Beatrix put her arm around Percival's shoulders. "Come on, old friend. We need to get away and hole up somewhere to regroup. Then it's back to London. We have eighteen hours until we meet the others."

The trio sped down the halls and chambers until they reached the central hall. By then, it was 4:18 p.m. They were late and they knew it, yet there was no sign of anyone, not even Mr. Oseary or the strange man to whom he had been talking with.

"That's weird," Beatrix said as she looked around.

They walked over to the administrative office, but the light was off, and the door was locked. Ben cupped his hands around his face and peered through a crack in the blinds. "Nigel Geddings," he said, reading the nameplate on the desk. "It's funny he would leave without us being accounted for, don't you think?"

"The poor bastard's probably dead," Percival said. "Seen off by the pale bloke that Beatrix sent through the gateway." He glanced at Ben, who looked down and away from the others at the mention of Bram. It was a subject that neither Ben nor Percival wanted to broach just yet.

"Maybe. Maybe not," Beatrix said. "Maybe Geddings let him in. He was here before, you know, when Wendell disappeared. I saw the records."

"What are you implying?" Percival asked. "That he's working for the Enemy? So, he just so happened to be working at the same sodding place where Wendell flipped his lid and went in?"

Beatrix wheeled on Percival. "Not by accident, you id—" She caught herself, and then exploded with rage. "He was posted here where my dad was lost! We were right under the nose of one of Seraphim's spies, and you brought us here!"

Percival and Ben stood there, mouths agape, as they stared at Beatrix, who was seething with fury.

"What?" Beatrix yelled, her fists at her side.

"Your eyes," Ben said.

"What about them?"

"They just . . . changed."

"Changed? Changed how? What the hell are you talking about?"

"They turned to fire. A purple flame," Percival said. "It appeared and then disappeared just as quickly. It's the Andromeda in you, child." Percival eyed her warily. "Are you alright, Beatrix?"

Gray Witch. Star Child . . .

At that moment, Beatrix realized she was exhausted. "I'm fine," she said, her shoulders sagging.

Outside, headlights rolled past, illuminating the windows. Immediately on high alert, Percival peeked outside.

"Bloody bollocks. They found us."

Outside was a black sedan, its tinted windows concealing its occupants. The vehicle's very presence seemed to portend doom.

"We absolutely, positively can't catch a sodding break anywhere I swear," Percival muttered.

Suddenly, Beatrix was overcome with the urge to leave the castle. Before the others could stop her, she ran forward and burst out the front door. Her curly hair bobbed back and forth as she strode over to the car, then leaned over and rapped on the window.

"Oh, bloody hell, let's go!" Percival said to Ben, but he was already on his way to protect his sister from another self-imposed danger. When they tried to pull her away from the car, though, she shrugged them off and continued knocking on the window.

A moment later, the engine turned off, and the window slid down.

"Percival, I could hear your foul mouth and uncouth language from as far away as Dundee," the driver said. "I believe you're in need of a libation to calm your nerves. So, get in this car this instant, you ruddy scallywag!"

Incredulous at first, Beatrix broke into an amazed grin, and Ben whooped with excitement that they may have skirted another brush with death. Only Percival remained unmoved. He opened the back door for Beatrix and Ben, then climbed in after them. Only then did he address the mysterious chauffeur.

"Seppe, when this is over, I'm going to kill you."

Montavani snickered from the driver's seat.

"Where to?" Beatrix asked.

"To get this poor sod a drink," Montavani replied, smiling. "The Green Griffin, of course!"

The scream grew louder as Alex and Malik raced toward it, the ever-expanding black seeming to grow toward them the closer they got. The steel tubes of the synchrotron seemed distorted and bent. Liquified. Incredibly, Lightheart had become separated from them. One moment, he was there — the next, he was gone.

"You hear that?" Libby asked as they crept down the corridor.

"Yes," Fred replied, full of terror. The scream was farther down the tube. In the dark.

Libby took off at a trot. She had yet to draw her weapon, which surprised Fred. As he trailed Libby, he occasionally reached out to touch her shoulder while cowering behind her.

Libby took a chance and would be angry at herself later for her next choice. "Elias! Elias, are you there?"

"Here! I'm here!" Lightheart called out.

Their hope of rescuing the others reignited, Fred and Libby ran toward his voice. Libby was sprinting, and Fred, long strider that he was, couldn't keep up.

"Thank God! I can't find the others. Where are they? Did you see them?" Lightheart asked.

"Not yet," Libby replied. "Don't move. I can't see you in the bloody dark. I don't want to run over you if you're prone."

"We became separated. I lost Alex and Maylek!" Lightheart said.

Something about his pronunciation of Malik's name caused the hair to stand up on the back of Libby's neck. She eased her hand behind her back and flicked the safety switch on her sidearm. Then she felt for Fred in the dark and pulled his ear alarmingly close to her lips. "Hardingham, get down."

"What the—"

The tube was flooded with intense white light as a sinister laugh echoed throughout the synchrotron. Libby and Fred were temporarily blinded as a concussive force sent them hurtling backward onto the concrete floor.

Shielding her eyes with her fingers, Libby risked a peek at a figure standing tall and cloaked in black. He seemed taller than a human and darker than night. His face . . . was blank. And perched atop his head was a fedora.

The Hat Man.

It had been using the voice of Lightheart, who lay prone at the Hat Man's feet, unconscious.

"Fools who have been playing with things they don't understand," Luka said, shifting back to his regular doomsday tone. "Well, friends, it ends here. The day of death for you."

Libby drew her weapon and unleashed a salvo at Luka, but the projectiles stopped in mid-flight directly in front of his outstretched palm. He plucked the projectiles out of the air and then rubbed them between his gloved hands. Metal powder drifted down onto the concrete floor.

Libby crawled over to Fred to shield him from the coming onslaught, realizing these were likely her final moments. She closed her eyes tight and said, "It'll be over soon."

"Stop! Wait!" a weakened voice commanded.

Alex and Malik froze and groped to find each other in the darkness. The emergency lights could hardly cut through the blackness.

"Please! Don't go any farther down there!" the voice said.

"Who are you?" Malik, his voice shaky and full of fear.

"Dr. Abernathy," the voice replied, gasping. "Violet Abernathy. I work here."

"Dr. Abernathy!" Malik cried. "Where are you?"

"Here!"

Alex and Malik followed the voice until they found her lying on the floor.

Through gasps of fear and exertion, Dr. Abernathy continued. "Don't go any farther. There's something down there. It . . . it's not of this world."

"Mechanix," Malik said with disdain.

Abernathy looked at him in surprise. "What?"

"Malik!" Alex said. "We don't know what it is!" She turned back to Abernathy. "Can you walk?"

"Yes," Abernathy replied, though not with much confidence. They helped her to her feet, then set off down the semi-dark tunnel.

"There's no explanation for what's happening here," she said. "Something completely alien is among us! Look!"

She pointed to the ceiling. Fissures had appeared, outlined in blue-green light, and the walls were quivering, continuing the process of liquefaction.

"What the hell is this?" Abernathy asked. When she pulled out her phone to take pictures as they journeyed forward, Malik asked her to turn on her compass. The needle was spinning out of control.

"I'm Alex, by the way, Alex Thacker. And this is Malik Patel. We're both from New York," Alex paused to catch her breath as they ran down the dark hall. "We must find Professor Lightheart. He's our teacher, and we got separated from —"

A massive bright white light exploded down the hall in front of them. Although nearly two hundred yards away, they had to steady themselves to avoid being knocked over. The trio flattened themselves against the wall and peered down the hallway. In the distance, they saw a tall figure at the center of a ball of blinding white light.

"It's *him*," Malik said.

"Who?" Abernathy asked.

Malik turned to look at her, his expression blank. "The Hat Man."

The two groups were completely unaware that although the mission had failed, they were separated from one another in the same segment of the synchrotron tube and close to reuniting. The tube itself seemed to be coming apart as its walls continued to destabilize with liquid undulations. As the cracks and fissures progressed, they revealed something new. Beyond the fissures was what could only be described as one thing — space.

With Alex, Malik, and Dr. Abernathy on one side and Fred and Libby on the other, each party was cut off by the threat from the Hat Man. As for Lightheart, he was lying unconscious at the Hat Man's feet.

Malik's chest heaved as he inhaled and exhaled in large gulps. Then something in him began to grow. Something he had not experienced much in his fourteen years. His hands curled into fists, and his nostrils flared. Perhaps it was because he finally had a chance to play the hero, especially in front of Dr. Abernathy, but the feeling in his chest grew until his face burned, and he finally blew his top. Malik was furious. He was tired of being the victim, of being passive, of being reactive, of being bullied. Tired of being Malik Patel.

His legs churning as fast as they could go, Malik hurtled toward the light. As he closed in on the Hat Man, he let out his version of a rebel yell. (The others would later say it sounded like a girl screeching in horror at the sight of uninvited culinary vermin.)

When Malik was thirty yards away, the Hat Man turned his attention away from Libby and Fred and toward the running boy. Pulling an object from his pocket, Malik raised his arm to throw it at Luka. But when he glanced down at the last moment, he saw Lightheart, whose lips formed a single word: "Don't!"

It was too late, though. Malik flung the sphere at the Hat Man. During the entire ordeal, it had remained a quivering piece of cohesive matter in his Member's Only jacket pocket, though neither Malik nor the others, save Lightheart, knew exactly what it was. Malik had thrown a grenade at the Hat Man made of pure singularity. The results were devastating. But not to Malik.

The Hat Man managed to shield his malformed face with his arms before it hit him. When it struck, a fissure opened above him and the air itself was ripped asunder. The periphery of the crack was laced with blue-green light. Inside of the cavity was a starscape of bent space. The Hat Man seemed to bend and distort as he was siphoned into the starscape.

"Nooooo!" he cried as the fissure closed behind him.

The walls stopped quivering, and the fissures closed. The amber lights ceased flashing, and the fluorescent lights flickered back on. Malik stood there, his chest heaving and his body pumping with adrenaline. He remained there until Alex and Dr. Abernathy caught up with him.

Several yards down the corridor, they saw Libby squatting next to Fred, who was leaning against a wall with his knees drawn up in front of him.

"You have a concussion," Libby told him. "Wait here." She strode over to Malik, acknowledging him and his actions with a curt nod.

"We have a problem," Alex said, pointing down.

Only then did the others realize that Lightheart was gone. Lying on the floor where he had been was a black fedora.

"What in the name of all things sacred is going on here?" Dr. Abernathy asked. "And who are you people?"

Ignoring her question, Alex looked at Libby. "Dr. Lightheart is gone. Taken."

"Are you certain?" Libby replied.

"He was there at the Hat Man's feet." She leveled her gaze at Malik. "I saw his body distort, and he went in with him."

Libby was all business, her MI5 training having desensitized her to such developments. "That's that then. We'll deal with what it means later. For now, we have to leave. That Hat Man, as you call him, may not have been alone, and we don't have the firepower to go toe-to-toe with another of his kind."

"What about the mission?" Malik asked. "We're here, and there's no security. All the cameras I see are blown out and smoking. The storage pods are just down this hall. We can grab it and go. We need only a little according to —"

"Shut up, Malik!" Alex said, her eyes on Abernathy.

"Grab what?" Violet asked, her hands on the hips of her white lab jacket.

"Oh, bloody hell!" Libby said, fed up. "The antimatter. We're taking it. That's what. It's the only way to beat these damn beasts back to the place they came from. That's it and that's final."

Without realizing it, Libby had her front foot forward, her palm outstretched like a stop sign, with her other hand behind her back. It was a tactical position to show authority. And it worked. Only later would Libby have time to wonder how a top MI5 operator could get sucked into such a preposterous quest with such a motley crew and, on top of that, assume leadership of it.

Violet said nothing, sensing that with each passing moment, the day was not going in her favor, nor was it following the normal laws of nature.

"So, what now?" Fred asked, rubbing his concussed head.

"We have what we came for," Alex said. "The exact layout of the area and the location of the storage pods. Dr. Abernathy, how big are the individual storage vessels?"

For reasons she couldn't comprehend, Violet trusted these people, perhaps because they had saved her when doing so meant risking themselves. "They're very small, only six inches in length, and very light. And absolutely too dangerous to carry by hand."

"If only we could communicate with the other team to see if they were successful, we could kill two birds with one stone and swipe the stuff right now," Alex said.

The others pondered, for a moment, the risks and benefits of communication.

Malik had always viewed himself as the most intelligent person in any room or situation he was in. However, his humility and his abysmal self-image rarely allowed him the satisfaction of letting others know of his acumen. So far, he had deduced many things from his experience at the Diamond Light Source facility, some of it inaccurate but some of it spot on.

First, Malik deduced that the Hat Man was, in fact, Luka, the leader of the vicious Mechanix, Seraphim's deadliest agents. Malik also figured that Luka's presence in the tube had somehow destabilized the cohesion of matter on Earth. The loss of atomic and molecular cohesion tore holes in the space-time continuum, generating separate realities superimposed on each other and allowing them to see elements of space through the fissures. Malik theorized that perhaps during the exchange, Luka had changed the properties of the entire synchrotron in a way that splintered them off into another realm or reality. Malik was convinced that somewhere another Malik and his companions had seen the event from the other side.

Malik knew that for a moment, he had glimpsed the Other Place.

There were two other theories Malik was so certain of that he viewed them as facts. First, Professor Lightheart had been taken against his will. Second, Lightheart was now dead. Malik felt genuine pain at the loss of his teacher and possibly a one-day future friend.

On both counts, however, Malik Patel was wrong.

CHAPTER 17

The Green Griffin

A T THE GREEN GRIFFIN IN DUNDEE, BEATRIX, BEN, Percival, and Montavani sat in an L-shaped booth in the corner. The tavern, being rough around the edges and having no conventional rules about the age of its patrons, allowed the children access as long as they stayed quiet and didn't annoy anyone. Percival sat there thinking as he sipped his precious pint of stout. Montavani allowed him a few moments of quiet revelry before addressing him.

"Still the Bastard for you, eh?" Montavani said, nodding to Percival.

Beatrix waited for the obligatory explosion from Percival.

"Mmm" was Percival's only reply as he held his glass slightly aloft to ensure its opacity. "Been with the Bastard since I was seventeen. No sense gettin' off that train now," he replied, referencing the illegitimate moniker of the aforementioned beer.

The tavern was nestled in the deepest corner of one of the darkest alleys in Dundee. Percival had grown up there and frequented such haunts as a rough-and-tumble twenty-something. The tavern was dim, smokey (pipes only), and just noisy enough to drown out conversation. Most importantly, they were all able to keep an eye on the entrance to see who was coming and going. It reminded Beatrix of the Prancing

Pony in Tolkien's tales. She expected Strider to come through the door at any moment.

Beatrix and Ben ordered coffees and water, as they were both exhausted and dehydrated. Their fish and chips were soon to follow.

The corner booth was flanked by Old World oil lamps, creating the aura of an eighteenth-century establishment. The table was thick and made of worn oak, as were the chairs. An old and infinitely melted candle burned at the center of the table, its wax having sealed it there eons ago. The faint smell of stale beer was mixed with that of the scent a nearby fireplace, which helped stave off the bitterly cold afternoon. Beatrix was in love with the place.

"Is it safe?" Montavani asked Percival.

Percival nodded, then patted the breast pocket of his velvet blazer without looking up.

"Well, then, all is not lost," Montavani said.

Ben, who had remained aloof since the adventure in the castle chamber, looked at Montavani. "Why did you come? How did you get here?"

Percival folded his arms and sat back with a wry smile.

Montavani lit his pipe, as he was prone to do when framing his thoughts. After a few puffs, he began. "The Verge, at least as you know it, was destroyed. Overrun by the Enemy. The attention attracted by your escapades on the road had a part to play in that, no doubt."

He looked at Beatrix.

"She had no choice, Seppe," Percival protested. "Don't hold her responsible for that, a'right?"

"Of course not, old friend. Be that as it may, destroying the reconnaissance elements of the Black Path was a necessary and exceptional feat. Obliteration of the mountainside was slightly more noticeable and possibly a bit excessive, but that's just me thinking aloud." Montavani's subtle attempt at humor fell flat, so he continued. "I had to come. I made my way to Glamis as fast as feasible." He gave an admonishing look at Percival that Beatrix picked up on.

Using alternate meridians, no doubt.

"I found you, and successful in your mission, no less. I left the original rythrax in safekeeping in New York." He gave Percival another knowing look. "I dared not try to take it through the portal, lest I be discovered instantly by the agents of the Black."

Beatrix was desperate to tell Montavani about her trip through the gateway and her "detour" to the "Other Place," complete with a run-in with a construct of Wendell. However, it didn't seem like the right time. Although she liked and admired Montavani, she wasn't certain how much she could trust him. She had begun to feel like a pawn. Years of self-deprecation and self-loathing had fine-tuned Beatrix's mistrust detector. Even now, faint footfalls of mistrust went pitter-pattering through her mind.

I'm a hypocrite; that's what I am. I haven't told anyone about my own "missing time" incident. I didn't instantaneously come through the meridian to Telegraph Cottage from the Verge. I was late. Percival said I was two minutes late. Okay, let's do some math.

Beatrix scribbled on an unused napkin as Percival and Montavani debriefed Ben.

Okay, so two minutes. One hour here is eleven years in the Divide or there about. So, if there are twenty-four hours in a day and sixty minutes in an hour. Wait, that's addition? No, crap. You multiply. Twenty-four times sixty is 1,440 minutes in a day. Multiply that by 365 days in a year and that's . . . 525,600 minutes in a year on Earth. Wendell was gone eight hours and was apart from us for eight-eight years! Oh, wait! That's messing me up. We need common terms. Four hundred and eighty minutes in eight hours. Yep. That means 525,600 minutes in a year times eighty-eight years is, whoa, 46,252,800 minutes. Better! Wow, this is getting hard! Are my calculations right? Where is Malik when I need him? Malik! Geez, I almost forgot! I hope he's okay. Dang, I really meant that!

Okay, whew, cross multiply, so let's try this.

She wrote the following on her napkin:

480 minutes (in 8 hours) = 2 minutes missing on Earth
46,252,800 minutes in 88 years (in Other World) X

Holy crap. There's no way this is right. But it's cool. Math is fun! Whoopee!

(92,505,600) = 2(46,252,600)
(x)480= 192,720

What now? Crap. Oh! Solve for "x" by dividing both sides by 1,440, moron! What the . . .?

"One hundred and thirty-three days," Montavani said. "You were missing for two minutes here on Earth, Beatrix. That's slightly more than one hundred and thirty-three days in the alter world." He smiled at Beatrix, his eyes full of empathy.

"One hundred and thirty-three days? How? You knew then! Why didn't it feel that long?" Beatrix stated.

"Yes, that and more," Montavani replied with a large exhale of smoke. He looked tired. "We can discuss this at length at a time more suitable."

"What about the others? What's happened to them? We need to get back to London. Are they okay?"

Montavani seemed transfixed on the candle, staring at it without blinking.

"I want to know about my friends," Beatrix pressed. "Alex and Malik. Have you heard from Professor Lightheart?"

Percival flicked his eyebrows at Montavani as if to ask if he were going to answer.

"I have had confirmation that Elias completed his mission. He communicated with me via encrypted text just before he achieved his objective. He also sent me the exact coordinates of the antimatter storage chamber."

With that, he popped a chip in his mouth and began chewing.

"Excuse me? *His* mission? *His* objective?" Beatrix caught herself speaking loudly and lowered her voice. "What do you mean by his mission? The mission was to determine the exact location of the chamber so we could use the rythrax device and go in to take the pods. In and out. That's it!"

"No, Beatrix. That was the mission you and your London team came up with, which I endorsed and still do. Elias had another mission that he was able to carry out."

Beatrix was furious. It felt like he was treating her like a child. Seeing her anger, Percival coughed several times, then waved to the barkeep for another pint. Ben put his hand on Beatrix's arm to calm her.

"My good man, another?" Montavani said. "I can't be toting you hither and yon through Dundee and the omniverse with you half in the bag. And you," he added, turning to Ben, "you've got quite a story to tell, I'm afraid. Running into the Emulator. Pale, sickly looking bloke he is, that Bram fellow." Montavani's eyes narrowed as he sipped his tea. "Yet, he was known to you somehow."

Ben shifted in his seat and then nodded. "Yes, sir."

"Bram is an unwritten who was brought forth from the blackest reaches of the uncharted multiverse. He's a phantom, that one, a pale-faced wraith pledged eternally to the dark altar of the one true enemy, Seraphim himself. Possibly more sinister than Luka and the Mechanix themselves." Montavani shrugged, then changed the subject as Ben processed the information regarding his "familiar" assailant.

When Beatrix stood to go to the powder room, Montavani said, "Well, by your experience, it looks as if you have been changed in the hyperfold as well." He nodded at her head, which caused Beatrix to blush. The omnipresent thicket of brown curls was a constant sore point. Beatrix excused herself and made a beeline for the restroom.

Beatrix closed the door to the restroom, which was not much bigger than a British phone booth and looked at her reflection in the shiny metal mirror. Noticing something out of place, she leaned in closer.

Running from the crown of her head all the way down to her chin, in a long thin strand, her hair was gray, almost silver. Beatrix grabbed it and held it out at its full length. She couldn't believe it.

Freakin' great! Five feet, one inch tall, check. One Pop Tart away from chubby, check. Glasses, check. Zits, check. Strand of gray granny hair, check! And somehow I'm considered special. The hope of humankind. This is a complete farce. If only Rosemarie could see this!

The thought of Rosemarie Crerar Voght caused Beatrix to laugh and snort despite herself. She blew her nose, checked her hair again, and then returned to the table. Percival and Ben were gone and only Montavani remained.

"They're warming up the car," Montavani said. "It's time to go. Your hair . . . you've been phasing."

"I've been what?"

"Phasing. Traveling through the lattice of meridians unconfined to normal gateways. It changes a person."

"Changes? How? What other changes might I expect?"

"Phasing through meridians has never been done. Only the Mechanix and you have ever done so — at least unaided. Or, of course, the Eidolon. Gliding through meridians can take one through many parts of the omniverse and can even age someone. Or make them younger. No one knows."

"Why did I go there? And why for so long? Will it happen again? If it's random, why did I wind up seeing him?"

"Who?" Montavani asked, his blue eyes wide and his eyebrows raised.

"Wendell. Or maybe not Wendell. It was like a hologram or a replica. Either way, it was meant to show me something."

"A construct. Real yet not real. You saw what you wanted to see. Wendell was there as you desired to see him."

"No," Beatrix replied. "That's not the case. He told me to go away. I wouldn't have wanted that. He also said, 'Shut the way,' over and over again. 'Shut the way.'"

"What else did he say?" Montavani asked, his interest piqued.

"He said I was one of several. Uh, thirteen. 'You are of the Thirteen.' Where have I heard that before?" Beatrix paused to think. "In New York! On Seventy-ninth Street! The simulacra said that and only that — thirteen. What does it mean?"

"It means that this world may be destabilizing, and Seraphim's plans are moving faster than we anticipated. If that's the case, we're facing unspeakable danger and imminent annihilation."

"Why?" Beatrix asked, plunking back down in the booth.

"The Thirteen are the last keepers of a secret faith. The rebellion against the dark altar. Me, Percival, and Wendell, wherever he is, are the last known surviving members of the Thirteen. We've lost ten so far, counting Wendell. We vowed never to mention the Thirteen unless the situation was dire, as in threatening the balance of the cosmos. There are consequences of doing so. In your world, the naming of the Thirteen would be our "Bat signal." But I suppose we have come to that. The final summoning of the Thirteen. There were to be twelve warriors led by a supreme. A phantom. An Eidolon with powers beyond all others and, in the raw form, perhaps greater than that of the Dark Master himself."

"Gee, you said you've lost ten so far and that you and Parfleet count as two. You left one out. Who or where is the thirteenth? We need to find him! Then we can shut the meridians, and everything will be fine."

Montavani didn't answer, just smiled sadly, his expression laced with contrition.

"Where do we find the last of the Thirteen?" Beatrix pressed.

"The last of the Thirteen . . . is the Star Child. Some legends call her Mortmaiden, which in the common tongue means Gray Witch or Soul Stealer. One who carries the stellar trait Andromeda."

Oh no.

"Is that me?" Beatrix asked.

Montavani didn't reply. He didn't have to.

"What did I do for a hundred and thirty-three days?"

Montavani didn't reply to that question either.

The trouble with a lie is that one has difficulty recalling what they said and when they said it. When the person who was lied to brings up information about the date or the event, the teller of the lie has no idea what they're talking about. There is no cognitive permanency of the information as there is with the truth. The liar can't remember. The speaking of a truth is not just the spoken word. Truth is experienced. Truth is done. It has a past, a present, and a future. A lie is a construct with no foundation in reality, so it can't be easily remembered.

On the other hand, not all lies are real lies, plain and simple. Lies of omission are damnable yet forgivable in certain instances. There are also cases where the past is clouded. The past can be true but misremembered. The past can also be obliterated by trauma and blocked out by the subconscious. In the case of Benjamin Voght, he was beginning to think this last explanation was the case.

By all accounts, Ben was a "good boy." He didn't lie, cheat, or steal. He was protective of his family and of anyone who was disadvantaged. But he couldn't shake the idea that somehow, he had unknowingly covered up a lie. He had had dreams of a childhood that differed from Beatrix's. In fact, they had nothing in common. Ben could remember images of his mother, but Beatrix never spoke of her. The subject being taboo, they never talked about their years prior to Wendell either. It was odd. Everyone had memories from when they were three. Ben realized he did, but Beatrix did not. He knew in his heart they were not siblings by blood. That was his first lie of omission.

Then there was Bram.

As soon as he saw him, Ben felt like he knew him. The recognition was mutual. Ben could only guess how that was possible. A tangled gossamer of logic began piecing together hypotheses in Ben's mind, the unraveling cobweb of theories making him shudder.

Where did I come from?

Ben pondered these things, then buried them deep. His only goal for the moment was to protect Beatrix at all costs. Even if the price was his own life. Ben knew her gifts could tip the balance in their favor.

These thoughts penetrated Ben's mind as he and Percival raced through the constructed meridian they had generated from the rythrax. Still bearing a lock of Beatrix's hair, they had pulled the car around and warmed it up as Montavani had told Beatrix they were doing. Then they headed into the alley behind the Green Griffin and, while standing in the snow and chasing away a rat, tore a hole in space-time and, within 0.0000000001 seconds, arrived at their destination—the Diamond Light Source antimatter chamber. Lightheart had come through for them.

"Grab it and let's bloody go, boy," Percival said. "We can't stay here! And be careful!"

They were standing in the closed and locked chamber housing a large number of capsules. They were six inches long and were made of metal with a transparent center, revealing a black substance that light couldn't penetrate.

Ben picked one up and held it aloft, fumbling it and nearly dropping it in the process.

"Sweet mother of pearl! You almost killed us and everyone within a hundred miles! Put it in the case with both hands this instant!" Percival said through clenched teeth. "My God, young man," he muttered.

Ben gulped. "Sorry."

They gathered six vials, and Percival placed them in a velvet-lined briefcase with individual recesses for each one. He checked them repeatedly before, with the skill of a pediatric neurosurgeon, closing the case.

"Now," Percival said, his anger in check, "let's get the bloody hell out of this sodding place and back to the Griffin for another pint. I hate this sneaking—"

The gear mechanisms on the vault door started moving, and a gasket released pressure. The door was opening. They had nowhere to run, and they had no time to use the rythrax.

"Oh no!—"

Percival's voice died in his throat when he was accosted with an unexpected view. Standing before him in the antechamber were Alex, Malik, and Fred. Beside them was a black woman who had been working the numeric keypad to open the vault. And standing to the group's right was a short woman with ginger hair and fierce green eyes. She was holding a weapon, and it was pointed directly at Percival's face.

"Drop it," she said.

"No! Don't!" the woman in the lab coat said with panic.

The temporary confusion from the adults was unnecessary. Ben had already sprinted past Dr. Abernathy and Libby to put Malik in a bear hug. He turned to Alex and gave her a more formal, quasi-awkward hug characteristic of teenagers who like each other as more than friends but couldn't admit it.

Fred lowered the wet cloth from his head. "Percival," he said, surprising everyone. "Hello. Is that it?" He motioned to the satchel.

"Yes," Percival replied as he stared straight down the barrel of Libby's .40 caliber Glock, then reached out and pushed it to the side. "Yes, this is it."

"Can we leave now?" Fred asked.

"Yes, we should," Percival replied. "What about her?"

For a moment, Violet was alarmed. She had seen this movie before. Where witnesses were "seen off."

"She comes with us," Libby said. She shot a look at Violet and said, "I'm sorry, but we have to."

"Where's the car?" Libby asked. "We need to hit the road."

Alex stepped away from Ben and Malik and fished some of Beatrix's hair from her pocket, then held out pieces to Violet and Libby.

"Hold out your hand, please."

Violet complied, taking the proffered hair. Libby just stood there with her mouth open, ready to explode at the idea of standing in an antimatter chamber with hair in her hand.

As Percival readied the rythrax, the air started to quiver around the group, and he yelled for everyone to pull in close.

The last thing Percival heard before the air tore open and the meridian appeared to consume them, was Libby cursing with a vehemence he had never heard from a woman before. It was a lasting first impression.

He took an immediate liking to her.

The exact logistics of what happened to the seven travelers from Oxfordshire will not be told here, but for the sake of completeness, below is a brief summary.

Percival had gathered the group as closely as possible in the Diamond Light Source antimatter storage chamber for the development of the temporary meridian (a trans-meridian) with the rythrax. It was a simple "boomerang" space-time arc that would take the companions back to the exact geometric point where the original meridian opened: the alley behind the Green Griffin.

However, in an effort to stand closer to Violet, Malik tripped and shoved Fred, who was sent flailing into Percival. This, in turn, caused the Scotsman, who too was flailing, to move his hand in an unorthodox manner as he tried to ensure the antimatter case did not receive a "mild jostling and kill them all," as he eloquently put it. The result was that the axis of the meridian changed by a few nanometers. This coordinate change moved the destination sixteen feet off the template arc and sent the companions careening through space (for 0.00000125 seconds) into the restroom of the Green Griffin, the very place where Beatrix had recently discovered her gray strands of hair: a five-by-five-foot water closet designed for single occupancy.

Although physically uninjured, the seven were quite shaken up psychologically due to being extremely compacted and knotted up in the loo. Percival himself was on the bottom of the human mass of tangled limbs, his head not two inches from the toilet seat. Not much more needs to be said here except that the web of obscenity woven by said Scotsman could be heard in the pub's parlor itself.

They had heard worse…but not much.

Hearing the commotion from his table, Montavani smiled. "It appears our heroic companions have returned." He took a last swig of ale and then smacked his hands on the table. "Time to take off!"

Anxious to see Ben, Beatrix followed him.

Good timing. I never got to ask you about Professor Lightheart and what his mission was. Well, I guess I can find out when I see him. Lightheart always had a soft spot for me. 133 days!

The travelers untangled themselves and then made quick salutations to each other, some expressing surprise at seeing Montavani (Malik and Fred) and others indifferent (Libby and Violet). Only Alex seemed downright disturbed, as if a plan had not been followed. Beatrix added another item to the ever-expanding list of Alex's strange behaviors.

They were ushered out into the back alley, where snow was falling. Beatrix saw two new faces and wondered who the women were. The short one was studying her. Only then did Beatrix notice someone was missing.

"Where's Professor Lightheart?" she asked.

No one replied, everyone looking away.

"I said, where's —"

A firm hand gripped hers. Beatrix looked up, surprised it belonged to Malik. "He's gone, Beatrix. Taken . . . to the Other Place."

Beatrix recoiled in horror and covered her mouth with her hands. "Taken?" She looked at Percival for answers. "Is that true? Are we sure?"

Percival nodded, barely able to meet her gaze. "Yes."

"People," Montavani said, "we must go. We have what we came for, and now we must return home."

"Where's home?" Beatrix asked. "You said the Verge was destroyed, and we certainly can't get back through the Telegraph Cottage meridian." Beatrix realized she was starting to cry.

Professor Lightheart is dead!

Montavani smiled warmly. "My dear, we have places everywhere. No! We'll set up shop in a place to complete the first leg of our mission, the closure of the prime meridian — New York City."

"What? Back to the city? Thank goodness," Malik said. "I need my humidifier and a fresh pair of socks."

"Not your home, you dolt," Montavani said. "We have a haven there, and we must lie low so we can move forward with our plan. The servants of the Black Path are likely surveilling us as we speak. We must go."

"How can we get back?" Ben asked.

Montavani smiled at him in response.

They used the same shady car rental place in Dundee to put the others in a follow-up vehicle. Alex rode with Violet, Libby, and Fred. Malik, Ben, and Beatrix rode in the back of Montavani's black behemoth. Percival, in no condition to drive after his escapades at Glamis and the Green Griffin, slept in the passenger seat. The trio of teens all fell asleep.

In the follow-up car, Fred drove as, to his delight, Libby sat in the passenger seat. Violet was in the back with Alex. As Violet slept, Alex looked out the window.

At that point, a peculiar conversation took shape in Libby's head as she recalled what Gran Olive had told her about Fred's relationship with his sister, Evelyn.

Evelyn is Alex's mother and a former MI5 Section 3 operator. A damn good one. That makes Alex Fred's niece, right? I've always been crap at figuring out relations. Okay, Fred. The same Fred Hardingham who had gone "rogue" in the United States with his niece in tow. The very niece who attends Festermunder School in Midtown Manhattan. The school Olive called "the evil place."

So, this Alex kid here. Little Miss Perfect with her ridiculous height and all, she lost her sister. What's her name? Gwen. Obviously, it had something to do with these portals and nonsense with these beastly otherworldly things. I have my own issues with the other brat, Beatrix, but this Alex is hiding some-thing. I've seen her body language. Her moves. Her reasoning. She has yet to panic one iota, not like the idiotic Patel kid. It's like she's trained for this.

"Say, Alex. It's Alex, right?" Libby said as politely as her persona could muster.

"Yes. Libby, right? Soames-Briggs. Where does the double name come from?"

"Never mind that right now. Let me ask you something. Why did your family choose that school in the States? Festen-munder?"

"Festermunder," Alex said. "Yes. A private institution in Midtown New York."

"Yes, that one," Libby confirmed while looking at Alex in the rear-view mirror. "So, why that school? It appears to have a less-than-stel-lar reputation."

She looks uncomfortable. Good.

"It was all we could afford, I guess. I don't know."

"Really? How much does it cost relative to similar schools? Surely, it must be pricey if it's in the city center, right?"

"Well, I'm not certain of that. My parents picked it, and I didn't ask them why."

She's upset. I got her.

"Would your sister — Gwen, is it? — would she have been enrolled at Festermunder had she been with you?"

Alex's expression darkened. "I . . . I don't know. Why are you asking me these things? That's private family business. Not yours! So, piss off!"

Libby spun around in her seat and leveled her intimidating gaze on Alex, and in one statement turned, the teenager's world upside down. "You are operational. On orders from your mum. You went there to investigate something that pertains to your sister. That's a fact."

Alex returned her glare for a moment, then turned and looked out the window, her gaze remaining fixed there for the rest of their trip to the train station in Edinburgh.

Once there, the group boarded the Eurostar train, splitting into three separate compartments for the journey back to Paddington Station. Fred and Percival said they would pull watch in the hallway as the others slept. By the time they boarded, it was 10:00 p.m., and it was raining.

It occurred to Percival that, as per custom, Montavani had provided no detail about the apparent pathway back to New York. It also occurred to him as he stood in the corridor that he and Montavani had not spoken of what to do about their little problem.

Dr. Violet Abernathy.

CHAPTER 18

Another World Under the Clock

B IG BEN (OFFICIALLY KNOWN IN THE U.K. AS THE Elizabeth Tower for sticklers) loomed before them as the eight members of the company tried to get through the square unnoticed. It was midnight, and the Westminster and Whitehall areas were quiet. No one up to any good was out and about in that area of town, and all of them knew it. Malik was most displeased with the situation.

"It's freaking freezing out here, man," he said as he struggled to keep up with the group. "I can't catch another cold. If I have too many absences due to illness, it will wind up on my permanent record!"

"Shut up, you fool!" Montavani said. "We have no use for your grousing now that we're almost there."

Beatrix urged Malik onward with a rare look of encouragement. Looking past him, she spied the top of the London Eye, which was just across the Thames. It was not operating at that late an hour but was beautifully lit for the holidays.

Standing under the edifice of Big Ben, Montavani gathered the group in close. Only Libby and Beatrix seemed intent on glancing around.

"Alright, we have a small issue. Not insurmountable but an issue nonetheless."

"What bloody issue?" Libby asked as her eyes continued to sweep the area.

"The issue, young lady, is one of real estate."

"Real estate?" Violet asked.

"Yes! As in location, location, location. I can't seem to recall the exact way into the warren of tunnels under this magnificent timepiece!"

"Sweet mother of pearl, Seppe," Percival exclaimed. "We're standing here, hangin' our arses out in the bloody wind, freezing, and you forgot the meridional pattern?"

"No, imbecile! I forgot which manhole cover it is!"

Only then did the others realize the entire square was pock-marked with manhole covers, up and down the sidewalk. At least twenty-five of them from the Westminster bridge to the Abbey.

Beatrix was still transfixed by the London Eye, not helping the others decide which manhole covers to check. As the hair on the back of her neck began to stand up, not with her eyes but with some sense of inner sight, Beatrix felt as if she was being watched from the London Eye. Specifically, from the top of the Ferris wheel. Looking inward, Beatrix glimpsed a shadowy figure.

As her inner vision tightened and focused, incredibly, she found herself on top of the Eye. In the topmost car, at the highest point of the wheel, was a little girl with blond hair, waving her arm. Beatrix realized the girl was motioning for someone but looking beyond her to the square. Beatrix looked back but couldn't tell where the girl was directing her attention.

Then an echoing voice broke free, shrill and soft.

"Alex. Make her stay. Not to come for me now. It's not time. The answer is at the school. Help her find it. Please tell her. I must go. Look beyond."

The little girl pointed back to the square, and Beatrix was astonished by what she saw. A blue light arced through the square in the shape of two triangles with their apexes touching. In the center was a blue dot that glowed brighter than the rest of the lines. In the square, the rest of the group was oblivious that a coordinate map was being drawn with luminescent energy fields right in their midst.

"The World Under the Clock . . . it waits."

Beatrix thought she was dreaming, and the stupor continued until she turned back and realized the vision was gone, and she was standing in the square again with the others who were still searching for the correct spot to enter the Underground.

"Just a moment, I think I found it!" Montavani called out. He bent down over the nearest manhole cover, searching for vibrations, then shook his head. "No hum! Damn!"

"It's here!" Beatrix called out, louder than she intended. Everyone stopped and stared at her. Beatrix was standing on a manhole cover. The moment she looked down at the carvings, she knew she was correct. The rusty iron had a small logo etched in the center circle that she knew all too well—two triangles and an infinity symbol. That did not surprise Beatrix in the slightest, but the wording beneath it shook her to her core.

The Voght Company
1943

Beatrix raised her hand to get the others' attention, then pointed down at the manhole cover bearing her name. The others scurried over, and Montavani squatted down to begin prying the lid. He was using the same red scissors from the Verge.

Crack! The cover slid to the side much louder than the group would have liked. The group huddled around the manhole and peered down into the gloom. A pale blue-white light was barely perceptible someplace deep down.

"It's bloody cold up here," Percival said, needing no prompting. The Scotsman heaved himself over the manhole and launched himself down into darkness below.

Fred gasped. "Blimey! Is he gone? Another wormhole?"

"Gone he is. But no, he's simply down in that hole under the street," Montavani said. "There are catacombs down there. Let's go. And don't, pray tell, interact with the 'below dwellers,' as they don't take kindly to the surface folk."

Beatrix opened her mouth to frame a question about said "below dwellers" but then thought better of it. One by one, the others dropped into the manhole. Then, with some difficulty, Montavani closed the lid over them.

Once down below, everyone, save for Percival and Montavani, was overcome with incredible fright. There was a two-second drop, after which they contacted a hard, slanted surface. Being next after Percival, Ben found himself careening through the darkness on a slick surface. The motivity created static electricity around his clothing, making iridescent sparks.

Behind him, Malik was whooping and hollering with a rare outburst of joy, having released himself from his fear for a few precious moments. It helped that as the slide spiraled down and around, they were able to gain some visibility due to the omnipresent blue glow and from the sparks of static. When they were finally able to ascertain what was going on, the revelry ended as they accelerated into a more vertical position and began to free fall. It was then that they realized they were in a clear tube.

Malik and Ben, both in free fall and approaching terminal velocity, looked up and saw Beatrix, Alex, and the flailing form of Fred Hardingham blasting down the over-sized test tube toward them. Behind them was Libby and Violet Abernathy, both terrified. Later, Violet agreed with Malik that, against the law of physics, the entire group had caught up to each other to become a human mass in free fall.

Beatrix realized they had entered a massive underground chamber that stretched on endlessly in every direction she looked. But she was too frantic to focus on the details of the chamber, fear consuming her and every other member of the human knot as they blasted down the tube.

Beatrix gasped as Fred's effeminate scream penetrated her ears. The ground was racing up to meet them. She shut her eyes tight as she prepared for the inevitable.

But instead of slamming into the embrace of a most horrible death, Beatrix felt herself decelerate as if someone had applied a set of giant air brakes. They slowed to a speed that suggested an invisible parachute had affixed itself to them, coming to rest with incredible delicacy on what could only be described as a large pile of laundry.

It was not clean.

Before anyone in the tangled group could utter a word, their attention was grabbed by a seemingly impossible thing standing before them.

It was not the prim and perfect shapes of Percival and Montavani that transfixed them. It was a being that stood between their leaders that caused their jaws to drop.

"What the bloody hell?" Libby reached for her sidearm. Finding nothing behind her back, she returned her attention to the source of her bewilderment.

"What the bloody hell?" the figure parroted in a plummy British accent. "Nice friends of yours, Seppe. Their manners are about what I would expect from associates of yours."

The figure stepped forward and sniffed. It settled in front of Malik, who was shaking. "You stink." Then the figure turned to Montavani in disgust. "The whole lot of them. They're ripe! What gives, Seppe? These sots are running with you now? This is the worst lot of travelers I've seen you bring through here in ages! At least since the incident with Dharmon Bundee and his folk with the stolen Alcubierre warp drive. This is worse than the Tunguska crap you pulled. Honestly."

Eons? Groups of travelers? Dharmon Bundee? Warp drive? Tunguska — the meteor? Beatrix thought. *What the . . .?*

The figure rolled his eyes at the assumed futility of the situation and exhaled as if preparing for a recitation. "I'm Gorff, watch warden of this precinct and door master of the hyperfold, pro tem. You are — unfortunately for myself and my kind — guests of this realm for a period of seven hours if needed with no more than three one-hour options to renew the arrangement. Therefore, you are allowed access to hyperfold travel through zones twelve and seven up to and including three times. Return to this precinct via customary dendrites via captive portals one and three is permitted. No requests for travel via alternate paths will be honored. Don't even try it."

The companions, who had only just then untangled themselves from the knot they were in, sat on the laundry pile and stared in near fetal disbelief at the form in front of them.

"What, ahem, I mean, who are you?" Ben asked.

Gorff looked askance at Montavani. "Not too bright, is he?" he muttered. Then he turned back to the group. "I am Gorff, door master —"

"*Pro tem*," Montavani corrected.

"*Pro tem*," Gorff said with mock emphasis and an eye roll, "of the Precinct 27 Hyperfold and Watch Warden here."

Gorff exhaled in futility and then looked straight at the group. The creature was no more than three and a half feet tall. It had gray-green skin and was bald but for a manicured beard that stretched past its chin and touched the top of an idiosyncratically worn black Metallica shirt. He wore dark-green pants that covered large brown boots and a mustard-yellow vest. Around his neck was a leather pouch that dangled from a tarnished silver chain. His eyes were large and curious.

Yielding to the numerous unasked questions about who he was and his origin, Gorff continued with a mild degree of humility. "In case you haven't already guessed, I'm not like you all. I am of the race of original celestial travelers called the Ghramling. We're their descendants. We're the Ghreimling. 'Dark dwellers' in the common tongue. Our kin are the stranded folk from the uncharted spaces—"

"Gremlins?" Malik blurted, as was his custom.

Percival drew a quick breath and whispered a perfunctory apology to Gorff for Malik's usage of the unintended epithet.

Gorff walked over to face Malik, who was still quivering. "No! Not like 'gremlin.' That term—nay, that epithet—was furnished by stupid legends and stories for little children. It's a term of disrespect! A downright slur! I would much prefer 'goblin'!"

"I'm soddy. I'm so soddy! I—" Malik looked at Percival for assistance, but it was Montavani who interceded.

"Tut, tut. I'm sure no offense was intended by the poor fool. It's no use sitting here on this stinking pile of laundry quarreling. We have things to accomplish and continuing to misunderstand each other is not a priority. Now, Steve, we need your help, and I must talk to you privately at once."

Percival raised an eyebrow and frowned. Only Beatrix seemed to pick up on the name. *Steve?*

"Alright. Fine. Let's retire for a moment to the downward chambers and have a bit of a meeting. These others can relax and eat something," Gorff said, still scowling at Malik.

Gorff led the way down a large, wide hall with walls made of glistening wet dark-gray bricks and stone. As they walked, Gorff came alongside Beatrix.

"Hello," he muttered without looking up at her.

"Hello," Beatrix replied hesitantly.

"Gorff," he offered by of introduction. "Friends call me Steve, which is my name in the common tongue."

"Pleased to meet you Gor—er, Steve," Beatrix said. "What is this place?"

"This is Precinct 27, the hyperfold—"

"No, I mean, how is it that this exists under the city? We could scarcely be a few hundred feet down. Where are the subways? How do Londoners not find this place?"

"Look at your watch," Gorff/Steve said. "What time is it?"

Beatrix looked at her *Star Wars* watch and drew in a breath. "The hands, they're spinning!"

"Exactly! You're in Oblivion," he said.

"Tell me about it. But really, what—"

"Oblivion. That's where you are now. You're physically present in Oblivion. The empty space. In the common tongue, you would call this place limbo."

"Limbo? Like purgatory?"

"No. Oblivion is timeless. It's an empty space. Your watch doesn't function here, as there is no counting of time here. This is the eighth day of the week. The twenty-fifth hour. Up there is the forest." Gorff pointed above them. "This is the place beyond the woods. The borderland to the Blank Reaches, where time is not counted. You of all people should know this. You're in the World Under the Clock."

Beatrix and Gorff lagged behind the group, which had forged ahead with Percival in the lead. "So, time doesn't count here? I'm not aging right now?"

"No. You're in Oblivion. There is no time. You passed into our realm in the tubes as you all fell."

"Then how old are you?"

"Me?" Gorff sighed. "I'm old."

"How old?" Beatrix asked, smiling as she looked at him out of the corner of her eye.

"Eight thousand seven hundred and thirteen years," Gorff said with resignation.

"Well," Beatrix replied, not knowing what to say, "at least you get to live a long life."

"Hmph." Gorff said. Her offhand comment seemed to puzzle him.

As the group followed their mysterious guide, Gorff fell silent, and save for the hushed whisperings of Percival and Montavani, no one else spoke. They were all exhausted.

The hall narrowed and widened several times; then the air began to feel lighter, accompanied by a light breeze.

"Thank the maker, we've got transport," Percival exclaimed. Beatrix and the others looked beyond his outstretched finger, their eyes coming to rest on a large platform sitting over a bottomless chasm.

"Someone watch Malik," Libby said as she approached the edge of the precipice to assess the platform. "What is it?"

"A windjet," Gorff replied.

"What does it do?"

"It's what we use to move through the catacombs at speed."

"Is it another portal, Mr. Gorff?" Fred asked with cringeworthy sincerity, eliciting an eye roll from Libby.

"No, Mr. Mister," Gorff said, full of sarcasm. "It's not another blimey 'portal,' as you call it. The windjet is what you think it is. PST technology is as old as time."

"PST?" Alex said.

"Pneumatic subterranean transport! An air car for you physicists in the group! Jiminy crimbles ghreleheim, Seppe, what kind of passengers have you drummed up this time, huh?"

Beatrix noticed that Montavani ignored the indigenous profanity and the implication of past adventures with other "passengers."

Mental note number 304 to ask about later.

Gorff urged the companions across the sky ramp onto the windjet platform. The vehicle sat on a semicircular track of polished metal. The windjet was about thirty feet long and covered with a flawless clear canopy that extended down to the body, which was a bold silver. To Beatrix, it looked like one of the flying cars from the cheesy 1970s cartoon *The Jetsons*. The windjet's silver body curved under toward the steel tube, and on its underside was a soft layer of bristles. As the group boarded, the windjet gently rolled back and forth.

"Let's go, one and all," Montavani urged. "Find a seat and buckle up."

Gorff sat in the pilot's chair at the front of the windjet. Beatrix noticed the chair seemed to have been designed for him, as it was higher up than the other bucket seats, which were in rows down the cabin. The console consisted of three buttons — red, green, and yellow — and a brass control stick with a circular knob on top.

"Alright," Gorff said as he turned around, "we'll be traveling very fast, and few of you are accustomed to the forces that will be put on your body. Not to worry; there's a G-force balancing system that will zero out the effect on you. But as we reach top speeds, we'll momentarily lose gravity, and some of you may be nauseous—"

"Oh no," Malik whimpered.

"If you need to pass out, then blimey pass out." Gorff looked at Fred when he said that. "Ready?"

"Mr. Gorff," Fred replied, "if I may ask—"

He never got to ask the question because Gorff hit the green button, and a clear tube materialized from the sides of the metal half circle, encasing the windjet. Seconds later, they were driven deep into their seats as the windjet exploded forward into the tube and the darkness beyond.

Beatrix felt a force on her chest like an elephant was sitting on it . The blackness gave way to a large open space that stretched hundreds of yards in every direction. She saw structures, stone outcroppings and countless windows resembling an underground city. The "cityscape" was visible infinitely up and down, making Beatrix think that Oblivion was aptly named.

How are we still under a city?

"This sucks," Malik said.

"Actually, you are correct, young man!" Gorff hollered back over his shoulder. "The PST tech blokes use push-pull mechanics. We're getting blown down the tube from hundreds of thousands of pounds of air pressure and pulled by the same amount from a negative pressure gradient from assimilated dark energy. So, yes, it rightly sucks!"

"Where is the negative air pressure generated?" Violet called out from the back row.

"From the gateway itself. The hyperfold aperture is opened on a schedule and with it comes fresh air. We have no idea how, and no one has ever been able to explain it," Gorff said.

As the windjet gathered even more speed, the travelers fell silent. The rush of air along the length of the tube provided a relaxing white noise. Gorff dimmed the cabin lights, and the only illumination came from the instrument panel and small sconces embedded in the garishly carpeted low walls of the fuselage. The inhabitants were all busy with their own thoughts and observations as, with a whoosh, the windjet accelerated even more. The passing lights from the subterranean cityscape became a giant blurred kaleidoscope.

Then gravity stopped.

Beatrix noticed it immediately, as she had been waiting for the moment by holding her necklace in her hand. The wooden token floated up from her palm. Her satchel rose off her lap and her hair began sticking up. A hypnotic effect took over as the inhabitants of the windjet became entranced. Beatrix's eyes rolled back into her head as she was overcome with extreme somnolence. Every small sound became a reverberating echo in the corners of her subconscious.

As Beatrix drifted, she seemed to awaken in the half-light of a partial dream. Malik, seated next to her, was drifting up and down in his seat in a zero-gravity trance. The others, including Parfleet, wore vacant expressions. Only Montavani appeared different as he sat there, asleep with his eyes open like small slits.

As the cityscape flashed by, it became distorted, the light and dark parts bending and blurring. A low hum started, progressing to a steady drone. It held on a certain frequency, a note that struck Beatrix with the flickering tongues of fear.

The windjet stopped, and the occupants, except for Beatrix, whip-lashed in slow motion, still catatonic. The droning became louder as the clear canopy retracted, exposing them to the dark of Oblivion.

"Ouy evah . . . ouy evah ti," a voice said. It was ominously deep and possessed such a malice as to make Beatrix shudder.

"Emoc!" it commanded. "Emoc!" it repeated, sounding even more dreadful.

Beatrix was suddenly carried forth from her seat, floating away from the windjet and leaving her companions behind. She found herself traversing the narrow channel of the sky bridge, continuing until the windjet and her friends were lost from sight.

Beatrix stood on the sky bridge over the empty chasm below. She had never felt more alone, as if she were the only inhabitant of the World Under the Clock.

Then he came.

A shadow materialized several yards ahead of her. It was undefined at first, Beatrix unsure if the shadow were a splinter in her mind's eye, but it felt real. The looming shadow was tall, taking the shape of a man.

"Emoc ot em. . . ."

Beatrix was afraid, yet she couldn't speak or move.

"Evig ot em! Evig ot em! Ylno I nac evas mih!"

Beatrix was entranced by the vile voice and the unintelligible words that it spoke. Although she couldn't understand the Shadow's commands, she was able to comprehend the words' context through her emotions. Dread. Dread and cold fear, coursing through her body. All Beatrix could see was an undefinable wall of darkness. A void without stars.

"Eht ecafrus lliw ton evas uoy. I ees uoy! Reah em! Reah em! Evig ot em."

"Give you what?" Beatrix muttered.

The looming shadow accelerated toward Beatrix and seemed to pass through her before it disappeared into black vapor, leaving a whispered word in her mind.

Ouy.

In the splinters of her mind, Beatrix saw a wall of stars rushing away to disappear in wall of blackness. Then the stars came rushing back. Only in reverse like a video of a celestial explosion being played backwards.

Now awake, Beatrix found herself back in her seat in the windjet, a single word on her lips.

"You."

Then Gorff was before her, startling Beatrix. "You have the mark."

"Yes," Beatrix meekly confirmed as she shook off the cobwebs of her dream.

"You've seen him?" Gorff inquired, not taking his green eyes off hers.

"Yes."

Gorff sat next to her on the edge of the bucket seat and sighed as he stared ahead into the kaleidoscope. "I, too, have seen him."

"Seraphim," Beatrix said.

"Yes," Gorff replied. "The Dark One. He has stirred in your mind, young one, has he not?"

Beatrix turned toward the creature, who was now a friend. "Yes. How do you know?"

"All those who have faced the Dark Star and his minions recognize the eyes of another who have seen it."

"Seen what?"

"The End of Time. The Beyond. The edge of the hypersphere. He shows it to all who see him. Yet here his spoken words are inverted as our world is 'counterspin' to his."

Beatrix was about to ask another question of the Ghreimling but thought better of it as the windjet slowed, and the others began to stir.

Is that the vision that Seraphim showed me? The end of time?

"The Great Apocrypha. Genocolypse. The Annihilation, they call it," Gorff whispered as he stared ahead into the abyss. Then he turned toward her. "The end is the beginning, the beginning, the end."

"We can stop it," Beatrix whispered. "We can destroy his gateways. The meridians. We can stop him. I . . . I . . . I can kill Seraphim."

"Child, if you truly believe that is the answer, then you have already failed." Gorff's eyes lost their mirthful appearance, replaced by sadness. "The Eidolon of the Thirteen, you are. Strong yet full of misplaced might. You may try, but no one can kill Seraphim. Nor should they even want to."

Nor should they want to?

"The hyperfold aperture has a fractional refresh rate of sixteen minutes between openings—"

"Does that mean it's open for sixteen minutes?" Malik asked.

"No, fool. Think of what you're saying," Gorff said. Seeing the hurt look on Malik's face, Gorff sought to placate him. "Look, young man, the aperture opens every sixteen minutes and then remains open for sixteen seconds."

"Which means . . .?"

"Which means we have four minutes to get you all in the bloody gateway before the template arc changes and the destination isn't the same! I really don't want you whisked away to Bogrii-7, as those asteroid belters are a rough lot to deal with," Gorff said as he continued down the narrow sky bridge with the group. "Seppe, you and Percival know about the Wheel Effect, of course, but for the rest of the bloody group, let me explain while we walk, but quickly now. We have only three minutes and forty-one seconds left in London for you."

The little company crowded close with Montavani and Parfleet in tow. Violet was in particular transfixed by everything Gorff said.

"The Wheel Effect was discovered ages ago. Many of the first travelers who mapped the hyperfolds did so at great peril. The large majority were lost to the uncharted reaches of the macroverse. Each leap into a meridian was blind. Many ghreleheim, my forefathers, were lost over the centuries as volunteer explorers. Each leap that was successful made the next one infinitely more dangerous. Some, like my uncle Freeb Mwoob, made six jumps and mapped them all prior to his disappearance."

Gorff paused for a moment and grew pensive, then shrugged and continued. "People, the meridians are not finite. They change and alter on set schedules. This information was paid for by the lives of our forefathers and by the risks taken by the travelers—as well as by students at your bloody Festermunder! Like Seppe. And you, Percival." Gorff turned to Beatrix. "And, of course, your foster-father, Wendell Voght."

Wendell!

"Mwoob was lost on a hyperfold jump that sent him somewhere to

M31, Andromeda. Lost but not without contribution. Yes, he discovered the New York-London-Verdun axis. He also found and retro-mapped the Franz Josef Land-Ulaanbaatar-Tucson axis . . ."

"Tucson," Percival said. "I spent a month there one night."

A brief sniff from Montavani resembled mirth.

As the group spilled out onto a wide platform, Gorff continued. "Of course, Wendell Voght discovered the Black Meridian."

"The Black Meridian?" Beatrix asked.

"The Dark Path in Scotland. To the Other Place."

Castle Glamis.

"But none of them saw as much as the greatest of all travelers, Peter Loren."

Who is Peter Loren? Beatrix mused.

The trip would take 0.000000031 nanoseconds, according to their guide. As Gorff bid the group adieu, he asked to hold Beatrix's satchel. She obliged him, and he opened it and took out her leather-bound journal. He slipped the pencil from the holder on the spine and then wrote something on the last page. He snapped the journal shut and placed it back in the satchel, which he also secured.

"Find your truth," he whispered. "But don't attempt to destroy him. You will not win. The path of creation also destroys."

Montavani walked over, holding a pair of red scissors. "Beatrix."

Her last feeling as the group jumped into the meridian was a blast of fear. Only then did she realize what had happened the last time. . . .

CHAPTER 19

The Sovereign Light Theater

Journal Entry: 0413
December 24, 2016
New York, New York
Sovereign Light Theater
188-A East 43th St.

We're back. The traverse went as expected. Less than a fraction of a second. We made an unceremonious arrival in the Onassis Reservoir on the Jetty. The old man didn't join us, much to the dismay of all. He claimed he would catch up as he had business elsewhere. The intra-terrestrial guide in London (a story in itself) was informative albeit a trifle difficult to communicate with, as he was extremely truculent with all but Montavani and, of course, Beatrix. I have discovered that the gateways are ever evolving and destabilizing. It seems clear now that they intend to try to implode the prime meridian at Festermunder. I need clear instructions on what I should do. If it closes, we lose possibly our only opportunity to go back for her. Do I need to consult our ally? Please advise. We dare not communicate in the clear. A new SOI is needed immediately. The Brit agent is suspicious and very tenacious. We're now holed up in a defunct theater in Midtown (West 43rd between 9th and 10th Ave) being used as a safe house.

On a personal note, I detest this prying and spying and would like to stop. Is there any chance I can?

Love to you and Daddy,

Alex

"The Sovereign Light Theater was originally a German Baptist Church built in 1890 in what is now known as Hell's Kitchen. It morphed into a more secular pursuit and became a discotheque in the 1960s before becoming a cafe. The Sovereign Light Cafe went out of business after six years, and the real estate was sold at auction at the massive haul of 11.1 million by a private equity firm. The firm was a British Holding called Coventry Brothers, a wholly owned subsidiary of a print media tycoon dating back to the nineteenth century: the Voght Company. The Sovereign Light Theater retained the moniker of the aforementioned cafe. The current manager/owner of said theater is also a teacher of history at Festermunder Academy in Midtown New York City: Mr. Elias V. Lightheart."

Malik continued reading the press clipping through the stained and dusty bulletin board glass in the foyer of the Sovereign Light Theater as Beatrix, Ben, and Alex stood looking over his shoulder, listening.

"Voght! Your family is rich!" Malik said. "Professor Lightheart was the caretaker? Poor old Lightheart. He'll never get to come back to this place."

"Yeah," Beatrix replied, nowhere near as excited as Malik. She was growing accustomed to being emotionally unmoved by new information even when she was sorrowful.

The Voght Company.

The name was once a nugget of importance and interest in an otherwise uninteresting life. Now Beatrix felt it was the bane of her existence.

Her moment of self-reflection was broken by Percival's Scottish drawl.

"A'right. Let me show you the place. But first some ground rules. No phones. None. They're to remain turned off and placed in this basket." He passed around a dusty wicker basket, and Beatrix, Ben, and Malik reluctantly turned theirs in. Alex surrendered hers in with a carefree smile, which Libby noticed and she glanced at Alex suspiciously.

"Take these," Percival continued. "They're analogue phones. You can use them to send simple texts. All calls must be under sixty seconds to be sure we ain't triangulated. That applies to you too, dearie," he added, looking at Libby.

She fixed Percival with a gaze so vile that he momentarily lost his momentum. "Old man, I'll keep my belongings to myself along with whatever else I choose. I know more than all of you bloody combined about counter-surveillance, and I'll tell you morons first off, if someone wants to track you, they'll find you and your dumbphones. Mine stays, Percival." It was the first time she had addressed him by name. As she eyed the rest of the group, her face softened slightly. "After your tour, I need to debrief you all and go over some security measures."

"Fine," Parfleet said in mock surrender, palms up.

Percival led the group out of the foyer, which had ticket counters hidden behind red curtains and brass casing.

They went through four open doors to a wider anteroom, from which they could see the theater beyond. The words "Sovereign Light Theater" were etched in brass around the doors in a Gatsby-Fitzgerald font that Beatrix appreciated. She felt an arm around her shoulder. It was Ben, who gave her a firm smile as if to say, "Our new home."

Beatrix nodded and gave him a half hug as the tour continued.

"The main theater," Percival announced. "It has an orchestra pit next to the stage. Then the mezzanine and then the balcony. The stage area is where we'll meet for meals and meetings."

The chairs were sapphire-colored velvet, and the floor was covered with a floral carpet. The running lights in the floors and sconces on the sides of aisle seats functioned perfectly. The ceiling was a captivating etching that looked like cosmic events and celestial bodies—comets, planets, stars, and the moon.

Beatrix looked askance at the ceiling and saw it as a whole rather than focusing on its parts. She was able to perceive two triangles touching apex to apex tethered together with an infinity symbol — the same thing she had seen in the Verge and in the library in Festermunder.

Festermunder. The mission. My goodness. I'm so tired of this, and we haven't really accomplished much at all, other than bringing that accursed antimatter over here. Meanwhile, Professor Lightheart is gone, and our leader stayed behind in London. Business elsewhere?

With Lightheart gone and Montavani having ditched them, Beatrix was at a loss as to the point of their misadventure. She dared not tell that to Alex, whom Beatrix still did not wholly trust, nor did she confide in Malik, as his heart couldn't take it. The only person she revealed her doubts to was Ben.

"What about Fred?" Ben whispered as the tour broke up, and the others looked for bathrooms and accommodations.

"Fred?" Beatrix replied. "You've got to be kidding me. He's super nice, but he's in way over his head. Besides, Libby has him right under her thumb. He can't even take a pee without her watching him."

"You like her?" Ben asked.

"Libby?"

Ben nodded as he sipped his water bottle.

"Yeah, I do. But she scares me."

As if on cue, Libby stepped out of the shadows in front of them. "Debrief in ten minutes!"

Mercifully, Percival insisted on serving a meal at the long table on the stage during the debriefing. Libby allowed it, but only because she was famished. Percival served shepherd's pie, and he even had the kindness to consider Malik's issues with beef and made him a vegetarian plate.

Percival sat at the head of the table and Libby at the foot. To Percival's right was Beatrix, then Ben, and then Malik. Across from them were Violet, Fred, and Alex. Beatrix couldn't help but notice a couple of empty seats, which could have accommodated Montavani, who was attending to other affairs, and Professor Lightheart, whom they had lost in Oxfordshire. Libby took 10 minutes to issue security measures about light, noise, texting, and web browsing.

"To Elias," Percival said as he lifted his glass of ale. Somewhat disjointedly, everyone, including Violet and Libby, raised their glasses out of respect for their fallen companion.

"May he find peace." Percival's voice broke and he cleared his throat. "It's Christmas Eve, so let's make this brief so we have time for rest, as I'm sure no one wants to engage in merriment this night. Regarding Lightheart—we have an issue. He's missing, and we can expect his anaphora to try to assume his role. But we can't have the bloody thing bumping around our world as we plan the final stage of our operation at the school."

"Anaphora?" Ben inquired.

"A type of simulacrum. They're not all the same. Some are more exact copies of the original in literally every conceivable detail. Others are merely essays in the understanding of replication. They're less reliable, easily spotted, and unlikely to do much more than create chaos. They're the epistropha."

Percival paused and took a swig of ale. "Wendell's simulacrum was an epistropha. A lesser one. A babbling mess of a man. Seppe sent him over in haste when he was taken. We had no time to delve into the intricacies of developing a reliable anaphora of Wendell to come back to the World Above."

"But you said he was sent back to warn us," Beatrix protested.

Percival gave Beatrix an icy look. "Child, there was more at stake than you can know. Just let us plan for Elias's arrival. In fact, he's probably skulking around the streets of New York as we speak."

"As what?" Libby asked. "An anaphora?"

Percival nodded.

"Then tomorrow, we set out looking for him. Agreed?" Libby looked around the group, their silence seeming to indicate consent.

"Right, Beatrix, Malik, and Percival you take west of Broadway, and Fred, Ben, Alex, and Violet can take the east side," Libby said. "There won't be a lot of folks out early Christmas morning, so it will make our job easier. We need to go over some of the places Elias frequented, as his simulacrum could remember some things, right?"

Percival nodded. "Yes, there are some implanted memories. But it's not that simple. If he has come back to us, we could all be in great danger."

"What kind of danger?" Fred asked. "I thought the anaphora would be no threat to us."

Percival's face reddened, his blood pressure about to explode. "Jiminy

Christmas this bloke! Listen, mate, you're supposed to be the MI5 investigator of the unexplained. Did you learn nothing over the past few days? There's a risk he's been followed back!"

"By whom?" Fred asked, coming close to the periphery of insolence (a rare thing for him).

"Them." That from Violet, who had remained mute throughout the conference thus far. Everyone turned to look at her. "Them," Violet repeated, "the agents of Seraphim. They're real. I saw one in the synchrotron. I felt the power throw me back when the big one came at me. They will tail Elias, will they not? The man we need so desperately is merely bait in a trap."

"Nonetheless, we need Elias's anaphora," Percival said. "We need to get back into that bloody Festermunder School to deliver the payload into the prime meridian, and Elias is our ticket. We can't get access to the area without his credentials."

"What credentials?" Alex asked.

Percival, who had less than absolute zero when it came to patience levels with Alex (and all British women, save Libby, whom he was slightly scared of), leveled his gaze on her and exhaled before speaking. "He has the cipher to the elevator access coded from his DNA, and it must be from a living host, i.e., we need Elias Lightheart alive."

Percival shot an accusatory glance at Libby, immediately canceling her utilitarian idea of toting in a corpse and using it as a biological locksmith.

"Alive and conscious," Percival added. "We may need his voice as well!"

"So if 'they' come," Malik said, "Beatrix can't take them all on, can she?"

Beatrix sneered at Malik and twisted uncomfortably in her seat.

Percival didn't reply.

Across the world, Montavani fretted.

The decision to allow Lightheart to be taken over to the Divide weighed heavily on him. Nothing of that magnitude had ever been attempted before. The risks were incalculable. The mission even more daring.

The fool, Lightheart. He wanted this.

In his heart, Montavani knew his friend would be taken to the dark spaces in the Deep and interrogated mercilessly by Luka and his agents. No one had ever emerged from their instruments and techniques fully intact. There was one major difference, though.

We have assets on the inside.

Montavani drew on his pipe and exhaled as he continued to muse, his thoughts bitter.

Hopefully, Elias can convince them he's come over to their side.

Montavani regretted that he—and to some extent, Percival—had had to lie to the rest of the company.

It's just too dangerous to give them any knowledge of Elias's attempt to cross over to the others. If they were captured, the plan would fail.

To make the ruse seem believable, Lightheart could have to commit completely to the exchange and possibly allow himself the horror of committing unsaid indiscretions in order to make good his turning to the Black. Also, information would have to be rendered, and that intelligence would have to be substantiated by the Mechanix lest Lightheart's posture as a defector not be believed.

He will be tested. Yes, he'll be tested to the edge of his morality and beyond.

Montavani was most concerned with Beatrix.

Oh, Beatrix, if you only knew all. . . .

Her role in the plan was vital yet not wholly sacrosanct to Montavani. Lightheart knew it better than most.

Seraphim is interested in anything to do with the girl. He was obsessed with the subject, and in truth, now he knows her name. Elias must not give her up completely, but it would be helpful if he could give them a nibble of truth in order to appear reputable. They just may keep him alive long enough for her to complete her mission. Then he can complete his.

Lightheart's mission was simple as it was complex: go deep undercover with the others and report back on the Enemies' intent from the inside.

Then there was the matter of the little girl.

The sister.

"Steve."

Montavani nodded, extinguished his pipe, placing it in his front coat pocket, and then turned to Gorff and winked as he buttoned his coat.

He then stepped through the meridian and was never seen in the World Under the Clock by any other Ghreimling again.

Alex had a problem.

On the outside, she was a smart, pretty, confident teenager. Everything had always come easily to her. Yet, ever since that day in the English countryside when Gwen was taken, she couldn't seem to shake the feeling that she was not enough.

When Gwen was lost, her family had been shattered. Although her parents never blamed her or Uncle Freddie, she couldn't help but feel responsible. That was why Alex felt compelled to do what her parents were asking, even if that meant going behind her friends' backs.

Friends.

The word stung as she thought of it. Alex so desperately wanted to be liked and respected by the group. But if they knew her motives . . .

Alex had climbed the ladder to the scaffolding above the darkened stage for a bit of privacy. Pulling out her non-confiscated phone, she began to text, doing her best to cover the screen with her hand.

> We're coming out tomorrow FYI
> Mum: Why?
> Looking for Lightheart — his whatever.
> Mum: Anaphora
> That
> Mum: He may be followed.
> What do I do?
> Mum: Get the information from him.
> Shouldn't I tell the others?
> Mum: ABSOLUTELY NOT!
> I hate this Mum!
> Mum: Lives are at stake Lexi.
> Gotta go some

The grip was fierce and strong. It belonged to Libby. It felt like the bones in Alex's wrist were about to explode.

Libby snatched the phone from Alex and read it. "You and I are going for a walk, young lady."

Including the events of the last few months, Alex had never been more scared for her life than she was at that moment.

Libby dragged Alex, who stood almost a head taller than her, out of the theater's service exit and onto the 44th Street sidewalk in the blistering cold. It was 1:12 a.m. on Christmas morning. They were alone.

Not letting go of Alex's wrist, Libby wheeled on her, her voice sharp. "I know about your parents. I'll give you two minutes to explain everything, no crap or I'll turn you over to Percival. Or I could just leave you out here."

"Libby—"

"And to tell you another thing, how dare you, you arrogant little imp, call me by first name? It's—"

"There's a problem—"

"Oh, damn right, there's a problem. The problem is, I'm in a foreign country without a visa or valid documentation following ghosts and witchery and whatever the hell else is being conjured up as speak and will likely end up extradited back to the UK .What the hell—"

"Libby!"

Libby was unaccustomed to being spoken to in such a manner, especially by a teenager, and she hesitated momentarily, which allowed Alex to wring her hand free. But she did not run.

"Please. I mean no harm. They—"

"They what?" Libby asked. "Out with it, Thacker!"

"Their plan!"

"What about it?"

"It's not going to work! It'll only make things worse!" Alex protested as steam issued from her mouth in the frigid air. "It's going to fail. Montavani and Percival, they're not telling us everything."

Libby folded her arms over the front of her hoodie, a brief but unspoken truce forming between them. "What? Tell me?"

"The prime meridian. In Festermunder. If they destroy it, we won't ever be able to cross it."

"Why would we cross over to the other accursed place?" Libby asked.

"My mum has studied this exhaustively, and I'm telling you that the gateway under Festermunder is the only way we can bring the fight to the other side. Do we really want to have another battle on our side, especially here in New York? We need to take the fight to them. We can too. That's the part of the plan my mum has been obsessed with."

"What's in it for you?" Libby asked.

Alex stared straight at Libby for a moment before speaking. "They have my sister."

"Gwen," Libby replied. "I read about her; your great-gran Olive told me the story. Wait." Libby took a second to frame her thoughts. "You said your parents are obsessed with the gateways."

"Yeah?"

"Did that begin before or after Gwen was taken?"

"I . . . I actually never thought about it. Why? What are you implying?"

"You need to learn some basic police work, Thacker. The sequence of events is crucial. If Gwen was taken following your parents' study of the gateways, then . . ." Libby trailed off as she looked west toward the New Jersey bluffs of Weehawken, which were dotted with lights.

"Oh my God! She was taken as a warning!" Alex said. "But surely they would have told me!"

"At some point, you'll need to sort that out with your parents, but don't worry about it now." It was as close to consolation as Libby could get. "Now, why did your great-grandma Olive call Festermunder evil? Was it the presence of the gateway or something else?"

"There . . . there's something evil there that doesn't sleep, and Professor Lightheart knew someth—"

Alex's sentence was cut off mid-syllable as she lost the ability to speak. The air felt thick and Alex and Libby felt like their ears had been stuffed with cotton. Movements slowed to a fraction of normal speed as they both felt mired in a stop-motion/still-life setting.

A piece of trash blew past, and some leaves crawled over the pavement.

Both women tried to utter a word of warning, to no avail. Words conjured in the mind couldn't be generated in time. The world had changed.

Libby watched as Alex spun slowly to look behind her down 44th Street, a trail of vaporous light dragging behind her movements. Alex's ponytail whipped around in slow motion.

What the bloody hell? Libby thought, though she couldn't connect her mouth to the words.

They both looked up as something blocked out all the light in the night sky. The stars shifted and winked out. It was blacker than black. The streetlights stood no chance of suppressing the shroud of darkness that fell over the street.

Alex and Libby both felt something heavy on them. A weight like an invisible low ceiling seemed to push them down. Slowly, without gravity playing its usual role, they both sank to the pavement.

The air was no longer breathable, and it became dreadfully hot. The thickness that had started moments earlier felt like solid matter that their lungs refused to inhale. Alex and then Libby felt the cobwebs of unconsciousness wrap around their minds as they began to pass out.

Then there was a light.

Clinging to her last strand of consciousness, Libby looked up see Beatrix standing over her and Alex. With her knees half bent and her arms above her head, Beatrix was pushing the blackness back up. Fully conscious now, Alex watched helplessly as Beatrix struggled with the shroud of darkness. Purple light emanated from her fingertips where she touched the black disc, and the blackness shrank as if Beatrix herself had balled it up like a piece of paper. She then crushed its remnants in her hands with a final flare of white-hot light.

The air became breathable again, and the temperature dropped. Libby and Alex both flexed their wrists and elbows as they regained mobility.

"Inside, now!" Beatrix said, her irises glowing purple

The fourteen-year-old honor student and the MI5 agent followed her back into the theater without a word.

Luka sat alone in a black sedan with tinted windows and watched, unblinking, the front of the Sovereign Light Theater. However, he never saw the exchange between Alex and Libby. He saw only the theater, nothing else.

CHAPTER 20

Anaphora and Epistropha

DARKNESS SURROUNDED EVERYTHING. THICK AND IMPEN-etrable. A blackness with weight and mass. Lightheart felt the oppressiveness of the dark invade his very mind. He shut his eyes as if the internal void would somehow lessen the blanket of fear that meant to enshroud him.

Where am I? Am I dead?

No answer came. Only more silence.

I know where I am.

He remembered a white-hot explosion in the synchrotron. Then there was the fall. An endless pull into nothing. Totally unlike the other gateways he had traversed before. This was longer. And something else was different.

There were colors.

Everywhere during the fall, Lightheart saw vaporous tears and streaks in the void. They were frighteningly beautiful. Montavani had not told him of such phenomena.

Lightheart raised his arms to place his hands on his face and was surprised to find them unbound. He felt his body for injury and realized he

~ 265 ~

and his belongings were intact. Feeling around more, he realized he was lying on a soft bed. Relaxing somewhat, he reviewed his objective.

The peaceful moment came to an abrupt end as a red light snapped on, blinding him. Having been in the dark for untold hours, Lightheart had to squint for several seconds before he could safely look at the light. What he saw frightened him.

A black snake-like object extended from the ceiling, then coiled back as if readying to strike him. Its head featured a red robotic eye with blinking horizontal slits of black. The eye inched closer until it was in front of his face. Then a blue beam emitted from it, traversing his iris.

It's scanning me.

Montavani had warned thid would happen. In a realm of the real, and the simulacra, someone wanted to be certain of Lightheart's authenticity. He knew he must remain calm as the probe was sensing more than his identity. And sensing his stress level as well.

My anaphora. It's already back there! In my world.

Apparently satisfied with its findings, the red-eyed snake skulked back into the ceiling, and Lightheart was in the dark again.

Then Lightheart heard a knock (almost polite sounding), and an unseen door opened, flooding the room with soft light.

Expecting the worst, Lightheart was perplexed to see no one there. He swung his feet down to the stone floor and crept toward the doorway. An oil lamp burned on a stone wall out in a hall. Looking right and left, he saw more candles at intervals along the corridor. On instinct, he turned to his right and proceeded down the hallway.

Well, they know I'm here. I'm sure they're watching me and allowing me to explore.

As Lightheart wheeled around the corner, however, he stopped short. Two men in black cowls were crumpled on the floor. Standing over them was the reason for their unconscious state.

A young girl wielding some type of device.

Lightheart gaped in amazement as she held her finger to her lips to shush him.

"You've come," she said, looking past him. "Is this all there is?"

In the shadows of an alley in midtown Manhattan, Luka took a moment to think. To his knowledge, they had not arrived, which perplexed him. The mighty Bram had been taken to the inquisitors of Seraphim. There were rumors among the Mechanix that Bram had even been taken before the altar of the Dark Star itself to beg for clemency. But no one could be certain of that. Having never been seen, Seraphim was more powerful in the mind and need not be glimpsed to be feared. The Master was said to have never granted anyone an audience. No one except the old man had ever laid eyes on him. Not even Luka could make that claim.

He decided to wait.

Her patience beyond the breaking point, Beatrix marched ahead of Libby and Alex down the stairs to the concession lounge. The large, round room was carpeted and had a low ceiling, the perfect place for the discussion she felt was needed.

"Okay, right here, on Christmas, let's have it out," Libby said.

Beatrix wheeled on her and Alex, but what she said was unexpected. "Help me!" Beatrix said in a broken voice. Then she plopped onto the floor and began to cry. "Help me, please!"

Two arms squeezed her shoulders, then wrapped around her as she sobbed. A head pressed close to hers. "It'll be alright," a voice with a British accent whispered, repeating the words over and over until Beatrix ran out of tears. She couldn't recall ever being hugged like that, as if the giver needed it as much as the receiver.

Beatrix looked up and was surprised to see Alex sitting across from her. The arms around her shoulders belong to Libby.

Beatrix recoiled in shock, then relaxed. Libby sat upright as if the light in the room had changed and the maternal moment had passed. Beatrix wiped a huge plump tear from her cheek that threatened to cross onto her lips. "Sorry."

"It's alright," Alex replied.

An awkward silence spread as the three sat in a close circle, cross-legged on the floor.

"Truth time," Libby said. "We have to start looking out for each other, and we have to be able to trust each other." She ended her sentence looking at Alex.

Alex shook her head, but then, in response to a stern look from Libby, offered what amounted to her full penance. "Beatrix, I haven't been completely honest with you."

As she said it, Alex seemed to weaken, and her shoulders dropped. A burden had been lifted.

"Go on," Beatrix urged, her eyes red.

"I'm not just a regular student at Festermunder. I . . . I got into the school by unusual means."

"I thought you got in on an sports scholarship," Beatrix said, encasing the word in air quotes as she cited the oft-used and sketchy way private educational institutions attained certain gifted students by awarding them farcical aid packages based on dubious credentials. Beatrix assumed it was for something stupid like tennis.

"Uh, no. It's not at all like that. I'm actually rubbish at tennis," Alex replied, as if reading Beatrix's mind.

She's stalling.

"Alex, tell her or I will," Libby commanded.

Alex exhaled. "Fred isn't the only member of my family working for the British government. My mum and I are as well. I'm enrolled in the school to spy on it."

Beatrix's mouth fell open in shock.

"Not exactly accurate, Thacker," Libby said. "Your activities in the States aren't in any way sanctioned by MI5 or the Commonwealth. This casual investigation of the school is your family's mess—"

"No, that's not entirely correct," Alex said.

"Just what the hell are you talking about, Thacker?"

"The investigation of Festermunder was sanctioned by some offbeat departmental section that's cloaked in secrecy. I'm not sure what it's called, but someone came to us after all of Mum's requests to investigate my sister's disappearance were denied. They said her case was delegated to local law enforcement. It was very hush-hush. Mum was being drummed out of the Company, as they thought she was taking Gwen's disappearance too personally to carry out her duties effectively."

"Two questions," Beatrix said. "Why did they change their minds about investigating your sister's abduction? And what does Gwen have to do with Festermunder?"

Libby looked on in uncharacteristic silence, though impressed with Beatrix's police work.

"Right," Alex continued. "Mum was contacted by someone from a discretionary MI5 department who wanted to remain anonymous. But she figured it out by following him. I forget his name. Damn, what was it?"

"Please continue," Beatrix said with undue patience.

"Well, Mum was contacted by this bloke from Organizational Analysis or Analytical Organization — IS-1! Yes, that's it. And he had information he said he could trade for us about Gwen and similar phenomena, and we should look at a school in the states called Festermunder."

"Wait? IS-1?" Libby said. That was Management Analysis — the black box section of MI5 that had pools of resources (and agents) that couldn't be accounted for.

"Alex, does the name 'Manafort' mean anything to you?" Libby inquired.

"No, not really. Manafort. I can't recall — wait, yes! That was the bloke Mum kept having to meet for dead drops and information exchanges. That's him. Manafort, without a doubt. We need to contact him."

"That will be hard," Libby replied, "considering he's dead."

"Dead? How?" Alex asked.

"Probably from that wretch we ran into at Gran Olive's flat."

"I have another question," Beatrix said. "Why Festermunder? It's in the States, and Gwen disappeared in the UK, so I don't see a connection no matter what's happening down into the school's library."

"We had no idea either. Only that Mum was aware of the school long before Gwen and I were born. Festermunder being an issue was first, and this whole thing with Gwen came a decade or more later. It was then that Manafort became especially helpful to Mum when she began looking into Festermunder again with some new evidence or something."

"I checked your mother's records at MI5, Thacker. There are no records of her ever mentioning Festermunder. No investigation was ever sanctioned by the Company, and no record was ever made of working directly with the FBI."

"She wanted to follow up on her hunches in her free time," Alex said.

"I understand that this poor Manafort fellow was helpful in furthering the investigation, but that was only recently and after your sister disappeared, right?" Beatrix said. "She was interested in Festermunder years before Gwen and Manafort, correct?"

Was Manafort working for the Enemy? Did he want Evelyn to reveal something about Festermunder that the Enemy couldn't obtain on his own?

Alex nodded as Libby looked on with keen interest.

"But how did she learn about the mysteries surrounding the school?" Beatrix asked. "Who tipped her off about Festermunder and the meridian?"

Beatrix could hardly have prepared herself for the answer.

"That's easy," Alex replied. "Your foster father, Wendell Voght."

"Wendell?" Always desperate for any shred of information about her missing father, Beatrix sat bolt upright.

"In the early 2000s, immediately following 9/11, there was increased cooperation in intelligence gathering, even of the unexplained, between the FBI and MI5 as well as intelligentsia worldwide," Libby said. "So, it's not surprising that your mum would have been given shreds of information about Festermunder."

Alex nodded. "No. There was definitely an interaction between Mum and Wendell sometime in the late 1990s to the early 2000s."

"How?" Beatrix asked.

"A letter. Wendell sent an anonymous letter to MI5 in 2012. My only thought was that he didn't trust what would happen if he used traditional law enforcement in America. He may have been investigating Festermunder himself, as he was a former student there."

"How did your mom know Wendell wrote the letter if he wrote it anonymously?" Beatrix asked.

"We're British, Beatrix," Libby replied on Alex's behalf. "We invented the spy craft."

Libby had not meant the comment to be funny, but the three snickered anyway.

"Why would Wendell, who had already discovered and been using the meridians, send in any information that might expose them to scrutiny?" Beatrix asked. "It doesn't make sense."

"Perhaps he was creating a trail of breadcrumbs," Alex said. "He was smart. Wendell knew the trail would eventually lead back to him. A coded signal, of course. Maybe he wanted to find someone he could trust in case something happened."

A last-ditch warning, Beatrix thought. *We need that letter!*

"Wait!" Libby said. "There's something now! I saw a picture in your great-gran Olive's flat. I think your mother had a connection, Alex. Hold on."

Libby put her head in her hands, rubbing her temples as if willing herself to recall something would trigger a memory. "There was a large lady in a picture with your mum."

Libby sat bolt upright and reached for her phone. Although forbidden, she had kept it close. She thumbed through her pictures and screenshots until she found the one she had snapped a copy of in Gran Olive's flat, then passed her phone to Beatrix as Alex leaned in to look.

When Alex saw the picture, dated March 14, 1999, she sighed. It showed a young Evelyn Thacker standing next to Headmistress Grunnion-Paltine. Beatrix was dumbstruck when she recognized the third figure.

Wendell Voght.

Looking closer, she noticed something peculiar.

Twenty-something Wendell Voght and twenty-something Evelyn Thacker were holding hands.

On Evelyn's left hand was an engagement ring.

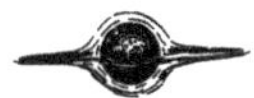

Christmas morning dawned cloudy and cold. The search party working east of Broadway, which included Ben, Alex, and Violet, worked their way between the long avenues seeking shelter from the wind that seemed to use every advantage the buildings afforded to assault them. Still woozy from his concussion in the synchrotron two days prior, Fred had started out with the group. But he was in no shape to deal with the physical hardship of walking countless miles with the mercury at 28°F. Worried about her uncle's health, Alex brought him back to the theater to rest, then set out again with Violet and Ben.

Libby had not been assigned to either search party, as announced she would stay back and look after Fred (much to his delight). Beatrix detected an almost imperceptible nod from Libby as if some unspoken plan were about to be hatched.

I like her. She thinks I'm a fool, though.

Percival was exceptionally jovial. "Merry Christmas, Beatrix. Merry Christmas, May-leck!"

"Merry Christmas," Beatrix mumbled.

"It's *Mah*-lik, emphasis on the Mah—"

"Oh shut it, fool. No one cares. It's Christmas!" Percival giggled and then slapped Malik on the back, causing him to cough. Beatrix looked at Malik and smiled as if to say she was sorry.

"Now, let's go find this sodding Elias doppelganger and bring him in before those hostile devils do," Percival continued. "There are surely about the place already." He buttoned his heavy coat over his omnipresent crushed-velvet blazer.

Percival peeked out the peephole in the theater door, then opened it and walked out into the street. "Clear."

Beatrix checked her watch, sniffed, then adjusted her sock hat and scarf. It was 6:48 a.m. on Christmas Day. She jammed her hands into her jacket pockets and felt a piece of paper. As Malik and Percival walked ahead toward the Hudson down West 44th Street, Beatrix pulled out the piece of paper.

> Beatrix,
>
> I'm going to recon Festermunder today. I'm going alone. I dared not tell Percival or Fred. I want to follow up on a hunch. I'm telling you because I trust you can keep a secret and not tell the others. Percival has the "goods" on him. If anything happens to me, please forward any information for my final arrangements to my father,

Admiral Joffrey Soames, whom I believe resides in Reykjavik, Iceland. I'll see you soon, I'm most certain.

LSB

There was little to do other than the obvious. Ben and Alex walked beside each other down East 58th Street toward the river with Violet following, her gloved hands jammed into her coat pockets. The wind was howling; the sky overcast.

"So, we're basically out looking for a random crazy man in New York on Christmas Day?" Alex said.

"We have to find the Elias anaphora in order to gain access to the critical levels of the school. There's no getting around it. We already have the bounty that you lifted from my place of work! Oh my God! My job. I'll never go back!"

"Easy, Dr. Abernathy," Ben replied. "We have to destroy the prime meridian at Festermunder, or there will be no lab in Oxfordshire to return to. The universe is counting on us. They—"

"Just don't know it yet," Alex said, finishing for him.

Violet opened her mouth to speak, then shut it while staring straight ahead. Alex and Ben turned to see what she was looking at. Ahead of them, at approximately head height, was the yawning maw of black star-riddled space.

The maw was irregular and shredded like a deformed starfish. It was wreathed with a blue-white aura that seemed to waver and move with gentle purpose. It seemed to beckon the companions closer. Violet was entranced, but Alex looked around while assuming a defensive posture, sensing a trap.

"It's so beautiful," Violet mumbled.

"Doctor, step back," Ben said. "Step back now! Don't go any closer!"

Ben placed his hand on his left temple as he was wracked by a fiery pain behind his eye. He bent over at the waist, holding his head with both hands in sudden agony. Alex went to him and put her arms on his shoulders.

"Ben! Ben! Are you alright?"

"It's so cold. My head. It feels frozen inside. Oh, my eyes!"

Ben tore himself away from the pain long enough to lunge at Violet, who was attempting to put her hand into the maw. The maw rose up and expanded, taking on the shape of a coiled predator, ready for a strike. The expansion of the aperture coincided with an explosion of white-hot pain in Ben's head. He went down, his vision turning black.

His last thoughts were about the pain and how he had felt it two days prior. In Glamis . . . with Bram.

Libby hated to breach protocol. Rules existed for a reason. She detested the skulking around and the dishonesty associated with disobedience. She wasn't certain what she was more concerned with: the attempted break-in and trespassing in Festermunder Academy or lying to her new-found companions.

That poor sod Fred couldn't take it.

The building loomed ahead as Libby pressed on ahead down 8th Avenue.

That's the scariest bloody thing I've ever seen in my life. Why would anyone put a school there? Come to think of it, why would any parent let their child go to this school?

The Festermunder School towered over her, brown and forbidding. A windowless sixty-story monolith. Even the front doors were solid, unlike the skyscrapers dotting Manhattan.

Good way to keep people out—or keep people in.

Libby bypassed the front door and continued around to the next street, then spied the alley between buildings. She noticed that Festermunder School had a physical plant out back with steam emanating from several vents. Dumpsters also dotted the alley. She picked her way down the alley and found it deserted. Finding the back door, Libby looked around once again before fishing out her lock-picking kit and sliding a file into the tumbler of the deadbolt. It opened with surprising, almost troubling, ease.

As soon as she stepped inside, the door shut behind her. Libby was inside Festermunder.

Libby scurried from the entrance hall into the hallway on the main level and began switching back and forth, from right to left. The dark wood beams contrasted with the light hardwood floors, making every hall look the same. Libby looked about in vain for a central room or set of elevators or stairs, increasingly determined to find a way out of the maze.

I've traveled too far to still be on the same floor. The building footprint isn't this big! This is more of that devilry that Percival and Beatrix are mixed up in!

Libby heard a low rumbling sound that became a faint hum that droned in her ears. She lowered herself to the floor and placed her ear to the hardwood. It sounded like a mechanical fan. It had a radiating quality that reminded her of a helicopter. The floor was also warm to the touch, almost hot.

Invigorated by her discovery, Libby set off again and then stopped about a hundred feet down the hallway. An elevator door was visible to her right.

It hadn't been there before.

That's bloody impossible!

The door was brass, creating a distorted reflection of her. A bell chimed, and the door opened, causing Libby to draw a short breath and assume a defensive posture. The elevator was empty. The red carpet inside beckoned her forward.

This is a trap as much as I've ever seen one.

Libby went into the elevator, and the door closed behind her.

Beatrix, Malik, and Percival were cold and having no luck west of Broadway searching for Elias's anaphora or "beta," as Percival referred to him. They had traversed the avenues all the way down to Union Square but had nothing to show for it. Malik was tired, and his complaining was beginning to wear on Percival. They began bickering, each of them determined to get the last word in. Malik, although pious to a fault, was relentless when he thought his points were grounded in logic. Beatrix was sympathetic to his plight. She even found out he celebrated Christmas and made a note to get him something.

That will have to be later when we go back up town perhaps. Right now, we're looking for a needle in a stack of needles.

As the bickering and one-upping continued on the corner of 7th Avenue and 14th Street, Beatrix began to zone out. Her companions' sniping began to sound hollow as if they were arguing in an aluminum vessel. She pulled her hoodie down tight against the cold, partially obscuring her eyes, which had begun to glaze over, then close. Had Percival or Malik noticed, they would have been transfixed by her eyes, the irises burning with a purple fire. This contrasted with the shock of gray hair that hung down over her face.

In her own void of semi-consciousness, as Beatrix probed her thoughts, she saw a twinkling starscape against the black of deep space. Standing there, yet aloof, she felt herself losing cohesion. She would describe the sensation later to Ben as "coming apart." She had felt the sensation before as a young child and most recently in the meridians. Her body began to particulate and dissolve. The physical disassociation had the effect of splitting into innumerable atoms. The particles began to spin off and travel away from Beatrix. From her vantage point, she was meshing with the matter of buildings, structures, trees, and other objects while accelerating. The speed was incredible and terrifying. In her subconscious, she sought to shield herself but couldn't. The periphery was a blur, but the vector of travel was a focused telescope sensing and penetrating the buildings and brownstones. Beatrix tried to shut out the vision, but she couldn't because it was inside her head. Blasting forth at a high speed, she was being drawn to something.

It was then that Beatrix encountered Lightheart's anaphora.

Casting herself blocks away and through buildings, she saw it crouching behind a dumpster near Battery Park in the Financial District. He looked confused and frightened. A stranger in a strange land.

Beatrix felt herself being ripped from her state of numbed cognition in response to Malik slapping her cheeks and Percival calling her name.

"Beatrix!" he said. "Beatrix, listen to me!"

When Beatrix came to, she noticed that Malik was holding her hand with both of his as if to console her.

"Malik, I'm good. I'm good, okay?" Beatrix said as she spun on Percival.

"I found him! In Battery Park!"

"What?"

"When I fainted. I 'traveled' there. Through buildings and everything."

Percival reached up and stroked his goatee, muttering something, then turned and hailed a cab simply by raising his hand and snapping his fingers. He spun back toward Beatrix, as close to anger as he was able to get with the beloved girl he swore to protect. "Beatrix, for the love of all things sacred, never do that again, please."

Satisfied with his rebuke, he grabbed Malik and Beatrix and led them toward the taxi, then directed the driver to Battery Park.

Libby's ears popped as she descended several floors in the elevator. The doors opened onto a round room flanked on the far side by large mahogany double doors. Libby strode across the rotunda to try one of the doors and was surprised as one of them opened.

Libby had just entered Festermunder's library.

Little did she know it wasn't the World Under the Clock.

She knew from Ben and Beatrix's stories that the gateway lay before her in the very room in which she was standing. Wasting no time, Libby strode to the nearest row of books and made her way toward the center of the labyrinth. She removed her ever-present hoodie, the room feeling stuffy and hot.

Although trained at threat detection, Libby failed to notice the plump form of Professor Gregory Brecourt peering from behind the book pile. He picked up his phone and typed a text message.

Brit agent. Take action?

Brecourt received three dots, then received a terse response.

Negative.

The Gnome scoffed to himself at the idiocy of the situation. He knew full well he would be held responsible for any outcome, good or ill. Now that the faculty and administration seemed to be dealing more and more with these "Dark Fellows," matters seemed to be much more cloak and dagger. His text from Headmistress Grunnion-Paltine perplexed him.

What is she thinking?

The retrieval of Lightheart's wayward anaphora proved to be absurdly simple. The cab driver dropped off the silent and recently defrosted trio of Percival, Malik, and Beatrix in Battery Park. Beatrix was able to triangulate the anaphora's position from memory, and they found him squatting behind a park bench next to a prostrate homeless person, who was unknowingly sleeping next to the replica of the cosmic traveler.

The cab driver had stayed; Percival seemed to trust the man and wanted the same ride back to the Sovereign Light Theater to diminish the number of people observing them. The driver let them out four blocks from the Theater. They led Lightheart's double the rest of the way to their new home on 44th and 9th.

Percival was the first to notice the black sedan with tinted windows parked across the street. Beatrix was next.

"Percival!" Beatrix said.

"Keep going, and don't look up!" he hissed.

The four of them ran through the door and vanished from sight as it slammed behind them.

Across the street, Luka's eyes remained fixed on the Sovereign Light Theater. He hadn't seen or heard anyone enter. Thus, he was certain his quarry was still afoot in the city. However, he, like Professor Gregory Brecourt, had been deceived.

Ark 884

Beatrix shook off the cold along with her overcoat. "How can you be sure we're okay?"

Percival uncharacteristically ignored Beatrix.

"Percival! I'm speaking to you. What's the deal? I saw the car just like you did, and I thought we were dead. How are we safe?"

Malik tapped the Scotsman on the shoulder, which succeeded in drawing Percival's ire, then his attention. "Mr. Perc—"

"I heard her, fool! Can't a man think without you consistently being a sodding nuisance?"

"Alright! That's enough! Why do you pick on Malik like that?" Beatrix asked. "He didn't do anything to you. Seriously, lay off him, and tell us what's up!"

Chastened by being spoken to by his charge like that, Percival relented. "Join me in the mezzanine in ten minutes," he said as he walked toward the basement stairs. "And bring along that sodding Hardingham fellow and the lady Brit. For Pete's sake, there better be fresh coffee. . . ."

Once everyone had refreshed themselves and was situated in the mezzanine, along with coffee or water, Percival stood with his back to the stage. He was leaning on the brass railing of the first row, overlooking the orchestra section.

Beatrix, Malik, and Fred, who was still groggy, were sprawled in blue velvet chairs in front of him.

"Where's Briggs, Hardingham?" Percival began.

"I dunno, man. I thought she went out with one of the groups."

Percival looked at Beatrix, who offered nothing.

"Mag-bloody-nificent. One more loose end. I'll handle that once I've completely sodding unthawed. The others are on their way back, and we can catch them up later. Now, the matter of the car across the street." He drew in a breath while thinking of how to frame his thoughts. "Historically, we've had problems with the integrity of our organization. Those of us who have traveled the meridians and have been to the Other Place were once part of a unified society. An enclave, if you will, of servants to our misguided perception of what was the greater good—"

"Servants of Seraphim, you mean," Malik corrected.

Percival seethed. "Patel, you insolent prat, if you interrupt one more time, you will be dismissed not only from this meeting but ejected from this sodding thea—"

"Alright, alright, I'm sure he didn't mean to be insolent," Beatrix said. "But you said you broke free from servitude, correct? How does this relate to the car outside?"

"Hold on a bit; I'll get to it. Servitude . . . yes, that much is true. But we dared not do anything about it in the clear. There were contingencies, plans, mind you, that followed every possible outcome of our intent at treachery. Every possible trajectory of our actions was projected, and we reconciled potential solutions. We had these encoded, and only a few of us had any knowledge of them in case we were penetrated by the Dark Fellows. There was the engineering of simulacra, as I was in the form of the mangy mongrel: Plan Domino. There was a plan, called Blue Falcon, for what we would do if Seppe or I were turned over to the agents of the Black. There was the plan to engineer a weapon styled like the prophecies told of the Phantom Thirteen or the Eidolon—"

"Percival!" Beatrix said as his words hit close to home. "What about the car? How does any of this relate?"

Percival hesitated, then continued. "You are currently not where you think you are as you sit here."

"What?" Fred exclaimed. "Do explain, man."

"You, Hardingham. And you, Patel. And you, Beatrix, are all part of Ark 884, also known as Plan Purple."

"Purple?" Malik said.

"Yes, purple, Master Patel, like the sodding color."

"What's Plan Purple?" Beatrix asked.

Percival sighed. "Plan Purple is misdirection. Using basic scientific principles of distorted space-time."

Fred, Malik, and Beatrix looked at Percival with their mouths slightly ajar, urging him to continue.

"Misdirection. Making something that is true appear to be quite false. Or making something false appear true. Allow me to explain. Yes, there is indeed a black sedan parked across from the Sovereign Light Theater. Yes, there in it dwells one of the Dark Fellows. Yet, he'll never see us, the ruddy bastard, for he can't. That, my dear friends, is Purple."

"Sir, do tell us what you're talking about," Fred pleaded.

"That sodding devil in the car is looking at a fully functional simulacrum of this theater. Completely intact and totally blocked by a blind curve of subluminal space-time. He can't see us here, coming or going, as we don't exist to him in this space or time as long as we're here. This place"—he pointed at the theater around him—"is cloaked by subluminal dark matter, also known as delta violet matter; thus 'purple.' Seppe slipped back twenty years and engineered it himself. We can't be found here because, technically, we're not here. As when we're here, we don't exist. As I said, we're covered by delta violet matter. We are covered by Purple."

"Then why did that black cloud come down on us outside?" Beatrix asked. "It was from them. I—"

"Tut-tut," Percival said, waving his index finger. "That may not have had anything to do with the sodding Dark Fellows at all. Remember, the meridians are destabilizing. They will gather near any of us who have traveled the gateways, as we're marked by their constituent matter. Dangerous as it may have been, the source was likely benign. Just as

Seppe says, the connections between ours and the Other Place are degrading. We'll see more of this, I'm sure."

"Two questions," Malik said. "What is Ark 884? And the antimatter. You said it had properties that cause an effect like Purple. What else happens?"

"Well," Percival rubbed his hands together in excitement, "Ark 884 is this place. One of over 24,135 safe zones around the cosmos that we have primed and created as part of Plan Purple."

The cosmos?

"The question now is not where is the theater, but when is the theater? We're in a construct of another place in the fabric of space-time."

"Like an alternate street or address?" Fred said.

"More like a cul-de-sac whose location is ever changing in space and time."

"Was that how the Verge was cloaked before it was destroyed?" Malik asked.

"Was? No, Patel, *is*. The Verge is there. Seppe destroyed a construct of Ark 212, but I assure you, the Verge is right where we left it, fully intact."

Montavani said he destroyed it, Beatrix thought. *Another half-truth. He said it was discovered by the Mechanix, so he had no choice. Where are they now then? Alive?*

"They're unwritten," Percival said, reading her mind. "All of them. Anyone caught in the cataclysm of closing an ark is erased from existence. Like a character deleted from a page late in a book, one ceases to exist from the earlier pages and drops out of the story."

"Why didn't you trap all of the Mechanix or even Seraphim in an ark and implode it then?" Malik asked.

Percival opened his mouth to speak, then closed it again, only to open it and pause, his eyes on Beatrix. "A conversation for later, Master Patel."

Fred raised his hand. "I have three questions."

"Then bloody ask them, you sod," Percival said. "This isn't grammar school."

"Where's Libby? And where on earth did you put Elias?"

"What's the third?"

"Is this 'Purple' only available to the good guys?"

Percival did not reply.

Bollocks!

Libby was lost. Deeply in the labyrinth of Festermunder's library, she had retraced her steps and was hopelessly turned around. She cursed under breath again at her own stupidity. Libby had even gone as far as to periodically extrude books from the shelves to mark her path, to no avail. Although the cavernous room was circular and set up in the shape of a wheel, the nonsensical bookshelf patterns disrupted her internal GPS. There were too many unexpected diagonals and switchbacks. In addition, the books she had pulled out were all being pushed back in by someone . . . or something.

The meridian is at the room's geometric center. How bloody hard could it be to find it?

Sweating now, Libby felt the spider legs of fear tinkling against the back of her neck as she broke into her half-crouched "tactical trot" toward what she assumed was the center of the library.

It was only then when Libby saw it.

The books and the shelves themselves began to bend and distort and waver, not unlike the walls of the synchrotron in Oxford. The Episcopalian red carpet began to fade to a dark gray and then to black. The distorted shelves faded and disappeared. Then the lights died.

Libby was overtaken by a darkness she had never experienced.

Looking at the floor, Libby saw an infinite cosmos of stars. The ceiling shone bright with stars, nebulae, and galaxies. Losing her equilibrium, Libby stopped and squatted down to look at the celestial transformation, scared but transfixed.

Then . . . a voice.

"Elizabeth. Don't move. I'll come to you."

"Who is this?" Libby demanded.

"It's I," the benevolent voice replied.

"Dad?" Libby said. "I'm scared."

"No."

Libby looked up through, and standing tall, wreathed in stars, his hand outstretched, was none other than Guiseppe Montavani—or so it appeared.

Taking the old man's hand, Libby allowed herself to be led to the doors to the rotunda, leaving the library behind. Looking over her shoulder, Libby saw that the room resembled an expanse of the cosmos, dotted with an infinite number of stars. She dared not look at her feet, as she felt she would fall into the void.

As the doors opened to the rotunda, Libby was greeted with an astonishing sight.

It was gone.

There were no walls, no ceiling, and no scarlet carpet. The world was white. Libby looked at Montavani for guidance, but he was no longer visible. Alone, Libby cast her eyes about the white expanse to get some sense of equilibrium. Struggling, she fell to her knees to put her hands on what seemed to be a solid surface. The incomprehensible surroundings caused Libby to become nauseous, as she couldn't perceive where she was relative to the floor and ceiling. There was no floor. No ceiling. No landmarks. It was beyond vertigo.

Squinting, Libby made fists with her hands and then released them as she choked down a mind-numbing sense of fear. At that moment, she heard in a voice in her head, calling her out of her cocoon of self-preservation.

Lady?

As Libby listened, the question was repeated.

Lady?

The voice had a familiar accent. Libby dared to open her eyes, looking once again onto the shapeless expanse of white.

In the distance was a child, a girl. She was running away, though she would turn and call back periodically.

Lady?

The child continued to call out until she faded into a blur.

The figure whom Libby assumed was Montavani returned and led her away. As she walked, Libby was encumbered by a wave of exhaustion. Collapsing into a heap, Libby lay unconscious. She was picked up and carried.

The room changed yet again. The walls morphed back into the solid wood and stucco halls of Festermunder's fourth-floor Science and Physics Hall. Libby was carried down the hall, still asleep.

They entered Room 433, which had a nameplate that said "Dr. Null" on it affixed to the door. It was the electro-physics lab. A large metallic box, large enough to house several people, was opened, and Libby was placed inside it. Then the door closed with a thud and a click. The outside of the box was labeled "Faraday RF Cage: 1300 k/joules."

When Libby awoke to the still blackness of her metal tomb, Headmistress Grunnion-Paltine turned the lights off and closed the door to Room 433, then skulked away.

Alone with Percival in the hall behind the stage of the Sovereign Light Theater, Beatrix decided it was time to come clean. But in exchange, she wanted information.

"Libby," Beatrix said.

"Tell me," Percival replied, "where is she?"

"She went down to Festermunder. To do a recon of the place."

"What?" Percival nearly exploded. "Girl! Do you know what this means? We're blown! She should have been back hours ago. It's 8:23 p.m.!"

Beatrix was thrown off balance, having rarely witnessed Percival's ire directed solely at her.

"Is that all? Did she tell anyone else? Did she take anything?" Percival demanded, red blooming across his face.

"No, she only told me in a note. She said it was to reconnoiter the area. She's MI5; she'll be fine. She's not a loose cannon—"

"Not a loose cannon?" Percival belched out through clenched teeth. "That's all she is! She's an agent sworn to the Her Majesty's Crown on the run in New York with the biggest lot of sodding fools this side of Bunbury—"

"What's Bunbury?" Beatrix asked.

"Nothing! I sodding made it up." Percival smirked and then caught himself. "The woman is bloody fierce, and she'll stop at nothing to clear her name from this."

"One thing was funny," Beatrix said.

Dread swept across Percival's face. "What?"

"Her note. It said, 'Percival has the goods, all of them.' She also listed notification of final arrangements for her father in Iceland if something were to happen."

"The goods? She said those words? Next-of-kin? Sodding Iceland? Beatrix!" Percival put his hands on her shoulders, then let them drop.

Beatrix drew in a quick breath. She realized her mistake.

As she pondered her error, Percival placed his satchel on a nearby table. He opened it; then a few seconds later, he closed it. It was open long enough for Beatrix to discern that one of the six antimatter vials was missing.

"Bollocks! Well, you have to hand it to her. She made off with a tube of our payload from Oxfordshire. British!" Percival cursed.

Beatrix stood with her palms outstretched to apologize.

"I heard everything," Ben said, startling them both as he entered. "Libby plans to destroy the prime meridian at Festermunder. What do we do?"

"We do nothing until we've blimey thought about it. It's obvious that Briggs failed in her plot—"

"How do you know?" Ben asked.

Percival walked away, motioning for the others to follow. "Proof."

Shuffling down the back steps off the stage to his dressing room, Percival was followed by Ben and Beatrix as well as Fred. (Violet had to lie down from exhaustion due to her experience with the maw.) After unlocking the door, he peeked inside before opening it fully. There on the floor, covered with a quilt and fast asleep, was Lightheart's anaphora.

Percival closed the door and locked it, then waved for Ben and Beatrix to follow him down the hall to Beatrix's dressing room. Once there, Beatrix plopped onto her bed, and Ben sat on a bean bag chair. Fred sat on a director's chair. Percival cracked his knuckles as he remained standing.

"Libby failed. She has been gone for twelve hours now, according to my calculations. But we now have proof that the meridian is still intact."

"Lightheart?" Ben and Beatrix said in unison.

"Yes. If the prime meridian were destabilized and closed, he would not be here and the original Elias Lightheart would be trapped in the Divide. His anaphora would cease to exist. It would be . . . erased.”

“The antimatter,” Ben said, “what would happen to Festermunder and the library and all?”

“There would be an EMP effect. A huge electromagnetic pulse and infrared tsunami. Fryin’ electronics and radiation effects on anyone near it. That’s why I was so sodding incensed! The depositor will need a radiation suit! No, Briggs never made it. It’s also readily discernible”—he swallowed thickly—“that we may never see her again.”

“What?” Fred stood up with indignation. “My God, man. We just write her off?” Fred’s ears were red, and his face flushed. Beatrix wasn’t sure if he was angry or on the verge of tears.

“I won’t have it!” he continued, waving his arms. “You hear me? That’s flat!”

“He’s right,” Beatrix said. “We can’t leave Libby there. If there’s even a chance—”

“If she’s even alive,” Percival said. “The school is not cloaked by Purple. Trust me, there is other devilry afoot at that accursed place. Ask me how I know some time. We know the prime is still there and still active, and our mission is to seal it. I see no reason why we can’t fancy a look for Miss Briggs while we’re at it.”

Beatrix, Ben, and Fred nodded their understanding.

“Tonight,” Percival added.

There is an axiom in the military that states: “Before a battle starts, plans are everything. After the battle begins, plans are worthless.” Percival knew this well by substituting the term “bollocks” to the idea of launching a clandestine assault on Festermunder School that very evening. After all, it was Christmas night, and no one, save Fred, felt up to the mission. Yet, they gathered once again around the table on the stage of the Sovereign Light Theater, wrapping up plans for that very thing.

Beatrix was puzzled at Ben’s behavior. He seemed very unenthusiastic about going to the school, which was unlike him—so was disagreeing with his sister.

He's not been the same since Glamis. With Bram.

Beatrix's thoughts were interrupted by Alex, who tapped her shoulder to let her know Percival was finalizing plans and desired her attention. Malik was taking notes on a small yellow legal pad and continuously clicking his pen on and off.

"Patel, kindly stop clicking that sodding pen before I send it and you to the infernal regions," Percival, his teeth clenched into a smile. "Aye, we need to get down to the school. Although I don't like it, we have to take the subway there. I don't want to risk another cab." He looked around the table at the others to be certain he had their attention. "We take Mr. Professor in a wheelchair down to the school, as we have to use him to the lower levels—"

"What will happen to him after that, Percival?" Violet asked.

"We'll stash him somewhere. Now, the roster. I'll need you students to get around the place. I don't know the school, so I have no sodding idea how to find my way around. But you"—he pointed at Beatrix—"you will be staying here."

Beatrix opened her mouth to speak, but Ben shut her down. "He's right, Beatrix. We can't risk losing you. You're too valuable."

"I agree, Beatrix," Alex added. "You have to sit this out. You can't be compromised."

As her companions clamored about her importance to the cause, Beatrix pushed her chair back and stood. Holding her coffee cup in her right hand and placing her left hand on her temple, she furrowed her brow and closed her eyes.

With her coffee cup sitting on the palm of her right hand, Beatrix's eyes opened and flashed a deep luminescent purple. The cup rose three inches off her palm before it inverted. Though still full of hot coffee, the liquid did not come out. The others stopped talking, transfixed by the spectacle. Beatrix rotated her fingers around the mug's circumference, then flicked her hand, and the cup flew across the room and slammed into the back curtain. It passed right through it, crashing into the stage's brick back wall. Smoke curled up from a smoldering hole where the cup had cut through the curtain. Even more miraculously, floating in the air above Beatrix's hand was a perfect sphere of quivering coffee.

As if breaking from a trance, Beatrix looked up, and the coffee dropped onto the table.

"I wish to go," Beatrix said, looking at Percival for ten full seconds.

"She goes," he agreed, holding her gaze. He turned to Violet. "Doctor Abernathy, we need you here to watch the theater and make sure we stay cloaked with Purple. Agreed?"

"Agreed," Violet replied, still staring at Beatrix, who had defied all the known laws of physics with a coffee cup not thirty seconds prior.

"Patel, you stay with the good doctor."

"No," Malik said.

"Beg your sodding pardon?" Percival grunted.

"No."

"See here, Patel, you—"

"I'm going. I've been in on this since Wendell disappeared, and unlike anyone else here, I've studied the schematic of the school and the library. That's final." Malik had rarely shown such obstinance in the face of anyone. Most of it was false bravado, but Beatrix thought it was sweet. Although he had no chance, she knew Malik adored her, and she feared he might do something stupid to impress her.

"Sodding fine! But I want it on record that I think it's a bad idea."

It was settled. Percival, Fred, Alex, Malik, Ben, and Beatrix would take Lightheart's anaphora and break into Festermunder, where they would attempt to close the prime meridian and find Libby Soames-Briggs. Beatrix wished more than ever that Montavani were there. She had questions that wouldn't go away. Why were they doing this? If Wendell was in the Divide, why close off her only access to him? Why had he asked her to shut the way?

Across the city, in Room 433 of Festermunder Academy, Libby awoke to the pitch black. Seeking to conserve air, Libby closed her eyes and prayed a rescue would come while she could still breathe.

CHAPTER 21

Up Through the Downside

"THE DARK FELLOWS," PERCIVAL SAID ONCE THEY were on the train, interrupting her thoughts.

"What about them?" Beatrix replied.

"They won't find us," Percival said, patting the breast pocket of his crushed-velvet blazer. "We're cloaked."

Her eyebrows rose in response to that revelation. Then she looked around at the train car. It was devoid of passengers save for her, Ben, Malik, Alex, Fred, and Percival. Normally, it would have struck Beatrix as odd, being on an empty train at 9:00 p.m. on Christmas night in Manhattan, but her recent experience with interstellar adventure had taught her many things, not least of which was not to be surprised by anything that happened.

Percival didn't need to tell them that things were slightly different regarding the subway. They hadn't left the theater at all to go to the nearest subway platform. Percival led them back down the hall toward the boilers in the basement. Behind them was a nondescript door with a sign on it that said, "Janitor." It led down some stone steps to a subway platform. There were no people present. In fact, the door they used to access the platform disappeared too. All that remained was blank subway tile on three sides and the track ahead of them.

The train lurched ahead and picked speed, heading south toward Festermunder. The lights flickered on and off, and Percival and Ben each reached out a foot to steady the wheelchair in which Lightheart's simulacrum was sleeping.

Malik elbowed Beatrix, who had been staring at her Doc Martens, lost in thought, as if to say, "You good?" She ignored him, focusing on her brother instead. She couldn't help but notice he seemed unwell. His face was pale and ashen.

He's changed. What did Bram tell him?

The gentle rocking of the subway train began to slow. Fred looked up and then bolted to his feet with rare audacity. "We're here!"

The platform was vastly different from the one under the Sovereign Light Theater. Stretching out in every direction was a spider web of tracks. The network was incomprehensible. As in London, there was no way such a network should have existed under "real time" Manhattan. Instead of trains, however, bolts of bright light blasted down the various pathways. As soon as everyone disembarked, the subway car in which they had been riding disappeared into a yellow mass of plasma and exploded away from them with such force that it sent Lightheart's wheelchair caroming into a brick wall. Fred caught up to it and pulled Lightheart back to the group.

"Beatrix, you're with me," Percival said. "You too, Alex. Ben, you and Patel go with Fred to find Briggs." Percival checked his jacket pocket, which held the five vials of antimatter.

Expecting a protest from Ben, Beatrix was surprised when he agreed with a slow nod.

"Now, listen very sodding carefully," Percival said. "We'll head to the library — Alex, Beatrix, and me. We'll have to move swiftly to avoid detection. We'll send you a signal when we're prepared to deliver the payload into the meridian. Once we do, we'll only have a few moments to get out. We do not want to be near that thing when it goes off."

"What's the signal?" Fred asked.

"I'll come up with something you can't mistake, you noodle-necked moron. Now put these on and let's go; we're running out of time."

With that, he tore Lightheart's wheelchair out of Fred's hands and strode over to a hallway that held a bank of six elevators. The elevator doors were made of shiny brass, and they distorted Percival's reflection as he parked Lightheart in front of the nearest elevator.

With Alex's help, Percival pulled Lightheart to his feet in front of the control panel. "This is why we went to all the sodding trouble of bringing him," Percival said. "Here goes."

As he placed the simulacrum's hand on the panel, everyone held their breath. Seconds later, the black screen chirped to life and opened.

"Now what?" Alex asked.

"Stick his hand inside?" Malik suggested.

Alex eased Lightheart's hand into the chamber while Percival steadied him. Nothing happened at first. Then, with a jolt, a clicking sound began, and small spider-like projections emerged, poking at Lightheart's hand.

Beatrix drew a breath. "Percival," she said, as if in warning.

"It's sensing his DNA," Alex said, "to confirm a match."

As if hearing the conversation, the spider paused and looked up at the group with its single red eye, then resumed its high-speed work. It chirped once and disappeared before the doors of all six elevators opened.

Beatrix turned to Ben. "Be safe, okay?" Ben nodded and gave her a one-armed hug.

Percival rolled Lightheart's simulacrum into the elevator, accompanied by Beatrix and Alex. Fred, Ben, and Malik got into the next elevator. Malik looked at Beatrix as if he were about to cry. Beatrix's gaze was on her brother as the doors closed.

"Okay, Master Patel, where to look?" Fred whispered as Malik and Ben peered around the corner of the eight-floor lobby.

The halls were deserted. The low lighting gave off an eerie glow. The beige stucco walls could scarcely outline the shadows of the trio as they conferred against a wood column. Fred fingered a dimmer switch and toyed with turning up the lights, but a barely perceptible head shake from Ben stopped him.

"We've gone from room to room from the twelfth floor down, which has taken the better part of an hour," Fred said. "Have you any clue where she might be?"

The question was put to Ben, but Malik answered while looking at his Casio timepiece. "We have no access above the twelfth floor. No one does. There's no way to get to the higher levels that anyone has heard of—and I've been here since pre-K—not even for the faculty. Sixty floors and only twelve are accessible. We have to work our way down."

"As far as that accursed library?" Fred asked.

"No. Percival, Alex, and Beatrix will have that area covered," Malik replied.

Ben looked up at the mention of Beatrix but said nothing.

"What shall we do?" Fred asked. "Agent Soames-Briggs is here, and she needs our help! The signal will be coming any moment. Jiminy Christmas!" Fred wrung his hands with worry but not for himself.

"I say we—"

"What was that?" Fred snapped.

Malik froze in mid-sentence, and Ben had lowered himself to a crouch, instinctively shielding his smaller friend.

They heard it again. A shrill voice. Louder this time. It sounded like an adult, and it seemed to be coming from the next room. Then it was gone and the lights went out.

That was enough for Malik and Fred. They bolted to the stairwell across the lobby and flung the door open. Ben followed, keeping an eye out for threats.

Seldom ever achieving such haste, albeit with little grace, Fred bounded down the stairs. As the trio approached each successive platform, the window in the fire-retardant stairwell door revealed light, but as soon as Fred reached for a door handle, the lights on that floor would go out. Fear drove Fred and Malik, and Ben followed, vowing to protect them.

When they made it to the landing of the fourth floor, this time, the lights didn't go out when Fred reached the door. Panting with exertion, they opened the door and slipped into a dimly lit alcove.

"Fourth floor, science and physics," Malik said between breaths. "Beatrix hates this floor."

Ben looked at Malik frowned.

"Let's have a bit of a look around, shall we?" Fred said, indicating Malik should lead.

The heat pumps must have been left on over the holidays, as the place was sweltering. As they followed the carpet down the left side of the hall, Malik stiffened and pointed. Six doors down on the left, a door was ajar. However, that was not as surprising as the figure who stood tall and forbidding in the hallway — Headmistresses Grunnion-Paltine.

"Oh dear!" Fred exclaimed.

"Oh $%#!" Malik muttered. "We're dead!"

The trio turned to run but were hit by a shockwave that knocked them to the floor. They struggled to their feet, only to be struck down again. An unseen hand of dreadful force dragged them down the hall, straight toward Grunnion-Paltine.

Only Ben was strong enough to break free into a sprint, but went flying, his body careening down the hall, tumbling end over end until he rolled to a stop by the water fountain. Sensing he could do nothing against this new enemy, he sprinted to his right and back toward the stairwell, out of view.

"Master Patel," Headmistress Grunnion-Paltine said, her body seething with malice and shrill voice echoing down the hall. Fred, who was lying on his side, cowered, then stood as if to shield Malik from what was coming. But what came next couldn't have surprised them more.

After wheeling Lightheart's simulacrum out of the elevator and into the rotunda outside Festermunder's library, Percival hesitated, then strode over to the series of doors. Beatrix stopped and touched his arm as if to ask him what the plan was.

Percival leaned in. "We leave him here for now and get him on the way back if we fail. He'll still be here. I'll drop the payload and, Alex, you deliver the signal."

"What's the signal?" Alex asked.

"How much time do we have?" Beatrix said before Percival could answer.

"The signal will occur when we drop the antimatter in. Moments after that, all hell will break loose. All lights and electronics will be fried, and I'd wager some other blasted devilry will be afoot too."

It was then that Beatrix looked through the contents of the duffle bag he had given her to carry while on the subway.

Radiation suits? A Faraday box! Resistant to electromagnetic pulses. We learned about this in Professor Null's horrible physics class. He was always having coffee with Professor Lightheart.

"What's in here?" Beatrix asked, patting the metal box as Percival peered through a peephole in the library door.

"Walkie-talkies and flashlights," he replied without looking. "Let's go."

The door opened silently, revealing the library just as Beatrix remembered it — as if the destruction that Ben had caused in his confrontation with Luka never happened.

It even smells clean.

The trio strode past the shuttered office of Dr. Gregory Brecourt, a.k.a. the Gnome, and moved past the book chute and its ever-expanding pile of weathered hardbacks beneath its beaten copper eaves. In true Festermunder fashion, considering computers existed, there was no reason to have so much in print.

What are they worried about? That the Library is gonna get hacked? Stupid school.

Beatrix lifted a book off the pile, but as she went to open it, Alex clamped it shut. "Beatrix, we have to hurry."

Percival looked uncharacteristically worried as he kept an eye out for threats and spoke without looking at them. "Let's move! I'm sure there are watchers about and more besides!"

They headed deeper into the library toward the center, where they knew the prime meridian was. The whole time Beatrix couldn't shake a terrible feeling of incongruity.

Something's not right here.

Beatrix looked around and realized Alex was no longer with them.

Ben raced downstairs and burst from the fire exit into the library rotunda. Sprinting over the scarlet carpet, he scarcely noticed Lightheart's simulacrum dozing in his wheelchair off to his right. As Ben swung the door open, Lightheart's doppelganger spoke.

"The books. They're not what they seem."

Ben nodded and then entered the library. The heat was stifling, and the silence in the room was deafening. He couldn't hear the others.

"They've got to be here!" Ben whispered.

As he started toward the outer shelves leading to the center, Ben glanced at the book chute. The beaten copper of its metal sides shone in the dim light as books continued to fall.

The books, they never stopped. Their source unknown. In the age of the Internet and cloud-based storage, it never made sense why more and more books were added to a library restricted to the faculty and only students who were for detention.

Walking over to the pile of worn and tattered books scattered across the floor, Ben grabbed a brown one at random and opened it to the middle.

What he saw stunned him.

Names. Only names.

Flipping through the pages, Ben only saw names. He picked up another book and found the same. No stories, no text, and no periodicals. The titles and authors were there — Shakespeare, Joyce, Twain — but there was nothing in the pages but names.

Picking up a red book and flipping in vain through its pages, Ben stopped, noticing something he hadn't seen before.

Dates!

The years spanned anywhere in time — 1588, 1832, 1971, 1698.

As the minutes ticked by, Ben broke into a sweat as he searched for his quarry.

2016!

Ben flipped through the book until he found November. Then there it was.

Nic Stooch: 11/28/16 status closed
Becker McTeel: 11/28/16 status closed
Darby St. Vincent: 11/28/16 status closed

The missing! The simulacra! Nic, Darby, and Becker are listed here on the day they went over to the Other Place!

Ben was bewildered not to find Lightheart's name in the register, as he had clearly gone over too. Then he remembered Montavani's words: "Elias completed his mission. He went over deliberately. Stooch and the others did not. They're part of the Taken."

Ben shuddered at the thought. Then he looked at the book's title page and saw a stamp that appeared to be fresh.

Updated January 1, 2016

Ben realized it was not a registry of those who had gone over in the past. It was an index of who was next. On a hunched, he turned to the back of the book. When he read what was written there, he cried out in anguish.

December 2016
Beatrix Gray Voght (status: open)

"Boy!" a voice yelled so loudly that it echoed in Ben's mind. Turning around, Ben saw a dark shape step out from the darkness and into full view.

The Hat Man.

Malik Patel was screwed, and he knew it.

All his life he had just wanted to make a difference. To be somebody. To be wanted by someone. To be needed. To be part of a group. To not be the third wheel. This entire escapade was completely outside of his character, and now he was going to die. Tonight. Right there. At this school. On Christmas.

I mean, who dies on Christmas? Who freakin' does that? I've never even kissed a girl!

Tears streamed down his cheeks as Malik stood in the shadow of Headmistress Grunnion-Paltine, waiting for the blow that would end his life.

HGP stood six feet tall and at least 280 pounds. She towered over Malik, her eyes gleamed dark and evil in the low light. Her gap-toothed smile sadistically on full display. Fred, on the floor behind Malik, did his best to sum up their predicament.

"Oh, bugger."

"You have no place here," HGP said to the MI5 agent. "You know nothing about what you're trifling with, you skinny toad!" She turned to Malik. "You realize that you are in a highly volatile situation. One far beyond your slimy grasp. I assure you, young fool, no one will miss you when you disappear."

With a burst of speed, the headmistress raised her python-like arms above her head. Malik noticed her hands were covered with mechanical gears and knobs that coursed with green sparks as she brought her arms down and her wrists collided. The ensuing explosion blew Malik end over end through the nearby elevator doors.

Except there was no elevator, only an empty shaft.

Malik spun through the blackness, completely disoriented. The last thing he remembered was the air rushing past, a green-blue light, and a pile of books.

Ben bolted between the nearest bookshelves to his left, not looking back to see where the Hat Man was. Slamming into a bookshelf at top speed, he caused it to tip over.

Not again!

The shelves begin to topple like dominos. Then he heard a scream above the din.

Alex!

Ben wheeled about and retraced his steps, his chest burning with exertion like never before. A concussive blast of clear plasma obliterated the bookshelf that Ben had just passed, sending books and papers flying.

Another scream. This time Ben was positive it was Alex. But he also had another thought.

Find Beatrix.

Ben circled a shelf and sprinted toward what he understood to be the center of the cavernous library, and at that moment, his world was upended by a blast of sonic waves rippling through the carpet. It flipped him end over end until he landed flat on his back, the wind knocked out of him.

The Hat Man was standing over him. Ben closed his eyes and raised his hands in front of his face.

Beatrix, I'm sorry!

"Hey, you!" a shrill British voice said from behind the monster in black. "Piss off!"

Hovering over the carpet with unseen feet, the Hat Man's turned toward Alex and issued a death stroke of distorted dark matter at her. Alex dove onto the carpet, narrowly avoiding the blast, but it was only a matter of time.

Without the antimatter, we have no defense, Ben thought.

He hopped to his feet and sprinted right, paralleling the aisle that the Hat Man had followed Alex down. Turning and turning, he couldn't seem to make headway as he heard more blasts farther down toward what he thought was the center of the library. He stopped to catch his breath, his chest heaving in the growing heat.

Ben was lost.

Kerplunk!

Malik fell onto the pile of books. Miraculously, he was unhurt, even though he knew he must've fallen at least four stories plus the unknown distance to the underground library. However, he didn't have much time to ponder his good fortune.

"Sodding imbecile!" a familiar voice drawled in a Scottish accent. Percival darted out of the shadows and grabbed Malik, pulling him down from the pile.

"What?" Malik asked, sounding hurt. He had almost died and expected sympathy. Receiving none, he looked past Percival and saw Beatrix. Her eyes were still flaring a faint purple, and her left hand was facing the book pile, palm out.

Accustomed to Beatrix's burgeoning powers, Malik realized she had done something to decelerate his fall, saving his life.

Beatrix walked over to Malik and hugged him. "Good job not dying."

Malik swallowed, his saliva thick in his mouth. "Thanks."

"Excuse me," Percival said. "Is now the time for reunions of departed friends, or are we trying to complete this sodding mission? This place is full of evil, and the sooner we get our arses outta here, the damn better. And—"

He was interrupted by a blast and a scream.

"The Dark Fellows. They're afoot! Let's drop this sodding payload and get out before that dratted hat-wearing devil shows up."

"I can't find Ben," Malik said.

Beatrix's eyes widened; then she turned and made off into the depths of the library, not waiting to see if the others followed her.

CHAPTER 22

The Door
of Night

EADMISTRESS GRUNNION-PALTINE LOOMED OVER FRED. "Get up, fool."

She yanked Fred by the arm with such force that he caught air before landing on his feet, albeit disoriented. Grabbing his collar, she marched toward the door of Professor Null's electro-physics lab, then threw him into the wall when she noticed something more important than the spindly MI5 agent she had just caught.

"You!" HGP said to a figure who stood eighty feet down the hall in front of the open elevator shaft. "You have no place here, you old fool! You lost your opportunity ages ago! You will be swallowed in the meridian from whence you came if you come any closer; I promise you."

She smashed her mechanical gloves together, and they sparked green as she prepared to hurl a plasma ball at the interloper. Bracing herself with one foot back in a crouch, HGP screamed as she unleashed a green blast so intense the recoil nearly knocked her off balance. The green ball sizzled as it blasted down the hall toward the shadowy figure in front of the elevators.

The figure stood resolutely with one similarly gloved hand up, palm outstretched, and deflected the plasma ball. The green particles collected in a cloud in front of the figure and fell back into his hand in the form of a small green ball. The entire move was a study in nonchalance.

"It would be good of you to cease with your tomfoolery this instant, Lucinda," the figure said. "I have no quarrel with you, and I would think you should have none with me, knowing our history."

As Montavani's voice boomed down the hall, it startled Fred.

Realizing she was no match for Montavani, HGP took off in the opposite direction and disappeared. Fred was surprised that Montavani did not give chase, nor did he come forward to convene with Fred. He merely gave him a two-finger salute and a smirk before he stepped into the open elevator shaft and disappeared with a flash of green light.

In a daze from everything that had just occurred, Fred heard a knocking sound in the classroom behind him, and he turned to investigate. The sound was consistent but getting weaker.

Fred entered the classroom and saw a large Faraday box. He tried the handle, but it was locked. Tilting a louver so he could see inside, Fred peered through a small square of tempered glass. The face staring back at him caused his heart to leap into his throat.

Libby.

Ben was running out of time and energy. The heat and the thickness of the air in the library was overcoming the reserves of the all-star lacrosse player. Summoning his remaining strength, he heaved himself to his feet and continued running, all the while primed for another blast or scream.

He didn't have to wait long.

A scream erupted as another missile of distorted space flashed over Ben's head, vaporizing a fire extinguisher. He spotted a blond ponytail as Alex sprinted down a row. Ben followed.

She finally broke into full view thirty yards or so in front of him. Risking a glance over his shoulder, Ben saw a large figure blocking out all the light as it moved toward him.

"Alex!" Ben shouted, knowing that stealth at that point was pointless.

Alex glanced back as she continued to race forward.

Ben picked up the pace. "Alex!"

The process continued until Alex rounded a corner to her right and began running in concentric rings around the circular rows. Ben cast another glance over his shoulder but did not see his pursuer. Turning forward again, he saw that he had made it to the cyclone fencing. He was at the center of the library.

The prime meridian! If only I had the antimatter, I could end this!

Ben skirted the crates and shelves inside the fencing that were used to obstruct the view from outside. Then he came upon the oculus. It was dormant just as it had been that night in detention. Black as the door of night. Glancing across its circumference, he saw Alex. She was poised on the edge of the ring, the toes of her shoes extended over the chasm as she looked down.

"Alex, please take a step back," Ben said.

Alex, her face never more beautiful than it was at that moment, looked sad.

"Alex? What are you doing? Step back. You're scaring me."

Alex fixed her eyes on Ben's. "Don't think badly of me," she said.

Then she jumped.

Beatrix sensed it first. As they walked along the outer edge of the circular library, working their way toward the center, she sensed rather than saw a white-hot flash of light. The flash was also in her head.

Beatrix doubled over in pain, clutching her forehead with both hands. Malik patted her back, not knowing what else to do or say.

"Sweet mother of sodding Pearl!" Percival said. "The prime meridian! It's been ignited! What the bloody hell? It better not be that Brit agent."

"Is it the signal?" Malik asked. "Are we good? Maybe she did our dirty work for us."

"No," Beatrix said between breaths, still clutching her head. "It's something else."

She stood up, secured her satchel over her shoulder, then took a hard right toward the oculus. Malik and Percival followed. As he ran, Percival removed the small case that contained the vials of antimatter. He urged the others to don their radiation suits and they complied. Then all continued their dash.

Beatrix stopped short so quickly that Percival rammed into her. After he excused himself with an epithet, Beatrix continued. "This way," she said.

In her head another voice called.

Shut the way.

But this time, it did not seem altogether right.

Ben stood on the edge of the oculus and watched in horror as Alex jumped into the void. At first, his eyes refused to accept what they had just seen, and he stood there transfixed, not believing what had just happened. A low rumbling starting from the depths suddenly became a roar, and the void exploded with the most beautiful sight that Ben had ever seen.

It was full of stars.

Blue, white, yellow, and amber. Colorful nebulae were also visible against the cosmic backdrop.

On his hands and knees, Ben watched as the small universe began to rotate. As it did, the ceiling seemed to part, and the points of the pyramidal symbols shifted in opposite directions. The infinity symbol disappeared into the stonework as light broke through. The pyramids spun so quickly that they disappeared in the expanding light.

Ben leaned out over the void to get a better view of the opening to the oculus. Nothing could have prepared him for what he saw.

The face staring back looked panicked, which surprised Fred. He had only known Libby for forty-eight hours, but that entire time, she had appeared supremely confident and intimidating. Also, in Fred's private estimation, she was the most fiercely beautiful creature on Earth.

But now she looked terrified.

"Miss Briggs!" Fred hollered.

Libby motioned him closer. Then she held up her phone. On it was written a single word.

"Keys!" Fred shouted. "Where?"

She typed another message.

> Look around idiot. Hurry.

"Right!"

Fred set about looking for the keys to the Faraday box. He rifled through the teacher's desk and personal items, turning up nothing.

"Keys, keys! If I were a blimey set of keys, where would I be? Jiminy Christmas, where would the keys be?"

Fred felt a glimmer of hope when he saw Libby's tote bag by the door of the box. He rifled through it as Libby watched through the glass, shaking her head as if to say, "Forget it."

Fred produced a zippered pouch and, curious, opened it to reveal a six-inch cylindrical tube filled with a black liquid. He drew a breath as he realized what it was—the antimatter that Libby had filched from Percival.

Libby held her phone to the window, and what was written on it froze Fred blood unlike anything had before.

> Freddie I'm running out of air.

Fred held his hand to the glass, covering Libby's own.

"I'm going to get you out! I promise!"

Fred was quite sure that Libby couldn't hear a word he said. So, putting his mouth closer to the window, for the first time in his life, he spoke three words that he had never said to anyone other than his gran Olive or his cat, Moresby: "I love you."

With that, Fred turned and trotted down the hall, his heart racing in his chest and a tube of antimatter in his right hand containing enough concentrated energy to tear a hole in the universe.

Fred knew who had the keys to get to Libby out, and he was determined to get them from her—or die trying.

Beatrix flew past the gates as Percival and Malik strove to keep up. She saw Ben crouching as he looked up at the top of the oculus.

"Ben!" Beatrix whispered.

"She's gone," Ben said. "I don't understand it. She jumped in. No one forced her. She apologized, and then she jumped."

Ben was crying.

Beatrix hugged him and then looked up. The sight caused her to step back.

"Holy *&$#," Malik said.

The exclamation elicited a rare referendum of approval from Percival. "You said it, mate."

The hole in the oculus revealed the expanse of the inside of the Festermunder building. It appeared to be hollow yet full of stars. On the walls were a seemingly infinite number of apertures that opened and closed, arcs of colorful energy jetting in and out of them.

The network! This is what Lightheart theorized, Beatrix thought. *He tried to map these. They're in the manuscript! I saw the sketches. He said no one was aware of them except for Wendell. I saw these on the computer!*

"Percival?" Beatrix said without looking away from the network. "What do we do now?"

Percival didn't get a chance to answer.

A concussive blast shattered the air and sent them spinning in all directions.

"Gray Witch!" a voice boomed.

Beatrix turned and saw her tormentor, who was standing on the other side of the void. Even the star stream parted slightly as if to emphasize that his malice could divide the cosmos.

"You will come with me, or they will die."

"Luka!" another voice said.

The Hat Man turned and saw Percival standing on the other side of the void. "Mongrel!" Luka said. Eyes suddenly appeared on the faceless monster that blazed like red coals.

"Well, it looks like you have yourself buggered up in another one of your classic failures! Tryin' to scare children into doin' your bidding? Listen, mate, your dark master will not be charitable once he realizes your true aim."

Luka seemed to expand in height. "I serve the Master of the Black Path and none other. You and the old man will be tortured ceaselessly and watch your companions die for nothing!"

"Oy! You have tried to cheat and betray your Master, but he expected that," Percival replied. "His watchers are now massing in the Divide for you, waiting for you to fail their test. You pitiful bastard! Do think you can turn her to your aims and defeat Seraphim? You don't understand your peril. Be gone from here, lest you be banished to the Black Reaches, you dratted devil."

Betrayal? Luka's gone rogue?

"Their death will be on your hands, mongrel," Luka replied, unmoved by Percival's warning. "All of them."

"It won't be for nothing," Beatrix said. "Do it, Percival. End this and take this devil with it."

A blast exploded from Luka that separated Beatrix and Ben on the left side of the void with Percival on the right. Malik was nowhere to be seen.

"You! Gray Witch! They lied to you!" Luka whispered.

"Do it, Percival!" Beatrix screamed.

Percival had put his hand into his front pocket as he absorbed a blast in the chest from Luka.

He's going to do it!

"All lies. You're Eidolon. The old man lied to you. You're Phantom. You know what that means?"

"Shut up!" Beatrix screamed as she began to cry.

Luka laughed, a deep guttural doom-filled sound. Beatrix's eyes flared violet, and she couldn't stop her tears.

"They didn't tell you!" Luka said, still laughing as he shot another blast at Percival to keep him from reaching his glasses case, which was two yards away from his prone body.

"Stop it! Please! He's still breathing!" Beatrix pleaded. "I'll do anything!"

Beatrix felt a searing pain in her head, and she clamped her hands over her ears as the world moved in slow motion.

"The simulacra. There's a reality that you don't grasp. They're using you, fool!"

"Get your voice out of my head!" Beatrix screamed.

Luka laughed. "The old man wants to shield you from the truth."

"What truth?" Ben asked as he struggled with a similar pain in his head and body.

"Boy, you are not what you think you are, and neither is your sister!" Luka screamed over the noise of the star stream as it continued to flare. He sent a bolt of dark energy into Ben that picked him up and suspended him over the void.

"Tell me!" Ben yelled as he struggled to escape.

"Shut up, Ben! Stop it, please!" Beatrix cried.

"Tell us now before you kill us!" Ben screamed.

"Ben, stop! I beg you." Beatrix wailed.

"You, boy, are of the other world, passed here through the meridians whole as you are. Bram gave you this gift, which you have thrown away. You are complete."

Ben's mouth fell open in shock.

Bram. A gift?

"Stop it!" Beatrix screamed.

"You, Gray Witch, are not what you think either. You're powerful, but you're nothing. A soul-stealer but a pawn. Your template is firmly enslaved thanks to your self-styled father. Think you're real, do you?" Luka laughed.

"Girl, you are but a copy. A facsimile of something else that is only real in the Other Place. A hidden slave who will be found and eliminated; then you will be unwritten. You are not Beatrix. You are the soul-stealer! A mutation. You are the Gray Witch! Know you not what 'Eidolon' means in the common tongue?"

Beatrix's eyes flared purple one last time as her heart broke, and she prepared to die.

I knew it. I have no identity. I'm not me. I'm nothing. I always knew it.

"It means 'ghost.' I am your only hope. Go ahead, destroy the gateway. You will never see him again!"

Luka lowered his voice. "Come with me. You will give me the map to the stars that you have hidden in your mind, and we can find your template and sanctuary for you. You can find your father. With your powers, we can finish the new world and end the war."

A war?

"So you can enslave Earth and take everyone and everything you need to create Utopia? Go ahead and kill me first, but . . ." Beatrix hesitated as something occurred to her.

"But what, young fool?" Luka bellowed, his anger rising again.

"But . . ."

"Speak, fool, or die!"

Beatrix stood up straight and swept the wisp of gray hair back, her irises flaring brilliant purple once more. "But… you…you can't kill me."

For a moment, Luka seemed to hesitate. Then a small, diminutive voice called out. It even sounded skinny. "Hey!"

Luka turned, and behind him stood Malik, trembling, and holding something in his right hand.

Beatrix's satchel.

Beatrix screamed with such force that the books on the nearby shelves exploded and crisscrossed the star stream over the void. "Noooooooooooooooooooooooooo!"

But it was too late. Malik intended to strike down Luka with an empty leather satchel.

Only Malik wasn't stupid. Nor was the satchel empty.

Beatrix's satchel was full of the antimatter that Percival had slipped into it.

The force of the concussion could be felt as far as Harlem. Richter scales at Columbia University later recorded a Level 5 tectonic disturbance.

Luka did not assess the threat from Malik quickly enough. The moment the antimatter hit him, it caused an immediate destabilization of the matter constituting his body, and he transmuted into dark energy. Slammeding into the void with unspeakable force, his body was atomized as it hit the surface. The particles appeared to coagulate into humanoid form for a moment before they disappeared once again.

The impact sent Malik careening over the meridian. He hit Ben, and his momentum carried them to the far edge of the void.

They almost made it.

"I have not killed a man in a good deal of time, but it wouldn't trouble me in the slightest if I were to break my streak with you," a high-pitched voice called down the back hallway of the fourth floor.

Fred did not need to find Headmistress Grunnion-Paltine. She had found him.

Fred swallowed as he walked to the center of the hall. HGP stood at the other end, not sixty feet away. It was a standoff.

"The keys, begging your pardon. I need the keys to the box. Then I'll be out of your way. You won't see us again, I promise."

For a second, Fred thought he was in luck, for HGP reached into the left side of her cardigan and pulled out a ring of keys. She threw them on the floor in front of her, not thirty feet from Fred.

"Want to have a go at it, Limey?" she asked. Her cheeks rosy, she smiled, revealing her worn, gapped teeth. "We play American football here."

She bent over and assumed a three-point stance in the middle of the hallway. Reluctantly, Fred did the same. HGP's left hand came off the floor, and her fingers twitched as if she were waiting for someone to say "hike." Fred laid a hand behind his back like he was one of the Olympic speed skaters he had seen once when watching the Winter Games with Gran Olive.

"Say when," HGP said, her nostrils flaring.

With more bravado than he thought he had, Fred began counting, "One . . . two . . . two and a half . . . two and three quarters . . ."

Before he reached three, HGP was galloping toward him like a giant rabid Doberman.

Fred took off toward HGP as well, and as they closed in what seemed like slow motion, HGP realized too late that Fred was playing the role of Ferdinand the bull. He had no intention of fighting. Fred's hand was behind his back, concealing something.

At the last second, Fred turned and slid through HGP's gigantic leg gap. He leaped to his feet, but instead of brandishing the keys he had just grabbed, he pointed at her as if to say, "Look."

All characters and events in this publication are fictitious and any resemblance to real persons, living or dead, is purely coincidental.

The cover was designed by Anthea Savidis.

Caught off balance, only then did HGP realize why Fred had kept his left hand behind his back. He was holding an empty test tube.

"What is this?" she asked.

He had thrown the contents of the antimatter tube all over Headmistress Grunnion-Paltine.

At first, she couldn't understand what was happening. Then she screamed, and her mechanical gloves smoked and fired off green and orange sparks. Her skin turned red, and she hollered as it burned. HGP fell to her knees and tried to get up to go after Fred, but went to her knees once more. She turned a nearby fire extinguisher on herself and used the cloud of sodium bicarbonate to cover her retreat, sprinting back down toward the elevators, cursing and screaming the whole way.

Fred Hardingham had won at American football.

Beatrix was almost too late.

She lunged and somehow managed to hold on. A barely conscious Percival was clutching her ankle with one hand and an overturned bookshelf with the other.

Ben and Malik were dangling from Beatrix's hands, Ben from the right and Malik from the left.

"Somebody help us!" Beatrix screamed.

Tendrils of the starscape wrapped around Ben and Malik's ankles. The rest of the void turned black. It was pulling them in. The force of gravity was impossibly strong. The prime meridian was destabilizing and turning into a black hole.

The harder Beatrix pulled, the stronger the void seemed to get. Her shoulders felt like they were being pulled from their sockets. Her arms screamed in pain. The burning in her muscles was unbearable.

Ben looked up at Beatrix, his face contorted with pain and sadness.

Beatrix screamed in pain, and her eyes flared purple as she sobbed. She couldn't lift him. It was no use. She wasn't powerful. She was useless.

"Beatrix?"

"No!" Beatrix yelled.

"Beatrix, let me go," Ben said.

"No!" Malik cried.

"Beatrix, you have to let me go!" Ben insisted, tears running down his cheeks. "Just let me go, Beatrix."

"No! You're all I have!" she yelled through her sobs.

Ben turned and looked at Malik. "Take care of her."

"No! No!" Malik cried. "Please, you're my best friend. Don't do this to me!"

With his last ounce of strength, Ben looked up at Beatrix. "Find me."

Then, using his other hand, Ben pried Beatrix's fingers off his wrist.

He fell.

And then he was gone.

"No! Ben! No!" Beatrix screamed. Her strength seemed to return as she flung Malik with such force that he flew back over her head and slammed into the cyclone fence.

"Oh no . . . what have we done?" Beatrix asked, shaking and sobbing as she lay on the edge of the void.

The space in the void began to distort. In a daze, Beatrix couldn't tell if what she was experiencing was real or a nightmare.

A large, dark mass blocked out many of the stars. As it took form, she realized it had a body. And a face. Yet not a face. Beatrix could only make out its shape against the stars.

Emoc ot em. Emoc ot em. Come to me. I ees ouy. I see you.

Beatrix grabbed her head with both hands and closed her eyes. "Get out of my head!"

Xirteab.

A low droning hum began from the depths of the void. It grew louder and louder until it was deafening. The shape of the man became known to her.

Seraphim.

Then it happened. The tension. The years of anxiety. The misplaced anger. The fact that she was nothing. Only a copy. A pawn. With her fingers burrowed in her hair, Beatrix screamed the only word that meant anything to her.

"Ben!"

Beatrix stood and tongues of purple flame blasted forth from her eyes and fingernails, exploding into the void toward the dark figure. The result was cataclysmic. The energy of the impact rocked the library and sent a white-hot beam of star material up through the oculus. The starscape faded to black, and the void transformed to an amorphous dark gray.

The meridian appeared dormant.

Beatrix collapsed. Hands grabbed her shirt and stood her upright. They belonged to Malik. He was battered and bruised, and his eyes were red with tears. Beatrix noticed something else. Malik's hair was sticking straight up. She felt the tickle of static electricity.

Static charge! EMP! This place is about to be fried!

"Malik!" Beatrix said. "Where's Percival? We have to go right now!"

"He's here!" Malik said, pointing to a nearby row.

Confused, Beatrix saw nothing; then she looked down and realized why. A pug was urinating on the nearest remnant of the recent melee — a smoking black fedora.

"Parfleet, lead us out," Malik said. "This place is about to go off!"

Beatrix cast a last glance at the void. She thought of Alex and Ben. Then she began to sob.

Ben!

The space inside the void was completely lifeless, the temperature dropping.

"Beatrix!" Malik said. "We need to leave."

With that, the two companions took off at a trot, following their canine guide out of the library. Parfleet the pug was much more of a guide than his human simulacrum and was able to sniff out a quick path out of the labyrinth without cursing.

They burst forth into the rotunda and found Lightheart's replica sitting in his wheelchair, surprisingly alert.

"Time to go, Professor!" Malik called out with false cheerfulness, then grabbed the handles and pushed the wheelchair toward the freight elevator. They jumped in, and the doors closed just as a sonic blast from the library sent out a shockwave. The lights in the elevator went out.

"Oh no!" Malik said. "How stupid are we?"

"Just wait," the simulacrum said.

Beatrix and Malik looked at him, waiting for more information. When none was forthcoming they looked at each other.

"Well, we're screwed," Malik said. "No one will find us here. At least no one we want to see."

The buttons were half-lit, and Beatrix tried them all.

"Some type of auxiliary must be protecting the circuitry here," Malik said. "There shouldn't be any lights on if this was an EMP."

Thump.

Something crashing into the door made all of the occupants jump.

Thump.

The banging continued. Someone was forcing the door.

"Crap!" Malik cried. "It's her. I know it. We've come this far only to freakin' die!"

"It could be Fred or Libby!" Beatrix said.

"It's Grunnion-Paltine, man. She's coming to end us!"

Parfleet was going crazy, squealing and barking.

"Get behind me," Beatrix commanded. Malik and Lightheart's double did as ordered. Beatrix stood in a half crouch position with Parfleet gnashing his teeth at her feet. As the doors were pried apart, her eyes glowed fluorescent violet.

Before Beatrix could react, a blinding blast of green light surrounded them, and a gray vapor wafted through the air. Beatrix and Malik coughed and sputtered. When the smoke cleared, they winced when they heard a voice.

But it wasn't the voice they expected.

"Oy, ya mad bastard! I done told ya about doin' that blimey thing when I'm not ready. I should let Beatrix blow yer arse to smithereens!"

Percival was back in human form.

The object of his ire laughed, pretending to cough. "Well?" Montavani said. "Ready to go?"

Fred fumbled with the keys, trying to find the correct one. Two dozen were on the ring, and they all looked the same. Libby reappeared at the window, looking weaker.

"C'mon, Freddie, you blimey fool!" Fred said as he kept trying keys.

The hair on the back of his neck began to stand up. But for perhaps the first time, it wasn't because of fear. This was something else.

Static!

Blue sparks leaped across the computer screens in the room. Then the lights started sparking.

The signal!

Fred felt stinging pain as he struggled on, finally producing the last untried key. Holding it aloft, he said a prayer, then stuck it into the lock.

It clicked. Fred yelped with joy before he turned it, flipped the lock, and hoisted the door open. The rush of air into the box was nearly strong enough to make the door slam, and Fred had to put his body weight against it. He peered inside.

"Miss Libby?"

The static-charge shockwave was barreling down the hallway toward room 433. Fred climbed into the box and slammed the door on just as the EMP hit. The Faraday box was consumed with hot blue lightning for twenty seconds before it died down.

Fred turned and found Libby next to him. He tapped her head. "Miss Libby," he said. After nudging her with the greatest of care, Fred became agitated and more emphatic, calling her name louder and louder. Realizing she could be gravely hurt or worse, Fred grew frantic. "C'mon, Miss Libby. Please! Please don't be dead. Oh, bugger, I finally love a girl, and she doesn't last three days because of me. Fred, you dope! Please, Miss Libby, wake up!"

In the dark of the box, a light came on. It was Libby's phone. The LED screen chirped to life to show the battery life was down to ten percent, but the phone worked! Fred knew an EMP effect would have fried all electrical devices outside the box. The light also revealed Libby's face. Fred picked up the phone and held it out to her.

It was the most beautiful face he had ever seen.

Her eyes opened.

"Hardingham, you moron. If you don't get that bloody light out of my eyes this instant, I'll punch you in the throat with it!"

"Libby!" Fred yelled. He reached out to hug her, but Libby stuck her finger in Fred's chest.

"Stop moron! See if your key works from the inside before we celebrate like fools and then suffocate. There must be a fail-safe in case some idiot teenager gets locked in here."

Fred held up the key, thanking his luck he hadn't left it in the latch. It worked. The door cracked open, and air rushed in. Fred helped Libby get up, and she actually accepted his assistance, as she was weak from hypoxia.

They exited Room 433 and proceeded toward the elevator.

Libby Soames-Briggs never mentioned that she heard everything Fred Hardingham said that night.

Surprisingly, neither group had any trouble leaving Festermunder School that night. They all walked unchecked into the frigid night air and trekked down 8th Avenue toward the Sovereign Light Theater without incident. There, they found Libby and Fred arriving from the opposite end of the street. All of them were too tired and despondent to greet each other with much more than a cursory acknowledgement.

Beatrix took one last look at the night sky. Seeing that the stars were veiled, she went into the Sovereign Light Theater and closed the door.

CHAPTER 23

The Stolen Star

IT WAS THE DAY AFTER CHRISTMAS.

Beatrix reluctantly accepted the offer to meet Montavani for coffee at the Drip. She had slept like a rock, blackout tired and compartmentalizing her anguish over the night before. Percival suggested he tag along in pug form so as to not attract unwanted attention.

"There'll be watchers all over the school for the next few days, trying to figure out what happened, so we should be relatively safe for a bit," he said prior to being transformed.

At the Drip, Beatrix took up her normal corner seat in the L-shaped booth that was up against the window looking out on Broadway. Parfleet curled up on the ledge of the windowsill and began dozing.

Once their coffees arrived, Montavani waited for Beatrix to speak.

Beatrix also waited—a powerful lesson she had learned from Montavani himself.

"Beatrix, I'm sorry. But all is not lost—"

"Not lost? *Not lost?* Did we shut the way? Is it destroyed? Alex is lost, and my brother is gone. Gone! I'll never see him again. My life is over. And I'm just . . . just . . . I don't even know what to say. And where the hell were you? We needed you?"

"I'm marked. I can't be present in or near the meridians for any significant amount of time, or Seraphim's agents will track me and bring danger to you. Percival and I elected to keep that from you lest something happen and that information could be used by the Enemy. With the help of the rythrax, I'm able to be present for only moments before I can be discovered. But, I say again, everything's not lost."

"How?" Beatrix asked.

He exhaled. "Alex left of her own free will. When you search your thoughts, you will realize you already know why. She's fearless and high minded and shouldn't be faulted for deceiving you. And you . . . you're no different today than you've always been. Yes, you are powerful. Capable of incredible mastery over matter and space and time. Luka, as evil as he is, never lied to you. You are, in fact, the Eidolon. We're at war, Beatrix. You—"

"I'm a copy! A fake! Luka said so. I'm nothing. I was unique, but it was stolen from me!"

Montavani held out his hand, indicating Beatrix should lower her voice.

"You are what you are. You're still unique, Beatrix. You're Starlight. No one is like you. You have thoughts. A free will. Use them. Understand them. And then, we have work to do."

Montavani blew on his coffee to cool it before he continued. "Do you think last night was a failure? In the last week, we have brought grave problems on the Enemy. You conquered Luka."

Beatrix shivered at the mention of his name. "Is he dead?"

"Dead?" Montavani raised his eyebrows. "He's neither dead nor living. Luka is an Incomplete. He will not be reduced to atoms and spun off into the unwritten spaces. No, Luka will be reconstituted. For now, he need not be concerned with facing you again soon. He was here without his Master's leave, and for that, he'll be brought to the altar of the Dark Star itself and face Seraphim and his counselors. I shudder to think of what that will mean. But no, Beatrix, Luka is not dead, only vanquished for a time."

"Why did he come here without Seraphim's knowledge?"

Montavani scoffed. "Luka wanted you for himself. He desires mastery over the Master he serves faithfully yet hates. Seraphim knew. Trust me, he sees all. It's likely he wanted to probe the situation. To test you. To be certain his mastery over the Andromeda particle. I suspect you have given him pause — and closed off an important resource by gaining control of the meridian by unconventional means."

Beatrix raised her eyebrows causing her glasses to slip halfway down her nose. She pushed them back up. "Unconventional means? What do you mean?"

"When you held Ben over the void and he freed himself from your grasp, you transferred to him elements of the Andromeda particle. When he made his traverse to the Divide, he made the meridian impassable to Seraphim's agents, but not us, thus opening a multitude of opportunities throughout the universe, some of which you may have seen."

Beatrix summoned the courage to ask the question she had dared not face yet. "Was . . . Ben . . .? Is he . . .?"

"Is Ben what?"

Beatrix sighed. "Ben wasn't my brother, was he?"

Montavani closed his eyes, then took a sip of his coffee. Setting his mug down, he placed both hands on the table and looked into Beatrix's eyes. "No."

Beatrix nodded with resignation.

"Your brother, as you know him, is real, but you have no biological relation. Ben is flesh and blood and born free in the Divide. He was sent here along with your furry friend to protect you from the coming cataclysm."

Beatrix smiled and patted Parfleet, who continued to doze. "Did Ben know?"

"About your relationship? He suspects things. Has dreamed of things. Images of a past life. He will come to know more in time now that he possesses a part of the Andromeda particle, wherever he is. Ben loves you, Beatrix, and love transcends blood. In my opinion, blood and blind loyalty are meaningless next to those of us who care for one another based on merit and good deeds. Ben proved he's willing to die for you. You idolize Ben, and he idolizes you. Everyone needs a hero, a person they can nearly worship. For some, it's a parent, a sibling, or a mentor. For others, it's a foster father or a friend. It's called agape."

"Why?" Beatrix asked as she readjusted Parfleet, who was becoming recalcitrant.

"He's driven to be a good person. When you held him over the void, he was perfectly willing to be taken into the Black Path just so Master Patel would live."

"Malik," Beatrix said with a mild sense of admiration. "Ben would've laid down in traffic for Malik. It's like he knew that Malik needed a chance at a good life. Up until then, Ben's life was charmed."

"I suppose Ben is not unlike Wendell ultimately," Montavani said.

"I know. I guess I thought maybe Wendell was always going to be there for me. I shouldn't have assumed that would be the case with Ben either. But what about me? Who am I if I'm not Ben's sister? You said Luka never lied to me?"

"You, Beatrix, are the Star Child, pure stellar energy harnessed into a simulacrum." Montavani hesitated. "I'm reluctant to say more. You're only a child, but you possess eons of knowledge, though you know it not."

"How?"

"The Keepers. You were created from celestial material that Seraphim had been collating from around the universe to be used for a dark and unknown purpose. He had taken children from this world and others to experiment for his dark purposes. That's why Festermunder was important to him. There was an endless supply of test subjects and a direct way to funnel them to the Other Place.

"The star material . . . we were able to steal it. Many of my comrades died doing so. In fact, we"—he motioned to the pug sleeping on the windowsill—"are the last of our kind."

"The Thirteen?" Beatrix asked.

"There were twelve Keepers, and the thirteenth warrior was prophesied for eons. The Andromeda element would be in this one, whom we call the Eidolon, capable of sustained and unspeakable power. The known laws of the universe do not apply to this being. No one knew this, of course, until the process was complete. Rumors spread, and we couldn't suppress them. You were given the priority to be located and taken by Seraphim's agents. Above all else, they wanted, and still bitterly desire, to recover the Stolen Star. Legends arose over the years as we sought to hide you. They call you the Gray Witch."

At the mention of the name, Beatrix started playing with her long shock of gray hair.

"False prophecies of the death and destruction the Eidolon could bring were created to make everyone scared of you. To make the goal of finding and hunting you down seem of dire import to those in the alter world. They called you 'Mortmaiden' in the common tongue. Once our brotherhood was penetrated by Luka's agents, Wendell and I sent you here."

"It's like how the villagers rose up against the monster in *Beauty and the Beast*," Beatrix said. "But why here? And why now?"

"Why not some other time and place? Like why New York and why the Festermunder School?" Montavani added.

"Yes. It seems way too convenient."

"That was Wendell's folly. He let his love for you overpower logic and good sense. But I also think he wanted to give you an opportunity to have a way out. A loophole so that one day you could assume your old self. A normal life."

"Where is Ben now?" Beatrix asked nervously.

"I suspect Ben is exactly where he chooses to be in the Divide, which means I have no idea. Only time will tell."

Beatrix was getting upset, so she calmed herself by looking out onto the street and petting Parfleet. "I don't care what I can do. I just want to be real. I want my identity back. Wherever it is, I want the real me. You owe it to me to help me. I want to find Wendell!"

"I'll help you," Montavani replied.

"Ben. He may not be my brother, but I love him and he's all I know. I want him back!"

Montavani took a sip of coffee before he replied, "Beatrix, do something for me."

Beatrix raised her eyebrows as if to ask him what it might be.

"Make it stop."

"Make what stop?" Beatrix asked.

"Your way. Your feeling of being less. You are consistently more than you think you are. You cannot choose *what* you are, but you are *who* you choose to be."

"How will that get my brother back? Am I supposed to just be okay with that? Because of me, he's gone!"

"Beatrix, make it stop." Montavani turned to look out at the street.

Beatrix felt drawn to the street. She got up and went out into the frigid, cloudy morning. The shock of gray hair blew in the wind on top of her black curls.

Be more than you think you are.

Beatrix turned and looked uptown, then downtown before she walked toward the center of the crosswalk.

You are who you choose to be.

Standing in the center of the crosswalk, Beatrix felt compelled by a feeling. She balled her hands into fists and scrunched her eyes shut, then relaxed them.

Make it stop.

She opened her eyes.

The world had stopped.

Pedestrians were frozen in place, as if someone had hit "pause" on a movie. The cold, muddy water splashed by a taxicab stopped in an arc of liquid. Nothing moved. Even the birds were frozen in the air.

As Beatrix looked around, it seemed as if all of the atoms and electrons and every particle of matter had stopped vibrating.

The uptown and downtown view was as still as a tomb.

Someone approached from behind Beatrix, causing the hairs on the back of her neck to stick up.

"Beatrix."

She turned and ran toward the voice. She wrapped her arms around the figure and sagged under a tidal wave of happiness she had not expected to feel that or any other day.

"You're here! Are you real?" Beatrix stood back and looked at Ben. He was pale had a small shock of gray hair on the side of his head.

"I'm okay," he replied.

As tears ran down her face, a thought occurred to her. "Wait! What's my favorite book, what do I think is gross, and who is the most annoying person on earth?"

"*The Mysterious Benedict Society*. People who go barefoot indoors, and Malik."

Beatrix threw her arms around Ben and buried her face in his sweatshirt.

Festermunder. Headmistress Grunnion-Paltine. Rosemarie. Finding

Wendell. Alex lost to the void. Her companions all gathered at the Sovereign Light Theater—Percival, Malik, Fred, Libby, and Violet. Seraphim. It would all be there waiting for Beatrix when she was ready.

The search for the Stolen Star could wait.

Ben Voght had returned, and she did not ask how or why. For the moment at least, all was right with the only world Beatrix knew.

THE END